Mary Balogh is a *New York Times* bestselling author. A former teacher, she grew up in Wales and now lives in Canada.

Visit Mary Balogh online:

www.marybalogh.com
www.facebook.com/AuthorMaryBalogh

Praise for Mary Balogh:

'Ms Balogh is a veritable treasure, a matchless storyteller who makes our hearts melt with delight'
Romantic Times

'Balogh is truly a find'
Publishers Weekly

'Balogh is the queen of spicy Regency-era romance, creating memorable characters in unforgettable stories'
Booklist

By Mary Balogh

Mistress Couplet:

No Man's Mistress
More Than a Mistress

The Secret Mistress (prequel to the Mistress Couplet)

Huxtables Series:

First Comes Marriage
Then Comes Seduction
At Last Comes Love
Seducing an Angel
A Secret Affair

Simply Quartet:

Simply Unforgettable
Simply Love
Simply Magic
Simply Perfect

Bedwyn Series:

One Night for Love
A Summer to Remember
Slightly Married
Slightly Wicked
Slightly Scandalous
Slightly Tempted
Slightly Sinful
Slightly Dangerous

Survivors' Club Series:

The Proposal
The Arrangement
The Escape

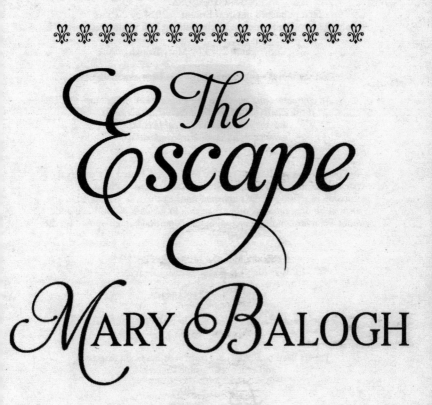

The Escape

MARY BALOGH

piatkus

PIATKUS

First published in the US in 2014 by Dell, an imprint of Random House,
a division of Random House LLC, a Penguin Random House Company,
New York, USA
First published in Great Britain in 2014 by Piatkus
Published by arrangement with the Bantam Dell Publishing Group

Printed and bound in Great Britain by CPI (Group) UK Ltd,
Croydon CR0 4YY

Papers used by Piatkus are from well-managed forests
and other responsible sources.

MIX
Paper from
responsible sources
FSC
www.fsc.org
FSC® C104740

Piatkus
An imprint of
Little, Brown Book Group
100 Victoria Embankment
London EC4Y 0DY

An Hachette UK Company
www.hachette.co.uk

www.piatkus.co.uk

To Melanie McKay

who bid upon and won the package I donated to the
Charity Royale auction in Regina, Saskatchewan,
Canada. Proceeds went to My Aunt's Place,
a homeless shelter for women and children.

One item of the package was the right to have her
name used as a character in my next book.
Melanie asked that the name be her sister's
rather than her own.

My heroine in this book is, therefore,
Samantha McKay (nee Saul).

The
Escape

1

❧

 The hour was approaching midnight, but no one was making any move to retire to bed.

"You are going to find it mighty peaceful around here after we have all left, George," Ralph Stockwood, Earl of Berwick, remarked.

"It will be quiet, certainly." The Duke of Stanbrook looked about the circle of six guests gathered in the drawing room at Penderris Hall, his country home in Cornwall, and his eyes paused fondly on each of them in turn before moving on. "Yes, and peaceful too, Ralph. But I am going to miss you all damnably."

"You will be c-counting your blessings, George," said Flavian Arnott, Viscount Ponsonby, "as soon as you realize you will not have to listen to Vince scraping away on his v-violin for another whole year."

"Or the cats howling in ecstasy along with the music it creates," Vincent Hunt, Viscount Darleigh, added. "You might as well mention that too, Flave. There is no need to consider my sensibilities."

"You play with a great deal more competence than you did last year, Vincent," Imogen Hayes, Lady Barclay, assured him. "By next year I do not doubt you will have improved even further. You are a marvel and an inspiration to us all."

"I may even dance to one of your tunes one of these days, provided it is not too sprightly, Vince." Sir Benedict Harper looked ruefully at the two canes propped against the arm of his chair.

"You are not by any chance harboring a hope that we will all decide to stay a year or two longer instead of leaving tomorrow, George?" Hugo Emes, Lord Trentham, asked, sounding almost wistful. "I have never known three weeks to pass by so quickly. We arrived here, we blinked, and now it is time to go our separate ways again."

"George is far too p-polite to say a bald no, Hugo," Flavian told him. "But life calls us hence, alas."

They were feeling somewhat maudlin, the seven of them, the members of the self-styled Survivors' Club. Once, they had all spent several years here at Penderris, recuperating from wounds sustained during the Napoleonic Wars. Although each had had to fight a lone battle toward recovery, they had also aided and supported one another and grown as close as any brothers—and sister. When the time had come for them to leave, to make new lives for themselves or to retrieve the old, they had gone with mingled eagerness and trepidation. Life was for living, they had all agreed, yet the cocoon in which they had been wrapped for so long had kept them safe and even happy. They had decided that they would return to Cornwall for a few weeks each year to keep alive their friendship, to share their experiences of life beyond the familiar confines of Penderris, and to help with any difficulty that may have arisen for one or more of them.

This had been the third such gathering. But now it was over for another year, or would be on the morrow.

Hugo got to his feet and stretched, expanding his already impressive girth, none of which owed anything to fat. He was the tallest and broadest of them, and the most fierce-looking, with his close-cropped hair and frequent frown.

"The devil of it is that I do not want to put an end to any of this," he said. "But if I am to make an early start in the morning, then I had better get to bed."

It was the signal for them all to rise. Most had lengthy journeys to make and hoped for an early departure.

Sir Benedict was the slowest to get to his feet. He had to gather his canes to his sides, slip his arms through the straps he had contrived, and haul himself painstakingly upward. Any of the others would have been glad to offer a helping hand, of course, but they knew better than to do so. They were all fiercely independent despite their various disabilities. Vincent, for example, would leave the room and climb the stairs to his own chamber unassisted despite the fact that he was blind. On the other hand, they would all wait for their slower friend and match their steps to his as they climbed the stairs.

"P-pretty soon, Ben," Flavian said, "you are going to be able to do that in under a minute."

"Better than two, as it was last year," Ralph said. "That really was a bit of a yawn, Ben."

They would *not* resist the urge to jab at him and tease him—except, perhaps, Imogen.

"Even two is remarkable for someone who was once told he must have both legs amputated if his life was to be saved," she said.

"You are depressed, Ben." Hugo paused midstretch to make the observation.

Benedict shot him a glance. "Just tired. It is late, and we are at the wrong end of our three-week stay. I always hate goodbyes."

"No," Imogen said, "it is more than that, Ben. Hugo is not the only one to have noticed. We *all* have, but it has never come up during our nightly sessions."

They had sat up late most nights during the past three weeks, as they did each year, sharing some of their deeper concerns and insecurities—and triumphs. They kept few secrets from one another. There were always some, of course. One's soul could never be laid quite bare to another person, no matter how close a friend. Ben had held his own soul close this year. He *had* been depressed. He still was. He felt chagrined, though, that he had not hidden his mood better.

"Perhaps we are intruding where no help or sympathy is wanted," the duke said. "Are we, Benedict? Or shall we sit back down and discuss it?"

"After I have just made the herculean effort to get up? And when everyone is about to totter off to bed in order to look fresh and beautiful in the morning?" Ben laughed, but no one else shared his amusement.

"You *are* depressed, Ben," Vincent said. "Even I have noticed."

The others all sat again, and Ben, with a sigh, resumed his own seat. He had so nearly got away with it.

"No one likes to be a whiner," he told them. "Whiners are dead bores."

"Agreed." George smiled. "But you have never been a whiner, Benedict. None of us has. The rest of us would not have put up with it. Admitting problems, asking for help or even just for a friendly ear, is not whining. It is merely drawing upon the collective sympathies of people who know almost exactly what you are going through. Your legs are paining you, are they?"

"I never resent a bit of pain," Ben said without denying it. "At least it reminds me that I still have my legs."

"But—?"

George had not himself fought in the wars, though he had once been a military officer. His only son had fought, though, and had died in Portugal. His wife, the boy's mother, perhaps overcome with grief, flung herself to her death from the cliffs at the edge of the estate not long after. When he had opened his home to the six of them, as well as to others, George had been as wounded as any of them. He probably still was.

"I will walk. I *do* walk after a fashion. And I will dance one day." Ben smiled ruefully. That had always been his boast, and the others often teased him about it.

No one teased now.

"But—?" It was Hugo this time.

"But I will never do either as I once did," Ben said. "I suppose I have known it for a long time. I would be a fool not to have done so. But it has taken me six years to face up to the fact that I will never walk more than a few steps without my canes—plural—and that I will never move more than haltingly with them. I will never get my life back as it was. I will always be a cripple."

"A harsh word, that," Ralph said with a frown. "And a bit defeatist?"

"It is the simple truth," Ben said firmly. "It is time to accept reality."

The duke rested his elbows on the arms of his chair and steepled his fingers. "And accepting reality involves giving up and calling yourself a cripple?" he said. "You would never have got up off your bed, Benedict, if you had done that from the start. Indeed, you would have agreed to allow the army sawbones to relieve you of your legs altogether."

"Admitting the truth does not mean giving up," Ben told him. "But it does mean assessing reality and adjusting my life accordingly. I was a career military officer and never envisaged any other life for myself. I did not *want* any other life. I was going to end up a general. I have lived and toiled for the day when I could have that old life back. It is not going to happen, though. It never was. It is time I admitted it openly and dealt with it."

"You cannot be happy with a life outside the army?" Imogen asked.

"Oh, I can be," Ben assured her. "Of course I can. And

will. It is just that I have spent six years denying reality, with the result that at this late date I still have no
idea what the future *does* hold for me. Or what I want
of the future. I have wasted those years yearning for a
past that is long gone and will never return. You see? I
am whining, and you could all be sleeping peacefully in
your beds by now."

"I would r-rather be here," Flavian said. "If one of us
ever goes away from here unhappy because he c-couldn't
bring himself to confide in the rest of us, then we
m-might as well stop coming. George lives at the back
of beyond here in Cornwall, after all. Who would want
to c-come just for the scenery?"

"He is right, Ben." Vincent grinned. "*I* would not
come for the scenery."

"You are not going home when you leave here, Ben,"
George said. It was a statement, not a question.

"Beatrice—my sister—needs company," Ben explained with a shrug. "She had a lingering chill through
the winter and is only now getting her strength back
with the spring. She does not feel up to moving to London when Gramley goes up after Easter for the opening
of the parliamentary session. And her boys will be away
at school."

"The Countess of Gramley is fortunate to have such
an agreeable brother," the duke said.

"We were always particularly fond of each other,"
Ben told him.

But he had not answered George's implied question.
And since the answer was a large part of the depression
his friends had noticed, he felt obliged to give it. Flavian
was right. If they could not share themselves with one
another here, their friendship and these gatherings would
lose meaning.

"Whenever I go home to Kenelston," he said, "Calvin
is unwilling to let me to do anything. He does not want

me to set foot in the study or talk to my estate agent or visit any of my farms. He insists upon doing everything that needs to be done himself. His manner is always cheerful and hearty. It is as if he believes my brain has been rendered as crooked as my legs. And Julia, my sister-in-law, fusses over me, even to the point of clearing a path before me whenever I emerge from my own apartments. The children are allowed the run of the house, you see, and run they do, strewing objects as they go. She has my meals served in my private apartments so that I will not have to exert myself to go down to the dining room. She—they both go a fair way, in fact, toward smothering me with kindness until I leave again."

"Ah," George said. "Now we get to the heart of the matter."

"They really do fear me," Ben said. "They fairly pulsate with anxiety every moment I am there."

"I daresay your younger brother and his wife grew accustomed to thinking of your home as their own during the years you were here as a patient and then as a convalescent," George said. "But you left here three years ago, Benedict."

Why had he not at that time taken possession of his own home and somehow forced his brother to make other provisions for his own family? That was the implied question. The trouble was, Ben did not have an answer, other than procrastination. Or out-and-out cowardice. Or—something else.

He sighed. "Families are complex."

"They are," Vincent agreed with fervor. "I feel for you, Ben."

"My elder brother and Calvin were always very close," Ben explained. "It was almost as if I, tucked in the middle, did not exist. Not that there was any hostility, just . . . indifference. I was their brother and they were mine, and that was that. Wallace was only ever interested in a future in politics and government. He lived in London, both before and after our father's death. When he succeeded to the baronetcy, he made it very clear that he was not in any way interested in either living at Kenelston or running the estate. Since Calvin was interested in both, and since he also married early and started a family, the two of them came to an arrangement that brought them mutual satisfaction. Calvin would live in the house and administer the estate for a consideration, and Wallace would pay the bills and draw on the proceeds but not have to bother his head about running any of it. Calvin did *not* expect—none of us did—that a loaded cart would topple onto Wallace near Covent Garden and kill him outright. It was too bizarre. That happened just a short while before I was wounded. I was not expected to survive either. Even after I was brought back to England and then here, I was not expected to live. *You* did not expect it, George, did you?"

"On the contrary," the duke said. "I looked into your eyes the day you were brought here, Benedict, and knew you were too stubborn to die. I almost regretted it. I have never seen anyone suffer more pain than you. Your younger brother assumed, then, that the title and fortune and Kenelston itself would soon be entirely his?"

"It must have been a severe blow to him," Ben said with a rueful smile, "when I lived. I am sure he has never forgiven me, though that makes him sound malicious, and really he is not. When I am away from home, he can carry on as he has since our father died. When I am there, he no doubt feels threatened—and with good reason. Everything is mine by law, after all. And if Kenelston is not to be my home, where *will* be?"

That was the question that had been plaguing him for three years.

"My home is full of female relatives who love me to distraction," Vincent said. "They would breathe for me if they could. They do everything else—or so it seems. And soon—I have already heard the rumblings of it— they are going to be forcing potential brides on me because a blind man must need a wife to hold his hand through all the dark years that remain to him. My situation is a little different from yours, Ben, but there are similarities. One of these days I am going to have to put my foot down and become master of my own house. But how to do it is the problem. How do you talk firmly to people you love?"

Ben sighed and then chuckled. "You are exactly right, Vince," he said. "Perhaps you and I are just a couple of dithering weaklings. But Calvin has a wife and four children to provide for, while I have no one besides myself. And he is my brother. I do care for him, even if we were never close. It was a sheer accident of birth that made him the third-born son and me the second."

"You feel g-guilty for having inherited the baronetcy, Ben?" Flavian asked.

"I never expected it, you see," Ben explained. "There was no one more robust or full of life than Wallace. Besides, I never wanted to be anything but a military officer. I certainly never expected Kenelston to be mine. But it is, and I sometimes think that if I could simply go there and immerse myself in running the estate, perhaps I would finally feel settled and would proceed to live happily ever after."

"But your home is occupied by other people," Hugo said. "I would go in there for you if you wanted, Ben, and clear them all out. I would scowl and look tough, and they would toddle off without so much as a squeal of protest. But that is not the point, is it?"

Ben joined in the general laughter.

"Life was simple in the army," he said. "Brute force solved all problems."

"Until Hugo w-went out of his head," Flavian said, "and Vince lost his sight and every b-bone in your legs got crushed, Ben, not to mention most of the bones in the rest of your body too. And Ralph had all his friends wiped off the m-map and his pretty looks ruined when someone slashed his face, and Imogen was forced to make a d-decision no one ought ever to have to make and live with her choice f-forever after, and George lost everything that was dear to him even without leaving Penderris. And half the w-words I want to speak get stuck on the way out of my mouth as though something in my brain needs a d-dab of oil."

"Right," Ben said. "War is not the answer. Life only seemed simpler in those days. But I am keeping you all from your beauty rest. You will all be wishing me to Hades. I am sorry, I did not mean to unburden myself of all these petty problems."

"You did so because we invited you to, Benedict," Imogen reminded him, "and because this is precisely why we gather here every year. Unfortunately, we have not been able to offer you any solutions, have we? Except for Hugo's offer to remove your brother and his family from your home by force—which fortunately was not a serious suggestion."

"It never matters, though, Imogen, does it?" Ralph said. "No one can ever solve anyone else's problems. But it always helps just to unburden oneself to listeners who *really* listen and know that glib answers are worthless."

"You are depressed, then, Benedict," the duke said. "Partly because you have accepted the permanent nature of the limitations of your own body but do not yet know where this acceptance will lead you, and partly because you have not yet accepted that you are no longer the middle brother of three but the elder of two, with certain decisions to make that you never expected. I do not fear that you will despair. It is not in your nature. I believe my ears are still ringing from the curse words you used to bellow out when the pain threatened to get past your endurance in the early days. You could have achieved the peace of death then, if you had only had the good sense to despair. You have only upward to go, then. You have, perhaps, rested upon a plateau overlong. Moving off it can be a frightening thing. It can also be an exciting challenge."

"Have you been rehearsing that speech all d-day, George?" Flavian asked. "I feel we ought to stand and applaud."

"It was quite spontaneous, I assure you," the duke said. "But I am rather pleased with it. I had not realized I was so wise. Or so eloquent. It must be time for bed." He laughed with the rest of them.

Ben positioned his canes and went through the slow rigmarole of getting to his feet again while everyone else stood.

Nothing had changed in the last hour, he thought as he made his slow way upstairs to his bedchamber, Flavian at his side, the others a little ahead of them. Nothing had been solved. But somehow he felt more cheerful—or perhaps merely more hopeful. Now that he had said it aloud—that his disabilities were permanent and he must carve out a wholly new life for himself—he felt more able to *do* something, to create a new and meaningful future, even if he had no idea yet what it would be.

But at least the immediate future was taken care of and did not involve one of those increasingly awkward and depressing visits to his own home. He would start out for County Durham in the north of England tomorrow and stay for a while with his sister. He looked forward to it. Beatrice, five years his senior, had always been his favorite sibling. While there with her, he would give some serious thought to what he was going to do with the rest of his life.

He would make some plans, some decisions. Something definite and interesting and challenging. Something to lift him out of the depression that had hung over him like a gray cloud for far too long.

There would be no more drifting.

There was really something rather exhilarating about the thought that the rest of his life was his for the making.

2

❧

*S*amantha McKay was restless. She stood at the window of the sitting room at Bramble Hall, her home in County Durham, and drummed her fingertips on the windowsill. Her sister-in-law was lying on the daybed in her room upstairs, incapacitated yet again by a sick headache. Matilda never had ordinary headaches. They were always either *sick* headaches or migraines, sometimes both.

They had been sitting here together quite companionably just half an hour ago, Samantha stitching at her embroidery, Matilda repairing the lace edging of a tablecloth. Samantha had remarked on what a fine day it was at last, even if the sun was not actually shining. She had suggested casually that perhaps they should go out for a walk. She had almost turned craven and left it at that, but she had pressed onward. Perhaps, she had suggested, they should walk out beyond the confines of the park today. Although the grounds surrounding the house were always referred to as the park, such a word glamorized what was in effect merely a large garden. It was perfectly adequate for a sedate stroll among the flower beds or for sitting out in on a warm day, but it did not offer nearly sufficient scope for real exercise.

And real exercise was what Samantha had begun to crave more than anything else she could think of. If she did not get out beyond house and garden soon and walk, *really* walk, she would . . . Oh, she would scream or throw herself down on the floor and drum her heels and have a major tantrum. Well, she would *feel* like doing all those things even though she supposed she would not actually *do* anything more extravagant than sigh and yearn and plot. She was nearly desperate, though.

Matilda, predictably, had looked reproachful, not to mention shocked and sorrowful. It was not—or so she had proceeded to explain—that she did not feel in need of a good walk herself. A true lady must, however, learn to master her base desires when she was in deep mourning. A true lady kept herself decently confined to her home and took the air in the privacy of her own park, shielded behind its walls from the critical eyes of the prying world. It was certainly not seemly for a lady in mourning to be seen out *enjoying* herself. Or to be seen at all for that matter, except by her close relatives and servants inside her own home and by her neighbors at church.

Captain Matthew McKay, Matilda's brother and Samantha's husband of seven years, had died four months before Matilda delivered herself of this speech. He had died after suffering for five years from the wounds he had sustained as an officer during the Peninsular Wars. He had needed constant tending during those years, or, rather, he had *demanded* constant tending, and the role of nurse had fallen to Samantha's almost exclusive lot since he would admit no one else to the sickroom except his valet and the physician. She had hardly known what it was to sleep for a whole night or to have more than an hour here and there outside the sickroom during the day. She had almost never had the chance to go beyond the garden walls. Even a stroll in the garden had been a rare treat.

Matilda had come to Bramble Hall for the final couple of months of her brother's life, after Samantha had written to her father-in-law, the Earl of Heathmoor, at Leyland Abbey in Kent, to inform him that the physician believed the end was near. But the burden of care upon Samantha's shoulders had not been lightened, partly because by that time Matthew really had needed her, and partly because he could not stand the sight of Matilda and always told her quite bluntly when she appeared in his room to take herself off and keep her Friday face out of his sight.

Samantha had been very close to the point of collapse by the time Matthew died. She had been exhausted and numb and dispirited. Her life had felt suddenly empty and colorless. She had had no will to do anything, even to get up in the morning or clothe herself or brush her hair. Even to eat.

It was no wonder she had allowed Matilda to take charge of everything, though she had written to her father-in-law herself within an hour of his son's death.

Matilda had insisted that the second son of the Earl of Heathmoor be mourned according to the strictest rules of propriety, though she had not needed to insist— Samantha had put up no fight. It had not even occurred to her that she might or that the rules of which Matilda spoke were excessive as well as oppressive. She had allowed herself to be decked out from head to toe in what must surely be the heaviest and gloomiest mourning garments ever fashioned. She had not even insisted upon being fitted for the new clothes. She had allowed herself to be cloistered within her home, the curtains always more than half drawn across the windows out of respect for the dead. She had allowed Matilda to discourage any visitors who made courtesy calls of sympathy from coming again, and to refuse every invitation that was extended to them, even to the most sober and respectable of social gatherings.

Samantha had not missed mingling with society in

the form of her neighbors for the obvious reason that she never had mingled with them. She hardly even knew them beyond nodding at church on Sunday mornings. She had been at Bramble Hall for five years, and almost every moment of those years had been devoted to Matthew's care.

For four months now she had not cared for anything beyond the numbness of her own all-encompassing lethargy and exhaustion. If truth were told, she had been rather glad that Matilda was there to take charge of all that needed to be done, even though she had never liked her sister-in-law any better than her husband had.

But numbness and exhaustion could last only so long. After four months, life was reasserting itself. She was restless. She was ready to fling off her lethargy. She needed to get out—out of the house, out of the park. She needed to walk. She needed to breathe real air.

She gazed outdoors, her fingers drumming, and then looked down at her widow's weeds and grimaced. She felt the blackness of every ill-fitting stitch of them like a physical weight. She had tried reasoning with Matilda earlier. Surely, she had said, it would be harmless to go out for a walk along country lanes that were rarely traveled. And even if they did encounter someone, surely that person would not think any the worse of them for strolling sedately in the countryside close to their own home. Surely whoever it was would not dash off to spread the word throughout the neighborhood that the widow and her sister-in-law were kicking up a lark, behaving with shocking levity and disrespect for the dead.

Had she really hoped to draw a smile from Matilda with her exaggeration? Had Matilda *ever* smiled? What she *had* done was stare stonily back at her smiling sister-in-law, deliberately set aside her unfinished mending task, and announce that she had a sick headache, for which she hoped Samantha was satisfied. She had withdrawn to her room to lie down for an hour or two.

Samantha was glad Matilda had never married. Some poor man had thereby been saved from a life of abject misery. She did not even feel guilty at the uncharitable thought.

Her downward glance at her blacks had also encountered the eager, hopeful expression of a large brown shaggy dog of quite indeterminate breed, a stray that had turned up literally on her doorstep two years ago looking like a gangly skeleton, and had taken up residence there after she fed him out of sheer pity and then tried to shoo him away. He had steadfastly refused to be shooed, and somehow, by means quite beyond either her comprehension or her control, he had taken up residence *inside* the house and grown more bulky and more thick-and-unruly-coated but never sleek or shiny or graceful as any self-respecting dog ought to look. He was seated at Samantha's feet now, his tail thumping the floor, his tongue lolling, his eyes begging her to please, *please* do something with him.

Sometimes she felt he was the only bright spot in her world.

"*You* would come walking with me if I asked it of you, would you not, Tramp?" she asked him. "Respectability notwithstanding?"

It was a fatal question—it had contained a word beginning with the letter *w*. Actually, it had contained more than one, but one of them also had the letters *a-l-k* attached to it. Tramp scrambled to his feet in his usual ungainly manner, yipped sharply as if under the illusion that he was still a puppy, panted noisily as though he had just run a mile at top speed, and continued to gaze expectantly upward.

"How could your answer be anything but yes?" She laughed at him and patted his head. But he was having none of such mild affection. He circled his head so that he could first slobber over her hand and then expose his throat for a good scratch. "And why not? Why ever *not*, Tramp?"

It was clear Tramp could think of no reason at all why they should deprive themselves merely because Lady Matilda McKay had a sick headache as well as strange notions about air and exercise and correct mourning etiquette. He lumbered over to the door and gazed up at the knob.

It was unseemly for a lady to walk alone beyond the confines of her own park—even when she was *not* in mourning. Or so Samantha had been taught during the year she had spent at Leyland Abbey while Matthew was away in the Peninsula with his regiment. It was one of the many dreary rules of being a lady that her father-in-law had felt it incumbent upon himself to teach the woman his son had married against his wishes.

Well, she had no choice but to go alone. Matilda was flat on her daybed upstairs and would not have accompanied her anyway—it was the very idea of the walk that had put her on the daybed. If Samantha set one toe beyond the boundary of the park and Matilda and the Earl of Heathmoor found out about it . . . Well, even if she dug a hole all the way to China and disappeared down it, she would not escape their wrath. And the earl *would* hear about it if Matilda did. There were many miles of countryside between County Durham in the north of England and Kent in the south, but those miles burned up a few times each week with messengers bearing Matilda's letters home and the earl's letters to Bramble Hall.

Why had she allowed this to happen? Samantha asked herself. She was beginning to feel like a prisoner in her own home, under the guardianship of a humorless spy. Matthew would not have tolerated it. He had exercised a sort of tyranny of his own over her, but it was not his father's. He had hated his father.

"Well," she said, "since I was foolish enough to use the forbidden word in your hearing, Tramp, it would be nothing short of cruelty to disappoint you. And it would be the ultimate in cruelty to disappoint myself."

His tail waved, and he looked from the doorknob to her and back again.

Ten minutes later they were striding along the path at the west side of the house toward the garden gate, which they passed through to the lane and meadows beyond. At least, Samantha strode in quite unladylike but equally unrepentant fashion while Tramp loped along at her side and occasionally dashed off in pursuit of any squirrel or small rodent incautious enough to rear its head. Though perhaps it was not lack of caution but merely contempt on their part, for Tramp never came close to running his prey to earth.

Ah, it felt so very good to breathe in fresh air at last, Samantha thought, even if it must be filtered through the heavy black veil that hung from the brim of her black bonnet. And it was glorious to see nothing but open space about her, first on the lane, and then on the daisy-and-buttercup-strewn grass of a meadow onto which they turned. It was sheer heaven to allow her stride to lengthen and to know that at least for a while the horizon was the only boundary that confined her.

There was no one to witness her grand indiscretion, no one to gasp in horror at the sight of her.

She stopped occasionally and gathered buttercups, while Tramp frolicked about her. And then, her little posy complete, she strode along again, a thick hedge to one side, all the fresh beauties of nature spread out on the other, the sky stretching overhead with its high layer of clouds through which she could see the bright, fuzzy disk of the sun. There was a brisk, slightly chilly breeze fluttering her veil about her face, but she did not feel the discomfort of the cold. Indeed, she relished it. She felt happier than she had felt for months, even perhaps for years. Oh, definitely for years.

She was *not* going to feel guilty about taking this hour for herself. No one could say she had not given her husband all the attention she possibly could while he lived. And no one could say she had not mourned him properly since his death. No one could even say she had been glad of his death. She had never, ever wished him dead, even at those times when she had wondered if she had any reserves of energy left with which to tend him and be patient with his endless peevishness. She had been genuinely saddened by the death of the man she had married just seven years before with such high hopes for a happily-ever-after.

No, she was not going to feel guilty. She *needed* this—this pleasure, this peace, this quiet restoration of her spirits.

It was precisely as she was thinking these tranquil thoughts that her peace was shattered in a sudden and most alarming manner.

Tramp had just returned with the stick she had thrown for him, and she was bending to retrieve it with one hand while she held her posy in the other, when it seemed that a thunderbolt came crashing down upon them from the heavens, only narrowly missing them. Samantha shrieked with terror, while the dog went into a frenzy of hysterical barking and leaped aimlessly in every direction, bowling Samantha right off her feet. Her buttercups went flying about in a hail of yellow, and she landed with a painful thud on her bottom.

She gaped in mingled pain and terror and discovered that the thunderbolt was in fact a large black horse, which had just leapt over the hedge very close to where she had been standing. It might have kept on going, since it appeared to have landed safely enough, but Tramp's barking and leaping and perhaps her own scream had sent it into a frenzy of its own. It whinnied and reared, its eyes rolling wildly and fearfully, as the rider on its back fought for his seat and brought it under control with considerable skill and a whole arsenal of curse words most foul.

"Are you out of your *mind*? Are you quite *insane*?"

"Bring that blasted animal under control, woman, damn it."

Samantha shouted her rhetorical questions and the man bellowed his imperious command simultaneously.

Tramp was standing his ground and barking ferociously, alternately with baring his teeth and growling in a fearsome manner. The horse was still prancing nervously, though it was no longer rearing.

Woman?

Blasted animal?

Damn it?

And why was the man not leaping from the saddle to help her to her feet and assure himself that he had not done her any fatal injury, as any true gentleman would?

"Tramp," she said firmly, though certainly not in obedience to the rider's command. "That is quite enough!"

A rabbit chose that moment to pop up on the horizon, ears pointed at the heavens, and Tramp dashed off in joyful pursuit, still barking and still convinced he could win the race.

"You might have *killed* me with your irresponsible stunt," Samantha shouted above the din. "Are you *quite* mad?"

The gentleman on the horse's back glared coldly at her. "If you are unable to control that pathetic excuse for a dog," he said, "you really ought not to bring him out where he can upset horses and livestock and endanger human life."

"Livestock?" She looked pointedly to left and right to indicate that there was nary a cow or bull in sight. "*He* endangered human life? Your own, I suppose you mean, since mine clearly means nothing to you. Allow me to pose a question. Was it you, sir, or was it Tramp who chose with reckless unconcern to jump a hedge without first ascertaining that it was safe to do so? And was it you or he who then hurled the blame upon the innocent person who was almost killed? And upon a dog which was happily at play until he had the life virtually scared out of him?"

She got to her feet without taking her eyes off him— and without wincing over what felt like a bruised tailbone. Perhaps it was a good thing he had *not* dismounted to help her up, she thought as wrath took the place of terror. She might have smacked his face, and that must certainly be against the rules of propriety for a lady, not to mention a widow in deep mourning.

His nostrils flared as he listened to her, and his lips compressed into a thin line as he looked down at her as though she were a nasty worm it might have been better that his horse had trodden upon.

"I trust," he said with stiff formality, "you have not come to any great harm, ma'am? I assume not, though, since you are quite capable of speech."

She narrowed her eyes and bent upon him her most cold and haughty stare, though she was aware that the thickness of her veil probably marred its full effect.

Tramp came dashing back without the rabbit. He had stopped barking. She rested a hand on his head as he sat panting beside her, eyeing horse and rider eagerly as though they might be new friends.

Samantha and the rider regarded each other for a few silent moments, which nevertheless bristled with mutual hostility. Then he abruptly touched his whip to the brim of his tall hat, turned his horse, and rode away at a canter without another word, leaving her the clear victor of the field.

Well.

Well!

Her bosom still heaved with ire. *Woman,* indeed. And *blasted animal.* And *damn it.*

He was a stranger—at least she thought he was since she had certainly never set eyes upon him before. A thoroughly disagreeable stranger. She fervently hoped he would keep on riding until he was far, far away and never return. He was no gentleman despite his looks, which suggested the contrary. *He* had done something unpardonably reckless, with results that might have been fatal had she been standing six feet farther to the east. Yet *she* and *Tramp* were to blame. And though he had asked, or rather *trusted,* that she had taken no harm, he had not got down from his saddle to find out at closer quarters. And then he had had the effrontery to assume that she must be unharmed, since she could still talk. As if she were some kind of *shrew.*

It really was a shame that good looks and elegance and an overall appearance of masculine virility were wasted on such a nasty, cold, arrogant, villainous sort of man. He *was* good-looking, she admitted when she thought about him, even if his face was a trifle too lean and angular for true handsomeness. And he was young-ish. She guessed he was not much above thirty, if he was even that old.

He had an impressive vocabulary, almost none of which she would have understood if she had not spent a year with Matthew's regiment before they were sent off to the Peninsula. And he had used it in a lady's hearing—without apologizing, as the officers of the regiment had always done quite effusively when they realized they had cursed within half a mile of a lady's ears.

She sincerely hoped she would never encounter him

again. She might be tempted to give him the full length of her tongue if she did.

"Well, pathetic excuse for a dog," she said, looking down at Tramp, "our one foray into the peace and freedom of the outdoors almost ended in disaster. Behold my posy scattered to the four winds. Father-in-Law would lecture me for a fortnight if he were to hear about this adventure, especially if he knew I had scolded a gentleman instead of hanging my head meekly and allowing *him* to scold *me*. Do not, I pray you, breathe a word of this to Matilda. She would have a migraine and a sick headache combined—after berating me, that is, and writing a long letter home. You do not suppose they can be right, do you, Tramp? That I am not a proper lady, I mean? I suppose my origins are against me, as the Earl of Heathmoor was pleased to inform me with tedious regularity once upon a time, but really . . . *Woman* and *damn it*. And you a *blasted animal*. I have been severely provoked. *We* have been."

Tramp, apparently more forgiving than she, fell into step beside her and refrained from offering an opinion.

3

❧

*G*uilt and shame quickly hurled cold water on the embers of Ben's fury.

The humiliating truth, he admitted, was that he had frightened himself more than half to death when he jumped that damned hedge. He had been back to riding for some time, having discovered that he could both mount and dismount with the aid of a special block. He had learned to ride with some skill and confidence despite the fact that he did not have as much power in his thighs as he had used to have. But today was the first time since his cavalry days that he had challenged himself to jump a fence or hedge.

Perhaps it had been the reaction to that admission he had made to the Survivors at Penderris that he had taken his recovery as far as it could go. Perhaps he had needed to push himself to one more level of achievement just to prove to himself that he had not simply given up. The open meadows bordered by hedges in which he had been riding had tempted him. The hedges were high enough to be a challenge but not high enough to make the attempt to jump one of them entirely reckless. And so he had chosen this particular hedge, set his horse directly at it, and soared over with at least a foot to spare.

The rush of exhilarated triumph that had accompanied the jump had quickly converted to sheer, blind terror, however, and his mind had been catapulted back to that most hellish of black moments in the tumult of battle when he had been shot, his horse had been shot under him at the same time and had fallen on him before he could draw his foot free of the stirrup, and then another horse and rider had come crashing down on top of them both.

He had thought it was happening all over again. There had been that sense of falling, of losing control, of staring death in the eyeballs. Pure instinct had kept him in the saddle and set him to bringing his horse under control, and he had soon realized that the source of the whole near catastrophe was a damned maniacal hound, which was still leaping about, barking ferociously, long after all danger was over. And there was a woman, an ugly old crone, dressed from head to toe in hideous black, seated at her ease on the grass below the hedge, surrounded by wildflowers and not doing a blessed thing to control the beast.

Had he been at liberty to stop and consider, of course, he would have realized a number of other things, as he did now while he rode away from the scene of his guilt. She would not have been sitting on the ground gathering flowers just for the sheer pleasure of it. It was a chilly, blustery day. She must, then, have fallen or been knocked down. Her dog would not have behaved as it had if he had not come flying over the hedge without any warning. And he might easily have killed the woman if he had taken the hedge just to the right of where he had. The fault for the whole debacle had been, in fact, entirely his.

As she had not been shy about pointing out.

Something else had quickly become clear to him—two things, actually. She was not an old crone. She was in fact a youngish female, though he had not been able to see her face through the hideous funereal veil that covered it. And she was a lady. Her voice and her demeanor had both given evidence of that fact.

Not that his guilt would have been lessened even if she *had* been a crone. Or a beggar woman. Or both. He had yelled at her, and he could not be sure he had not used some inappropriate language while doing so. He certainly had when fighting for control of his mount. He had not gone to her rescue. Not that he could have done so literally, of course, but he might have shown considerably more concern, perhaps even explained why he could not get off his horse.

In short, he had behaved badly. Quite abominably, in fact.

He briefly considered turning back and begging her pardon, but he doubted she would be delighted to see him again. Besides, he was still feeling too irritated to make a sincere apology.

Pray God he never saw the woman again. Though he supposed it altogether probable that she lived in the neighborhood since she was out on foot with her dog— unescorted. And she was obviously in deep mourning for someone.

Good Lord, *he* had been terrified. How must *she* have felt when horse and rider erupted over the hedge a mere whisker from where she stood? Yet he had ripped up at her for walking and exercising her dog in a public meadow.

After he had ridden into the stables at Robland Park and dismounted, he was still feeling considerably out of sorts. He made his slow way to the house.

"Ah, you are back safe, are you?" Beatrice said, looking up from her knotwork as he lowered himself to a chair in the drawing room. "It concerns me that you insist upon riding alone, Ben, instead of taking a groom with you as any sensible man in your circumstances would. Oh, I know, I know. You do not have to say it, and I can see your brows knitting together in vexation. I am acting like a mother hen. But with Hector gone to London already and the boys back at school, I have no one to fuss over but you. And I cannot ride with you as I am still under physician's orders to coddle myself after that chill. Did you have a pleasant ride?"

"Very," he said.

She rested her work on her lap. "What has ruffled your feathers, then? Apart from my fussing, that is."

"Nothing."

She raised her eyebrows and resumed her work.

"The tea tray will be here in a moment," she told him. "I daresay you are a bit chilled."

"It is not a cold day."

She laughed without looking up. "If you are determined to be disagreeable, I shall make a companion of my knots."

He watched her for a short while. She wore a lacy cap on her fair hair. It offended him somewhat, though it was a pretty confection. She was only thirty-four, for God's sake, five years his senior. She behaved like a matron—which was exactly what she was, he supposed. It was longer than six years since he had been wounded, and sometimes it seemed that time had stood still since then. Except that it had not. Everything and everyone had moved on. And that was, of course, part of his recently acknowledged problem, for he had not. He had been too absorbed in trying to put himself back together so that he could pick up the threads of his life exactly where he had left them off.

The tea tray was brought in, and Beatrice set aside her work to pour them both a cup of tea and to carry him his, together with a plate of cakes.

"Thank you," he said. "I must smell of horse."

"It is not an unpleasant smell," she told him without denying it. "I shall be back to riding myself soon. The doctor will be calling here tomorrow, for the final time, it is to be hoped. I feel perfectly restored to health. Relax there for a while before you go to change your clothes."

"Is there a widow living in these parts?" he asked her abruptly. "A lady? Still in deep mourning?"

"Mrs. McKay, do you mean?" She lifted her cup to her lips. "Captain McKay's widow? He was the Earl of Heathmoor's second son and died three or four months ago. She lives at Bramble Hall on the far side of the village."

"She has a big, unruly dog?" Ben asked.

"A big, *friendly* dog," she said. "I did not find him unruly when I paid a call upon Mrs. McKay after the funeral, though he did insist in quite unmannerly fashion upon being petted. He came to lay his head on my lap and looked up at me with soulful eyes. I suppose he ought to have been trained not to do such things, but dogs always know who likes them."

"She had him in a meadow not very far from here," he said. "I almost bowled them both over when I jumped a hedge."

"Oh, goodness gracious," she said. "Was anyone hurt? But—you *jumped a hedge,* Ben? Where is my hartshorn? Ah, I have just remembered—I do not possess any, not being the vaporish sort, though you could easily make a convert of me."

"What the devil was she doing out unchaperoned?" he asked.

She clicked her tongue. "Ben, dear, your language! I am surprised to know she was. I have never seen her outside her own house except at church on Sundays. Captain McKay was very badly wounded in the Peninsula and never recovered his health enough to leave his bed. Mrs. McKay nursed him almost single-handedly and with great devotion, from what I can gather."

"Well, she was out alone today," he said. "At least, I assume it was the lady you named."

"I am surprised," she said again. "Her sister-in-law has been staying with her for some time. I have very little acquaintance with her, and it seems unfair to judge a near stranger, but I would guess she is as much a stickler for propriety taken to an extreme as the earl, her father, is. He is *not* my favorite person, or anyone else's that I know. Had he lived a couple of centuries ago, he would have joined forces with Oliver Cromwell and those horrid Puritans and sapped all the humor and enjoyment from everyone else's life. I am surprised Lady Matilda did not insist that Mrs. McKay remain at home behind closed doors and curtains."

"You sound indignant," he said.

"Well." She set down her cup and saucer. "When one arranges a quiet dinner with the soberest of one's neighbors, including the vicar and his wife, with the intention of extending the hand of sympathy and friendship to two ladies who have recently lost a husband and brother, and one has been turned down and made to feel that one's very existence is frivolous and contaminating, then one can surely be excused for being slightly ruffled when one is reminded of it."

He grinned at her until she caught his eye and laughed.

"The answer to my invitation was written by Lady Matilda McKay," she said. "I like to believe that Mrs. McKay would have declined it in a far more gracious manner, if she had declined it at all."

The grin faded from Ben's face. "I owe her an apology."

"Do you?" she asked. "Did you not apologize when it happened? She was *not* hurt, I hope?"

"I do not believe so," he said, though he remembered that she had been sitting on the ground when he first became aware of her. "But I ripped up at her, Bea, and blamed her for the near catastrophe—and her dog, which is an ugly brute if ever I saw one. I owe her an apology."

"Perhaps we will see her at church on Sunday," she said. "I would not go riding up to the doors of Bramble Hall, if I were you. For one thing, you have not been introduced and it would be vastly improper. For another, I do believe the sister-in-law might well have an apoplexy if she discovered a single gentleman on the doorstep. Either that, or she would attack you with the nearest umbrella or knitting needle."

He could just forget about the whole episode, Ben supposed a few minutes later as he made his slow way upstairs to change out of his riding clothes. But he hated to recall that he had behaved in a manner unbecoming a gentleman—and that was a bit of an understatement.

He definitely owed her an apology.

Samantha and Matilda went to church as usual the following Sunday. It might have amused Samantha that Sunday service had become the big outing and social event of her week, if it had not also been so pathetic. For so it had been for the past five years, even though she had been only nineteen when she first came to live at Bramble Hall. And the situation was not about to change, despite the fact that she no longer had Matthew to tend at home.

She sat beside Matilda in their usual pew at the front of the church, her prayer book on her lap, and turned her head neither to the left nor to the right, though she would dearly like to have seen which neighbors were also present. She would have liked to nod genially to them as she had always done in the past. But Matilda sat rigidly still, and, foolishly perhaps, Samantha felt constrained to match her piety, if that was what it was.

It was only after the service, then, when they had risen to pass down the aisle and out to the waiting gig, their faces properly hidden behind their veils, that she saw *that man* again. It was how she had been thinking of him, with growing indignation, for two days.

That man.

He was sitting in the pew across the aisle and one row back from hers. He must have been able to see her all through the service. He was still sitting, not jumping to his feet as soon as her eyes alit incautiously upon him, as any proper gentleman would have done, especially one who had treated her so ill. And it was not that he had not noticed her. His eyes were directly upon her.

How *dared* he?

He was not wearing his hat inside the church. His face was narrow and angular, as she had observed at their first meeting. He had a straight, finely chiseled nose and slightly hollowed cheeks, a firm chin and hard blue eyes beneath midbrown hair. He must have been exceedingly handsome in his youth. He was not a youth now, though. It was hard to guess his age, but his face bore evidence of having looked upon a great deal of hard living, perhaps of suffering. It was still handsome, however, she conceded grudgingly, perhaps the more so for not being boyish.

It would have been more satisfying if he had been ugly. All villains ought to look the part.

She would have looked away with deliberate disdain and continued up the aisle, but she had hesitated a moment too long, and the lady beside him, who *was* on her feet, spoke to her. She was Lady Gramley. Of course she was—this was her usual pew.

"Mrs. McKay," she said kindly, "how do you do?"

"I am well, thank you, ma'am," Samantha replied. She could feel Matilda's hand firm on her back. Good heavens, was it improper for a grieving widow even to exchange pleasantries with her neighbors at church?

"Perhaps you will allow me the pleasure of presenting my brother, Sir Benedict Harper," Lady Gramley said. "Mrs. McKay, Ben. And Lady Matilda McKay."

And *finally* he considered getting to his feet, though he was in no hurry even now. He looked to one side, away from Samantha and Matilda, and picked up two canes, which he arranged on either side of him. They were not ordinary canes. They were longer and had handpieces partway down, with leather loops through which he slid his hands. They circled his arms as he grasped the handpieces and hoisted himself to his feet.

Had he fallen from his horse since she last saw him? Samantha wondered hopefully and unkindly. But no. Those canes must have been specially made. She had seen nothing like them before.

Even when he was slightly hunched over them, she could see that he was tall and thin. No, not thin. *Lean.* There was a difference. And his well-fitting, fashionable coat and pantaloons, over which he wore highly polished Hessian boots, emphasized his pleasingly proportioned physique. He was an attractive man, she admitted without feeling in any way attracted. She felt as irritated with him as she had been two days ago. More so, perhaps, because now she could see that he had had an excuse for not jumping from his horse to rush gallantly to her rescue on that day, and she did not want him to have any excuse at all.

"Sir." She inclined her head with as much frosty hauteur as she could muster. She was aware of Matilda slightly curtsying and murmuring his name.

"Ma'am," he said, inclining his head. "Lady Matilda."

Benedict. It was far too pleasant a name for him. It sounded like a blessing—a benediction. She wondered if there was any profane word in existence that he had *not* used in that meadow. She doubted it.

"My brother has been kind enough to give me his company at Robland Park for a few weeks before I join my husband in London for the second half of the Season," Lady Gramley explained. "Perhaps we may call upon you one afternoon, Mrs. McKay? I have not spoken to you since soon after your husband was laid to rest, and I would not have you feel that your neighbors are neglecting you in your grief."

Samantha felt uncomfortable, for no longer than three weeks ago the Earl and Countess of Gramley had invited her and Matilda to dinner and Matilda had persuaded her that it would be unseemly to accept, that Lady Gramley ought not even to have suggested such a thing. Samantha had been surprised, but she had still been in the grip of lethargy and had allowed her sister-in-law to send a refusal, politely worded, she hoped. Even so, she thought it good of Lady Gramley not to have taken offense.

"That would be delightful," she said, though she could have wished that the lady's brother was not included. But perhaps she could suffocate him with courtesy if he came and show him what true gentility was. It would be a fitting revenge. It was more likely, though, that he would make an excuse *not* to come. "We will look forward to it, will we not, Matilda?"

"We are still in deep mourning, ma'am," Matilda reminded Lady Gramley, as if their heavy blacks were not hint enough. "However, there can be no objection to receiving an occasional afternoon call from a genteel neighbor."

Oh, good heavens. It was no wonder Matthew had been the black sheep of his family and had detested the lot of them, his sister included. Matilda was calling a

countess a genteel neighbor as though she were confer-
ring some great favor upon her.

Sir Benedict Harper had not removed his eyes from
Samantha's face. She wondered how much he could see
of it. And she wondered if he felt embarrassed at seeing
her again. Did he recall calling her *woman*? She recalled
it, and she bristled at the memory.

Samantha inclined her head again and moved on. The
whole encounter had taken less than a minute, but it
had left her with ruffled feathers. *Would* he accompany
Lady Gramley when she called? Would he dare?

She inclined her head civilly to a few other members
of the congregation and offered her hand to the vicar
and a comment on his sermon. Matilda praised him at
greater length and with stiff condescension. And then
they were in the gig and on their way home.

"Lady Gramley appears genteel enough," Matilda
observed.

"I have always found her both kind and gracious,"
Samantha said, "though I have not had many dealings
with her over the years. Or with any of my other neighbors, for that matter. Matthew needed almost all my
time and attention."

"Sir Benedict Harper is crippled," Matilda said.

"But not bedridden." He could even ride, Samantha
thought. "Perhaps he will not accompany his sister if
she calls on us."

"It would be tactful of him not to," Matilda agreed,
"since he is a stranger to us. It is a pity we could not
have avoided the introduction."

For once Samantha was in accord with her sister-in-
law. It did not happen often.

Matilda was as different from her brother as it was
possible to be. A self-avowed spinster at the age of
thirty-two, who had long ago professed her intention
of devoting herself to her mother in her declining years,

she seemed to lack any softness or femininity. Her father was next only to God in her esteem. Matthew had been three years older, handsome, dashing, charming— and quite irresistibly gorgeous in his scarlet regimentals. Samantha had met him at an assembly when his regiment was stationed a mere three miles from her home. She had been seventeen years old, young, naïve, and impressionable. She had tumbled headlong into love with Lieutenant McKay, as he had been then, as had every other girl for miles around. It would have been strange, perhaps, if she had not. When he married her, she had thought herself the happiest, most fortunate girl in the world, an impression that had remained with her for four months until she discovered that he was shallow and vain—and unfaithful.

Yes, he had been very different from his sister. Of the two, she would take Matthew any day of the year. Not that she any longer had a choice in the matter. The thought brought a stabbing of grief.

The severe wounds he suffered in battle had destroyed Matthew in more ways than one. He had been a difficult patient, though she had always tried to make allowances for his pain and his disabilities and the deteriorating condition of his lungs. He had been demanding and selfish. She had devoted herself to his care without complaint even though she had fallen out of love with him before he went away to the Peninsula.

His death had caused her real grief. It had been hard to watch the destruction of a man who had been so handsome and vital and vain—and to watch him die at the age of thirty-five.

Poor Matthew.

Matilda reached over and patted her hand. "Your grief does you credit, Samantha," she said. "I shall tell Father so when I write to him tomorrow."

Samantha reached beneath her veil and dashed away

a tear with one black-gloved hand. She felt guilty. For there was relief mingled with the sadness she felt at Matthew's having to die. She could no longer deny that fact. She was free at last—or would be when this heavy ritual of mourning was at an end.

Was it wicked to think that way?

4

✤

"I wonder," Ben said, "if Mrs. McKay has told her sister-in-law what happened a few afternoons ago."

"I really do not know the lady," Beatrice replied, "but I must confess that she strikes me as being a bit of a battle-ax."

They were traveling toward Bramble Hall in an open carriage, with the blessing of Beatrice's physician, who at last had pronounced her fully restored to health. It was a sunny day and quite warm for springtime. Two days had passed since their encounter with the McKay ladies at church.

"I did not behave as I ought to have when I first encountered Mrs. McKay," Ben said. "I really do need to make amends, Bea. Yet if I blurt out an apology over tea, I may embarrass her before her sister-in-law. I cannot help agreeing with you about the lady, even though we spoke with the two of them for what was probably no longer than a minute on Sunday, and it was impossible even to see their faces. Have you ever seen facial veils quite as black and heavy as theirs? I wonder they can see out. One half expects them to walk into walls."

"Perhaps their grief is great," she said. "Poor Captain McKay is said to have been exceedingly handsome and dashing once upon a time. War is a cruel thing, Ben, not that I need to tell you of all people that. It would have been kinder, perhaps, if he had been killed outright.

Kinder for him, kinder for his wife, kinder for his sister."

Dash it, would he ever escape from those wars? Ben thought irritably. What damnable fate was it that had set him to jumping that particular hedge at that particular moment on that particular day when he had jumped nothing on horseback in longer than six years? And what had led Mrs. McKay to walk just there when apparently she had scarcely set foot outside her own home since she moved there with her invalid husband five or six years ago?

Fate? He very much doubted it. And if it was, then fate was a damnably weird thing.

This visit he was about to pay was the last thing on earth he wished to be doing. One did not like to be caught out in ungentlemanly conduct, and one did not like having to beg pardon of the offended party, especially when she was as cold and haughty as Captain McKay's widow appeared to be.

"If I see even the glimmering of an opportunity," Beatrice promised as the carriage drew to a halt outside the front doors of Bramble Hall, "I will draw Lady Matilda away or at least out of earshot, Ben, so that you may make your peace with Mrs. McKay."

There was an instant response to the rap of the knocker against the door in the form of a deep, excited barking from within. The unruly hound, no doubt.

Bramble Hall was a solid stone house, a manor more than a mansion, but of pleasing proportions and set in gardens that were well tended even if not extensive. The interior too was handsome, Ben soon discovered, though the hall was paneled in dark wood and the sitting room into which they were shown was scarcely any lighter, since the dark wine velvet curtains were more than half drawn over the windows. The furniture was old and heavy and predominantly a dark brown. Dark-toned landscape paintings hung on the papered walls.

The ladies rose to their feet as the butler announced their visitors. They both, of course, wore black dresses that covered them from neck to wrists to ankles. Lady Matilda was also wearing a black lacy cap over her fair hair, tied in a neat black bow beneath her chin. Ben wondered uncharitably that she had not dyed her hair black.

Mrs. McKay's head was uncovered. Her very dark, glossy hair was styled in a tight coronet of braids about the crown of her head, the rest combed smooth, without a suggestion of a curl or ringlet to soften the severity. Her eyes were very dark too and large and long-lashed, her nose straight, her mouth generous and full-lipped, her skin dark-toned. She almost undoubtedly had some foreign blood in her veins, though he could not place her origin. Spain? Italy? Greece?

Her dress was of some heavy, rather stiff fabric and was ill-fitting and unbecoming. Nevertheless, it could not hide the fact, as her cloak had done on both previous occasions he had seen her, that she was generously curved and voluptuous of figure. She had the height to carry it too.

He had expected her to be ugly. She had *looked* ugly through her veil. She was, to the contrary, utterly, stunningly beautiful. And younger than he had estimated.

His impression of both ladies was gathered in a moment. Fortunately, he was prevented from staring overlong by the infernal hound, which looked every bit as ugly now as he had in the meadow a few days ago. He was prancing about them in the sort of orgy of undiscipline one might expect of an untrained puppy but not of a grown dog that lived inside the house. He seemed undecided whether to be ecstatic that they had come to visit or offended that they had dared trespass upon his domain. However, he seemed altogether willing to give them the benefit of the doubt if they showed the slightest tendency to play with him.

Beatrice laughed and patted his head. "What a lovely welcome," she said.

"Hush, dog," Lady Matilda commanded—to no effect. "Samantha, do have him removed."

"Sit, Tramp," Mrs. McKay said, "or you are going to have to be banished to outer darkness."

The dog did not sit, but he did stop his prancing to look up at his mistress, panting, tongue lolling, and then he padded off to plop himself down in the shaft of daylight that beamed through the narrow gap in the curtains, his ears cocked lest he miss someone offering further entertainment.

Wretched hound. Without him, Ben might well have cleared that hedge and ridden back to Robland without even realizing that he had frightened the devil out of a lady and narrowly missed killing her. He would not even have known that an apology was in order. And he would have glanced at those two black-shrouded females in church with absolutely no wish whatsoever of making their acquaintance.

"Lady Gramley," Mrs. McKay said, stepping forward to offer a hand to her guest, "I do beg your pardon for Tramp's bad manners. How kind of you to call upon us. You were not very well the last time you did so, I recall. I was touched that you came at all. I do hope you have recovered your health. We have been very dull with only each other for company, have we not, Matilda?"

She turned to Ben after Bea had assured her that she had made a full recovery from her stubborn chill. Mrs. McKay's expression changed imperceptibly from warmly welcoming to coolly gracious as she shook his hand too.

"Sir Benedict," she said, "it was good of you to accompany your sister. Do have a seat."

She glanced at his canes but did not try to steer him to a chair, he was relieved to discover. Some people did.

A polite conversation ensued before a tea tray was brought in. Mrs. McKay poured, and her sister-in-law carried the tea and a plate of sweet biscuits to their guests. The dog came and snuffled first at Beatrice and then at Ben. He seemed to prefer the latter, even though Bea patted his head again and Ben most decidedly did not. He plopped down at Ben's feet and rested his chin on one of Ben's boots.

The animal must be as thick as a plank. Had not Bea said he knew who liked him?

"Samantha," Lady Matilda said, "do call a servant to remove that dog. He really ought not to be allowed to roam at will, especially when you are entertaining visitors. You know my thoughts on the matter."

He must be the ugliest dog in creation, and Ben had certainly not taken kindly to his decision to favor him with his company. Yet when it came to a choice between a battle-ax of a woman—yes, he had decided, Bea had hit upon quite the right description of Lady Matilda McKay—on the one hand and a gangly, drooling, undisciplined, undiscerning dog on the other, the decision was not even difficult.

"If the dog—Tramp, is it?—is no bother to Mrs. McKay," he said, "he certainly is not to me, Lady Matilda. I beg you to allow him to remain where he is."

Mrs. McKay shot him a glance that defied interpretation. Suspicion? Resentment? Reproach? It was surely not gratitude.

Quinn, Ben's valet, would probably be polishing dog

drool off his boot tonight and not looking too happy about it.

"He appeared on my doorstep two years ago," Mrs. McKay explained, "a determined, decrepit vagabond who would not go away even after I had fed him. My husband said, quite rightly, I suppose, that he would not go away *because* I had fed him. But how could I not have done? His long legs were like bent sticks, his ribs were all quite visible, his coat was dull and tufted, and he had such a look of longing and hope in his eyes that . . . Well, I would have had to be made of stone to turn him away. He lived on the doorstep for a while. How he got from there into the house and became master of all he surveyed I do not know, but he did."

"He would not have done so if I had been living here with you at the time, Samantha," Lady Matilda said, "as I would have been had Mother not suffered palpitations with every word that reached us about Matthew's condition. Even now I would urge you to send him to the stables and make him stay there. Animals do not belong in a decent house, as I am sure you would agree, Lady Gramley."

"You will think me a thorough weakling, I daresay, ma'am," Mrs. McKay said as a maid removed the tea tray. "I love him, you see. How anyone *could* love an ugly, impudent fellow like you, Tramp, I do not know, but I do."

She contrived to look at the dog, Ben noticed, without also looking at him. Her every word was directed to Bea, as though he did not exist. She was obviously very vexed with him.

"Pets become as much a part of one's family as the other persons in it," Beatrice agreed. "While our spaniel was still alive, one of my sons once accused me of loving her more than I loved him or his brother. And my reply was that sometimes she was easier to love. I was smothering my son with hugs while I was saying it, I hasten to add."

Ben had spoken scarcely a word. At this rate he was going to feel worse when he left than he had before he arrived. For if he did not apologize now, he never would, and he would forever feel in the wrong—as he was, dash it all.

Mrs. McKay might be a considerable beauty, but he really could not like her, perhaps because she had held up a mirror in which he had seen the ugliest side of himself. He caught Beatrice's eye and raised his eyebrows. Good manners probably dictated that they leave very soon.

"Lady Matilda," she said, "I fear I have eaten too many of those excellent biscuits and would welcome some exercise before the drive back to Robland Park. Would you be willing to take a turn on the terrace with me?"

Lady Matilda looked anything but willing. However, she was a lady and her social manners prevailed.

"I shall fetch my bonnet and cloak," she said and left the room.

Beatrice drifted after her, having asked Mrs. McKay apologetically and rhetorically if she minded. That lady looked as if she *did* mind, though she answered politely enough to the contrary. She looked down at the hands clasped in her lap when she and Ben were alone together, and silence descended, apart from one contented sigh from the dog, who had looked interested in the stroll on the terrace but had decided against making himself one of the party, perhaps because its number was to include Lady Matilda.

Clearly Mrs. McKay had no intention of breaking the silence.

Ben cleared his throat. "Mrs. McKay," he said, "I believe I owe you an apology."

"Yes." She raised her eyes and looked so directly into his own that he felt himself move his head back an inch or so even though she was some distance away from him. "You believe correctly, sir."

Well. Had he expected her to simper and assure him that he had done nothing to offend her?

"What happened the other day was entirely my fault," he said. "I ought not to have jumped that hedge without knowing what was on the other side. And when I *did* jump it and almost killed you, I certainly ought not to have thrown the blame upon you and ripped up at you as I did."

"We are in perfect accord upon *that*," she assured him, her chin up, her eyes steady, her whole manner disdainful. She continued. "I suppose it would be a bit absurd if every rider felt obliged to dismount and push through a hedge before he jumped it just to make sure that some stray pedestrian was not strolling along on the other side. He could, perhaps, cry out a *tallyho!* as he came, but that might sound rather peculiar. What happened was an accident. No one was to blame for *that*, at least."

The fairness of her response only cast him more abjectly in the wrong.

"But someone was certainly to blame for what followed," he said. "I was, in fact. My immediate reaction to throw all the blame upon you and your dog when you were both clearly innocent of any offense was unjust and unpardonable. I hope you *will* pardon me, nevertheless, ma'am, when I assure you that I am thoroughly ashamed of myself. And I beg forgiveness for the appalling language I am sure I must have used in your hearing, though I hope none of it was directed at you personally."

She was still looking unwaveringly at him, and it struck him that those dark eyes of hers were a quite lethal weapon. He had to resist the urge to move his head back another inch and lower his own eyes.

"Except for one *damn it*," she said, "which was added after you had called someone *woman*. Since I was the only female present, I was led to understand that you meant me."

He grimaced. Dash it all, he did not remember that.

"What caused me most indignation, however," she added, "was the fact that you did not get down from your horse when you saw that I had been knocked over—even though the knocking was done by my own hysterical dog rather than by your horse. Unfortunately, I was forced to relinquish much of my wrath when I saw you on Sunday and understood why you had not dismounted."

"I ought to have explained at the time," he said. "I ought to have shown far more concern for the fright you had taken and the harm I may have done you. I ought to have—" He sighed with frustration and ran his fingers through his hair. "Well, the long and the short of it is that I behaved atrociously in every imaginable way. I understand that you are offended I even had the effrontery to present myself here. I will, in fact, remove myself without further ado."

He reached for his canes.

"I spent a year with my husband in proximity to his regiment," she told him. "I heard a thing or two that ladies are not supposed to hear. Officers have voices that must carry on a battlefield. Unfortunately, they also carry when they are *not* on a battlefield. I am not a green girl, Sir Benedict, and I must admit, with some reluctance, that I admire your courage in coming here to speak to me face-to-face. I did not expect it. I take it

Lady Gramley did not really feel any burning need to stroll on the terrace with poor Matilda? I believe she ate only one biscuit."

"I was afraid," he said, "that if I blurted out my apology in your sister-in-law's hearing, I might compound my offense by informing her of something she does not know about."

"Good gracious, you are absolutely right," she said. "Matilda would have an apoplexy if she discovered I had been beyond the walls of the park without an escort—or even with one."

"You will forgive me?" he asked her.

"I swore I never would." Her eyes moved to his canes. "Is it hard for you to ride?"

"Yes," he said. "But that very fact makes the lure of doing so irresistible. That hedge was the first obstacle I had jumped since . . . Well, since my great fall more than six years ago. I was inclined to think afterward, in light of what happened and what *almost* happened, that it would also be my last. But I have decided it will not be. The next time I shall choose a higher obstacle, but I will be sure to approach it with a *tallyho!* on my lips."

"You were not born this way, then?" she asked him. "There was an accident?"

"It was called war," he told her.

Her eyes came back to his, and a frown creased her brow for a moment.

"Well, at least," she said, "your injuries, though severe, were confined to your legs. Unlike my husband's."

He pursed his lips but did not answer.

The dog lumbered to his feet suddenly, crossed the distance to his mistress, set his chin on her lap, and gazed up at her. She patted his head and then smoothed her hand over it while he closed his eyes in ecstasy.

"That was insensitive of me, I suppose," she said,

sounding a little annoyed. "*Were* your injuries confined to your legs?"

A bullet below the shoulder, not so very far from the heart. A broken collarbone. Several broken or cracked ribs. A broken arm. Cuts and bruises in too many places to name. No significant head injuries, the only miracle associated with that particular incident.

"No."

She looked at him as though she expected him to enumerate all his hurts.

"Those of us who were wounded in the wars are not in competition with each other to discover who suffered most," he told her. "And there are many ways to suffer. I have a friend who led his men into a number of desperate battles and emerged each time without a scratch. He led a successful Forlorn Hope in Spain and survived unscathed, though most of his men were killed. He was lauded by generals and awarded a title by the Prince of Wales. Then he went out of his mind and was brought back to England in a straitjacket. It took him several years to recuperate to the point where he could resume something resembling a normal life. I have another friend who was both blinded and deafened in his very first battle at the age of seventeen. He was raving mad when he was brought back home. His hearing came back after a while, but his sight did not and never will. It took him a number of years to put himself back together so that he could live his life rather than merely endure what is left of it until death takes him. It is never easy, ma'am, to decide which wounds are more severe than others."

She had lowered her gaze again while he spoke. She pulled on the dog's ears and then rested her forehead briefly against the top of his head. But she got abruptly to her feet when Ben had finished speaking and turned away to take a few steps closer to the window.

"I am so tired," she said in a voice that vibrated with some strong emotion. She stopped abruptly and started again. "I am mortally *weary* of war and wounds and suffering and death. I want to *live*. I want to . . . to *dance*." She tipped her head back. He suspected that her eyes were tightly closed. Then she laughed softly. "I want to dance. Only four months after my husband's death. Could I possibly be more frivolous? Less sensitive? More lost to all decent conduct?"

He looked at her in some surprise. "Has anyone accused you of those things?" he asked her.

She lifted her head and turned to look at him over her shoulder. "Would not everyone?" she asked in her turn. "You are not married, Sir Benedict?"

"No."

"If you had been and you had died," she said, "would you have been shocked if your widow had wanted to dance three months later?"

"I suppose," he said, lifting one finger to rub along the side of his nose, "at that point it would not have mattered much to me, ma'am, what she did. Or at all, in fact."

She smiled at him unexpectedly and was suddenly transformed into a woman of vivid prettiness. And she must be, he thought, even younger than he had supposed when he walked into the room earlier—and decades younger than he had thought her when they first met.

"But even before my death," he added, "I would have wanted to know that she would live again after I was gone, smile and laugh again, dance again if she so desired. I suppose that, being human, I would have liked to think that she would grieve for a while too, but not indefinitely. But could she not have remembered me fondly while she smiled and laughed and danced?"

"Will you come again?" she asked him abruptly. "With your sister?"

"You will surely be happy to see the back of me," he said. For his part, he could hardly wait to make his escape.

"No one comes," she said. "No one is *allowed* to come. We are in deep mourning."

Her vivid smile was long gone. He wondered if he had imagined it.

"Perhaps," he suggested unwillingly, "you would like to call upon my sister at Robland Park? It would be an outing for you and perfectly respectable. Or does deep mourning not allow that?"

"It does not," she said. "But perhaps I will come anyway."

It occurred to him suddenly that for the past few minutes she had been standing while he had been sitting—and that he had stayed far longer than etiquette allowed.

"Beatrice will be happy to hear it," he said, reaching for his canes and slipping his arms through the straps. "Her own activities have been curtailed by the persistent chill she contracted before Christmas. I thank you for the tea and for listening to me."

He could not thank her for her forgiveness. She had not given it.

He hoisted himself upright, aware of her steady gaze. He wished he did not now have to shuffle out of the room in his ungainly manner while she watched.

"We have something in common, you know," he told her, stopping abruptly before he reached the door. "I want to dance too. Sometimes it is what I want to do more than anything else in life."

She accompanied him in silence to the front door and the waiting carriage. Beatrice was already standing beside it with Lady Matilda. They all said their farewells, and the carriage was soon on its way down the driveway.

"Well," Beatrice said on an audible exhalation, "*that* was a gloomy afternoon if ever I have spent one. I do not wonder if that woman has ever laughed, Ben—I am confident she has not. What I do wonder is if she has ever smiled. I seriously doubt it. She spoke of her father with the deepest reverence. I pity poor Mrs. McKay."

"She asked if we would come again," he told her. "I suggested she call on you at Robland instead. It seems, though, that neither receiving visitors nor paying calls is quite the thing for ladies in mourning. Was my social education incomplete, Bea? It seems a peculiar notion to me. But she did say she might come anyway. I hope you will not disown me for making so free with your hospitality."

"She might come?" she asked him. "But *will* she, do you suppose?"

Ben shrugged for answer. But he recalled the unexpected passion with which she had told him that she wanted to *live*. That infamous stroll in the meadow had probably been her way of breaking loose, at least for a short while. And he had ruined it for her.

"Did you make your apology?" Beatrice asked him.

"I did." He did not add that forgiveness had not been explicitly granted.

"Then duty is satisfied for now," she said. "It is a huge relief, I must say. And perhaps they will not come."

"She wants to dance," Ben said.

"What?" She turned her head to frown at him. "At the assembly next week, do you mean?"

"No. She wants to *dance*, Bea. I do too. *I* want to dance."

She tipped her head slightly to one side. "We will certainly go to the assembly if you feel up to it," she said, "though I doubt you will be able to dance to even the most stately of the tunes, Ben. You do very well walking with your canes. I am prouder of you than I can possibly say. But dancing? I think it wisest to put it from your mind, dearest, and concentrate upon what you *can* do."

Ah, literal-minded Bea! He did not try to explain.

5

❧

Samantha scarcely set foot over the doorstep for the rest of the week. It rained almost without ceasing—though that was not strictly accurate. She might almost have enjoyed an honest-to-goodness rain. This was drizzle and mist and heavy gray skies and chill temperatures. Pea soup weather, she could remember her mother calling it, the sort of weather that seeped beneath doors and around window frames even when they were tightly shut and made one feel damp and cold and miserable despite a fire crackling in the hearth and a woolen shawl drawn about one's shoulders.

She did not even go to church on Sunday, a rare omission. Matilda had a head cold as well as one of her headaches and submitted to being sent back to bed with a hot brick for her feet. Samantha might have gone to church alone, as she had done for five years, but Matilda became agitated when she suggested it, and she was actually quite glad to avail herself of the excuse not to go out.

She had seen no one but Matilda and the servants since Tuesday. The visit of Lady Gramley and Sir Benedict Harper seemed weeks ago rather than merely days. But when she had broached the idea of their driving over to Robland Park one day next week to return the visit, Matilda had looked pruneish, as Samantha had fully expected she would. It was a courtesy to pay an occasional call upon a neighbor in mourning, she had explained, but no one would expect a return visit. Indeed, most people of any gentility would be surprised and even shocked if it happened.

Samantha simply did not believe her. Not any longer. And even if Matilda was right about social expectations, how could she possibly submit to remaining inside the darkened house for another eight months with only the occasional foray into the garden for fresh air and one weekly attendance at church? She would go out of her mind with the tedium of it.

She was going to pay that return call, she decided between journeys up and down stairs as she tended to the invalid, a long-familiar role that did nothing to lift her spirits, though she was always careful to be cheerful when she was in her sister-in-law's room and seeing to her comfort by turning and plumping her pillows or straightening the bedcovers or moving her glass of water closer to her hand or laying a cool cloth on her fevered brow or closing the almost invisible gap between the curtains that was letting in a flood of hurtful light.

She was going to go to Robland Park even if it meant going alone. Indeed, she would far prefer to go without Matilda. Good heavens, she had allowed herself to become a virtual prisoner in her own home since Matthew's death. And she had somehow relinquished her role as lady of the house.

She liked Lady Gramley, who was refined and elegant with the easy manners of a true lady. She had always been kind, though even after five years of living here Samantha scarcely knew her or any of her other neighbors. She hoped it would be possible to make something of a friend of Lady Gramley in the future, even though there must be a ten-year gap in their ages.

Sir Benedict Harper was a different matter. She had felt considerable antipathy toward him before his visit, and it was only with the greatest reluctance that she had admitted to herself that it had been handsome of him to call on her and maneuver matters in such a way that his apology was made to her alone. He had been sensitive enough to realize that it was altogether possible Matilda knew nothing of her escapade that day. And his apology itself had been irreproachable, for he had taken all the blame upon himself. It had been unhandsome of her, on the other hand, to withhold the words of forgiveness for which he had asked. But it was hard to forgive someone who had ruined the only hour of true freedom she had enjoyed in at least six years.

And now she felt like the guilty one. Perversely, she resented him for that. But he was merely visiting at Robland Park. Perhaps he would be gone soon and she need never see him again. Perhaps he would be out riding again when she called on Lady Gramley.

She remembered with some embarrassment her passionate outburst in Sir Benedict's hearing. Whatever had possessed her? She had told him she wanted to *live*. She had even told him she wanted to dance. But she knew what had caused her to speak so. He was more than half crippled. He had suffered other injuries, all courtesy of the late wars. If she had had to encounter a stranger, even under the circumstances in which they had met, did he have to be yet another wounded soldier?

She could positively scream!

But he wanted to dance too. She wished he had not said that. The words had unnerved her, for they had expressed such an impossible dream that she had wanted to weep. The last man on earth over whom she wished to shed tears was Sir Benedict Harper.

But he wanted to dance.

Matilda came down to sit in the drawing room early the following afternoon, though she still had a wretched cold, poor thing. She sat near the fire, a shawl drawn closely about her shoulders, a handkerchief clutched in one hand and never too far from her reddened nose.

Samantha mentioned casually that since the rain had stopped at last perhaps she would take the gig and return Lady Gramley's call.

"Your sense of duty is misplaced," Matilda said. "But you will not go, of course, especially since I am unable to accompany you. Matthew would forbid it if he could, God rest his soul."

Quite possibly he would not have done. He had made great demands on her time and presence while he was ill, it was true, but he hated the puritanical, straitlaced attitudes of his family. It was a measure of his annoyance with *her,* after she had kicked up a fuss over his infidelity, that he had decided against taking her to the Peninsula with him or permitting her to go home to her own father, but had sent her to Leyland Abbey to live for that year instead. It was undoubtedly the worst punishment he could devise. It had been downright mean.

"There is an assembly in the village in a few days' time," Samantha said. "Attending *that* would be scandalous, Matilda. I do not, however, have the least intention of going. Paying a courtesy visit to a neighbor who paid one here last week, on the other hand, must be quite unexceptionable. And as for going in the gig myself, I did it every Sunday while Matthew lived, until you came a short while before his death, that is, and he never once voiced any objection."

"Then he ought to have done," Matilda said sharply before pausing to blow her nose. "*Father* would not have allowed it."

"The Earl of Heathmoor was not my husband," Samantha retorted, "or my own father. Oh, Matilda, let us not quarrel. How tedious this topic is! I need air and a change of scene. And I really ought to show a courtesy to Lady Gramley, who has called here twice since Matthew's funeral despite the fact that she was not at all well the first time. I am going. I daresay I will not be gone long. The bell pull is within your reach. If you need anything at all, Rose or one of the other servants will bring it."

Her sister-in-law looked thin-lipped and mulish as Samantha got to her feet. No doubt she would inform her father about this in her next letter home. Well, so be it. The rules he imposed upon his family, even at this distance, were Gothic, to say the least. Samantha was no longer going to accept them without question. She could show respect for the memory of her husband without incarcerating herself in her own home and being slavishly obedient to a family whose standards of propriety went far beyond what society demanded.

These thoughts caused her only a fleeting moment of uneasiness. Bramble Hall, which Matthew had been convinced would be made over to him while he lived, still belonged to the earl. But it had been willed to Matthew—except that Matthew was now dead. It would be her home for life, though, he had assured Samantha shortly before his passing. His father had to look after her since she had no fortune of her own and no relatives who would be glad to take her in, and he never shirked his responsibilities. It would suit his purpose to perfection to keep her far away here in the north of England in a house he had never lived in himself. The very last thing he would want was to have her living as a pensioner at Leyland and as a constant thorn in his side. Her future was quite secured.

* * *

Sir Benedict Harper was riding around the corner of the house at Robland Park as Samantha drew the gig to a halt before the front doors. He looked splendidly virile on horseback, she could not help but notice, his disability not at all apparent. She could have wished, though, that she had come earlier or that he had extended his ride longer.

He reined in his horse beside her and swept off his hat. "Good afternoon, Mrs. McKay," he said. "You are making the most of this welcome break in the weather too, are you? So is Beatrice, I am afraid. She is out on a round of sick visiting with the vicar's wife."

"Oh." How very unfortunate, and what an anticlimax after all the fuss that had preceded her coming here. "Well, no matter. At least I have had an outing. I would have had no excuse for it if I had known Lady Gramley was from home."

"There is no need for you to go away," he told her. "If you will give me a few minutes to stable my horse, I will join you. A groom is already on his way to see to your gig. Do go inside. No, I beg your pardon. That would not do, would it?"

He looked about him.

Samantha ought to announce her intention of leaving immediately. Matilda would be horrified if she stayed, and on this occasion her sister-in-law might be justified. Besides, she had no wish for another conversation alone with the gentleman. On the other hand, she desperately wanted to prolong her outing for at least a little while.

"Why do you not stroll among the flowers here?" he suggested. "There is even a seat over there."

He put his hat back on, touched his whip to the brim, and rode away before she could answer him. She hesitated for only a moment before getting down from the gig and leaving it in the care of the groom.

Matilda would say this served her right, coming to

call and finding Lady Gramley from home. Matilda would certainly believe that she ought to drive away without further ado now that she had made the discovery.

Oh, *stuff* Matilda McKay and her father, the Earl of Heathmoor, too. Samantha was mortally sick of measuring her every move by what they would think. She could perfectly understand why Matthew had left home as soon as he was old enough and had never gone back there to live. Even when he had come home from the Peninsula, dreadfully wounded and expected to die at any moment, he had begged to be taken somewhere other than Leyland. His father had sent them here, to one of his smaller properties, the one most remote from Kent.

Sir Benedict Harper looked at his best on horseback. He looked at his worst when walking, she thought as he came from the stables a few minutes later to join her. He walked with the aid of his canes, though he did not use them as crutches. He really was walking, slowly and painstakingly, and looking rather ungainly as he did so. It would be far easier, surely, and more graceful to use crutches—except that one needed one sound leg for crutches, did one not?

She could not help feeling a reluctant admiration for a man who clearly ought not to be walking but was. Matthew had never made any effort to overcome any of his disabilities or even to control his peevishness. Perhaps this man really would dance.

She went to meet him.

"Come and sit in the garden," he said.

"Oh, look," she said, tipping back her head. "The sun has come out. It would be a great pity to miss all its brightness by being cooped up indoors. Perhaps I am fortunate after all that Lady Gramley is from home. There has been so little sunshine lately."

And she would have missed it even if there had been. She could perfectly understand how a prisoner must feel, incarcerated in a dungeon year after year. Impulsively, she tossed her heavy veil back over the brim of her bonnet and was rewarded with bright sunlight and warm, delicious air.

"Lady Matilda did not wish to accompany you?" he asked.

"She has the most dreadful head cold," she said. "I do hope I am not carrying the infection here with me. She was huddled beside the fire in the sitting room when I left. She would not have come anyway, though. She considers such social calls improper while we are in deep mourning."

They had reached the flower garden and were soon seated side by side on the wrought iron seat she had seen earlier. He propped his canes beside it.

"Your husband was an officer," he said. "He died of wounds sustained in the wars, did he?"

"Most of them healed," she told him, "though some of them left him scarred. He lived in a darkened room because of them and would not see anyone except his valet and me. He had always been proud of his good looks. His worst injury, though, was a bullet lodged somewhere inside his chest, close to his heart. It could not be removed without killing him. It affected his lungs as well as his heart and made it progressively more difficult for him to breathe. There was never any hope of his making a full recovery."

"I am sorry," he said. "You have had a difficult time of it."

"Those words *for better or for worse* are no idle addition to the marriage service," she said. "Some of us are called upon to live up to what we have promised. Yes, I have had a difficult time of it. So have thousands of other women, wives and mothers and sisters. And for their men, life has been no easy matter either. Some of them die, as Matthew did. Some live on with permanent disabilities and pain. You must have had a difficult time of it too."

"Even though only my legs were affected?"

She turned her head sharply in his direction. It was unkind of him to remind her of that foolish assumption.

"That was shortsighted of me," she said. "You did admit there was more than that. Much more?"

He smiled at her, and she could see that he must once have been very handsome. He still was, but there were cares worn into his face now where once there must have been pure youthful charm. As there had been with Matthew, though she did not suppose Sir Benedict had ever been as breathtakingly good-looking as her husband.

"The years of my convalescence were the worst of my life," he said, "and also, strangely enough, the best. Life has a habit of being like that, giving and taking in equal measure, a balance of opposites. Beatrice would have had me here to nurse back to health, but she had young children at the time, and it would have been unfair to foist the burden of my wounded self upon her. I was fortunate enough to be brought to the notice of the Duke of Stanbrook. He took me and a number of other wounded officers into his own home, Penderris Hall in Cornwall, hired the best doctors and nurses, and kept some of us there for longer than three years while we healed and recuperated. There is a group of us, seven in all, who still meet there for a few weeks every year. Those five men, including the duke, and one woman are my closest friends in the world. They are my chosen family. We call ourselves the Survivors' Club."

"Are two of its members by any chance the hero of a Forlorn Hope who was brought home in a straitjacket and a young blind man?" she asked.

"Hugo, Lord Trentham, and Vincent, Viscount Darleigh, yes," he said.

"And one of the members of your club is a woman?"

"Imogen, Lady Barclay," he said. "She was in the Peninsula with her husband, who was a reconnaissance officer. A spy, in other words. He was captured while he was not in uniform, and he was tortured, partly in her presence. Then he died."

"Poor lady," she said.

"Yes."

"I wonder," she said, "if there is anyone of our generation or the generations directly above and below our own whose life is unaffected by the wars. Do you think there is?"

"We are all always affected by the major events of history," he said. "It is unavoidable. Who was it who said—" He stopped and frowned in thought. "It was John Donne in one of his essays. *No man is an island entire of itself.* That was it. There is always some poet or philosopher who has captured in brief and vivid words the greatest truths of human existence, is there not?"

"Are *you* a philosopher, Sir Benedict?" she asked.

"No." He laughed. "But I fear I *am* being a bore. You told me last week that you are tired of sickness and suffering and death—or something to that effect. You told me you wanted to *live,* specifically to dance. Has it been a long time since you danced? Tell me of the last time— or the last time that was memorable. Where was it? When? What did you dance? And with whom?"

"Goodness." She found herself laughing back at him. "Can I remember that far back? Oh, let me see. When was it? There were a few regimental balls before the regiment was sent to the Peninsula. I did not particularly enjoy them."

It was during those balls she had seen Matthew dance

with other women, both married and single. Not just dance, though—every officer danced with ladies other than their wives, of course. It was what was expected at any ball. Matthew had openly *flirted,* and all those wives and others had responded and been flattered and flirted right back. She had *hated* those balls and having to smile and dance and pretend to be finding nothing distasteful in her husband's behavior. She had hated the looks of kind sympathy in the eyes of some of the other officers with whom she danced.

"The last memorable dance was at an assembly when I was still living at home," she said. "Several of the officers billeted nearby were there and sending flutters of excitement through the hearts of every girl in attendance. How the other men must have hated the sight of scarlet regimentals. I had not thought about that before now. Lieutenant Matthew McKay, with whom I already had something of an acquaintance, singled me out for two dances. One was the Roger de Coverley. I can remember the sheer joy of dancing it. I was very much in love, you see. And he asked me that same night if I would marry him, though he had to talk to Papa before he could make an official offer, of course."

He was smiling at her, she saw when she turned her head toward him. Oh, goodness, when had she last indulged in happy memories?

"When was the last time *you* danced?" she asked him.

"I suppose it was at one of those regimental balls you did not enjoy," he said. "In fact, I know it was. I waltzed with my colonel's niece. I was waltzing for the first—and only—time. The waltz was very new then. There is no lovelier dance in the world for sheer romance."

"Was there a romance between you and the colonel's niece?" she asked.

"Oh, yes." He smiled softly. He was no longer looking at her but was gazing over the flower beds, and she knew that he too was lost in happy memories for the moment. "I had known her for a month and believed she was the other half of my soul."

"What happened?"

"War happened." He laughed softly. "We cannot get away from it, can we? Tell me about your home and your family."

"My father was a gentleman who lived contentedly in the country with his books," she said. "He was a widower with one son when he met my mother during a rare visit to London. She was twenty years younger than he, but they married and had me. My mother died when I was twelve, my father when I was eighteen."

"After you were married?" he asked.

"Yes."

He had died after a short illness during the year she was living at Leyland Abbey. Her brother, John, had not written to tell her about it until Papa died, and even then he had delayed a day or two until there was no possibility of her getting there in time for the funeral. She had wanted to go anyway. The house was to be sold and all its contents disposed of. There had not been anything of great value there, but there were several items she would have liked to retrieve as mementos, some things of her mother's in particular, which could have been of no interest to John. But he said in his letter that there was no need for her to go, and the Earl of Heathmoor, her father-in-law, who of course had read her letter before giving it to her, had agreed. As far as he was concerned, the less contact his son's wife had with her humble, even shady, past, the better for the whole McKay family.

"And your brother?" Sir Benedict asked.

"John?" she said. "He is my half brother, eighteen years older than I. He had left home before I was born.

He is a clergyman with a living twenty miles from where our father lived. He has a wife and family. I do not see them."

John had resented his father's remarriage. He had hated both Samantha and her mother, though he had never said so, of course. He was a man of the cloth, after all, and clergymen did not admit to feeling hatred.

"It is your turn," she said. "Tell me about your family."

"There were four of us children," he told her. "Beatrice is the eldest. Wallace, who inherited the baronetcy on our father's death, was a member of Parliament destined for brilliance. He was already making a rapid climb up the political ladder when he was killed by a vegetable cart that overturned on the streets of London. I inherited from him, but only a few scant days after I heard about it, I was wounded in the Peninsula. Calvin, my younger brother, had been in sole possession of Kenelston Hall, the family seat, for a number of years. He was Wallace's appointed steward there. He remained there with his wife and children and continued in that role after the double disasters. It was expected that I would not survive my injuries for very long, you see. I was not expected even to survive the journey home to England."

"He expected to inherit, then," she said. "Is he still living in your home?"

"Yes." There was a slight hesitation before he continued. "He is an excellent steward."

She turned her head to look at his profile. "And do you spend most of your time there too," she asked, "now that you have recovered?"

"No."

He did not elaborate. He did not need to. Obviously his brother had usurped his home and his estates and had made it difficult for Sir Benedict to oust him by doing an excellent job of running them. At least, that was what she guessed must have happened.

"Do you suppose," she asked after a brief silence, "there is anyone on this earth for whom life is easy?"

He turned his face toward her and regarded her curiously. "One does tend to assume that life must be far easier for others than it ever is for oneself," he said. "I suspect it rarely is. I daresay life was not meant to be easy."

"How very unkind on the part of whoever invented life."

They exchanged smiles, and she realized that she was enjoying this slightly improper visit more than she could have expected. He was really quite a pleasant companion.

"Life has been difficult for you for a long time," he said. "It will get better, I daresay, once the pain of your husband's passing has receded more. What do you plan to do when your mourning period is over?"

"I will make an effort to become better acquainted with my neighbors," she told him. "I will try to make real friends among them and to find useful ways to spend my time."

It sounded dull enough. In reality, it would be infinitely more delightful than anything had yet been in her adult life—if she disregarded the dizzy euphoria of the early months of her marriage.

"Will Lady Matilda remain with you?" he asked.

"Heaven forbid!" she exclaimed before she could stop herself. She set the fingertips of one hand over her mouth and gazed ruefully at him. "No, I believe she will feel obliged to return home to care for her mother. The Countess of Heathmoor suffers with palpitations and her nerves. We have an uneasy alliance, I am afraid, Matilda and I, and it becomes more uneasy by the day now that the early numbness of my bereavement has worn off. Matilda is so very correct in all she says and does, and I am sometimes a trial to her."

"And she to you?" He was smiling again. "You will not go with her to your father-in-law's home, then?"

"Oh, no," she said. "I lived there for a year after Matthew's regiment was sent to the Peninsula." She only just stopped herself from saying more.

He raised his eyebrows.

"I would not wish to return," she said. "And I have no doubt my father-in-law shares my sentiments."

"I do not have an acquaintance with the Earl of Heathmoor," Sir Benedict said.

It was not surprising. When he went to London, that den of all iniquity, the earl divided his time between the House of Lords and his clubs. He rarely attended any of the entertainments of the Season, and his womenfolk were not permitted to attend any. As soon as the spring session ended, he withdrew to Leyland and stayed there until duty called him forth again. He attended the Church of England, but one would never guess it from his attitudes and behavior. He was the quintessential Puritan. Anything that smacked of pleasure must by its very nature be sinful. Anything that ran counter to his sober principles and rules must be of the devil, and anyone who disobeyed him was the devil's spawn. He ruled his family with an iron fist, though to be fair, physical violence was rarely if ever necessary.

"I do not believe you would enjoy such an acquaintance," she said.

"You may rely upon my discretion not to tell anyone you just said that, ma'am," he said, his eyes twinkling with amusement. But he continued to look at her, and the smile faded from all but his eyes. "When I spent those years at Penderris Hall with my fellow Survivors, I had six confidants. They understood my thoughts and feelings because they were experiencing similar ones.

They knew when to advise, when to laugh at me or ca-jole, when merely to listen. They knew when to draw close and when to keep their distance. I believe it was only after I had left there that I fully understood how blessed I had been—and still am. I can say anything in the world to those friends, and they can say anything in the world to me without fearing censure and with the sure knowledge that what is said will remain confiden-tial. We all need people to whom we can speak freely. I have my sister too. We have always been close even though she is five years my senior. The older we get, however, the less wide that gap appears."

Was he telling her that he knew and understood all the things she had not put into words? That he under-stood her loneliness and sense of isolation? She only partly understood them herself. She had always been lonely and had always denied it, even to herself. To admit it would be to allow self-pity a toehold in her consciousness. And there was something almost shame-ful about loneliness, as if one must be unlovable as well as unloved.

"I envy you," she said. "It must be lovely to have close friends."

Too late she realized what she had admitted. For surely Matthew ought to have been such a friend.

"I am afraid," she said, "that I must already have committed that dreadful social faux pas of outstaying my welcome. We must have been sitting here for close to an hour. Matilda will be having forty fits. Perhaps forty-four if she ever discovers that Lady Gramley was not here."

She got to her feet and waited for him to rise too.

"Do you ride?" he asked as they began the slow walk up to the terrace.

"I learned as a girl," she told him, "though I did not have the chance to ride often. My father owned only the ancient beloved mare that pulled our gig at a speed roughly equivalent to a brisk stroll. Matthew insisted I ride more often after we were married, and I became quite proficient in the saddle, though it was not something that was encouraged when I was at Leyland. I have not ridden since I came to Bramble Hall."

"There are several horses in the stables here," he said. "Bea was commenting just yesterday that they are not exercised as often as they ought to be. She was indisposed over much of the winter and has only now been cleared for regular activity. Will you ride with me one day? Perhaps the day after tomorrow?"

"Oh," she said. "I—"

She was about to decline—for all the usual and obvious reasons. But she remembered the fright and exhilaration of those rare rides in her childhood, and the wonder and joy of riding what she had called a *real* horse after her marriage.

She was overwhelmed by temptation.

What would Matil— No! She did not *care* what Matilda would say.

"I shall ask Bea to ride with us, of course," he added.

"I would *like* to."

They spoke simultaneously.

"I shall choose a horse for you, then," he said, "and have a groom lead it over to Bramble Hall when we come."

"Thank you." She turned her head to look at his face in profile. She could tell from the set of his mouth that walking was not easy for him. It was very probably painful too, but he moved at a steady, though slow, pace, and he uttered no complaint.

She wondered what other injuries he had suffered.

She was so glad she had made this visit, she thought a few minutes later as she drove away in the gig, a groom having brought it up to the terrace for her. She was even glad Lady Gramley had not been here, for it was unlikely they would have sat out in the garden in the brightness of the sunshine, feeling the heat of it on their faces and bodies.

And she was glad she had had the courage to agree to ride with Sir Benedict—and Lady Gramley.

She felt really quite restored in spirit.

Perhaps she was coming alive again.

But whatever would Matilda say?

6

❧

"It is quite fascinating to observe how differently various people are affected by their infirmities," Beatrice said over a late tea. "Some people are an inspiration. They remain smiling and cheerful while suffering the most dreadful afflictions. Others make one feel as though one were being sucked into a black hole with them, poor things."

"You look exhausted," Ben said.

"But glad to be back to my parish and community duties at last," she assured him. "How did you enjoy your ride?"

"Very well indeed," he said, "for the five minutes it lasted. I was just riding out when I spotted a gig coming along the road in the direction of the house. It looked to me as though the lone occupant was dressed in unrelieved black. So I turned around and came back."

"Mrs. McKay?" she said. "Without Lady Matilda?"

"The lady has a head cold."

"And so Mrs. McKay was able to escape alone." She smiled at him. "You were not so lost to all conduct as to entertain her in here alone, I hope, Ben?"

"We sat outside in the garden for all of an hour," he told her.

It was a bit surprising, actually, that he had even turned back from his ride, since he might easily have escaped without her seeing him. And he certainly could have stopped her from staying. It had not been her suggestion. But then he was the one who had suggested that she call at Robland. He had felt sorry for her, cooped up in that gloomy manor with the battle-ax.

"Poor lady," Beatrice said. "I do not suppose her sister-in-law is good company even when she is in the best of health. Mrs. McKay must be very lonely. I wish I had been here."

"If ever the topic should arise, Bea," he said, "you have been complaining just recently that the horses in the stables are in need of more exercise than they are getting."

"Oh?" she said in some surprise. "*Have* I been so slandering my grooms? I am obliged to you for reminding me, Benedict, as I have no recollection of saying any such thing. And why *should* the topic arise?"

"I said as much to Mrs. McKay before she left here," he explained.

"Oh?" Her cup paused between the saucer and her lips.

"I asked her to ride with me the afternoon after tomorrow," he said, "but I suspect there is no suitable mount in the stables at Bramble Hall."

"I do not doubt you are right." She placed her cup back in its saucer and set both aside. "And she agreed?"

"Yes."

She rested her elbows on the arms of her chair and regarded him with a slight frown. "I doubt her sister-in-law will allow it," she said. "*If* she has power over Mrs. McKay, that is. But is it wise anyway, Ben? I can see no reason why a recently bereaved widow ought not to take the air on horseback if she so desires, but in the lone company of a single gentleman?"

"I did say I would persuade you to join us," he said. "Will you, Bea? Are you feeling up to it?"

"I certainly will be," she said, "if the alternative is for

you to ride out alone with a lady, Ben. It would not be at all proper, even if she were not in deep mourning."

"She is lonely, as you just observed," he said, "and restless."

Though why he should have taken it upon himself to try to alleviate that restlessness, he did not know.

"It is hardly surprising," she said. "She has been virtually incarcerated at Bramble Hall ever since she arrived. I suppose it was a labor of love, poor lady, nursing Captain McKay, and clearly he was desperately ill, but I always thought it selfish of him not to insist that she go out occasionally, even if only to take tea with a neighbor. She never did. It is perfectly understandable that by now, with the first wave of her grief passing off, she would be longing to flutter her wings."

"Yes."

She fixed him with a direct stare. "You are not making a flirt of Mrs. McKay by any chance, are you, Ben?" she asked him. "You have not conceived a tendre for her? I have been hoping for some time that you would recover your interest in women and in courtship. You have been a hermit for too long. I have been hoping you would marry before you turn thirty, though you have only a few months left in which to make me happy on that score. But I am not sure a recent widow is a wise choice, especially given the identity of her father-in-law. Of course, she is quite astonishingly lovely. She must have foreign blood to account for her dark coloring. *That* would not endear her to the Earl of Heathmoor, I daresay."

"Beatrice," Ben said in some exasperation, "I have met Mrs. McKay four times, including our disastrous encounter in the meadow and our brief meeting at church. We are to take a ride together the day after tomorrow—in your company. I do not believe we will be having the banns called this week or even next."

She laughed. "She *is* very beautiful. Though the black clothes she wears are unbecoming, to say the least."

"Agreed."

"If you sat outside in the garden," she said, "I suppose she kept that hideous veil over her face."

"She pushed it back over the brim of her bonnet, actually."

She regarded him in silence for a few seconds longer and then shrugged. "I know," she said. "You do not need to say it aloud. You are no longer nine years old or even nineteen. You are quite capable of living your own life, and even if you are not, you would not thank me for trying to live it for you. Very well, I will not. But what *are* you going to do with your life, Ben? You have appeared to . . . to drift aimlessly in the years since you left Cornwall. I have sworn to myself that I will say nothing, but here I am saying it anyway and annoying you."

He *was* irritated by the question, since he still did not know the answer. And he hated that in himself. He had always used to think of himself as a firm, decisive man. He had planned out his life when he was fifteen, and he had not deviated from that plan until a bullet and other assorted catastrophes had stopped him almost literally dead in his tracks six years ago. Now he felt as if he had been set adrift without a compass on an ocean that stretched vast and empty in every direction. He had come here with the firm intention of making plans and then launching them into effect. He was still determined to do it—tomorrow. Was it only recently he had made the discovery that tomorrow in fact never comes?

But Beatrice was someone who had always genuinely loved him. Her concern was real. She had a right to ask and a right to be answered.

"For the first year or so," he said, "my whole focus was upon surviving. Then it was upon the monumental task of getting up from my bed and somehow becoming mobile. And finally, and until very recently, it has been upon walking again and getting my life back as it was before so that I might proceed to live happily ever after according to the original plan. I must be very stubborn or very dense or both. I have only recently faced the truth—that neither my body nor my life will ever again be as it once was. I was a man of action, a soldier, an officer. Now I am none of those things. The trouble is, though, that I do not know what I am instead or what I will be. Or what I will do. I am in a bit of a bleak place, Bea, though I do not even know where that is." He laughed softly.

"You will return to Kenelston after you leave here?" she asked him. "You will make an effort to settle there at last?"

"I thought I might travel first," he said, plucking out of the air one of the ideas he had half considered. "I have done a little of it in the past few years. I have spent time in Bath, at Tunbridge Wells, in Harrogate, in other places. I thought I might see something of Scotland, the Lake District, Wales. I have even thought I might try writing a travel book. There are plenty of them for walkers. As far as I know there are none for people who cannot walk or who cannot walk easily or far. Yet there must be any number of people who would travel if they could do so without having to be ruggedly fit and healthy."

"Have you ever done any writing?" she asked, her eyebrows soaring.

"No," he admitted. "But I must do something. It does not make me comfortable to admit that I am an aimless nobody living nowhere. I must and will find a new challenge, and my eyes and my brain and my hands work well enough even if my legs do not. I may discover a hidden talent as an author. I may find myself traveling all over the world and penning dozens of books for my adoring readers. Can you not see my name writ large in gold on a leather cover?"

She shook her head, though she did answer his grin with a short bark of laughter. "Your challenge *could* be to run Kenelston for yourself," she said, "and to make it your home. It is yours, after all. But you do not have the heart to supplant Calvin, do you? I could simply shake that boy for his blockheaded selfishness. Though he is no longer a boy, of course. He ought to have made other arrangements for his family as soon as poor Wallace was killed and everything passed to you. It is not as though Father had left him without funds. But he kept very quiet instead and continued on as if Wallace were still alive. And of course your lengthy indisposition made it easier for him to become entrenched. But Kenelston is *not* his, and he has no business having the full run of it and allowing those unruly children of his to dash about inside it as though there were no such thing as a nursery wing there—and no such thing as discipline. Do let me have a word with him."

The idea of having to enlist the help of his sister to fight his battles for him was appalling.

"Thank you, Bea," he said, "but it suits my purpose to travel for a while until I can see my way forward to a more settled future. And since Kenelston will need a steward while I am gone, Calvin and Julia and the children might as well stay where they are. He *is* a very good steward, you know. And he loves the work."

She clucked her tongue and poured herself another cup of tea. She looked at him, teapot held aloft, but he shook his head.

Actually, he thought, perhaps he was using Calvin as an excuse. Perhaps it suited him as well as it did his younger brother to leave matters as they were. He was not perfectly convinced that the sedentary life of a country gentleman would be quite to his taste. It was a rather startling thought. He had not admitted as much to himself before.

"Begin your travels in London when I go there to join Hector," she suggested. "Come with me. Perhaps we will find you a pretty young lady who was not widowed a few months ago and who does not have a fire-breathing dragon for a father-in-law."

He laughed. "Thank you for the offer—for both offers. But London is the last place I want to go. And if I want a pretty woman, or any woman for that matter, I will find one for myself. I do not, though, as it happens."

But, surprisingly, he looked forward to riding with Mrs. McKay two days hence even though Beatrice would be with them. Perhaps it was because a widow still in deep mourning seemed a safe enough companion. His life had been almost entirely womanless for longer than six years. Apart from his sister and his sister-in-law, and his fellow Survivor Imogen, he had had virtually no dealings with any lady in all that time. He had been celibate for longer than six years.

It would all have seemed incredible at one stage in his life. He had fancied himself in love half a dozen times before being sure of it with the colonel's niece. And he had enjoyed a lusty sex life with women of another sort.

No longer, though.

But he missed the companionship of women. It was something he would like to have again, provided there was never any question of courtship. There could be no such question with Mrs. McKay. She still had eight months or so of mourning to live through before she could consider remarrying. And she would not consider him anyway, even if she were free to do so. She had just buried one husband who had been incapacitated by war. She certainly would not be tempted to take another.

She was a safe female companion, then. And he looked forward to seeing her ride—if, that was, nothing happened to prevent the outing. Inclement weather, for example. Or her sister-in-law's intervention.

"*W*hen I wrote to Father today," Matilda said, "I omitted all mention of your visit to Robland Park yesterday, Samantha. I thought about it last night and was forced to the conclusion that it was not a totally unpardonable breach of etiquette for you to return a call that had been made upon you last week by a countess, though I do wish you had waited until I could accompany you."

Samantha kept her head down as she worked a new flower into the design of the cloth she was embroidering.

"I daresay Lady Gramley was gratified to see you," Matilda added.

"I hope you sent my love to your mother," Samantha said at the same moment.

"I did," Matilda told her, "since you directed me to do so when you came to my room after breakfast to inquire after my health. I did not mention your visit, Samantha, because Father might see the matter differently from my more liberal view, and I would not wish to make you the object of his displeasure."

Samantha wove the silk thread invisibly through her work at the back of the cloth before cutting it and changing to a different shade. She seethed at the condescension of Matilda's words. She ought to just keep quiet until the subject was changed. But why should she? Anyway, Matilda was going to have to know her plans.

"Lady Gramley was not at home," she said. "Sir Benedict was just returning from a ride and was kind enough to keep me company in the garden for a while so that I would not have to drive back home immediately."

"It is to be hoped no one saw you there, Samantha," Matilda said. "Perhaps now you understand the folly of acting impulsively and contrary to the advice of your husband's sister."

"We had a very pleasant conversation," Samantha told her. "I am going riding with him tomorrow. He is going to have a horse from the Robland stables brought over for me."

Some imp of mischief led her to omit adding that Lady Gramley would be riding with them. She looked up when there was no immediate response to her words. Her sister-in-law was gazing back at her with red-tipped nose and ashen face and cold eyes.

"I must very adamantly advise you against such a thing, Samantha," she said. "Indeed, I take it upon myself to speak even more strongly on behalf of Matthew and Father. I forbid you to do this."

"Matthew liked me to ride," Samantha said, lowering her head to her work again. "If he *could* speak now, I daresay he would tell me to go, since he no longer has need of me in the sickroom. I need air and exercise. Quite desperately."

"Then I will walk with you in the garden," Matilda said.

"No, you will not," Samantha told her. "That is a very bad cold you have. You need to stay by the fire and out of drafts. And I need exercise that is more vigorous than a stroll in a confined area. A walk is not enough. I want to *ride*. And that is what I will do tomorrow. Oh, dear, did I say the forbidden word?"

Tramp, who had been lying in the shaft of sunlight that beamed through the window, looking for all the world as if he were comatose, had scrambled to his feet and was now standing before Samantha's chair, making pathetic little whining sounds and gazing fixedly and hopefully up at her.

"I used the word *walk*, did I not?"

His tail wagged. Yes, indeed, she had.

"Oh, very well." Samantha got to her feet. "We will go into the garden and find a stick for you to chase. Though that is not a fair game at all, you know, for you never throw the stick for *me* to chase."

"Samantha," Matilda said sharply before her sister-in-law could escape from the room to fetch her bonnet and cloak. "I must categorically forbid you to go riding tomorrow. You may say, if you will, that I have no power to command you, but indeed I do. I stand as Father's representative here."

Samantha stopped and turned to face her. "I *do* say that you have no right to command me, Matilda. It is insufferable that you would try. Your complaints and advice I will listen to. You have every right to express them. You have no right to *tell* me what I must do, or, more important, what I must *not* do. Nor does the Earl of Heathmoor. He is not *my* father."

Though he did own the home in which she was living.

She stayed outside in the garden for longer than an hour, to Tramp's great delight. She was feeling very close to the end of her tether. The past five years had been difficult ones, but though Matthew had been a demanding, often querulous patient, she had made allowances for his pain and discomfort. Besides, he was her husband. She had not been happy during those years, but she had been too busy and usually too exhausted to feel any great unhappiness.

The four months of her bereavement had been difficult ones too in a different way. They might have been less difficult if she had been able to respond to the very touching outpouring of sympathy and good wishes of neighbors with whom she had had no chance to become well acquainted before Matthew's death.

She might have made some friends, or at least a few friendly acquaintances, during these months. She had not been allowed to accept the overtures of her neighbors, however, and she had meekly given in to Matilda's directions on what was correct. She could do it no longer. She was beginning to feel quite mutinous.

I must categorically forbid you to go riding tomorrow . . . I stand as Father's representative here.

Oh, it was intolerable.

Finally even Tramp was tired of playing. He came and lay at her feet as she threw his stick once more, and then rested his chin on his paws.

"Ingrate!" she said. "You might at least have fetched it one more time before making your wishes known. It was a perfectly decent stick. Now I will have to search for another the next time you insist upon this game."

He heaved a sigh of unrepentant boredom.

"We had better go back inside, then," she said. "I have been avoiding the inevitable. Why did I have to marry into such a horrid family, Tramp? No, don't answer. I know why. It was because of the fatal combination of scarlet regimentals and a handsome face. He was *very* handsome, you know, and very dashing. You were not acquainted with him in those days. And it was not his fault his family is so horrid."

She thought of avoiding the sitting room when they went back inside and taking her outdoor things up to her room, where she would find something to keep her busy. But there was no avoiding Matilda forever, and she was not going to start hiding inside her own home. She left her outdoor things in the hall and opened the sitting room door, prepared somehow to make peace.

The room was empty.

She breathed a sigh of relief and crossed the room to pull the bell rope.

"Bring a tray of tea, will you, please, Rose?" she said when a maid answered her summons. "Do you know if Lady Matilda was feeling unwell again? Did she go back up to her room?"

Rose flushed and looked uncomfortable.

"I think she is up there, ma'am," she said, "but not to rest. She sent Randall down to the cellar to fetch her trunk and her big valise, and she sent for her maid to pack them."

Samantha stared at her. "Right. Thank you, Rose," she said. "Never mind about the tray for a while. I shall call for it later."

The maid scurried from the room.

All was bustle and activity in Matilda's room. Her trunk, two valises, and three hat boxes were open on the floor, and it seemed that every garment she possessed was piled either on her bed or on chairs—except the chair on which Matilda herself sat, her back ramrod straight, her lips set in a thin, straight line.

"What is this, Matilda?" Samantha asked. It was a rather foolish question, of course. It was perfectly obvious what *this* was.

"I shall be leaving for Leyland tomorrow morning," Matilda said without looking at her. "I shall take the traveling carriage and some servants."

Samantha walked farther into the room. "I am sorry it has come to this," she said. "Are you sure you are well enough to travel?"

"I will not remain here," Matilda said. "I know what is due my family and the memory of my brother, Samantha, and I will not sully either by remaining with someone who does not."

"And this is all because I choose to return the calls of my neighbors?" Samantha asked her.

"I hardly call riding out with a single gentleman who is staying with one of your neighbors *visiting*, Samantha," Matilda said. "Even if you were not in deep mourning I would call it both vulgar and scandalous."

"Vulgar and scandalous." Samantha sighed. "Did I neglect to mention that Lady Gramley will be riding with us?"

"That fact makes no difference," Matilda said. "I hope your conscience will persuade you to remain at home tomorrow, Samantha. But whether it does or does not, the intention was there and the determination to persist even after I had spoken to you quite sternly on behalf of my father. I will not remain after such an insult—an insult not to me, you will understand, but to the Earl of Heathmoor, your husband's father."

"Very well," Samantha said. "I see there is no point in my saying anything further. I shall make arrangements for the carriage and the coachman and a few other servants to be ready in the morning."

"It is already done," Matilda said. "I beg you not to exert yourself on my behalf."

And the thing was, Samantha thought a short while later when she was back in the sitting room, prowling about as though there was no comfortable chair upon which to sit—the thing was that she had been left feeling guilty, as if she really had behaved quite outrageously enough to be shunned by all decent folk.

Vulgar and scandalous—good heavens!

Oh, she was very angry again. Quite furious, in fact. For two pins she would hurl every ugly ornament on the mantelpiece onto the hearth and shatter them into a million pieces. But she doubted she would feel any better afterward.

Surely—oh, *surely*, other newly bereaved widows were not expected to stay in a darkened home for a whole year, discouraging visitors and never returning any calls they did receive. Surely they did not cut themselves off from all exercise and social activity, even if they *did* avoid more frivolous entertainments, like assemblies and picnics.

Surely the way she had been living here with Matilda was not *normal*.

Perhaps she was wrong. Perhaps her restlessness did denote a waywardness, a lack of respect for the man who had been her husband for seven years and for his grieving family. *Were* they grieving, though? Beneath the outer trappings of mourning, that was. None of them had come to Bramble Hall even once during the five years Matthew had been here, except Matilda at the end. None of them had come for the funeral. It was a long way, of course, from Kent to County Durham and would have caused an uncomfortable delay in the proceedings. Nevertheless, she had personally sent word to the earl and countess by special messenger, and they could have got word back to her just as quickly to delay the service. They had not done so.

Matthew had been the black sheep.

Oh, no, she decided, tugging firmly on the bell pull again, she was *not* going to feel guilty. And she was not going to try to persuade Matilda to change her mind. Good riddance to her. She was not going to send word to Robland Park to cancel tomorrow's ride either.

She was *not* going to feel guilty.

But of course she did.

"Bring the tea tray in, please, Rose," she said when the maid answered her summons.

She was not hungry either, though. Or thirsty.

❧

7

"It is going to rain," Beatrice observed at breakfast the next morning. She had looked up briefly from the letter she was reading.

Ben glanced toward the window and agreed that rain was a distinct possibility. It had been a pretty miserable spring so far, at least in this part of the country. It looked as if they were not going to be able to ride with Mrs. McKay after all. Perhaps it was just as well. He did not doubt the battle-ax would disapprove since she did not believe even a sedate visit to a neighbor was seemly. Though he did think it was high time Mrs. McKay thumbed her nose at the heavy restrictions that were being imposed upon her.

Perhaps the rain would hold off.

"How can boys spend such a vast deal of money when they are supposedly at school becoming the scholars of the future?" Beatrice asked, her eyes back on her letter. "And why do they apply for extra funds to their mothers rather than their fathers, who would demand an accounting of what had already been spent?"

"Precisely for that reason," he said. "I daresay the price of sweetmeats has risen since I was at school."

"Hmm," she said. "But having rotten teeth pulled is just as painful."

It started to rain in the late morning, a light drizzle at first, which might or might not turn into something more serious. By the time he had finished his luncheon, however, Ben was forced to admit that the rain had taken the first option. It was going to be too wet to ride.

He was disappointed. He went upstairs to do his daily exercises. He would not neglect those, even though he had accepted the reality that he would never recover more than very minimal use of his legs. He would not risk losing what little he had accomplished, however. At least he could get about on his own legs. Besides, there were other parts of his body that needed to be kept in good working condition.

The vigorous activity did not rid him of his restlessness. He was in a crisis period of his life, he realized.

He found his sister at the escritoire in the drawing room, writing to both of her sons and her husband.

"I feel bad about not sending word over to Bramble Hall," he told her.

"But Mrs. McKay will hardly expect us in this weather," she said without looking up.

"No," he agreed. "But I thought I would go over there anyway and make our excuses in person. Would you care to come with me?"

She brushed the feather of her quill pen over her chin and looked toward the window. "You must know how you tempt me, Ben," she said. "Letter writing was never one of my favorite activities. I daresay that proves I am not a proper lady. I must finish these now that I have started them, however, or I will put off doing so indefinitely. You do not need my company, do you? The McKay ladies will be each other's chaperon."

"You make me sound like a big bad wolf," he said.

"I daresay you appear that way to at least one of the ladies," she said. "Oh, dear, I do not usually take virtual strangers in such dislike. Convey my respects to them, if you please, Ben."

"I shall." He bent over her to kiss her cheek. "Give

my love to my nephews and tell them not to get up to any more mischief than I did in my day."

She snorted rather inelegantly. "I shall tell them *from their Uncle Benedict*," she said, "to be good. And frugal."

He laughed and made his slow way out of the room.

$\mathscr{S}$amantha had lain awake half the night. She rose early in order to have breakfast with Matilda and try to send her on her way with some civility. But her sister-in-law neither came down to eat nor had a tray sent up to her room. And when she did come downstairs, she was dressed for travel and the carriage was awaiting her outside the front doors, already laden with her baggage.

"It is going to rain," Samantha said. "I wish you would reconsider, Matilda, and postpone your departure at least for a few days."

Matilda was looking pale and unwell.

"I would not remain here another hour even if snow threatened," she said, smoothing her already-smooth leather gloves over the backs of her hands. "Father will be displeased with you, Samantha, and Mother will be disappointed. But neither of them will be surprised, I am sad to say. Father warned Matthew how it would be if he insisted upon condescending so low as to marry a Gypsy."

Fortunately, perhaps, she swept out through the doors and down the steps before Samantha could frame an answer. A footman handed her into the carriage. She did not look back or turn her head once she was seated. It was fortunate because Samantha's temper had snapped, or would have done if she had been left with any audience. As it was, she stood in the doorway and watched the carriage set off on its long journey, positively quivering with suppressed fury.

"I am *one quarter* Gypsy," she muttered to the empty air. "Better than one hundred percent McKay."

Her grandfather, a Welshman about whom she knew nothing except his nationality, had married a Gypsy, who had given birth to Samantha's mother before returning to her own people, never to be heard of again. And that sad and obscure little incident of history had had its effect upon the granddaughter of that ill-fated union. So had the fact that their daughter, Samantha's mother, had run away at the age of seventeen from Wales and the aunt who had raised her and had ended up in London, where she had been eking out a living as an actress when Samantha's father discovered her and married her.

"I am one quarter Gypsy and one quarter Welsh and half obscure English gentility. I am the spawn of a Welsh actress, who, like all members of her profession and nationality, was only one short rung up the ladder of wickedness from the devil himself. Or so my father-in-law once described her."

Heavy clouds loomed overhead. It would be a miracle if it did not rain by noon. Irony of ironies, she would probably not be going riding this afternoon after all. It was a horribly depressing thought that she might after all be compelled to spend the rest of the day respectably alone and indoors.

But the first thing she did when she went back inside was to stride into the sitting room and fling the heavy curtains back as far as they would go. She was going to change them. She was going to choose something lighter in both texture and color. She looked about the room with a frown. *Everything* needed changing. In five years she had not really noticed how gloomy a house this was.

Matilda was at this very moment carrying stories of

her wickedness to Leyland. *Wickedness!* For five years she had devoted every moment of her days to the care of the Earl of Heathmoor's son. She had endured five years of disturbed nights without complaint. She had given every particle of her energy and patience. By the time Matthew died, it had seemed there was nothing of herself left. That, she supposed, was why she had felt so empty. And yet, in the eyes of the earl and his precious daughter, she was wicked and of no account because of her birth—and because after four months of real mourning she was ready to reach out to her neighbors for comfort and friendship and to partake of some quiet outdoor exercise.

She was angry. She was so furious, in fact, that she eyed those hideous ornaments on the mantel again and would surely have hurled them if doing so would have made her feel one iota better. They were not worth her ire—the McKays, that was. But no matter how firmly she told herself that, she felt hurt anyway.

Thank goodness she was so far away from them and they were sure to be as happy about that as she was.

And of course it rained.

At first it merely drizzled, leaving the cruel hope that it would not come to anything but would stop before afternoon. It rained more heavily instead and showed every sign of having settled in for the day.

Matilda would call it a just punishment.

After toying with her food at luncheon, Samantha went back into the sitting room and tried embroidering. But when her silk knotted and her fingers pulled at the knot without their customary patience and it snarled to such a degree that she was forced to cut the thread and undo the work she had already done, she set the cloth aside. She tried reading but realized after she had moved her eyes determinedly over two whole pages that she could not recall a single word. She even indulged in a little weep while Tramp set his chin on her lap and gazed mournfully at her. But whoever had said that a good cry made one feel better obviously had never tried it himself. She ended up with a blocked nose, swollen eyes, a soggy handkerchief, and a more wretched misery than ever.

Self-pity was a dreadful affliction, she thought, irritated with herself as she kissed the top of the dog's head. She would not put up with it one moment longer. She dried her eyes, blew her nose loudly, and glared at her embroidery before picking it up and tackling it once more with firmness of purpose.

Fifteen minutes later her thoughts were interrupted by the sound of the knocker banging against the front door. She looked up in surprise, her needle suspended above the cloth. Matilda? No, of course not. Lady Gramley and Sir Benedict Harper? Hardly. They would not ride in this weather, and it was unnecessary for them to come to make their excuses. Samantha could not have failed to notice that it was raining. The vicar? He had not been back since Matilda had kept him talking on the step one afternoon until the cutting wind persuaded him to leave.

"Sir Benedict Harper, ma'am," the butler announced as he opened the door. He sounded a little dubious, but the gentleman came past him before she could decide whether it was proper to admit him or not, or—more to the point—whether she cared that it was not.

"Sir Benedict," she said, setting aside her work and rising to her feet. "You surely did not ride over?"

She was pathetically glad to see him.

"I came by carriage," he said, acknowledging a tail-wagging Tramp with a quelling glance. "Good afternoon, Mrs. McKay. Your sister-in-law is still indisposed, is she? I am sorry. I would not have—"

"She has gone," she told him. "She left this morning.

She would not remain here any longer to be contaminated by my wicked self."

Oh, dear, she ought not to have phrased it quite that way. She ought to have invented an illness in the family that had taken Matilda away. It would not have been difficult. The countess was always ailing. It was too late now, though.

He stood still, gazing at her as the butler shut the door behind him. He glanced at the window, she noticed. It was fully visible for the first time in months.

"Gone?" he said. "Not to return, do you mean? This did not have anything to do with the fact that you were to ride with me, did it? Beatrice *did* agree to come with us, you know."

It was too late for evasion.

"Nothing short of complete isolation behind the black veil of our mourning for the next eight months would have suited Matilda's sense of propriety, Sir Benedict," she told him. "I am not sure by what exact rule book she and my father-in-law live, but I have never heard of anyone else's living by it, for which mercy I am truly thankful. The Earl of Heathmoor is a law unto himself and always has been. Perhaps the book is his own. Indeed, I believe it must be."

Her voice sounded brittle, she realized, even on the brink of hysteria. She was terrified he was going to go away again, which would, of course, be the best thing he could do—for both of them. He would not appreciate having to listen to her pour out all her self-pitying woes. And she needed time to compose herself before conversing with anyone.

"I came to explain why we could not go out riding," he said, "though I daresay the reason is self-evident. I came to see if Lady Matilda had recovered from her cold and to offer her my sister's good wishes for her restored health. I will take my leave, ma'am, since you have no companion or chaperon and we cannot withdraw to the garden as we did at Robland a couple of days ago."

It would be quite the right thing to do, of course. But she could not *bear* to be alone again. Not yet. How foolish to have allowed someone like Matilda to have discomposed her so very much.

"Please stay," she said. "Do sit down. I am *sick* of propriety and even sicker of my own company. And why should I not entertain a guest who has been kind enough to call upon me despite the pouring rain?"

"Perhaps," he suggested, "because that guest is a single gentleman and you are a single lady without a companion."

She sighed. He looked uncomfortable standing there leaning on his canes. He must be desperate to leave. But loneliness and low spirits had made her selfish, not to mention indiscreet.

"Did you come, then, just to inform me that it is raining and to inquire after Matilda's health?" she asked him.

He hesitated. And then he took her completely by surprise. "Hang Lady Matilda's health," he said. "And your house has windows. They are not even almost completely covered by curtains today. I came to see you."

And if she had thought *he* looked uncomfortable a few moments ago, it was nothing like what she felt now. The very air in the room felt as if it had been charged with something dangerous.

But—*hang Lady Matilda's health*. She could not help but smile.

"Oh, do sit down," she said. "Why *should* you leave just because Matilda is not here?"

He made his slow way to the chair she had indicated

and sat. She reseated herself and they stared at each other.

Now what? At least in Lady Gramley's garden the day before yesterday there had been flowers to look at and the sky and the house. And there had been sounds even if she had been unaware of them at the time— birds, insects, wind, grooms in the stables. Here even Tramp was silent. He had stretched out before Sir Benedict, his chin on the man's boot.

"Did you love him?" he asked abruptly.

She raised her eyebrows. Had she expected him to talk about the weather? He was talking about Matthew? It was a horribly impertinent question. It demanded a sharp set-down.

"I was head-over-heels in love when I married him," she said. "Such euphoria cannot be expected to last forever, of course. There is really no such thing as happily ever after, Sir Benedict."

"How long had you been married before he was injured?" he asked.

"Two years," she told him. "I spent the first year with him and the second, after his regiment was sent to the Peninsula, at Leyland Abbey in Kent with my in-laws."

"And you fell out of love because of his injuries?"

"No." She gazed broodingly at him for a few moments. She ought to repel him by telling him how impertinent and intrusive his question was. "It did not take me long after my marriage to discover what I ought to have realized before. He could not live without the admiration of men and the adulation of women. He was handsome and dashing and charming. Everyone adored him. But he—"

Ah, she really ought not to be talking so about her own husband.

"But he adored no one except himself?" he suggested.

How could he have guessed that? But he was exactly

right. Matthew had seen everyone beyond himself as nothing more than an attentive, admiring audience. She doubted there had ever been anyone in his life whom he really knew or wanted to know, herself included. Even during the last five years he had seen her as he wanted to see her, an obedient and attentive wife, created for his comfort. He had never *known* her. Not even half.

"His wounds did not change him?" he asked.

"Oh, they did. Or perhaps they changed only the circumstances of his life rather than his essential character." She turned her gaze on the fire. "His nose had been cut by a saber and broken. His face was not very badly disfigured after it had healed, but he refused to be seen by anyone except his valet and me. He would not have a mirror in his room. He was crushed by what he thought of as the loss of his good looks, as though they were his very identity. If his health had been good apart from that relatively minor disfigurement, perhaps he would have recovered some of his old confidence and swagger. But his health was *not* good."

"Beatrice tells me you were devoted to him," he said.

"How could I not be?" She looked back at him. "He was my husband, and I cared about him. I ought not to have said anything negative about him. He is not here to contradict me or to retaliate with a listing of all *my* shortcomings."

"Sometimes, as I told you a couple of days ago," he said, "one needs to speak from the heart to people who understand and can be relied upon to keep a confidence."

"And I can rely upon you?" she asked. "Even though you are little more than a stranger to me?"

"You may rely upon my discretion."

She believed him. She remembered what he had said about his friends at Penderris Hall.

"He did not deserve such a very harsh and prolonged

ending to his life," she said. "I never ever wished that for him."

"And you do not deserve to be left feeling guilty that you are still alive," he said. "I told you about Hugo, Lord Trentham, who went out of his mind after successfully leading a Forlorn Hope in Spain. His chief torment—it plagued him for years after and still does to a certain degree—was that he survived intact while all his men either died or were horribly injured. Yet he led that attack of volunteers from the front with extraordinary courage. You must forgive yourself for being alive, Mrs. McKay, and for wishing to go on living."

"And for wanting to dance?" She half smiled at him.

"And even for wanting to ride."

"Enough of me and my petty miseries," she said with a slight shake of her head. "What of you? Why exactly are you staying in such a remote corner of England with your sister? It seems a very retired sort of life for a gentleman of your age."

"My age?" He raised his eyebrows.

"Your face has known suffering," she said, feeling the heat of a flush in her cheeks. "You could be any age between twenty-five and thirty-five. Or even—"

"I am twenty-nine," he said. "Beatrice needed a few more weeks at home to recover from her indisposition over the winter, but it was necessary for Gramley to go up to London to take his seat in the House of Lords. Their boys are away at school. I had nothing better to do with my time, so I came here to keep her company."

"Lady Gramley is fortunate to have such an attentive brother," she said.

"You are not so fortunate in your brother?" he asked. "Your half brother?"

"John is a clergyman and has the charge of a busy parish and of a wife and three children," she told him.

"And he was opposed to our father marrying my mother."

"Why?" he asked. "Just because she was not *his* mother?"

"At least partly for that reason, I am sure," she said. "His mother had been much respected and beloved by all her neighbors."

He was looking closely at her. "And your mother was not?"

She ought to just say yes or no and leave it at that.

"My mother was an actress when my father met her in London," she said. "She was also the daughter of a Welshman and a Gypsy. It was not a combination designed to endear her to her stepson. Or to the more genteel of my father's neighbors, especially when she was so much younger than he and so beautiful and vibrant."

"Ah," he said and regarded her in silence for a few moments while she waited for him to continue. This was the moment, perhaps, when he would recover his manners and take a hasty leave—or as hasty as he was able without making his distaste too obvious. "That would explain your vividly dark coloring. I have wondered where the foreign blood came from. It comes from your Gypsy grandmother."

"It is not really foreign blood, though, is it?" she said. "There have been Gypsies in Britain for generations. But there has not been much intermarriage and they have kept their distinctive looks."

He regarded her quietly again, but there was a slight smile on his face. She could not decipher its meaning.

"Is she still living?" he asked. "Your grandmother, I mean? Or your grandfather?"

"My grandmother left to return to her own people when my mother was an infant," she said. "I know nothing of my grandfather except his nationality. My mother left Wales at the age of seventeen and never went back. She almost never talked about her past. Perhaps she would have done if she had lived longer."

Silence stretched between them again.

"Perhaps," she said, "you feel the need to leave now, Sir Benedict?"

"Because I am compromising your virtue?" he asked. "Or because you are half Gypsy and may compromise mine?"

"One quarter," she said testily. "I am one quarter Gypsy."

"Ah, well, I am reassured, then," he said. "One half might have been difficult to overlook."

She looked sharply at him. His face was sober, but there was laughter in his eyes.

"Has it dogged you through your life?" he asked. "The fact that you have Gypsy blood, that is? And it is impossible for you to hide it. It may be only one quarter of your heritage, but it accounts for almost the whole of your looks."

She lifted her chin and said nothing.

"All your very *beautiful* looks," he added. "I am sorry. I have embarrassed you on an issue about which you seem sensitive. Yes, Mrs. McKay, I do feel the need to take my leave. But for propriety's sake. *Your* propriety."

She had been feeling uncomfortable with him and irritated that he had somehow persuaded her to reveal such private aspects of her life. How did he *do* that? Was it just that she was unaccustomed to having social dealings with anyone? But she was not ready yet to be alone.

"Why did you want to see me?" she asked him. "It is what you admitted a few minutes ago—that you came to see *me*."

"I did not expect to find you here alone," he protested.

"But you did. And you stayed."

"I did," he agreed. He lifted a hand to rub a finger along the side of his nose. "I certainly did not want to see you last week. I had wronged you horribly and I hated having to come to make my apology. I did not much want to see you two days ago, but since I was the one to suggest that you call on Beatrice, it would have seemed mean to sneak away on my horse and have you find no one home at all."

"You saw me coming, then?" she asked him. "You were returning from your ride?"

"I was just setting out, actually," he said. "And, yes, I saw you. And I enjoyed our conversation in the garden. I suppose I have been starved for female company, entirely by my own fault, and you seemed a safe companion."

"Safe?"

"You are a widow and only partway through your mourning period." He grimaced. "I apologize. I am making a mess of this. I am not interested in any flirtation. I am not in search of a wife. I—"

"And if you were," she said, "you would be searching in the wrong place. I am *not* in the market for a husband."

"No," he said. "Of course not. I enjoyed your companionship a few days ago, Mrs. McKay. It is not often one can relax with a member of the opposite sex who is not a relative."

"And so I am safe because I am a recent widow," she said. "But what if I were *not* still in mourning?"

He stared at her for a few moments.

"Then you would not seem safe at all," he said.

"Why not?"

"I would be tempted to . . . engage your interest," he said.

"My affections, do you mean?"

"Affection is not always necessary."

She settled her back against the cushions behind her. "You mean you would be tempted to seduce me?"

"Absolutely not." He frowned. "Seduction is one-sided. It suggests a certain degree of coercion or at least of deception."

Samantha could actually feel her heart thumping in her chest. She could hear it pulsing in her ears. "Sir Benedict," she said, "how has our conversation come to take this turn?"

He smiled at her suddenly, and there was a strange fluttering low in her abdomen, for it was a smile of considerable charm. It was almost boyish—except that it was not really boyish at all.

Oh, this was absolutely not safe! How dared he? She really ought not to have let him stay.

"I believe it must have a great deal to do with the absence of Lady Matilda," he said. "I doubt we would have spoken of much other than the weather and the state of one another's health if she had been here."

"No, indeed," she agreed fervently. "But we need not worry anyway, need we? I am a recent widow and so I am safe company."

"How old are you?" he asked.

"What a very unmannerly question," she said. "A woman never tells, sir. Younger than you, though. I believe my first impression of you was an accurate one after all. All that language and bad temper! You are no gentleman."

But she spoiled the effect of her words by laughing. He smiled back at her.

"I am going to ring for the tea tray," she said, getting to her feet. "Would you like something other than tea?"

"Sherry, if there is any."

She pulled the bell rope. Tramp raised his chin for a moment, sensed that her rising did not offer any treat for himself, and lowered it again onto Sir Benedict's right boot. Silly dog. Did he not realize that the man did not like him?

She gave the order to Rose but did not immediately sit down again. She felt uncomfortable and moved to the window, where she stood looking out. The rain had not eased.

He would be tempted to engage her interest if she were not a recent widow, he had openly admitted. She ought to have crossed the distance between them there and then and slapped his face. Or she ought to have demanded that he leave.

But it was by far the nicest thing anyone had said to her for a long, long time.

Oh, dear, she feared she would hug to herself the memory of his impudent words for days to come. How pathetic she was!

8

❧

*B*en had been aware almost as soon as he entered the room that Mrs. McKay had been crying. There had been no trace of tears left, it was true, but a slight redness and puffiness about her eyes had betrayed her. He had set out to distract her with conversation and had ended up coming very near to flirting with her.

That had *not* been his intention when he had decided to come. Well, of course it had not. He had expected a very dull, very formal visit with two ladies, not one. He really ought to have left immediately after he knew she was unchaperoned.

But she had been crying. And it had been apparent that she did not want to be alone. So he had stayed— very unwisely. Being alone with her here felt very different from the way being alone with her two days ago in Bea's flower garden had felt.

Dash it all.

He had not wanted a woman in six years—not women in general, and not any woman in particular. He had even been a little uneasy about it. Had his injuries included the death of his sexual appetites? But he had been only a *little* uneasy since he knew he could never offer himself in marriage to any woman—not his broken self, anyway, and he was never going to be fully healed. He really could not bear the thought of offering himself outside of marriage either, since no amount of money would completely compensate for the physical revulsion any woman must surely feel if she was forced to be intimate with him.

He watched her in silence as she stood at the window. Her very dark, almost black hair was dressed in a simple knot at her neck. A few tendrils had pulled loose at the sides. They were uncrimped and hung long and straight to her shoulders. Her face was beautiful anyway. It needed no adornment. Her hideous black crepe dress could not hide the lush curves of her figure or the elegant perfection of her posture.

She had Gypsy blood, and she was sensitive about it. She had half expected he would want to leave once he knew.

She was, he thought, a woman desperately in need of a friend. And friendship was something he was quite happy to offer—for a short while, at least, until he went away.

The maid returned with a tray and set it down on a table before withdrawing. Mrs. McKay turned her head to acknowledge its arrival though she did not immediately move from the window.

"It is a dreary world out there," she said. "It makes one thankful after all to be indoors with a fire burning in the hearth."

"It is not dreary." He drew his canes toward him and pulled himself to his feet as she watched. The dog scrambled up and looked at him, tail waving expectantly. Ben crossed the room to Mrs. McKay's side. "Above the clouds, you know, there is nothing but blue sky and sunshine."

"A fine consolation, indeed," she said, turning her face back to the window and looking up, "when it is impossible to get up there to see."

"A hot air balloon?" he suggested.

"Ugh!" She shuddered. "There would be rain on the

way up to the clouds, and then the mist and dampness of the clouds themselves."

"And the glory of the sunshine when we burst through to the other side," he said.

"We? Would we go together, then?"

"Oh, I think so," he said. "I *was* a military officer, of course, but I do not believe I could bellow *I told you so* quite loudly enough for you to hear me from down here."

"It would be horribly cold despite the sunshine," she said. "Have you never seen snow on mountaintops when it is warm on the plain?"

"You are determined to be pessimistic," he told her. "We would take fur robes with us and huddle together inside them."

"Together?"

She turned her head again. Her face was very close to his.

"One of the best sources of heat," he explained, "is body heat. I daresay it would be very chilly indeed up there."

"But we would be warm and snug together inside our furs."

"Yes. We would enjoy double our individual body heat."

He could almost feel her breath on his face. *And* her body heat. And here he was flirting again, but far more blatantly this time. Though he had not meant to. He had meant to cheer her up, to coax a smile or a laugh out of her.

"Where would we go?" she asked.

"Far, far away." His eyes dipped to her lips when she moistened them with her tongue.

"Ah." Her voice was a breathless whisper. "The very best place to go."

"Yes."

"Together."

"Yes."

Her eyes roamed over his face. They were large and dark and long-lashed and fathomless.

"It is longer than six years since I was kissed properly," she said.

"Properly." He swallowed. "And for me too—the same length of time. Perhaps we were both kissing for the last time on the same day at the same hour, more than six years ago, but we were kissing other people, not each other."

"Your colonel's niece?"

"Your husband?"

They both smiled.

"It is far too long a time," she said.

"Yes."

"Perhaps," she said, "we ought to do something about it."

He tried to think of all the reasons they should *not*— or at least all the reasons *he* should not.

"I am sorry." Her cheeks flushed and she turned her head rather jerkily to gaze through the window again.

He tipped his head slightly to one side and kissed her. And one thing was immediately certain. His sexual appetite had *not* been killed or even suffered damage. Her lips were soft and warm and moist. They were parted and slightly trembling. She turned fully toward him, and her hands came to rest on his shoulders.

He opened her mouth with his own and slid his tongue inside. She sucked it inward and pressed it to the roof of her mouth with her own tongue. He felt a pleasure so exquisite that he almost forgot about his cursed canes.

And then her face was a few inches away and her hands were on either side of his face, her fingers pushing into his hair. Her eyes were luminous and steady on his, her lips full and rosy and still moist and still inviting.

"I am sorry," he said. "I am handicapped. I cannot hold you."

"Perhaps that is a good thing at this precise moment." She smiled suddenly and looked young and very pretty. "Or perhaps it is just that we are both starved and *any* kiss would feel good."

"A lowering thought."

She dropped her hands to her sides, still smiling. But reality was intruding.

"I really ought not to have stayed when I discovered that Lady Matilda had gone," he said. "You will be horrified when you relive this afternoon after I have left."

"You presume to know my thoughts, do you?" she asked him. "My *future* thoughts? This was a horrid day before you came, Sir Benedict. I do not at all regret that Matilda has gone, but I do resent the fact that she left me feeling as if I were somehow in the wrong. And then it rained and I knew we could not ride. And the rain was dreary and I felt restless and lonely and utterly self-pitying. Self-pitying people are not pleasant company, even to themselves. And then, when I was at my lowest ebb, you came. And you somehow coaxed me into talking to you as though you were a trusted confidant. And then you flirted with me. For a few moments you bore me off with you to the sunshine above the clouds in a hot air balloon, wrapped together in warm furs and bound for a place far, far away. And then you kissed me. I am no longer at a low ebb. You can have *no idea* what I will feel after you have left. But I do assure you it will not be horror."

Good Lord! He thought she might find later today that she had deceived herself. He felt distinctly uncomfortable himself. This was *not* the way a gentleman behaved.

"Your sherry will not be getting cold," she said, moving past him, "but my tea certainly will. Shall I put some biscuits on a plate for you?"

"Just one," he said as he followed her more slowly across the room. "Thank you."

She fetched him his biscuit and sherry while her dog settled at his feet again.

"How old were you when you married?" he asked.

She smiled at him as she sat down and picked up her cup and saucer. "You are good at arithmetic, are you, Sir Benedict? Let me save you the bother of doing mental calculations. I was seventeen. Matthew and I were together for a year before his regiment was sent to the Peninsula. I spent the next year at Leyland Abbey. After Matthew was brought home, we came here, where we lived for five years before his passing a little over four months ago. That makes me twenty-four."

"You saw through my ruse, did you?" He laughed. "So you have been unkissed and celibate since the age of eighteen."

"I can do arithmetic too," she said as the flush deepened in her cheeks. "You have been unkissed and celibate since the age of twenty-three."

He sipped his sherry. "This is not a very proper conversation for a respectable drawing room, is it?"

"This has never been called a drawing room," she told him. "But you are quite right. Matilda would have an apoplexy if she could hear us. So would Lady Gramley, I suspect."

"Lord, yes." He put his plate down on the table beside him, the biscuit untouched. He set his sherry glass beside it, only two sips gone from it, and got to his feet again. "I believe I left common sense, not to mention my manners, outside in the rain when I stepped into Bramble Hall a while ago, Mrs. McKay. My being here alone with you *is* improper and would surely cause talk, even scandal if anyone were to learn of it. It must not happen again. I would not make you the object of unsavory gossip among your neighbors."

There was a twinge of something to her smile. Scorn? Sadness?

"You are perfectly right," she said. "But I will not regret this afternoon for all that, and I hope you will not. You have lifted my spirits when they were terribly low, and you have made me feel like a woman for the first time in years. I will remember our conversation and our kiss, brief and relatively innocent though it was. I will relive it far more often than I ought, I am sure. But you are right nevertheless. It must not be repeated. Will you give my regards to your sister?"

"I will," he promised as she pulled the bell rope and then directed the maid to have Sir Benedict Harper's carriage brought up to the door. "I am sorry about the ride. Perhaps we can try again on a better day. With Beatrice, of course."

He reached out a hand to her and she took it.

"Do come to call upon Bea whenever you feel lonely," he said. "She will be delighted. You could perhaps accompany her from time to time when she visits the sick. No one could argue that that is not an unexceptionable activity for a widow in mourning."

"Thank you," she said. "You are kind." And yet there was an edge to her voice now that he could not quite interpret.

He turned and made his way to the door. He felt clumsy, even grotesque, knowing that her eyes were upon him.

He sat in the carriage a few minutes later and raised a hand to her as she stood in the open doorway of the house, the dog beside her, wagging its tail.

So much for offering her his friendship for a while. He had ruined that possibility by being damned selfish and flirting with her and even kissing her. Continuing to visit her alone was out of the question now that he knew she *would* be alone. It was a shame. She needed companionship. So did he. But a single man and a single woman could not be companions without courting scandal. And justifiably so, it seemed.

Perhaps he could find her other companions, ones who were neither single nor male.

*T*wo days later Lady Gramley paid Samantha an afternoon call, bringing with her Mrs. Andrews, the vicar's wife, and cheerful conversation and practical suggestions for how Mrs. McKay might involve herself in village life without in any way compromising her status as a newly bereaved widow. Before they left, Samantha's name had been added to the list of official visitors to the sick, and she had become a member of two committees, one for organizing the church summer bazaar, and one for decorating the altar. She had been urged to pay social calls at Robland Park and the vicarage whenever she wished and was assured that she would soon find herself invited elsewhere too.

"I spoke with my husband about your situation, Mrs. McKay," Mrs. Andrews told her, "and he assured me that neither church nor society would ever frown upon a widow involving herself in good works and the quiet exchange of companionship with her peers, even during the early months of her bereavement. And you may believe me when I tell you that the vicar is a stickler for correct behavior."

Samantha suspected that Sir Benedict Harper was behind this visit, and she was grateful. Being busy in a way that was useful to others would surely still her restlessness and help her fulfill her desire to live again, not merely to exist from day to day. And perhaps making new friends here was not going to be so very hard after all.

But Sir Benedict did not come again. Neither was he at Robland Park when Samantha went there for tea, perhaps because she went by invitation and he knew about it in advance. When she saw him at church, he inclined his head politely but neither spoke nor looked fully at her.

She had relived their conversation and his kiss— especially his kiss—for the rest of the day after he left. She had lain awake half the night dreaming of it— ironic, that. And she had watched through the windows for him all the following morning and from the garden during the afternoon, when the rain had finally stopped long enough for her to take Tramp outside for some exercise.

But long before it was borne in upon her that he would not come again, she had succumbed to guilt. She had encouraged him to stay when he would have left after discovering that Matilda was no longer with her. She had encouraged him to flirt with her, though it had not been deliberate. And she had quite explicitly invited his kiss.

She had behaved quite shockingly badly. It was no wonder he did not wish to see her again. And she surely would not wish to see him again if she were not so lonely and so restless.

It would be for the best if she never saw him again, she decided. And then she learned that soon he would indeed be gone. Lady Gramley was planning to leave soon to join her husband in London. And her brother, she reported to a group of ladies at the vicarage one afternoon two weeks after his visit to Bramble Hall on that rainy afternoon, was going to do some traveling about the British Isles, starting in Scotland.

Samantha told herself quite firmly that the news did

not depress her in the slightest. It was nothing to her. She had put memories of that afternoon firmly behind her. Soon he would be gone, and she could devote herself to her new life here at Bramble Hall without the distraction of expecting to see him wherever she went. She intended to be active and busy while she lived out the remainder of her year of mourning.

Perhaps she would even be happy.

9

❧

$\mathscr{A}$ little over a week later, the carriage that had conveyed Matilda to Leyland Abbey returned to Bramble Hall, driven by a different coachman, with different outriders accompanying it. Samantha recognized the coachman from five years ago, but the other men were strangers to her. They were all large, burly men, as servants hired to guard travelers often were. They all also seemed particularly surly of disposition. That was what working for the Earl of Heathmoor did to people, Samantha thought. One of them handed her a letter that bore the earl's seal.

She took it from him and felt immediately chilled. She did not want any more dealings with Matthew's family, and this was hardly going to be a friendly missive. And why had other servants returned in place of the ones who had gone with Matilda? She took the letter into the sitting room and closed the door. She shooed Tramp off her favorite chair, upon which he was strictly forbidden to take up his abode—just as he had been strictly forbidden to enter the house once upon a time—and seated herself there in his place.

She did not want to break the seal on the letter. She had been feeling reasonably happy of late. She had friendly acquaintances. She had places to go, things to do while all the time preserving her respectability and her obligation to be in mourning for what remained of the year. She did not want to be plunged back into

gloom and guilt. For one moment she considered tossing the note on the fire and forgetting about it. Matthew would have done just that. But the trouble was
that she would *not* forget it. It would be better to read it
now and then somehow put it out of her mind.

She broke the seal with a terrible sense of foreboding.

She read the letter through without stopping and then
bent her head over her lap and shut her eyes very tightly.
After a few moments she could hear Tramp panting
nearby and could smell his less-than-sweet breath. A
cold, wet nose nudged at her hand and he whined. She
set her hand on his head.

"Tramp," she said.

He licked her face and whined again, in obvious distress.

"Oh, Tramp."

Stunned despair at the unexpectedness of it all en-
gulfed her. The Earl of Heathmoor was displeased
by the scandalous goings-on of his daughter-in-law as
reported to him by Lady Matilida. *That* was hardly a
surprise. Neither was the long-winded eloquence with
which he chastised her. It was the punishment that
made her feel rather as if she had been punched hard in
the stomach, though he did not call it punishment. If his
daughter-in-law did not know how to behave without
the firm guiding hand of a man, and clearly she did not,
then he must insist upon her removing to Leyland Abbey
without delay. There he would himself impose the necessary discipline to halt the wayward behavior that
would surely bring censure and even ruin upon the good
name of his family if allowed to continue.

If there had been no more than that, Samantha might
well have burned the letter after all and dealt with her
seething wrath as best she was able. But there *was* more.

For of course—oh, foolish, foolish, *foolish* of her to
have relied upon Matthew's expectations—Bramble Hall

was not hers. It had never been made over to Matthew, and if it had been willed to him, the bequest meant nothing when he had died before his father. The house belonged, with all its furnishings and all its servants, to the Earl of Heathmoor, and now, his second son being deceased and his son's widow not to be trusted to remain here and uphold his good name, he was sending his third son to live here. Rudolph and his wife, Patience, would arrive to take up residence within a fortnight. The house would be made ready for them during the intervening weeks. The earl's head coachman and his head groom, with other trusted servants, had been given instructions to convey Samantha to Leyland with just one day of rest between their arrival at Bramble Hall and their departure. She would make herself ready to accompany them.

He made them sound like jailers. They *looked* like jailers.

"Tramp," she said, "why did I not see this coming? Am I an utter idiot? I never *dreamed*. I thought he would be happy to leave me here, out of sight and out of mind."

For a few moments she sat with tightly clenched eyes while he whined and licked her face again. Then she lifted her head and gazed into his mournful eyes only inches from her own.

"I would rather kill myself than live at Leyland Abbey again," she told him. It was only just an exaggeration.

She got abruptly to her feet and paced the room, the letter still clutched in one hand. Whatever was she to do? She would be swallowed whole if she went to Leyland. She would never be free. But what was the alternative? She had never had to consider any. Matthew had assured her that she would have a home here for the rest of her life, and she had believed him. Oh, she ought to have *known* . . .

She stopped pacing after a while and clutched the windowsill with her free hand to prevent herself from falling. She inhaled and then found it impossible to exhale until the breath shuddered out of her in slow, jerky spurts, and then she seemed to have forgotten how to breathe in again. Her vision blackened about the edges. And then air wheezed in again. She willed herself to *wake up*. Right now this minute. This had to be a nightmare. But of course it was not.

She had to get out of the house, from which some force had surely sucked most of the air. The ceiling was pressing down upon the top of her head. And the house was no longer hers in any way at all. Rudolph and Patience would be here within two weeks. She turned and ran upstairs for her bonnet and cloak and outdoor shoes, Tramp thumping along at her heels.

The garden did not have enough air either. She strode along the side path without hesitating and out through the gate and along the lane beyond it until she saw a cart swaying beneath a large load of hay coming in her direction. She struck out across a field and then over a meadow—the very one in which she had met Sir Benedict Harper once upon a long time ago.

Robland Park was still a fair distance away, but she knew suddenly that it was her destination, that it had been from the start. No one could help her, but she needed the company of a friend, and Lady Gramley was the closest thing to a friend she had had for many years.

She strode onward, Tramp frisking at her heels and occasionally dashing off in pursuit of some wild creature more fleet of foot than he and therefore not at all timid about showing its head. He never learned that lesson, poor, foolish dog.

Whatever would become of him? He would certainly not be allowed to accompany her to Leyland Abbey.

Oh, she would die if she was torn away from him. Surely she would.

$\mathscr{S}$amantha was not the only person in the neighborhood to have received a letter of some significance that morning. Both Ben and Beatrice had received one too. Their letters were beside their plates as they sat down to breakfast.

Beatrice's letter was from her husband's sister, fifteen years younger than he. Caroline, Lady Vere, was in imminent expectation of the birth of her first child and had been impatiently awaiting the arrival of her mother-in-law to help her through the ordeal of the confinement. But that lady had recently taken to her bed with some unnamed disorder of the nerves, and Caroline begged Beatrice, in closely crossed lines and with what seemed like near hysteria, to *please* come in her stead, since Vere very nearly had a fit of the vapors every time anyone so much as touched upon the coming event in his hearing and there was no one else to whom she could turn except her old nurse, who always scolded so and whose hands shook with some sort of palsy.

"I had hoped to spend at least another week or two at home before going to London," Beatrice told Ben with a sigh after sharing with him the contents of her letter. "Now it seems I must set off for Berkshire without further ado—today if at all possible. I could be there the day after tomorrow if there are no unexpected delays. I would not put poor Caroline through the terror of being alone except for her apology for a husband and a nurse who has always terrorized her. Men are always useless under such circumstances, you know, especially the expectant father himself, who always entertains the illusion that *he* is the great sufferer at the very heart of the crisis."

"Then you must go," Ben said, laughing.

"But what about you?" she asked with a frown. "I cannot expect you to remove yourself from Robland at a moment's notice when I specifically invited you here to keep me company. You are welcome to stay on alone, of course, but it seems very inhospitable of me to abandon you."

"I will not hold it against you," he assured her, "since Lady Vere's need of your company appears to be greater than mine. I shall be perfectly comfortable here on my own, Bea. And I daresay I will be off myself within a week at the longest."

"To Kenelston?" she asked hopefully.

"Still not to Kenelston," he said. "Probably to Scotland. I have never been there, you know. It is reputed to be very scenic and beautiful, as are Ireland and Wales and numerous parts of England. Perhaps eventually, when my adoring public is begging for more books, I will even venture abroad."

"And never settle down, I suppose," she said, still frowning. "Has it not occurred to you, Benedict, that that is the whole cause of your restlessness?"

"Not settling down? It is a somewhat obvious conclusion, I suppose," he admitted. "If I were settled, I would not be restless. If I am restless, I cannot be settled."

"I should know better by now," she said, getting to her feet after setting her napkin across her plate, "than to try to discuss your personal affairs with you."

"Alas," he said, "I have no affairs to discuss."

"Ah, these double meanings," she said. "Who invented the English language, I wonder? He did not do a stellar job of it, whoever he was."

"Perhaps," he said, "he was a she."

She gave a bark of laughter. "On the assumption that women are by nature muddleheaded? I cannot stay to argue. I must get busy if I am to leave as close to noon as possible. The bulk of my things can be sent directly to London in a few weeks' time, of course."

Ben reread his own letter after she had left the breakfast parlor. It was from Hugo Emes, Lord Trentham, one of his fellow Survivors. Hugo was getting married, to Lady Muir. Ben was genuinely pleased at the news. He had wondered if Hugo would go after her when they all left Penderris. She had sprained her ankle down on the beach when they were all staying in Cornwall, and Hugo had found her and carried her up to the house like the brawny giant he was, scowling all the way, Ben did not doubt. He had fallen head-over-ears in love with her, as she had with him, if Ben was any judge of female sensibilities. But Hugo had felt restrained by the fact that though titled and enormously wealthy, he was a man of middle-class origin, while she was the sister of the Earl of Kilbourne and the widow of a viscount. And so he had let her go without a fight, the idiot, when her brother came to fetch her a few days later. Obviously, though, he *had* gone after her. They were to be married at St. George's on Hanover Square in London.

The letter was an invitation to the wedding, though Hugo did not hold high expectations of Ben's being there.

I did not have Lady Gramley's direction, he had written, *and neither did anyone else. I wrote to Kenelston for it, but by the time your brother's reply reached me, far too much time had passed and it seems impossible that you could be here even if you felt inclined to tear across half the country just for my nuptials. Imogen is coming from Cornwall, though, and Flavian, Ralph, and George are already here. I have not heard from Vincent yet.*

Ben felt a longing to be there too, even if it *was* London. It looked as if he might be the only one of the Survivors not to attend Hugo's wedding. And he was the first of them to marry. Was he also the only one who ever would? They all liked to think they were healed and ready to take on the world again, but in truth they were a deeply damaged lot. Not that self-pity was their besetting sin. They had all fought hard against that particular trait.

The wedding was in a week's time. He could get there for it if he set out without delay. The lure of seeing them all again when they had parted not so long ago, not expecting to be together again until next year, was almost overwhelming. And they would be gathering for a happy event. It really *was* happy. Ben had liked Lady Muir very well indeed, and it had seemed to him that she and Hugo were perfect for each other despite the obvious differences of social status and temperament.

For a moment he felt a wave of envy. It was not jealousy. He had not fancied Lady Muir himself. It was just envy that two worthy people had found each other and connected with each other's heart, for undoubtedly it was a love match. And so they would marry and settle to a lifetime of shared passion.

Perhaps he *would* go, Ben decided. Not today, though. There would be too much chaos if both he and Beatrice were preparing for a hasty departure. He could still arrive in time if he left tomorrow morning, though it would mean traveling in longer stages than he found comfortable. He would not need to stay in town for long, just long enough for the wedding and a leisurely visit with his friends. He could still go to Scotland after leaving there, making his slow, meandering way back north, writing down his impressions as he went.

Was it absurd to imagine that he could write? It probably was, but he could at least try. He had to do *something*.

Beatrice left just before one o'clock. Ben waved her on her way and smiled at the sight of her traveling carriage piled high with baggage while more followed in a smaller conveyance. And the bulk of her belongings were to follow her to London?

He went back inside and upstairs to the room adjoining his own where he did his daily exercises.

He had made the definite decision by the time he was finished that he would go to London, that he would surprise Hugo by turning up at the last minute to make their number complete, assuming, that was, that Vincent was going. Partly, he knew, it was procrastination that drove him. Although the idea of setting out for a tour of Scotland excited him in the abstract, the prospect of actually setting out alone, no particular destination in mind, was less appealing. Perhaps Ralph or Flavian could be persuaded to join him. Or even Vince. It might be interesting to add the observations of a blind traveler to his book.

He was coming out of his room after washing and changing out of his sweaty exercise clothes when he heard the sound of voices in the hall downstairs. Beatrice's butler was informing someone that her ladyship was not at home.

"Oh," the other person said. And, after a pause, "When do you expect her back?"

It was a woman's voice. Mrs. McKay's. Ben prepared to step back into his room, where his valet was beginning to pack his bags. He had done a successful job in the past few weeks of avoiding her, of avoiding causing her any gossip in the neighborhood, for that was what it would have come to if he had continued to call upon her.

"She has gone away, ma'am," the butler explained, "and will not be back until the summer."

"Oh." Somehow there was a world of flatness in the single syllable.

Ben hesitated, his hand on the knob of his door.

"Should I see if Sir Benedict is at home, ma'am?" the butler asked.

Ben frowned and shook his head.

"Oh," she said, "I do not know. No, perhaps I ought to . . ."

This had not been intended as a social visit. Something in her voice told Ben that. There was distress beneath the flatness of tone.

"Who is it, Rogers?" he called loudly enough to be heard downstairs, and he made his way to the head of the stairs so that he could see for himself.

"It is Mrs. McKay, sir," the butler told him, "come to call on Lady Gramley."

The dog was with her. It barked once and wagged its tail at him. Why that wretched hound liked him, he had no idea. Perhaps because he had never kicked him in the chin when that part of his anatomy had rested on Ben's boot?

She looked up at him. Her dark veil had been tossed back over the brim of her bonnet to reveal a very pale face, even allowing for the fact that black tended to leach color from the skin.

"I am so sorry," she said. "I did not know your sister had gone away. I—I will not disturb you. I am sorry. Come along, Tramp."

"Did you walk here?" Ben asked.

"Yes," she said. "We were out for a stroll and I decided on a whim to call here."

"We certainly will not send you away without any refreshments," Ben said, beginning the slow descent of the stairs. "Will we, Rogers? Show Mrs. McKay into the small salon, if you please, and have a tray of tea brought there. And some brandy."

"I—" She did not finish what she had started to say. "Thank you. I will just drink a cup of tea and be on my way. I am sorry for being a nuisance."

She was over by the unlit fireplace, removing her bonnet, when Ben entered the room. Her dog ambled over to greet him, his tail wagging and his rear end wiggling. Ben eyed him with disfavor and scratched him beneath his chin.

"I am sorry . . ." she began.

"Yes," he said, closing the door behind him. "You have already made that perfectly clear, Mrs. McKay. What has happened?"

He felt resentful. If she had left this until tomorrow, he would have been gone and known nothing about it. She would have been compelled to cope alone with whatever was troubling her.

"Nothing has happened." She smiled, a sickly expression that reached no higher than her lips. "I did not know Lady Gramley was leaving for London so soon."

"She is on her way to Berkshire," he told her, "where Gramley's sister is expecting to give birth any day. Her mother-in-law was supposed to attend her, but she has been detained by illness. Beatrice left here just after noon, only a few hours after receiving her sister-in-law's letter. I am sure she is sitting in the carriage at this very moment thinking of all the people here to whom she ought to have dashed off notes of explanation. What is the matter?"

Something clearly was. She was making an effort to appear composed, but she looked as if she might shatter at any moment. And she was still standing.

"Nothing."

The door opened behind Ben, and a footman set down a large tray. Ben bent over it and poured a little brandy into a glass. He carried it across the room to her, supporting himself with just one of his canes.

"Drink this," he said.

"What is it?"

"Brandy," he said. "Sit down and drink it. I daresay your walk has chilled you."

"I did not notice," she said as she half collapsed onto a sofa.

"Drink it."

She took the glass, sipped the brandy, and made a face.

"Toss it back," he told her.

She did so and coughed and sputtered. "Oh, that is vile."

"Pay attention to the aftereffects, though," he told her.

She closed her eyes briefly. Her cheeks gained some color.

"He is throwing me out of Bramble Hall," she said, "and sending his son to live there."

She had not made her meaning at all clear, but it did not take much effort to decipher it anyway. He took the empty glass from her hand and returned it to the tray. He poured a cup of tea and carried it across to her.

He was presumably the Earl of Heathmoor.

❧

$\mathscr{S}$amantha took the cup and saucer from him with hands she schooled to be steady. Tramp was seated beside her, at attention, his ears cocked, his eyes intent on hers. He knew there was something wrong, the poor dear.

"Thank you," she said.

She was dreadfully upset that Lady Gramley had gone away. Although there were other ladies in the neighborhood to whom she supposed she might turn in her distress, none but Lady Gramley felt like a friend. Sometimes friendly acquaintances were simply not enough. Though *how* she had expected Lady Gramley to help her she did not know.

"Heathmoor is tossing you out without making any provision for you?" Sir Benedict Harper asked, seating himself across from her. "He is literally evicting you?"

"No. He has far too great a sense of family duty to do that," she said. "I am to go to Leyland Abbey in Kent. He has sent his own coachman and outriders back with the carriage Matilda took, and they have orders to escort me there. I am to leave the day after tomorrow. I do not know if their instructions are to coerce me if I will not go voluntarily or I try to delay, but I would not be at all surprised if they are. My father-in-law made it very clear in the letter he sent me that he sees me as a disgrace to his family and that I must be fetched to a place where he can keep a strict eye upon me and correct my waywardness."

"And this is because you returned Bea's visit that one afternoon and agreed to ride with her and with me a few days later?" He was frowning at her as if he did not quite believe his ears.

"They were not small matters to Matilda," she told him. "They are not small matters to Matilda's father. Heaven knows what I may get up to if I am left to my own devices here. I may even take it into my head to go about visiting the sick or arranging flowers on the altar at church."

She took a sip of her tea and discovered gratefully that it was both strong and sweet.

"Perhaps," he said, "it is not quite what you think. Perhaps your father-in-law's annoyance with you arises from a genuine concern that you will be lonely here without the companionship of his daughter. Perhaps he thinks you will be happier surrounded by your late husband's family."

She took another sip of tea. "I think not," she said. "But I am sorry to have made such a nuisance of myself. I came here, I suppose, to unburden myself to Lady Gramley, though to what purpose I do not know. I just did not know what else to do. I *do* not know what else to do."

"You do not believe you can find any sort of contentment at Leyland?" he asked her. "Even just temporarily, until your year of mourning is at an end?"

"Could you find any sort of contentment in a prison, Sir Benedict?" she asked in return. "Where even smiles are construed as sin, and laughter is unheard of?"

"And it is out of the question to go to your half brother?"

"Yes," she said.

John would perhaps not literally refuse her admission

to the vicarage if she turned up on his doorstep, but he would certainly make it clear that she was unwelcome, that she could not stay there beyond a few nights at the longest.

"Forgive my impertinence," Sir Benedict said, "but do you not have an independence? Can you not set up on your own somewhere?"

She stared blankly at him. Her father had left her a small legacy, which Matthew had appropriated. He had left her with a small income, enough for her personal needs since she had never been extravagant. But enough with which to set up her own establishment? She did not know and had never wondered. She had relied upon Matthew's assumption that his father would be happy to leave her at Bramble Hall. Oh, how foolish of her. How foolish! She ought to have been making plans. But *what* plans?

"I could not stay anywhere close to here," she said, "where at least I have some friendly acquaintances and some sense of belonging. Rudolph and Patience will be at Bramble Hall within a fortnight. They would make life very difficult for me if I remained here in defiance of my father-in-law's express wishes. And I could not return to the village where I grew up. I had a few friends there, but on the whole I was not well accepted because my mother was not. As for anywhere else, well, I do not *know* anywhere."

She swallowed awkwardly. She was suddenly very frightened. The world seemed a vast and hostile place. Whatever was she going to *do*?

"Starting a new life is never easy," he said, "especially when there is no obvious base of operations. You have the rest of today and tomorrow, then, to think of an alternative to Leyland Abbey."

"I cannot go there." She set down her cup and saucer and gripped one arm of the sofa. "I will not. Though I may not have a choice if I am right about those servants the earl has sent. They are all large, severe-looking men. However it is, though, I have to leave Bramble Hall. I expected it to be my home for the rest of my life. It is what my husband expected."

She dipped her head forward in an attempt to cling to consciousness. Tramp whined. She was going to be homeless. And friendless.

"I must count my blessings," she said, smoothing a hand over the dog's head as though to reassure herself by comforting him. "I am not penniless, after all. There are thousands upon thousands of people who at this very moment are both homeless and destitute. Oh, the despair of it. How do they go on, Sir Benedict? I must not despair. It would be wicked. I am not destitute. There must be somewhere I can live, some small country house I can afford."

She frowned in thought for a moment but was distracted when she realized he had got to his feet and come to sit beside her after propping his canes against the far side of the sofa. He took her right hand in both of his while Tramp stretched out at their feet. His hands were blessedly warm.

"I know how it is to feel homeless, even if I do not know how it is actually to *be* homeless," he said. "It is a wretchedly bleak and lonely feeling. But, as you say, you are not destitute."

She turned her head and looked at his finely chiseled features and slightly hollowed cheekbones, a strangely appealing, not-quite-handsome face—though his eyes were very blue. He had kissed her almost a month ago and then withdrawn from her life, though she was convinced he had sent his sister to befriend her and involve her in neighborhood and church activities.

"Do you have any other relatives apart from your half brother?" he asked.

"A few aunts and uncles and cousins," she said. "None to whom I have ever been close. They all shared my half brother's outrage over my father's marrying an actress of doubtful origin who was half his age."

"And there is no one else?"

There was the illusion of comfort in his grasp.

"There were friends, other wives, during the first year of my marriage," she said. "But I was not with them long enough to establish any lasting friendships before the regiment went to the Peninsula and I was sent to Leyland instead of going with them. No, there is no one."

How abject it sounded. After twenty-four years of living, she had no one to whom she could turn for help.

He raised her hand, and she felt the warmth of his lips and his breath against the back of it for a few moments.

"But I have taken enough of your time, Sir Benedict," she said. "You must be wishing me in Hades though you have been very kind. This is not your concern, and the longer I talk, the more pathetic I sound."

She spoke briskly, and she tried at the same time to repossess her hand. He tightened his hold upon it, however.

"I think," he said, "you had better marry me, Mrs. McKay."

She jerked her hand free then and leapt to her feet. "Oh, no," she cried in great dismay. "No, no, no. Oh, how very good of you. And how excruciatingly embarrassing. I was not in any way hinting at such a thing, you know." She set her palms against her cheeks. As she had suspected, they were hot with shame.

"I am perfectly well aware of that," he said. "But marriage to me would solve your problem, you know. And perhaps it would solve mine too."

"You *have* a problem?" She frowned down at him.

"An inability to steel myself to rid my home of my

younger brother and his family, who have usurped it," he said, smiling a slightly crooked smile, "and an impossibility of living there with them. A restlessness and a depression of spirits at the realization that I will never again be the man of action I used to be. An inability to forge a meaningful new life for myself and settle to it. Beatrice says it is all explained by the fact that I have no woman in my life."

"But you cannot solve a problem—not for either of us," she said, "by creating a new one."

"Marriage to each other would create a problem?" he asked.

"Of course it would." She stretched her fingers and then curled them into her palms at her sides. They were tingling. "It would be very improper for me to marry only five months after the death of my husband. Besides, I do not *wish* to marry again. Not yet, at least. The fetters of my first marriage were tightly binding and I want to be *free*. And if and when I *do* marry, I want it to be to a man who . . . who had no connection with the wars. Forgive me, but I am tired of the wars and what they did to so many people. And as for you, it is nothing but sheer gallantry that has put the idea of marrying me into your head. By your own admission you are not yet ready to settle to your own life, Sir Benedict, let alone take on the burden of someone else's. You are not ready for the bonds of marriage. Not with me, certainly, when I am as restless and needy as you are. We would drag each other down into a pit of unending depression if we were to marry."

"Would we?" He was still smiling that crooked smile. "I find you very attractive, you know. And lest you think that not a very strong motive for marriage, I would add that you are the *first* woman to whom I have been attracted in six years."

"I find you . . . personable too," she admitted. Good

heavens, how could she deny it? There had been that kiss, had there not? "But attraction is not everything, or even very much. I was attracted to Matthew . . . Oh, Sir Benedict, if we are only attracted to each other, then we should go to bed and have our fill of pleasure with each other. We ought not to *marry*."

His smile had disappeared and his face had flushed. Oh, dear, had she really just said what she knew she *had* said?

"An affair?" he said. "That would not solve your problem, ma'am. Not unless, that is, you are suggesting that I set you up somewhere as my mistress."

She doubted she had ever felt more mortified in her life. She stared at him and—laughed. And he stared back at her and laughed too.

"With a carriage of my own and four white horses to pull it?" she asked. "And diamonds as large as birds' eggs for my ears and bosom, and a bed draped in scarlet satin with scarlet velvet curtains about it and at the windows? With such inducements you might be able to persuade me."

"I believe," he said, "I might find the four white horses a trifle vulgar."

Incredibly, they both laughed again with genuine amusement.

And then that thought that had niggled at her a couple of minutes ago came to the forefront of her mind.

. . . *some small country house I can afford.*

She turned away sharply to the fireplace and stood with her hands on the mantelpiece, gazing into the unlit coals with unseeing eyes.

"Just a moment," she said, holding up one hand.

There was the little cottage.

Perhaps.

Her mother had grown up with her paternal aunt in southwest Wales before running away at the age of seventeen to become an actress in London. Not long before she died when Samantha was twelve, word of her aunt's death had reached her, and with it the news that she had been left her aunt's cottage on the coast. That cottage had passed to Samantha on her mother's death. She had not even realized it until, after her father's death, John had sent on a letter from the solicitor in Wales who was managing it. Mr. Rhys had written to inform her that the people who had been renting the cottage for a number of years had left and that he would see to its maintenance, using the accumulated rent money, until he received instructions either to rent it again or to sell it. John had taken it upon himself, he had informed her, to reply with the instructions that the solicitor proceed as he saw fit. Matthew had been brought back from the Peninsula then, and they had just moved to Bramble Hall. He had been desperately ill, and she had been unaccustomed to nursing him. She had set the letter aside, as well as any annoyance she might have felt with John for interfering in her business. It had not seemed important business, anyway. Certainly she had never written to Mr. Rhys herself, as she might have and probably ought to have done.

Her mother, when she had learned of the bequest, had described the cottage with open contempt as a "heap" and a "hovel" that was best left to crumble to dust. That had been a long time ago, maybe fourteen years, and her mother had been remembering it from years before that. It might well have deteriorated to nothing by this time, especially without renters to look after it properly. Besides, the cottage might as well be at the other end of the world for all the good it would do her. Wales! And West Wales at that. It was not even close to the border with England. Samantha had never been there. She knew no one there. As far as she knew, there *was* no one to know. No one connected to her, anyway.

But it was a house. Perhaps. *If* it still existed. It had existed in some form five years or so ago, though, otherwise the solicitor would not have written that he would sell it or rent it again if she wished.

She was desperately in need of a home—and she already owned one. *If* it was still standing. And *if* it was habitable.

And suddenly its very remoteness became its chief attraction. It was far away from Leyland Abbey.

Sir Benedict Harper was still sitting on the sofa when she swung around to look at him. He was gazing quietly at her. Gracious heaven, he had just offered to marry her. How very noble he was, and how different from what she had thought the first time she encountered him.

"I know where I am going to go," she told him. "At least for now. Perhaps forever."

Forever? Her stomach lurched.

He raised his eyebrows.

"I own a cottage," she told him. "My great-aunt left it to my mother, who grew up there with her. I believe it was a very old, dilapidated building even then. It is probably far worse now, but I have not heard of its falling down or having been demolished. It is mine now, and that is where I am going to go. Even a crumbling ruin would be preferable to Leyland."

"It is in Wales?" he asked.

"On the southwest coast, yes."

"And you intend to go there *alone?*" He frowned. "You will need to give the matter some careful thought, Mrs. McKay. It is a long way to go, through wild and lonely and possibly dangerous country. And who is to know what you will find at the end of it all? Perhaps the cottage really is uninhabitable."

"Then I will find one that is not," she said, "and rent it. At least I will be in a part of the world where half my heritage lies. And no one will find me there. No one will bother me. I will be able to live again."

"And dance?" But he was still frowning.

"On the beach, if there is one, as I daresay there is," she said. "On the edge of the world with all the wild power of the ocean looking on."

"And you intend to travel there alone and live there alone." He got slowly to his feet while Tramp sat up and watched, ever hopeful. "It would be sheer folly. The idea may seem appealing to you, and I can understand why. I can even applaud your courage. But consider the reality of leaving Bramble Hall behind and traveling alone and unaccompanied into such a distant unknown."

She did consider—for a few moments. And she was frightened—but undaunted. The alternative was far worse.

"Then you must come with me," she said.

Ben could not have been more effectively robbed of breath if someone had planted a fist in his stomach.

Then you must come with me.

They stood staring at each other, four feet apart. Color had flooded her cheeks while he feared it must have drained from his.

"Impossible," he said. "Who would be your chaperon?"

"You."

"But I am neither your father nor your brother nor your husband nor your betrothed. Nor female."

"So?" She raised her eyebrows.

"Your reputation would be in tatters," he told her.

Her lips curved into a half smile. "So?"

Oh, good Lord.

He went at the problem from a different angle. "I am hardly the ideal man to defend you should danger threaten." He looked down deliberately at his canes. "Unless, that is, we were assailed by a brigand obliging enough to come close enough to be clobbered."

"We will take a loaded pistol," she said, still with that half smile hovering about her lips and the color high in her cheeks, "and you may shoot him from a distance— while sitting."

"Between the eyes, I suppose."

"Where else?"

It struck him that she was actually enjoying herself, that her sudden realization that there was a solution to her dilemma awaiting her, in the form of a cottage that had been dilapidated even during her mother's girlhood, had made her giddy with relief.

"Mrs. McKay," he said, "*do* consider."

"Why?" she asked him. "I have had seven years of nothing but doing what is proper, Sir Benedict. And for what? I married in expectation of a lifetime of happily-ever-after and remained decently married after the disappointment and heartbreak that followed quickly upon the heels of my wedding. I spent a year at Leyland Abbey trying my hardest to be the sort of respectable lady my father-in-law insisted I be even while he disliked and despised me. I spent five long, weary years here, nursing a demanding, peevish invalid because he was my husband and I had promised on my wedding day to love and obey him in sickness and in health. I have observed every requirement of my mourning period but have still not satisfied my sister-in-law or the Earl of Heathmoor. I am facing the prospect of more years at Leyland while what is left of my youth dwindles into middle age and then old age and death. Where has *considering* ever got me? Perhaps it is time to do something *un*considered and impulsive. Perhaps it is time to take my life in my own hands and live it."

Her eyes flashed, and there was passion in every line

of her body. Who was he to tell her she was wrong? And perhaps she was not.

"I have one day in which to make a decision that will affect all of the rest of my life, whatever that decision is," she told him. "I have one day in which to make my escape—or bow to what seems my inevitable fate. I do not know where escape will lead me. On the other hand, I *do* know where bowing to my fate will. I would be a fool not to take a chance on escape. Perhaps this was meant to be, Sir Benedict. Why else would I have been left that cottage? It has seemed so useless to me since I learned it was mine that I have scarcely ever even spared it a thought. Yet now it is of crucial importance to my future. Do you believe that sometimes life points out a way for us to follow even if it does not force us into taking that particular path? I am going where life points me. I beg your pardon for trying to involve you. Of course you will not wish to accompany me. Why should you? You owe me nothing. You have been more than kind even to listen to me, and that kindness has led to my thinking of a solution for myself. I am going."

Oh, Lord. She looked like some kind of magnificent avenging angel. She could not *possibly* go striding off in the vague direction of Wales on her own.

Why the *devil* had he not ducked back into his room the moment he heard her voice? She would have remembered her cottage without his help once she had calmed down. How she got there would have been none of his concern.

It was not his concern now.

Perhaps this was meant to be, Sir Benedict.

Do you believe that sometimes life points out a way for us to follow . . .

Lord, Lord, Lord. Why had he not left for London and Hugo's wedding at the same time as Beatrice left for Berkshire?

"Even if I were to accompany you on your journey," he said, "what would you do at the end of it, without any servants except presumably a maid and without friends or a companion? What if the cottage needs a great deal of work before it is habitable, assuming it is habitable at all?"

She would find somewhere else to rent, in a part of the country where half her heritage lay. She had already said that.

"I suppose," she said, "there are servants there to be hired. And I can make friends. I do not fear being alone. I have been essentially alone for seven years and have survived. Are you thinking of accompanying me, then?"

His legs were aching from standing so long in the same position.

"How can I allow you to go alone?" he asked her.

Her eyebrows shot up. "You have no power to *allow* me to do anything, Sir Benedict," she said. "Or to prevent me from doing anything. You are not my husband."

"Thank the Lord," he said ungraciously.

Her chin went up a notch, but she relented and lowered it again. "How very unjust of me," she said. "I burst in upon you uninvited and unburdened myself of all my woes, yet now I am taking exception to your concern for my safety. It is kind of you to be concerned. But it is not your problem, you know. *I* am not your problem. I had better return home. Thank you for receiving me. I know you did not wish to do so. You have been avoiding me, and I do not blame you."

"For your own good," he told her, exasperated. "How long would it have been before the whole neighborhood was gossiping if we had become friends, Mrs. McKay, and had kept visiting each other without any sort of chaperonage?"

"Not long at all," she said. "I told you I did not blame you. And I *do* realize that it was you who gave Lady

Gramley the idea of bringing the vicar's wife to my home so that I could become involved in parish and community activities. I am grateful to you for that."

He was not really listening. He was thinking of traveling all day with her for a week or more in the close confines of a carriage. Of taking all his meals with her. Of their staying each night at the same inn. And he felt an unreasonable resentment, for she had not asked it of him after that first impulsive suggestion that he must go with her.

Good Lord, her reputation would be in shreds, and that was probably a gross understatement.

"You force me to very bad manners, Mrs. McKay," he said. "I am entertaining you in my sister's house, yet I am afraid I will have to sit while you stand."

"I ought to have noticed your discomfort," she said, seating herself on the sofa while he returned to his chair. "I am sorry. I have caused you nothing but discomfort since the moment of my arrival. I shall leave, and you must forget I was even here. You are going to Scotland, are you not? I have heard it is lovely there."

She got abruptly to her feet again, and her dog took up his position beside her, his tail waving hopefully.

Ben regarded her irritably. "I believe," he said, "I must have been a close personal friend of the late Captain Matthew McKay. I believe I must have promised him when he was on his deathbed that I would escort his widow to Wales, where he wished her to take up residence in the cottage she inherited before her marriage. I believe I must use my full credentials again and be known as Major Sir Benedict Harper."

She looked down at him, her eyes fathomless.

"We may just get away with it," he said, "without completely wrecking your reputation."

"You are coming?" She almost whispered the words.

"We had better take my carriage," he said. "But we

need to decide how we are to get you away from Bramble Hall tomorrow without causing a great fuss and bother among the servants, especially those burly strangers."

The dog flopped down onto all fours and proceeded to lick his paws. He had sensed further delay. Mrs. McKay's hands were clasped so tightly at her waist that Ben could see the whites of her knuckles. But then her eyes brightened and even sparkled.

"With great stealth," she said.

❧

$\mathcal{S}$amantha's longtime maid had left her service after Matthew's death, when she had married his valet. Her replacement was the young daughter of the cook, a cheerful girl who was well liked by all the other servants. Samantha liked her too, but she dared not confide in her or suggest taking the girl with her when she left Bramble Hall. Everyone in the house would know about it within minutes.

No one could forcibly stop her from leaving, of course, Samantha told herself. She was not a prisoner in her own home. Those servants from Leyland could not literally force her into the carriage and convey her all the way to Kent against her will. But, much as she tried to talk rational common sense into herself, she was not convinced that they would not do just that.

All the other servants at the house were technically the earl's too. He paid their salaries.

It would be best, she decided, if no one knew she was leaving or where she was going or with whom— especially with whom. There was no point in courting unnecessary scandal. The story of Sir Benedict's having been a close friend of Matthew's would not work here.

She had to wait until her maid had left her room for the night, then, before she could begin packing. The silly girl's head had been turned by the arrival of so many male servants from Leyland, and she felt impelled to discuss at great length the relative merits of each one with Mrs. McKay and to offer her own opinion on which was the most handsome but which had the most manly physique and which had paid her the most outrageous compliment even if he was not quite the best in either looks or build.

Samantha thought the girl was never going to leave. It was close to midnight when she began packing one large valise and one smaller one. But there was no great problem of room. It was amazing how much she was prepared to leave behind without any qualm of regret. She would leave all her mourning clothes except what she would wear for the first stage of the journey. She had been a dutiful wife to Matthew while he lived. She had mourned him for five months. She had nothing whatsoever with which to reproach herself.

It had been arranged that Sir Benedict Harper would send his valet with a gig at five o'clock in the morning. His man would leave the gig outside the side gate, come into the house through the side door, which Samantha would unlock ahead of time, and carry out her bags. She would accompany him back to Robland Park, where Sir Benedict and his traveling carriage would be waiting.

It seemed too clandestine a scheme to succeed, especially when there was a large, sometimes unruly dog to be smuggled out along with her and her belongings, for of course Tramp could not be left to the mercies of Rudolph and Patience. Besides, Samantha would no more leave him behind than she would her own child, if she had happened to have one. Tramp was family.

The scheme succeeded without mishap, however. At ten minutes past five Samantha waited a moment for an eagerly panting Tramp to finish his business at the side of the lane before shooing him up into the body of the gig with her baggage, and then seated herself beside the large, silent man who had spoken only to introduce himself as Quinn, Sir Benedict's valet. At a quarter to six she was being handed into an opulent traveling carriage in the stable yard at Robland. The house was still in darkness.

Tramp scrambled inside after her and settled on the seat opposite. He took up the whole space as if by right.

Mr. Quinn and the coachman loaded her bags and others onto the carriage in near silence. There were no grooms in sight. After a few minutes the carriage door opened again to reveal Sir Benedict. He looked about the interior.

"You have not brought your maid?" he asked.

"I am not sure she would have come," she told him. "I *am* sure she would have told all the other servants even if I had sworn her to secrecy."

"This *is* awkward," he said, but after another moment of standing there, he climbed inside slowly but with practiced skill and took the seat beside her.

The interior suddenly felt only half its former size. *This* felt very awkward indeed. Perhaps after all she ought to have escaped alone and traveled by stage or even post-chaise.

"Good morning to you, sir," she said briskly.

"Good morning, Mrs. McKay," he said. "I take it Quinn did not have to fight off all those burly servants in order to spirit you away safely from Bramble Hall? There are a couple of servants rousing here, but none of them have voiced any particular consternation over the discovery that I mean to set out on my travels this early and without waiting for breakfast. I do not believe any of them saw you. We will break our fast when we stop for the first change of horses. Will that suit you? Yes, good morning to you too, wretched dog. You do not need to beat the stuffing out of my cushions with your thumping tail. You are perfectly visible. And I notice that you have commandeered a whole seat for your personal use. If your mistress had indeed brought her maid, she would have had to sit up on the box with my valet and coachman."

He sounded deliberately, artificially cheerful just as she had done when she bade him good morning. He had seemed like a trusted friend yesterday. This morning he seemed like a stranger, which indeed he was.

The fever of excitement in which she had conceived this whole grand escapade yesterday had converted to a quite sick anxiety last night. She had been unable to sleep except in fitful snatches and with bizarre accompanying dreams. This morning she had been consumed by terror, as though she really were a convict making a daring escape under the very noses of a dozen fierce jailers. And now, seated inside the carriage with only a single gentleman for company, she was feeling tongue-tied and self-conscious.

Good heavens, they were going to be alone together for as many days as it took to reach the southwest coast of Wales and her cottage. And the same number of nights. And he had expected that her maid would be with her to lend some sort of respectability. His valet was with *him,* of course.

She felt physically sick again.

"I am not at all hungry, Sir Benedict," she assured him, her hands folded in her lap, her back straight and not quite touching the cushions behind her. As if a strictly ladylike posture and demeanor could miraculously make all proper.

The coachman put up the steps and shut the door with a decisive click, climbed up to the box while Mr. Quinn mounted from the other side, and within moments the carriage lurched into motion.

It was one of the single most panic-inducing moments of Samantha's life. She had to bite her lower lip in order to prevent herself from yelling to the coachman to stop.

Sir Benedict had turned his head and was looking

steadily at her. She had never particularly noticed until now how very narrow carriage seats were. Their shoulders were almost touching. Their faces were too close for comfort. And the world had grown light since she had come from Bramble Hall. There was no darkness in which to hide.

"You are having second thoughts?" he asked. "It is not too late to turn around, you know. I daresay we could smuggle you back into Bramble Hall without the servants there suspecting that you have been doing anything more startling than taking an early morning walk with your dog. Do you wish to return?"

The suggestion brought her to her senses.

"Absolutely not," she assured him. "I would not go back for any consideration. I am going to the only place I *can* go to be free. I am going to *live,* not merely exist at the pleasure of my father-in-law. If you have changed your mind about accompanying me, of course—"

"I have not."

"I feel guilty," she told him. "You were going to Scotland."

"I was going to *travel,*" he said. "And that is what I am doing. I could not and would not allow you to travel all the way to Wales alone."

"You are doing it again," she said. "Allowing me, not allowing me. I am very glad we are not married. I suspect you would be a tyrant."

"I hope I would know how to protect my wife, ma'am," he said stiffly, "even if it was sometimes despite herself. And you could not be more glad of our marital status or lack thereof than I am."

She pursed her lips.

"If we are going to quarrel all the way to Wales," he added, "it should be an interesting journey. Especially as we are still no more than a mile or two from Robland."

"Perhaps," she said, "if we do not converse, we will not quarrel."

And she turned her head away and half turned her body too so that she was looking out at the passing scenery. From his silence, she supposed he was doing the same through the window on his side.

Perhaps half an hour passed, though it felt more like an hour. Or three. It became more and more difficult to maintain her posture, to keep her chin from falling, to keep her eyes from closing. She envied Tramp, sprawled out and fast asleep and even snoring on his seat. And then, in a moment of lapsed concentration, she yawned hugely and audibly and felt instantly embarrassed.

"I suppose," he said, "you did not get a wink of sleep last night."

"Perhaps a wink," she said. "Maybe two. I had a great deal on my mind, Sir Benedict. It is not every day one sets off on a grand, life-changing adventure. Not if one is a woman, anyway."

"And not every man goes sneaking off every day with someone else's widow," he said dryly, "with nary a word to his family and friends. Why do you not take off your bonnet and set your head back against the cushions? And your back too. When I got into the carriage earlier, you looked so prim and starchy that I thought for a moment you had sent your sister-in-law in your place. The horses are still fresh and will carry us a fair distance before it becomes necessary for them to be changed. Your dog has not lost any time in catching up on his beauty sleep."

"Just do not utter any word that begins with *w*," she said, "especially with the letters *a-l-k* attached. You would soon discover how deeply asleep he is."

She took his advice—she seemed to have no choice in the matter since it was becoming increasingly difficult to remain awake. She pulled loose the bow of ribbon beneath her chin and removed her bonnet to hold on her lap. She leaned back with an inward sigh of relief. She would close her eyes for a few minutes.

She was more aware of him when she did so. She could feel his body heat down one side, though they were not touching. She could smell something that was distinctively masculine—leather, shaving soap, whatever. It was hard to distinguish individual smells, but they all added up to something rather enticing and altogether forbidden. He had kissed her once. There had even been tongue play, and it had been very pleasant indeed. A bit of an understatement that, though—*very pleasant indeed*. She wondered if he remembered. It had been almost a month ago. She doubted he had forgotten, though, for he had gone as long as she before that without kisses or anything else.

And she ought not to be thinking of such things now. Especially about the *anything else*.

She took refuge in other mental ramblings. Perhaps she ought to have left behind some sort of note for her father-in-law rather than slinking away like a naughty child who expected to be pursued. Would she be followed? But no one would know where she was going or how she was traveling. Perhaps she ought to have written to John, just to tell him she was quite safe and would write at greater length later. Though why she would do so, she did not know. John never wrote to her. He probably would not care if she went to the North Pole to live. Perhaps she ought to have left a note for Mrs. Andrews to explain why she must withdraw so soon from her committees and would be unable to do any more sick visiting. Perhaps . . .

She lost her battle with sleep at that point. Her thoughts floated away, and her head gradually slipped sideways until it rested against a warm, solid shoulder. She was vaguely aware of it, even of whose it was. She was even aware that it was not quite right to keep her head there, but she was too sleepy to act on the thought. It was a firm yet comfortable shoulder. She burrowed her head a little farther back to wedge it more securely between shoulder and cushion and slid the rest of the way into sleep.

*B*en sat very still and wondered if they would succeed in getting all the way to her new home without becoming lovers. He had wondered the same thing since yesterday afternoon. He had wondered it last night while trying to sleep.

. . . if we are only attracted to each other, then we should go to bed and have our fill of pleasure with each other.

She had actually spoken those words. After he had made her that asinine offer of marriage and before she had remembered that she owned a cottage—how could one forget that one owned a house?

He did not want them to become lovers. Well, he *did*. Of course he did. If he could shed all his clothes at this moment and plunge into a frigid lake, it would not surprise him at all if the water turned to steam. Good God, it had been longer than six years, and she was both beautiful and voluptuous and tantalizingly available.

But he did not *want* them to be lovers. For one thing, he was accompanying her in order to protect her from harm, not in order to debauch her himself. For another, he was a bit afraid of being anyone's lover. He did not want any woman to see him as he was, to witness the difficulties he would doubtless have—though in the last month, since that kiss had opened the floodgates of his restored sexuality, he had wondered if it would be possible to remain celibate for the rest of his life. But he did not want *her* to see him. She was physically perfect while he . . . Well, while he was not. And for yet another thing, she was a recent widow and it would not be right to begin an affair with her so soon.

But here she was, warm and relaxed with sleep, her head burrowed between his shoulder and the seat cushion, one of her arms through his, her ungloved hand resting on his upper thigh, fingers spread. Her little finger was a hair's breadth away from his groin. It really felt as though someone had pumped air from the tropics into the carriage. And it was all unconscious on her part.

He tried to think of other things and remembered suddenly that he had been planning to leave for London this morning. He would not be at Hugo's wedding after all. He had not even replied to the invitation. He felt a wave of regret bordering on loneliness, imagining his six friends all gathering in London for the festivities. They would miss him, but they would think he was still in the north of England with Beatrice.

Mrs. McKay smelled of something sweet and elusive. Gardenia? Actually, he was no expert on female scents, but this one must have been specifically designed to tease the senses of celibates.

He looked downward, past her shapely hand. His legs, encased in pantaloons and Hessian boots, looked almost normal. But when they stopped for a change of horses, as they must do soon, it would be evident that they were not normal at all. He would descend to the cobbles of the inn yard, taking many times longer about it than any normal man would, and then he would turn to hand Mrs. McKay down, all stiff pain and gallantry when, left to herself, she could have been down without his assistance and already seated in the coffee room. He would not even be able to offer his arm to lead her into the inn. He would need both for his canes and his twisted legs. She would no doubt reduce her pace in order to make him less conscious of his slowness.

Who was accompanying whom on this journey?

It was reality, though, and would never be any different. He had pledged himself to accept that, had he not? So, he was half crippled. His legs were only just better than useless. His legs were not *him*, however. His life did not lose worth just because he could not move as he had used to move—and as almost every other man on earth did. How long would it be until he fully accepted that?

He glanced across to the other seat, where the ugly hound sprawled in ungainly slumber. She loved the dog, ugliness and ungainliness notwithstanding.

He laughed softly to himself.

How the *devil* had he got himself into this coil? He wondered what his fellow Survivors would say when he recounted this adventure—or *mis*adventure—to them next spring.

They would not stop teasing him for a decade.

*T*raveling was one of the most difficult activities for Ben, a fact that underscored the irony of what he had decided to do with his life until something more meaningful suggested itself. Except that he knew his body well enough to understand how much he could demand of it. Normally he would travel in short stages, taking twice as long to get where he was going than anyone else would. And if he was traveling purely for pleasure, as he would soon be doing, he would take frequent days off.

This was different, however. Although he did not expect any pursuit, he still felt it wise to put as much distance between them and Bramble Hall as they could in the first day or two. One never knew when one would come up against someone who would know and recognize Mrs. McKay. Besides, it would be very much to his advantage to get this journey over with as soon as possible. He was not made of stone, after all.

By the end of the first day, he did not know quite how to sit still or how to keep a smile or at least a look of alert interest on his face as they conversed. And he did not know how he was going to descend from the carriage that final time. He did it, however, and even managed to stand at the reception desk of the inn his coachman had chosen long enough to pay for two bed-chambers, one for himself, Major Sir Benedict Harper, and one for Mrs. McKay, the recent widow of his military friend. He also reserved accommodation for the two servants as well as kennel room for the dog.

He supposed the explanation had not been necessary, since it could not matter to the landlord what the relationship was between the two people staying at his inn. Ben escorted a black-veiled Samantha to her room, made arrangements to join her later in the private dining room he had reserved, and collapsed on the bed in his own room before throwing one arm over his eyes.

He had long experience at enduring pain. He rarely took any medicine to dull it, and he rarely allowed it to slow him down or confine him to his bed. It was a fact of his life and always would be. All he could do to control it was avoid the sort of activities—like long days seated in a carriage—that would intensify it.

Quinn came within five minutes and silently pulled off his boots and set to work massaging stiff muscles and working out clenched knots until he could relax more.

"Does she know about this?" he asked.

"Good Lord, no," Ben said. "Why should she?"

They had talked determinedly through much of the day. And actually it had not been too difficult after a while. He had noticed that with her before. She was easy to talk to. She would always answer his questions and then ask her own in return. She neither monopolized the conversation nor expected him to do all the talking. They had exchanged memories of childhood. She remembered dancing barefoot in the grass with her mother and splashing and swimming in a stream with some other children from the village. He remembered swimming in the lake at Kenelston and climbing trees with the gamekeeper's two boys and engaging in sword fights with them, using the wooden toy weapons their father had carved for them all—Ben included.

They had even sat in companionable silence some of the time, watching the scenery go by on their respective sides of the carriage, alone with their own thoughts.

"You might suggest slowing the journey down," Quinn said. "Anyone would think from your speed that she was an underage maiden heiress and you a penniless nobody abducting her to Gretna Green."

"And so muddleheaded that I am taking her in quite the wrong direction?"

"You will be crippled before you get to the wilds of beyond," Quinn said, jerking his head in a direction that Ben guessed was meant to indicate the southwest coast of Wales.

"I think not," Ben said. "Give me half an hour, Quinn, and then come back to help me dress for dinner."

His valet grunted and withdrew. He had been a groom in the Duke of Stanbrook's stables at Penderris when Ben first encountered him. In those early days of all-consuming agony, only that particular groom was able to move him and turn him for the necessary washes and changes and treatments without his quite passing out from the pain. His Grace had pretended to grumble when Ben appropriated the groom to be his nurse and then his valet.

An hour later Ben descended to the private dining room, feeling considerably restored.

His first thought after opening the door was that he must have the wrong room. She was standing beside the table, which had been set for their meal, and she was wearing a high-waisted, short-sleeved evening dress of pale blue muslin. Her near-black hair was piled on her head in an intricately tied knot.

He stared at her, transfixed and aghast.

"What the devil?" he said, and he took an incautiously hasty step forward and shut the door firmly behind him.

She raised her eyebrows. "I left all my blacks at Bramble Hall, except what I wore today," she told him. "I will not wear those again. They were ordered from Leyland and sent to Bramble Hall without any consultation with me or any fitting with a proper modiste. They are ugly and impersonal and ill-fitting, and they in no way reflect the genuine sorrow I felt at the premature death of my husband. They are the mere ostentatious trappings of grief, designed to impress the world. I will not put on a meaningless show any longer. That part of my life is over, and the next part of my life has begun."

He took one step closer. "Have you forgotten," he said, "that we are traveling as a major and the *recent widow* of his military friend? Who has seen you dressed like that?"

"Like what?" she asked. "You make me sound as if I am dressed like a harlot."

"Like a young lady," he said between his teeth, "traveling with a gentleman who is not her husband. Who has seen you?"

Her cheeks had flushed. "The landlord showed me

where the dining parlor was," she said. "There were a few other people. I did not take much notice."

"You can be sure the *landlord* took notice," he said. "Good Lord, and you do not even have a maid with you."

"If you wish to go away, Sir Benedict—" she began.

"Stop talking nonsense," he snapped at her. "From now on, starting tomorrow, we are going to have to be husband and wife. That is the only solution."

"How ridiculous," she said.

"You will be Lady Harper from tomorrow on," he told her. "Oh, do not worry for your virtue. We will take separate rooms at the inns where we stay. My injuries make me restless and so make it imperative that I sleep alone. Not that we will be called upon to explain ourselves."

"I think, Sir Benedict," she said, "you are a bit stuffy. As well as tyrannical."

"What I *am*," he told her, "is concerned for your reputation, ma'am. And that is going to have to be *Benedict* and *Samantha* tomorrow. We will be husband and wife."

"I suppose," she said, "you would be happier if I were shrouded in black for the rest of my life."

"You may wear scarlet every day until you are eighty," he said, "after you have been delivered safely to your cottage and I have gone on my way."

"*Delivered*," she said. "Like an unwanted package."

The door opened behind him, and a maidservant carried in a large tray with their evening meal.

"Come and sit down," Mrs. McKay said to Ben. "You are in pain."

Well, it was all the result of being brought up short inside the door by her appearance. He was still in a lot less pain, though, than he had been an hour ago.

He moved toward the table without comment.

"You were in pain most of the afternoon, were you not?" she said after they had taken their seats and the girl had withdrawn. "I did not say anything then. It seemed like an impertinent intrusion upon your privacy. But perhaps I ought to have. Are you always in pain?"

"I make no complaint, ma'am," he said. "You must not concern yourself."

She clucked her tongue. "Matthew *always* complained," she said, "and I sometimes wished he had exercised a little more restraint. You will never complain, I suspect, and I will probably find your heroic fortitude just as irritating."

He laughed despite himself.

"Riding for hours in a carriage is not the most comfortable experience even for the most nimble," she said. "I suppose it is the worst thing in the world for you."

"Probably not the *very* worst," he said.

"You make me feel selfish and insensitive," she told him. "First my appearance and now this. We will not travel so far tomorrow or any other day after that. If we take two weeks, even three, to complete this journey, then so be it. We are in no particular hurry, are we?"

She might not be.

"I will not have you put yourself out for me," he said. "I have grown accustomed to my condition. No one else need be burdened with it."

She had taken his plate and was dishing out his food for him just as if she really were his wife and they were seated cozily at their own dining table.

"We will travel in a more leisurely fashion, beginning tomorrow," she told him. "Perhaps we are on our honeymoon. Do you suppose we are?"

Her sudden smile looked impish. He could have wished, though, that she had found some other subject to joke upon. Their honeymoon, indeed! Drat and blast it all.

"You told me earlier today, Mrs. McKay," he said, "that you were thankful I was not your husband. I replied in kind. I repeat that sentiment now. I have the feeling you would be one devil of a handful."

"A devil of a handful." She put down her knife and fork, set an elbow on the table, and rested her chin on her fist. "Indeed, Sir Benedict? How?"

Her voice had lowered to a throaty whisper, but her lips were curved up at the corners, and her eyes were dancing with mischief.

"Eat your dinner," he told her. He was feeling overheated again and there was not even a fire in the hearth.

❧

12

*A*fter that first day they traveled onward as man and wife. It was better that way, Samantha decided, for she could wear her own clothes again and forget about the ghastly oppression of her blacks. She had nothing particularly new and nothing very fashionable, but they were clothes she had chosen herself and, in a few cases, clothes she had made herself, and they suited her well enough. Wearing them again made her feel younger and more hopeful. They made her feel herself again.

She called him Ben. She had remarked—after one of their brief flare-ups—that *Benedict* made him sound like some sort of monk or saint and that no one had ever been more inappropriately named. Surprisingly, he had agreed with her and confided that he had always been uncomfortable with his name and far preferred the shortened form. She had told him that if he ever called her Sam she would have a temper tantrum. He had immediately called her Sammy and waggled his eyebrows at her. She had poked out her tongue and crossed her eyes in retaliation.

It actually felt good to act childishly. They had both ended up laughing.

After four days of travel, they crossed the River Wye into Wales. The land of her maternal forefathers. She had never expected that half of her heritage to mean anything to her and was surprised at the welling of emotion she felt at knowing that she was here at last.

She knew nothing about her mother's kin, except for her dead great-aunt, who had been Miss Dilys Bevan, pronounced *Dill-iss,* according to her mother. She had always assumed there were no other living relatives.

But perhaps there were.

Did she want there to be? But she knew the answer was no almost before her mind had asked the question. For if any were still living, then they had neglected her mother and therefore her. And that would be worse than if they did not exist.

But suddenly, going to her cottage to live took on new meaning. For perhaps there was more awaiting her than just a dilapidated hovel of a building. Perhaps there was a whole story. A whole Pandora's box, which she did *not* want to open. She must just hope it did not even exist.

She was feeling a little maudlin on the day they passed Tintern Abbey. They stopped to view the ruin, both of them having read and admired William Wordsworth's lengthy poem about it. The building and its unspoiled, deeply rural surroundings were every bit as lovely and romantic as they were depicted in that poem. Wooded hills rose on either side of the valley and the Wye flowed between, the abbey on its western bank.

Their days had settled into a certain routine. Samantha rose early each morning to take Tramp out for a walk before breakfast, and then they traveled until the horses were tired and must be changed or at least rested. They spent what remained of the afternoons either strolling in the vicinity of the inn where they had stopped or finding some local landmark of interest to explore. They would find somewhere comfortable to take their tea. Then Ben would write conscientiously in his journal, having called for pen and ink, while Samantha took Tramp for another walk. Then they would relax in their separate rooms until it was time to meet again for their evening meal.

They retired early in anticipation of the next day's exertions.

On this particular day they resumed their journey after visiting Tintern, in order to take rooms at an inn above the valley that had been recommended to them the night before. When they arrived there, though, it was to the disturbing discovery that there was only one room still available. It was a large and comfortable chamber, the landlord assured them when he saw Ben's hesitation, and there was a lovely view down into the valley and across it from its bay window.

"We will travel farther," Ben said. "My disability makes it difficult for my wife to share a room with me in any comfort."

But the closest inn, the landlord informed them, was at Chepstow, an uncomfortably long distance ahead when they had already traveled farther than usual today.

The journey was hard on Ben, Samantha knew. Though he never complained, she had learned to read his face and the tensions of his body, even his smile. What on earth had possessed him to believe that he could spend his life traveling and writing books about his journeys? But it was entirely her fault that he was doing so much traveling these days.

"We have come far enough," she said. "We must take the room, Ben. It will be just for one night."

"You will not be sorry, sir," the landlord assured him. "We have the best cook between Chepstow and Ross. You can ask anyone."

Ben looked as if he was about to argue. He was also looking rather pale and drawn. They had spent longer than they ought, perhaps, walking about the ruins.

"Very well," he said. "We will stay here."

The room was pretty and clean, and there was indeed a splendid view from the window, but it was *not* particularly spacious. There was no armchair or love seat or sofa, as Samantha had hoped there would be. She would have been happy to sleep on any of the three. The large, high bed dominated the room and occupied most of the floor space.

But good heavens, it was just for one night, she thought as they stood just inside the door, looking about them with great awkwardness. She spoke briskly. "I suppose if I lie very close to the edge on this side and you lie very close to the edge on that, there will be enough space between us to accommodate an elephant."

"If you roll over in the night," he said, "you had better be sure to roll the right way."

"And which way would that be?"

She turned to smile at him just as he turned *his* head to smile at *her*. And suddenly it seemed as if her words were written in fire on the air between them.

"I would imagine," he said, recovering himself, "elephants take exception to being awoken in the night."

"Yes." She crossed to the window, by far the finest feature of the room.

"Would you rather we went on to Chepstow after all?" he asked. "We still could."

"No, we could not," she said. "You are on the verge of collapse. It has been too busy a day. I shall go back down and make sure Tramp is properly accommodated. I shall have Mr. Quinn sent up to you."

He did not argue.

She spent an hour with the dog, at first sitting on some clean straw beside him, her knees drawn up almost to her chin, her arms wrapped about them, and then walking with him so that he could take care of business before settling for the night.

They had managed to rub along well enough together, she and Sir Benedict—Ben. They could talk and laugh and be silent together. They could enjoy doing a little sightseeing together despite the handicap of his not being able to walk fast or far. But he *was* a man, and she would have to be inhuman, she supposed, for that fact not to be affecting her, especially as they had, once upon a time, shared a kiss and soared together in imagination beyond the clouds in a hot air balloon, wrapped in furs against the chill of the upper atmosphere.

It was sometimes hard to ignore his maleness when they shared the close confines of a carriage interior during the daytime. Whatever was it going to be like to share a bed all night?

By the time she returned to the room, making a great deal of unnecessary bustle on the landing outside the door and then taking her time turning the handle, Ben was dressed for dinner and was sitting on the side of the bed, reading. He set his book aside and got to his feet. He did it more easily than usual, she noticed, perhaps because the bed was high.

"I shall leave you the use of the room," he said, "and see you downstairs in the dining room."

"Very well."

He was dressed smartly for dinner in black and white. She could have wished he did not look quite so attractive.

She donned a green silk gown and clasped about her neck the pearls her father had given her as a wedding present.

The only private dining parlor at the inn had been already spoken for by the time they arrived. There were just a few other people in the main dining room, however, and none of them were close enough to make conversation awkward. The food was excellent. At least, Samantha thought it probably was. She did not pay it much attention, truth to tell. She was too busy keeping the conversation going. It kept wanting to die, and they could not seem to hit upon a topic that required more than a question from one of them and a monosyllabic answer from the other.

Oh, what a difference having to share a bedchamber made. They had not had this problem on any previous evening. Not to this degree, anyway.

"If there had only been a private dining parlor available," he said eventually, "there might have been a chair upon which I could have spent the night."

"If you were going to do *that*," she said, "we might as well have continued on our way to Chepstow. *I* would have slept on the chair."

"Rubbish," he said. "I would never have allowed it."

"Perhaps," she said, "I would not have allowed you to dictate to me what I could or could not do."

"Are we back to bickering?" he asked. "But, really, Samantha, no gentleman would allow a lady to sleep on a chair in a private dining room while he enjoyed the luxury of a bed in a room with a view."

"Ah," she said, "the view. I had forgotten that. Undoubtedly, then, on this occasion I would have allowed you to have your way. An academic point, however. We do not have a private dining room and so neither of us is able to make the noble gesture of spending the night on a chair there."

"We both, in fact," he said, "get to enjoy the view."

She smiled and he chuckled, and Samantha gazed at him, arrested for a moment. She had been very fond of her father, but she could not remember ever joking with him or talking nonsense with him—or bickering with him. And though she must surely have laughed with Matthew during their courtship and the first few months of their marriage, she could not recall ever being deliberately silly with him purely for their mutual enjoyment.

It occurred to her that she *liked* Ben Harper, even if he did make her bristle with indignation on occasion—

and turn hot with longing at other times. It occurred to her that she would miss him when he had gone.

"He had a *mistress*," she said abruptly, and then she gazed at him in some surprise. What on earth had prompted her to say that? She set down her knife and fork, rested her forearms on the table, and leaned toward him. "They already had one child when he met and married me. Another was conceived during the first months of our marriage. I took that to mean that he did not care much for me at all and that I was not much good in the marriage bed."

She gazed at him, appalled. And she looked around furtively to make sure they were not within earshot of any other diners.

He looked from his knife to his fork and back again before setting them down across his plate and copying her posture. Their faces were not very far apart.

"I suppose," he said, "you have spent longer than six years imagining that you are sexually inadequate."

She half expected to see flames flaring up from her cheeks.

"No," she said. "Why should I allow my spirit to be crushed by someone I did not respect? I lost respect for my husband four months into our marriage. That is a terrible admission to make, is it not, to a virtual stranger?"

"I am hardly a stranger," he said. "And I am about to become even less of one. We are to spend the night teetering off the opposite edges of the same bed, are we not?"

"Have you ever had a mistress?" she asked him.

"Of long standing?" he said. "No. And never any children. And even if I had a mistress, I would dismiss her before marrying someone else. And no one would replace her. Ever."

"Was the colonel's niece very beautiful?" she asked.

He considered. "She was pretty. She was small and dainty, all smiles and dimples and blond curls and ringlets and big blue eyes."

"Such a woman would surely have been unwilling to follow the drum with you."

"But she was already doing so with her uncle," he told her. "She looked like a porcelain doll. In reality she was as tough as nails."

"Did you mourn her loss?"

"I cannot say I spared her more than a passing thought for at least two years," he said. "By then I was very thankful we had not married."

"I daresay she has grown plump," she said. "Small, pretty blonds often do."

His eyes laughed at her, and he reached across the table and took one of her hands in both of his.

"I believe, Sammy," he said, "you are jealous."

"Jealous?" She tried to withdraw her hand, but he tightened his hold on it. "How perfectly ridiculous. And how dare you call me that name when I have specifically asked you not to?"

"I think you want me," he said.

"Nonsense."

His eyes were laughing, but her stomach was clenched into knots. It was not true. Oh, of course it was true. He did not believe what he was saying, though. He was just teasing her. He was deliberately trying to make her cross—and was succeeding.

"I believe," he said, "you want to prove that you *are* good in bed after all."

"Oh!" She gaped inelegantly and jerked her hand from between his as she got abruptly to her feet. "How dare you. Oh, Ben, how dare you?"

Somehow she remembered to keep her voice down.

"You may have lost respect for your late husband," he said, "and you may have refused to allow his infidelity to break your spirit, but he hurt you more than you realize, Samantha. He was a fool. And one day you will be given proof of your desirability. But not tonight. You are quite safe from me, I promise, despite the situation in which we find ourselves. I will not take advantage of you."

She was almost disappointed.

"Go on up to our room now," he said, "since you appear to have finished eating. I will stay down here for a while."

She went without a word of protest, even though it could be said that he had issued a command.

He was a fool.

You will be given proof of your desirability.

I believe you want to prove that you are good in bed after all.

I think you want me.

And they were to spend the night together.

*N*ot only ought he to have written to Hugo, Ben thought as he drank his port, but he ought also to have written to Calvin at Kenelston. And probably to Beatrice. No doubt she would soon learn that Samantha had disappeared from Bramble Hall and that he had left Robland very early on the same day. He wondered if she would make the connection. But if she did, he did not believe she would share her suspicions with anyone.

Would anyone else make the connection? He doubted it, since he had taken care not to be seen with Samantha. No one would know that he had had more than a passing acquaintance with her, and it *was* known that he was about to leave Robland anyway.

He could still write the letters, of course. He could call for paper and pen and ink and write them now before he went upstairs. But he was reluctant to do so. There was something rather seductive about the idea of simply disappearing without a trace for as long as he chose. He could go where he wanted and do what he wanted without having to account to anyone. That was always the case, of course, but . . . Well, he wanted to be quite free to allow this adventure to develop as it would. He did not want friends and relatives murmuring in the background with either encouragement or disapproval.

Samantha was still up when he returned to their room, though he had lingered in the dining room long enough to give her the chance to be under the bedcovers and at least pretending to be asleep if she so chose. He had been hoping she would take that option.

She was sitting on the bed in her nightgown, her legs tucked to one side, only her bare feet visible beneath its hem, her arms raised to remove the pins from her hair. It was not a deliberately seductive pose. Nevertheless it did something uncomfortable to his breathing.

"I thought you would be asleep," he told her.

"Or feigning sleep, I suppose," she said, "curled up in a ball, breathing deeply and evenly, so that you could crawl by me and ease yourself in on the other side and do likewise?"

He shut and locked the door.

"I did consider it," she confessed, "but you would have known I was not really asleep, and then I would have known that *you* were not and we would have lain awake all night, each of us hoping that we were doing a better job of faking it than the other."

He laughed.

"Let me help you do that," he said, moving closer and propping his canes against the foot of the bed before sitting beside her. "I might say you are making a bird's nest of your hair, but I believe that would be insulting to the bird in question."

"Well," she said, lowering her arms, "you make me nervous, Ben, and I cannot for the life of me disentangle the last few pins. I believe they are lost in there forever."

He found and removed them, and her hair fell about her shoulders and down her back, heavy, shining, almost black Gypsy hair.

"I intended," she said, "to have it neatly braided before you came up. Could you not have stayed to drink the inn dry of brandy or port or whatever it is you drink after dinner?"

"Port," he said. "Brush?" He held out one hand, and she took a brush off the small chest beside the bed and handed it to him. He made a swirling motion with one finger. "Turn."

Her hair reached to her waist and almost touched the bed behind her. It smelled faintly of gardenia. Her nightgown was of white cotton and covered her as decently as her dresses did during the day. Except that it *was* a nightgown and she was obviously wearing no stays beneath it—or anything else, at a guess. And her feet were bare. And she was sitting on a bed.

He drew the brush through her hair. It slid downward from the roots to the tips.

"Two hundred strokes," she said.

He felt an immediate tightening at his groin. Two hundred?

"Every night," she added.

"Do you count them?"

"Yes. It was one way my mother taught me numbers."

She had been quite unaware of the double meaning of her words.

He counted silently.

"I was eighteen," she said when he was at thirty-nine strokes. "Barely. I had just had my birthday. I had been married a little less than four months."

He did not prompt her. If she needed to tell the story she had begun downstairs, then he would listen. He had all night, after all, and he knew from his experiences at Penderris that it was important that people be allowed to tell their stories.

Forty-five. Forty-six.

"I was so deeply in love," she said, "that I did not think the world was large enough to contain it all. Youth is a dangerous time of life."

Yes, it could be.

Fifty-one. Fifty-two. Fifty-three.

"I thought his love for me was just as all-consuming," she said. "I thought we were living happily ever after. How foolish young people can be. Shall I tell you why he married me?"

"If you wish." Fifty-nine. Sixty.

"He had always been the family rebel," she said. "He hated them all, particularly his father. But his father could never leave him alone. He had been at him to marry someone suitable—suitable in the eyes of the earl, that was. He had even named a few possible candidates. Matthew was eleven years older than I, you know. He met me at an assembly, found me pretty and eager—and, oh, how right he was about the latter! I was pathetically eager. I wore my heart not just on my sleeve, but on my nose and my forehead and my cheeks and my bosom and . . . Well. Suffice it to say that I made no secret of my adoration. I was pathetic."

"You were very young," he said. Good Lord, she was only twenty-four now. "You were being courted by a handsome military officer."

"Where was I?" she asked. He did not know where *he* was. He had lost count. Sixty-nine? Seventy? "He fancied himself in love with me, of course, or I daresay he would not have done what he did. But it also occurred to

him that it would be a splendid joke on his father
if he married me. I was the daughter of a gentleman of
no particular distinction. That would have been bad
enough in his father's eyes. He knew too, though, that I
was the daughter of an actress and the granddaughter of
some unknown Welshman and a Gypsy. And so he married me. He kept a decent silence about that part of his
motive until I discovered the existence of his mistress,
and then he told me about it—out of spite, I suppose,
though he laughed as he told the tale and invited me to
share the joke with him. It *was* funny, for it achieved
everything he had hoped for. The Earl of Heathmoor
was irate. When I refused to allow Matthew to touch me
after I made my discovery and then he refused to take
me to the Peninsula with his regiment and sent me to
Leyland Abbey instead, again out of spite, I was made
to feel that I was lower on the scale of significance than
the lowliest servant. But because I was a daughter-in-law
of the house, I must be subjected to a strict regimen of
reeducation. I was not quite nineteen when I went there."

He lowered the brush to the bed.

"I am *not* pleading for your pity," she said. "Heaven
forbid. My life is as it is. There are worse lives. I have
never been hungry or literally homeless. No one has
ever used physical violence on me worse than the occasional rap over the knuckles or smack on the bottom
when I was a child. And now I have been offered the gift
of freedom and a hovel of a cottage and a small competence with which to enjoy it. Do you understand what
a wonderful thing that is for a woman, Ben? I can be a
new person."

She turned to face him on the bed and tucked her feet
right out of sight.

"Then why the mournful look?" he asked.

"Do I look mournful?"

"I suppose," he said, "it is because you have been forced to bring the old person with you."

She grimaced. "Why *is* that? It is *such* a nuisance."

"But how could you ever feel joy," he asked her, "if you had not also known dreariness and suffering?"

"Is there ever joy?" Her dark eyes searched his face as though the answer was written there.

He opened his mouth to assure her that of course there was. But *was* there? When had he last felt it? When he arrived at Penderris Hall a few months ago for his annual stay there with his friends? That had been a happy moment, but had it been *joy*? He wished he had not used the word with her. It was a disturbing word.

And was that what his problem was? That wherever he went, he had to take himself with him? Was it in denial of that fact that he had decided to travel? The eternal quest to escape from himself, from the body that slowed him down, made him grotesque and ungainly, and stopped him from living the life he wanted to live?

"We have to believe there *is* joy," he said. "In the meantime, we have to believe that our lives are worth living."

She lifted one hand and set it against his cheek, her fingers pushing into his hair. Her hand was smooth and cool.

"It is ungrateful of me," she said, "to have been given freedom and a new life and yet to feel a little depressed. You will find a meaning for your life."

"I am going to be a world-famous travel writer." He smiled.

"You will find what you are searching for, Ben," she said. "You are a kind man."

"And the good and kind are rewarded with fulfillment and happiness?"

He was surprised to see tears brighten her eyes, though they did not spill over onto her cheeks.

"They should be," she said. "Life should work that way, though we know it does not always do so."

He released his hold on the brush, caught her by the waist, drew her against him, and kissed her. She wrapped her arms about him and kissed him back.

Their lips clung. Their breath mingled. She was warm, soft, fragrant, very feminine. He was aware, even with his eyes closed, of her nightgown and bare feet, of her hair loose down her back, of the bed beneath them. There was an increase of heat, a tightening in his groin again.

She slid her feet free of her nightgown and he somehow got his legs right up on the bed, and his hands were on her breasts, heavy and firm beneath the cotton of her nightgown, and her hands were under his coat, inside his waistcoat, warm against the back of his shirt.

She had lain down across the bed, and he had followed her, his hand beneath the hem of her nightgown, smoothing its way up the heat of her inner thigh. His tongue simulated in her mouth what he would like to be doing with her body. His weight was pressing against her breasts.

He had made her a promise downstairs just an hour or two ago.

But not tonight. You are quite safe from me, I promise, despite the situation in which we find ourselves. I will not take advantage of you.

He tried to ignore the voice in his head—his own voice. It could not be done, however.

He lifted his head and gazed down into her passion-heavy eyes.

"We cannot do this," he said.

She said nothing.

"We would regret it," he told her. "It would have been provoked entirely by this room. We *would* regret it."

Idiot, he thought. *Fool.*

"Would we?" She sighed, but he could see that she was returning to her senses.

"You know we would." He sat up, lowering the hem of her nightgown as he did so, and pushed himself to his feet without using his canes. High mattresses were always a blessing to him.

"And yet," she said, "it is quite acceptable for a widow to have an affair, provided she is discreet about it. I learned that when I was with Matthew's regiment. I think it would be a grand use of freedom—to have an affair."

"With me?" He did not turn to look at her.

"With a man who wanted one with me as much as I wanted one with him," she said. "Perhaps with you, Ben. One of these days. But not tonight. You are right about that. It would seem slightly sordid."

He drew a few slow breaths. "Now," he said, "if you would get beneath the covers and pretend to fall into an instant sleep to spare my modesty, I will slip out of a few of my clothes and climb in on the other side. And tomorrow and for every other night of our journey, we will continue on our way, even if the distance is a hundred miles, until we find an inn that can properly and separately accommodate us."

She got down from the bed, climbed beneath the covers so far to her side that it was a miracle she did not fall off, pulled the covers up over her head, and snored softly.

He smiled and made his way around to the other side.

"The only trouble is," she said when he was slipping out of his waistcoat, "that by the time *one of these days* comes along, you will be long gone from my life."

"Hush," he said, and she started snoring again.

He blew out the candle and climbed into bed, as far to his side as was possible.

He would be laughed out of any officers' mess tent, he

thought, if he was ever unwise enough to give an account of this night's doings—or absence of doings.

Not that he would ever again be in any mess tent.

He stared at the pale outline of the bay window.

He would never again be in any mess tent.

The army did not take cripples.

❦

$\mathscr{S}$amantha's first impression when she awoke was of warmth and comfort. She had surely just enjoyed her best night's sleep in a long time. And then, as she woke further, other impressions intruded. Her nose was virtually pressed against a naked chest that rose and fell to the steady rhythm of its owner's breathing. His body heat enveloped her and made her want to move her whole body closer though she was alarmingly close as it was. One of his arms was about her beneath the covers.

So much for a sleepless night as they each clung virtuously to their respective edges of the bed.

Samantha had never before slept with a man. *Slept,* that was, as opposed to having marital relations with. For close to four months after their marriage, Matthew had come to her bed almost nightly, but he had always returned to his own afterward. Somehow, this seemed almost as intimate as those brief sessions had been, perhaps because they were so long ago that she had forgotten just what real intimacy felt like.

They had come close to making love last night—until conscience had smitten him. She was not sure if she was glad or sorry.

He was sleeping. She could tell that from the deepness of his breathing and the warm relaxation of his body. She was tempted to fall back to sleep herself. But good sense prevailed. What she really needed to do was re-move herself from the bed, or at least from this particular part of it, before he too woke up. He might believe she had done this deliberately.

She considered her strategy. His arm was heavy across her. One of her legs was trapped beneath one of his. One of her hands was splayed across his chest. The other was resting on the side of his waist—she had only just realized that. It was full daylight. Goodness only knew what time it was. It might be dawn or it might be noon. She really had slept deeply.

She wriggled her leg free. She lifted her hand from his waist and removed her nose from his chest and then her other hand. She inched backward under his arm. She did it all in no more than five or ten minutes. He inhaled deeply, exhaled audibly, and fell silent. She edged back a little farther. If she turned now, she could swing her legs over the edge of the bed and sit up and then stand and be safe even if he then awoke and saw her in her rumpled nightgown, her unbraided hair in loose tangles about her head and shoulders and along her back. He would not know . . .

"I suppose," he said just as she sat up, in a perfectly normal, everyday conversational voice, "you did not sleep a wink all night."

"I slept a little," she admitted in a tone to match his own. She did not turn her head to look at him.

"Did I leave you enough room?" he asked. "I did not inadvertently touch you?"

"Oh, no," she said. "There was plenty of room."

"Samantha McKay," he said, "you will surely burn in hell one of these eternities. You are lying through your teeth."

She let out an enraged shriek and whisked her head around to glare at him. She grabbed her pillow and hurled it at him.

"You, sir," she said, "are no gentleman. You might at

least pretend to believe that we kept to our own edges of the bed."

He clasped the pillow to his chest. "I woke up at some time in the night," he said, "to find that I had rolled to the center of the bed and that you had done likewise. To be fair, I do not believe either of us was the aggressor. You grumbled some nonsense and grabbed me when I would have beaten a strategic retreat back to my edge, and, being the gentleman I am, contrary to your unjust accusation, I remained where I was and allowed you to burrow against me."

She shrieked again and grabbed for her pillow so that she could fling it at his head once more.

"And you," she said, "are going to *fry*. I did *not*. And if you had been the gentleman you profess to be, you would have moved, not just to the edge of the bed, but right off it onto the floor with your pillow."

"You were lying half on it," he said. "And being a gentleman . . ." He completed the sentence with a grin.

She stared down at him. He was enjoying himself, she thought, and so, strangely, was she. What had seemed horribly awkward and embarrassing just a minute or so ago had been turned into . . . fun. But oh, dear, he looked tousled and almost boyish. And attractive. It really would be wonderful to make love with him.

"What?" he said. "You have no answer?"

"You might have taken *my* pillow, then," she said.

"But you were lying half on that too."

"Poor thing," she said, narrowing her eyes. "And so you were doomed to spend the rest of the night in the middle of the bed with only half a pillow for your comfort."

"I am not complaining," he told her. He laced his hands behind his head and looked complacent. "Pillows are not the only source of comfort."

"Hmm." She got to her feet. "Turn your back and

pull the covers over your head. I am going to get dressed. I do not suppose anyone has fed and watered Tramp this morning or let him loose in the stable yard."

He did as he was told with great ostentation, and Samantha dressed quickly, a smile on her face, and dragged her brush through her hair before twisting and knotting it at her neck.

"I shall see you at breakfast in half an hour or so," she said as she let herself out of the room.

He snored softly beneath the bedcovers as she had done last night. She was laughing as she shut the door. How her life had changed in the span of a week. She scarcely recognized herself despite what had been said last night about having to take herself with her wherever she went. She could not remember a time when she had simply enjoyed someone else's company, when she had laughed and joked with that person and talked nonsense. And hurled pillows.

And shared a bed.

And felt a knee-weakening desire.

She was going to miss him dreadfully when they had arrived at her cottage and he had resumed his travels. But she would think of that when the time came.

Tramp greeted her as if he had been shut up all alone for at least a week in his perfectly comfortable stall.

*T*hey talked about the weather and the scenery. They talked about books—she had read a good many during the five years of her husband's illness, and he had read a fair number during the years of his convalescence and since. They talked more about their families and the homes where they had grown up, about their growing years, the friends they had had, the games they had played, the dreams they had dreamed. They talked about music, though neither claimed any proficiency on a musical instrument.

They carefully avoided any situation or topic that might ignite the attraction they undoubtedly felt for each other.

Sometimes they talked nonsense and laughed like silly children. It felt ridiculously good. Sometimes they bickered, though even those flare-ups usually ended in nonsense and laughter.

They talked with fellow travelers at inns where they stayed and at places of interest they visited. Ben began to think that perhaps he *would* enjoy traveling after all. He was sure he would have lingered in southeast Wales longer if he had been alone. He was fascinated by the new industries that were springing up—coal mines and associated shipping concerns and metalworks. He would have loved to make a few detours—into the Rhondda and Swansea Valleys, for example, to see the industries at work. Perhaps he would come back one day and add chapters to his book that were not concerned purely with pictorial beauty. But not yet. After he had seen Samantha settled, he would want to put as much distance as possible between himself and her.

"I have been thinking," he said the morning they left Swansea behind and proceeded toward West Wales, "that after you have taken up residence in your cottage I will take the route up the west coast of Wales rather than return the way we have come. I will see Aberystwyth and Harlech and Mount Snowdon, and then travel along the north coast."

Her dark eyes—those lovely, expressive eyes, which seemed to have come more fully alive since they left County Durham—looked steadily back into his own. She was wearing pale spring green today and looked young and wholesome and pretty. And desirable, though he tried to ignore that thought.

He was very glad they had not become lovers that night. It was going to be a lonely enough feeling, driving off on his own, without the added complication of having indulged in an affair with her.

Or would he regret not having reached for pleasure when it had surely been offered?

"There is sure to be some lovely scenery on that route," she said, half averting her face to gaze out of the window. "There already has been, has there not? Being in sight of the sea so much of the time smites me *here*." She tapped the outer edge of one curled fist against her stomach. "Or perhaps it is Wales itself that is affecting me. It really does feel like a different country even though most people speak English. But, oh, the accent, Ben. It is like music."

"Penderris is by the sea," he said. "Did I tell you that? It is at the top of a high cliff in Cornwall."

"With yellow sands, as there are everywhere here?" she asked.

"Yes. Sands far below the towering cliffs. I can only look down on the beach when I am there. But it is a beautiful sight."

"You do not swim, then?"

"I did once upon a time," he told her. "Like a fish. Or an eel. Especially in forbidden waters. The deep side of the lake at Kenelston was always infinitely more inviting than the river side, where the water was no deeper than waist high even to a boy. How could one even pretend to be a self-respecting fish there? But I have digressed."

She turned her face toward him while the dog snuffled in his sleep on the seat opposite and moved his chin to a more comfortable position. He saw in her face an awareness of the fact that their journey together was coming to an end.

"When we arrive in Tenby," he said, "there are going to have to be a few changes."

Mr. Rhys, the solicitor who was looking after her cottage, had his chambers there. Since she did not have the key to the house or even know exactly where it was, they were going to have to find him. And then everything would change. Either the cottage could be lived in or it could not. They must discover the answer to that question first and proceed from there. But there was no point yet in wondering what their next step would be if it turned out that it could not.

She raised her eyebrows. "You sound like an officer about to issue orders to your men. What are they, sir?"

"When we arrive there," he said, "you are going to have to revert to being the widowed Mrs. McKay, and I am going to have to be Major Sir Benedict Harper, friend of the late Captain Matthew McKay, escorting you as a result of that deathbed promise I made him. But you must have a maid, you know, to add some semblance of propriety to our having traveled so far together."

Her eyebrows stayed elevated while he frowned in thought. "She accompanied you as far as Tenby," he said, "but flatly refused to go one step farther from England or even to stay there. You will have been forced to send her on her way back to England by stage the very day we call upon your solicitor. You will need an instant replacement, of course, even before you move into your cottage. And you are going to need one or two other servants, I daresay—a housekeeper, a cook, or perhaps someone who can serve in both capacities, especially if the cottage is small. Perhaps a handyman. A companion."

"You do not need to concern yourself with those details, *Major Harper,*" she said, her back to the window now as she gazed steadily at him. "I shall manage. And I daresay Mr. Rhys will be willing to advise me."

He smiled apologetically. "I will worry."

"Why?" she asked him. "Because I am a woman?"

"Because everything here will be new and strange to you," he said. "Because you will be alone."

"And because I am a woman."

He did not contradict her. But it was not just that. It was something he *did,* organizing people and events, managing them. Or, rather, it was something he *had done* when he was an officer. It was something he enjoyed, something he missed, though he might, of course, have taken over the running of his own estate three years ago or any time since then.

"This feels like goodbye," she said softly.

"I believe you will be happy in this part of the world," he said. "You already seem to have a certain sense of belonging."

"I do." Yet there seemed to be a sadness in her eyes. *This feels like goodbye.*

Yes, she would settle here, provided the cottage was habitable. She would surely have some neighbors and would make friends, and after a decent time she would meet a worthy Welshman and marry and have children. She would be happy. And she would be free forever of the pernicious influence of Heathmoor and the rest of her in-laws.

And he would never know about any of it.

It would not matter, though. He would soon forget about her, as she would forget about him.

It just seemed at this moment that he never could.

14

❧

They reached Tenby early one afternoon on a cool, blustery day with white clouds scudding across a blue sky. It was a pretty, hilly town built above high cliffs, with views of the sea from a number of the front streets. They took rooms at a hotel at the top of the town and proceeded downhill to the chambers of Rhys and Llewellyn, their coachman having inquired about the direction while they were securing their rooms.

Mr. Llewellyn was not in, they were told, but Mr. Rhys would be pleased to see them if they cared to wait for a few minutes until he was free.

Samantha felt as fearful as if she had just stepped into the rooms of a tooth drawer. Much—perhaps the whole of the rest of her life—depended upon what happened in the next little while. If the cottage was not a viable home, then she did not know what she would do. If it was, then Ben would very soon be leaving.

She had tried not to think of that, and so of course she had been able to think of little else. She would miss him. Well, *of course* she would. But that simple realization did not begin to account for the deep pit of emptiness she sensed would be awaiting her when she watched his carriage drive away without her—forever.

She doubted she would see him again.

It was a gloomy thought to add to the dreariness of the fact that she was wearing her blacks again after swearing she never would. She was *not* wearing the veil over her face, however.

Mr. Rhys, a short, neatly dressed, white-haired man, who looked as if he surely ought to have retired years ago, came out of his room no longer than three minutes after they had sat down, his face wreathed in smiles. He extended his right hand to Samantha.

"Mrs. McKay?" he said. "Well, this *is* a welcome surprise. And Major Sir Benedict Harper? How do you do, sir?"

He shook them both heartily by the hand and ushered them into his office after instructing his clerk to bring in a pot of tea. He directed them to two chairs and took his place behind a large desk in a chair slightly higher than theirs, Samantha noticed with some amusement.

"I cannot say you resemble Miss Bevan, your great-aunt, Mrs. McKay," he said to Samantha. "I believe, however, that you do have a bit of the look of Miss Gwynneth Bevan, her niece, your mother. She was just a girl when I saw her last, but she showed promise of being a great beauty. I am delighted you have come in person. Miss Bevan's cottage, now yours, of course, has been unoccupied for a number of years, and I have been wondering lately if you had any new instructions for me. It is a year since I last heard from the Reverend Saul, your brother, who wrote as usual on your behalf. I would have been writing again soon, but this is so much better."

Samantha frowned. John had been conducting business with Mr. Rhys *on her behalf*? He had certainly not sent on any letter but that one not long after their father's death. Had he taken her silence on that occasion as permission to run her affairs for her?

"Is the cottage habitable, Mr. Rhys?" She felt as if she had been holding her breath ever since she arrived here.

"There may be a little bit of dust," he said. "I have

cleaners going in only once a month. I sent workers in a few months ago to deal with some damp in the pantry, but it was nothing serious. The garden is not as pretty as Miss Bevan always kept it. The flowers have been neglected, but I have made sure the grass is cut a few times each year. You may find the furniture a bit old-fashioned, but it is solid enough and of the best quality and it has been protected with covers. The inside probably needs a coat of paint, and the mats may be getting close to being threadbare. But I daresay I could get a decent price for it just as it is if you wish to sell it."

"Oh, but I wish to live there," she told him.

He beamed and rubbed his hands together. "I am delighted to hear it," he said. "Houses were made to be lived in, I always say, preferably by their longtime owners. There is still some of the rent money left in the account here. I have taken from it only what has been needed to keep up the house. And the rest of the money is intact."

"The rest of the money?" Samantha looked inquiringly at him.

"Miss Bevan was not in possession of a vast fortune," Mr. Rhys explained in his lovely precise Welsh accent. "But she was left a very tidy sum when old Mr. Bevan, her father, passed on. She did not spend much of it—she lived frugally all her life and always said she was contented as she was. And Mrs. Saul, your mother, never withdrew any of it. It has been sitting in an account here for many years now, gathering a nice bit of interest."

There was *money* as well as a habitable cottage? Why had she never known about this? Who *had* known? Papa? John?

She did not ask how much money there was. Neither did she ask any details about the cottage. She did not suppose either was of any significant size. But she did feel foolish for not knowing and wondered if the fault was her own. She had never asked—but her mother had talked so disparagingly about the property that she had made it seem like nothing at all.

Samantha was pleased, though, to know that there was a bit of money as well as the house. She had not been left penniless when Matthew died, but neither was she any more than comfortably situated. A few pounds more would be very welcome, especially if the cottage needed new rugs and a fresh coat of paint. She exchanged a look with Ben, and he smiled.

But all this meant, of course, that he would have no further reason to stay with her. For which fact he would surely be very thankful. She was really not his responsibility, after all.

The cottage was only a few miles along the coast, Mr. Rhys explained after the clerk had brought in the tea and a plate of sweet biscuits. It was close to the village of Fisherman's Bridge though separated from it by sand dunes, which hid the cottage from view. The beach in front of it had always been considered part of the property and was never used by anyone except the inhabitants of the cottage. He would not advise Mrs. McKay to go there today or even tomorrow. He would like to have the cottage cleaned up for her first and the grass cut and some coal and basic necessities of food brought in.

Ben told him the mythical story of his friend, the late Captain McKay, and of Samantha's maid leaving on the stage bound for England just that morning.

"A pity, that," Mr. Rhys said. "And you will be staying in Tenby for the next couple of nights, will you? At a hotel? That puts Mrs. McKay in a bit of an awkward position, doesn't it, even if she does have you for company and protection, Major. A lady needs her maid as well as a gentleman to lend her countenance. Let me see what I can do about finding a new maid. It should not be too difficult even at such short notice. The opportunities for good positions do not arise every day around here, especially for girls."

"Thank you, Mr. Rhys," Ben said. "That would set my mind at ease. I was deeply concerned, as you may imagine, when that wretched maid insisted that she would not stand for one more day of moving away from England rather than toward it."

He made a convincing liar, Samantha thought. And what did he mean by *that would set my mind at ease*?

"Wales is often seen as a wild, heathen outpost," Mr. Rhys said with one of his broad smiles. "And sometimes we Welsh are content to keep it that way. Though the southwest here is often referred to as little England. You will not find many people hereabouts who speak and understand nothing but Welsh."

"But it is a lovely, musical language," Samantha protested, "and I intend to learn it."

"Splendid." Mr. Rhys beamed at each of them in turn and rubbed his hands together again.

They took their leave as soon as they had finished drinking their tea.

"It *is* habitable, Ben," Samantha said as they were being driven slowly up a steep hill on the way back to their hotel. "I feel quite dizzy with the knowledge. Though I expect it is very tiny. I wonder what a *tidy sum* amounts to. Do you suppose I am vastly wealthy?"

"Probably not," he said. "But maybe it will be enough to buy you plenty of coal for your fires during the winters. They are supposed to be milder here than in other parts of the country, but if my experience of Cornwall is anything to judge by, they can be mighty damp and cheerless. And windy."

It was windy here today.

"I suppose that is the penalty of living close to the

sea," she said. "Oh, Ben, Mr. Rhys is so . . . *respectable,* is he not?"

"Of course," he said. "What did you expect? A wild heathen? He is as old as the hills too."

"He knew my great-aunt," she said.

"You know nothing about her but her name?" he asked. "Are you curious about her, Samantha? And about the rest of your heritage?"

"My mother almost never talked about her life here," she told him. "I think she was unhappy. Or perhaps just restless. She ran away to London when she was seventeen and never came back. Perhaps she intended to tell me more when I was older, but she died very suddenly when I was only twelve."

She had not answered his question about whether she was curious or not, though. She was a bit afraid to be curious, actually. She was afraid of what she might discover. Her mother had been abandoned by her parents, Samantha's grandparents. That at least she knew. She doubted she wanted to know the details.

Her great-aunt had owned her own cottage, though. That meant something at least. She had obviously not been penniless. Neither had her father, Samantha's great-grandfather, if he had left her *a tidy sum,* whatever that might be. But where had her money come from before that to purchase a cottage? She had apparently never been married. She had had enough money to live upon without the sum her father left her. She had been able to leave most or all of that to her niece, Samantha's mother, in addition to the cottage.

Samantha had always thought of her Welsh relatives as impoverished. Yet even a little bit of thought would have made her realize that her great-aunt could not have been penniless and that her money must have come from somewhere.

"Oh," she said with a sigh, "perhaps I am just a little bit curious, after all."

But they had arrived outside their hotel.

"Shall we rest for what remains of today and explore tomorrow?" Ben suggested. "Or would you—"

She interrupted him. "You are going to go to your room to lie down for a while," she told him. "I can always tell when you are in pain. You smile too much."

"I shall have to frown ferociously," he said, suiting action to words, "in order to convince you that I am hale and hearty."

He did not argue, though, about withdrawing to his room.

The day after tomorrow, Samantha thought as she closed the door to her own room, she was going to be moving into her own home. Her new life would begin in earnest. And Ben would start on his way up the west coast of Wales and the rest of *his* life.

Oh, dear, how could one's spirit be so elated and yet so depressed all at the same time? She had better take her mind off things by walking Tramp.

Two hours later, when Samantha was back in her room and sitting by the window, alternately looking at the sea and trying to read, there was a knock on her door. She opened it, smiling in anticipation of seeing Ben on the other side. But a thin, dark-haired, blue-eyed girl stood there instead.

She had been sent by Mr. Rhys's clerk, she explained, to be Mrs. McKay's maid and look after her clothes and fetch her washing water and do her hair and anything else that was asked of her, if Mrs. McKay pleased, but she was a good girl and Mr. Rhys himself could testify to that fact since her own mother's sister had been working for his wife's cousin for five years now and never any trouble, and *would* Mrs. McKay give her a chance, please, and she would never be sorry for she would do

anything Mrs. McKay pleased and besides, the clerk
had told her she must stay for the night even if not forever as the silly English girl who had been Mrs. McKay's
maid had gone away on the stage this morning and
abandoned her because she did not like Wales, though
what was wrong with Wales, who knew, for it was
surely a hundred times better than that England, where
there was scarcely a mountain or molehill to make the
land interesting and people could not sing to save their
lives, but anyway, it would not be respectable for Mrs.
McKay to be alone in a hotel without a maid even though
her dead husband's friend, who was both a major and a
sir, was here to protect her, though in another room of
course, and . . . and *would* Mrs. McKay consider her for
the job, *please*?

Samantha was not sure the girl had stopped once to
draw breath. Her eyes were wide with mingled eagerness and anxiety.

"You have the advantage of me," she said. "You know
my name."

"Oh," the girl said. "Gladys, Mrs. McKay. Gladys
Jones."

"And how old are you, Gladys?" Samantha asked.

"I am fourteen, Mrs. McKay," the girl said. "I am the
oldest of us. There are seven younger than me and none
of us working yet. I would be much obliged to you if
you would take me on so that I can give some money to
Da to help him feed us all. I am a good worker. My
mam says so, and she says she will miss me if I go into
service, but Ceris will do almost as well in my place. She
is a good girl too and she has just turned thirteen and
she is nearly as tall as me. But perhaps you would not
need me to live in just yet, and I could go back and forth
really easy because I live in Fisherman's Bridge, no more
than a bit of a walk from the empty cottage where you
are going to move to. Mam is expecting another of us in

a few weeks, and I would rather be there with her for the nights anyway until the new babe is in the cradle. After that I would be more than happy to live in. Though I will live in right away if you would rather and just have my half day to visit Mam and help Ceris out as much as I can."

Samantha stood back to let the girl into the room.

"I will be happy to give you a try, Gladys," she said, "while *you* give *me* a try. And I believe I will be able to do without your services at night at least for a while."

She thought of the maid she had had at Bramble Hall and how the girl had often kept her up late with her chattering. Gladys might well keep her up all night if she lived in.

"Oh, *thank* you, Mrs. McKay," the girl said, and she began immediately to attack Samantha's bags, which she proceeded to unpack even though she was going to have to pack everything again the morning after tomorrow.

Word was delivered to the hotel the following morning that a Mrs. Price, widowed mother of the blacksmith at Fisherman's Bridge, had gone over to the cottage to supervise the cleaners who had been sent in, to open the windows to air the place out, and to remove the covers from the furniture and do a bit of shopping and get fires lit in all the grates after the windows were closed again so that everything would be nice and warm and cozy for Mrs. McKay when she arrived the following day. Mrs. Price had expressed a willingness to be interviewed for a permanent position if Mrs. McKay so desired. She was an excellent cook and had held previous positions as a cook and housekeeper. She had the references to prove it.

And so the next phase of her life was about to begin, Samantha thought as she spent the afternoon with Ben and Tramp, sitting and taking short walks along the top of the cliffs above the sweep of Tenby Bay.

A phase that would not include Ben.

"Ben," she said in a rush after they had sat silently admiring the view for a while, "will you stay for a few days? After tomorrow, I mean?"

He gazed out to sea, his eyes narrowed against the brightness of the light sparkling off its surface.

"Oh, how selfish of me," she said. "Please ignore the question. You must be very eager to be on your way."

"If there is an inn at Fisherman's Bridge," he said, "I will stay for a few days. Until I am satisfied that you are properly settled."

"Did I force that upon you?" she asked him. "I am not your responsibility."

When he turned his head to look at her, he was frowning slightly.

"Oh, but you are," he said. "I promised my friend, your husband, on his deathbed that I would escort you here and see you safely settled. Remember? I always keep my promises."

And then, just when she felt that she would surely dissolve into tears, he grinned at her.

That grin was going to haunt her after he had gone. It always somehow had the power to turn her weak at the knees.

"I am going to take Tramp for a quick walk," she said, getting hastily to her feet.

The cliffs got lower as they traveled west along the coast the next morning, though they rose high above the sea again in the not-too-far distance. They had been told that the village of Fisherman's Bridge and therefore the cottage on this side of it were in the dip where the cliffs were at their lowest.

Samantha fully expected that the cottage would be no more than the hovel her mother had called it. But she would not be disappointed, she told herself. At least it was habitable. It would do for a while even if not forever. And this was such a beautiful part of the world she would surely not regret moving here.

And then, quite suddenly, just as they were approaching a line of rolling sand dunes, partly covered with grass, there it was. Or what must be it since there was no other dwelling in sight and the village must be beyond the dunes.

Except that it was not a cottage. Or not what she thought of as a cottage, anyway.

"Oh, goodness," she said.

Ben leaned sideways, his shoulder pressed against hers, so that he could see it with her out of the window on her side of the carriage.

It was a sturdy, square house of gray stone with a gray slate roof. It looked as if it must have at least four bedchambers upstairs and as many rooms downstairs. There was a porch at the front and a dormer window in the roof above it. A square garden surrounded it, bordered by a whitewashed wooden fence. There was a sizable barn in one corner. What had obviously been flower beds at one time were bare apart from a few weeds, but the grass had been newly scythed. Its green expanse was unmarred by either daisy or buttercup.

"That is *a cottage*?"

"Well," Ben said, "it is not a mansion, but it is not a hermit's shed either, is it?"

"It is a *house*," she said. "How on earth could my mother have called it a hovel? Do you suppose there is some mistake?"

"No," he said. "The carriage is turning toward it. Your new maid would say something if this was the wrong place, even though I notice that the sight of Quinn awed her into silence when she met him in the stable yard this morning and I have not heard her voice from up on the box, have you?"

"My great-aunt could really not have been impoverished," she said. "I always assumed she was."

A large woman in a dark brown dress with a voluminous white apron and matching mob cap had appeared on the steps outside the porch, a welcoming smile on her face. Mrs. Price, Samantha assumed. She dipped into a curtsy as the coachman lowered the steps and handed Samantha down at the garden gate. Mr. Quinn opened it. Gladys was clambering down from the box, unassisted.

"Welcome, Mrs. McKay," Mrs. Price said. "Everything is ready for you, even at such short notice. I kept everyone's nose to the grindstone yesterday until everything shone and not one speck of dust or dirt remained. And I came over early this morning to get some baking done so that you would have something nice to eat as well as having the smell of cooking in the house. There is nothing so homely as that smell, is there? And is that you, Gladys Jones? Your mam said you had gone off to see if you could be Mrs. McKay's maid. Come inside, ma'am. The gentleman has hurt himself, has he?"

The interior lived up to the outside, Samantha discovered over the next half hour. There were four sizable square rooms downstairs—a parlor, a dining room, a kitchen, and a book room. There were four large bedchambers upstairs and one small one at the head of the stairs, and there was the attic room with its dormer window in the roof. A hallway bisected the house downstairs and contained the staircase, which ran straight up to the landing above.

The architect, whoever he had been, had lacked imagination, perhaps, but Samantha loved the dimensions of the rooms. The furniture, though old and heavy and predominantly dark in color, just as Mr. Rhys had described it, nevertheless looked comfortable. Yesterday, no doubt, there had been a smell of age and even mustiness here, but the opened windows and the fires and the baking had taken care of that.

Finally, Mrs. Price bustled off to the kitchen to fetch some of her newly baked cakes and a pot of tea. Gladys was thumping about in the main bedchamber above the parlor, where Samantha sat with Ben.

"I cannot quite believe it," she said, spreading her hands on the soft old leather of the chair arms.

"That the cottage really exists?" he said. "Or that it is habitable? Or that it is really quite large? Or that it actually belongs to you? Or that you are here at last? Or that you have a beach all to yourself and a view to entice you to your front windows for a lifetime? Or that your life has changed so drastically in such a short time?"

"Oh, stop," she said, laughing. She rested her head against the back of her chair and closed her eyes briefly. "All of those things. Oh, Ben, it is as if I have been snatched away from my life and deposited here in heaven. It really feels like heaven."

"I daresay," he said, "the Earl of Heathmoor did you a favor when he took Bramble Hall away from you and summoned you to Leyland Abbey. You may never have given this cottage a serious thought if you had not been desperate for escape, or, if you had, perhaps you would never have thought of coming here."

"This *was* fate, then?" She opened her eyes to look at him. "Something that was meant to be?"

But Mrs. Price came bustling back into the room, bearing a large tray, before he could answer her.

"I did not know if you liked currant cake or seed cake or bara brith best, Mrs. McKay," she said. "So I made all three and you can have your pick. I daresay the major likes all three. Men usually do. I am sure you must both be ready for a nice cup of tea. You would not prefer coffee, I hope? Nasty, bitter stuff, if you were to ask me. I never have it in my own house. My man did not like it either and nor does my son. But I can get some to bring tomorrow, if you like it. If you want me to come again, that is. I wouldn't mind coming in each day to get your breakfast and staying until I have cooked your evening meal, though I would rather not live in. My son would starve since he has not found a wife for himself yet, and I can never seem to sleep sound in any other bed but my own."

"Shall we give your suggestion a try?" Samantha said. "And I am happy to drink tea. Bara . . . brith, did you say?"

"This dark full-fruit loaf," Mrs. Price said, indicating the slices of it on the cake plate she had brought in before pouring them each a cup of tea. "There is no cake to compare with it for richness of flavor. That dog is gnawing on a soup bone and drinking his water in the kitchen. I do like a dog in the house, and a cat too, though I have never seen a dog quite like this one."

"And never will again, Mrs. Price, it is to be fervently hoped," Ben said.

Mrs. Price laughed. "Can I get you anything else before I go back to the kitchen?" she asked.

"You have always lived here, have you, Mrs. Price?" Samantha asked. "The village is not far away?"

"Just over those sand dunes," Mrs. Price said, pointing west. "And behind here is Mr. Bevan's land and the big house, though you can't see it from here."

Mr. Bevan's land.

The big house.

"He is your grandfather, I expect, Mrs. McKay, isn't he?" Mrs. Price said. "I wasn't sure who was coming here, though I was told it was the owner. But you look as if you must be his granddaughter. He married a Gypsy lady, you know. But of course you know. You have the look of one yourself, though it sits well on you, I must say. I'll get back to the kitchen. I have some soup cooking and some bread rising."

"Is there an inn in the village, Mrs. Price?" Ben asked as she turned to leave.

"Oh, yes, indeed, sir," she told him. "It is a nice, tidy place too. Nothing fancy, but it serves up a good dinner, it do, and is always clean. The stables too. My brother owns it."

"Thank you," Ben said. "I shall probably stay there for a few nights until I am sure Mrs. McKay is properly settled here. I promised her late husband, my friend, that I would, you know."

Samantha took a bite of the bara brith when she was alone with Ben. It really was delicious, but she did not have much of an appetite. She set her plate aside and looked at him. He was gazing steadily back at her.

"He has land," she said, "and a big house. He is still alive."

"Yes."

"Yet he sent my mother here to live with his sister," she said. "He let her go to London at the age of seventeen and did not go after her. He did not go to her wedding or to my christening or to her funeral. It could not have been poverty that caused any of those things, could it?"

"Has imagining that he was poor comforted you over the years?" he asked.

"I have not needed comforting," she told him. "I have not thought of him or wondered about him."

But she knew as she stared at him and as he sat looking silently back that she must have done even if it had not been conscious. And she knew that the conviction that her grandfather had been poor was the only thing that had satisfied the hurt of being cut off from her mother's family at the same time as she was being shunned by her father's.

"I suppose," she said, "it was because she was the daughter of the Gypsy who abandoned him. My mother, I mean. And because I was her daughter. If he knew of me at all, that is."

"Are you going to be sorry you came?" Ben asked.

She looked beyond him to the window, which faced south. Through it she could see the land beyond the garden fence dipping away to the west and then rising again over the dunes. Through the dip she could see the sea and a strip of golden sand—just a stone's throw from her own house. The house itself was warm and cozy. A clock on the mantel ticked steadily. It would be lulling when she sat here alone. If she sat by the open window, she would be able to smell the salt of the sea. She would be able to hear it too.

And it was all *hers*.

It was her heritage.

"No." She opened her mouth to say more and shut it again.

"But—?"

"I am a bit afraid, perhaps," she admitted. "Afraid of Pandora's box."

He got slowly to his feet, abandoned one of his canes, and reached out his free hand. She set her own in it, and he led her to the window.

"Look at the sea, Samantha," he said. "I learned the trick when I was at Penderris. It was there long before we were thought of. It will be there long after we are forgotten, ebbing and flowing according to the law of the tides."

"Our little affairs are insignificant?"

"Far from it," he said. "Pain is not insignificant. Neither is bewilderment or fear. Or conditions like poverty or homelessness. But somewhere—*somewhere*—there is peace. It is not even far off. It is somewhere deep inside us, in fact, ever present, just waiting for us to look inward to find it."

She turned her head to look at his lean profile.

"It is how you learned to master your pain," she said with sudden intuition.

"It was, at last, the only way of doing it," he admitted. "But I sometimes forget. We all do. It is human nature to try to manage all our living for ourselves without drawing upon . . . But I am sorry. I did not intend to be so obscure. Just don't be afraid, though. Whatever you discover here, the knowing cannot bring you any real harm even if it feels painful, for these things *are* whether you know them or not. And perhaps the knowing will bring you some understanding and even perhaps some peace."

He continued to look out through the window, and she continued to look at him.

His pain, she thought, was fathoms deep. He had learned to master it. But he was still adrift in life. Unlike her, he had not found his home. But, also unlike her, he had learned not to fear.

"You *will* stay for a while?" she asked him. Oh, she hoped she was not being selfish. But just for a few days . . .

"I will stay," he said, lowering his eyes to hers. "For a while."

❧

15

𝒯he village of Fisherman's Bridge consisted of just one street worth speaking of. It followed the coastline for perhaps a mile. There were no high cliffs here, only a sea wall with golden sands stretching beyond it to the water's edge.

The inn was halfway along the street on the seaward side, the stables beside it rather than behind, where they would have obstructed the view from the dining room and taproom windows. There was a room available, and the landlord was delighted to let it to Major Sir Benedict Harper. It was quickly clear to Ben that the man knew exactly who he was. News traveled fast in small places. He knew too that Ben had come with Mrs. McKay, who was taking up residence in old Miss Bevan's cottage beyond the sand dunes. He asked if it was true that she was the granddaughter of Mr. Bevan, and Ben confirmed that she was. There was no point in denying it. It was no secret, after all.

But who the devil *was* Bevan? It appeared that he was some sort of landowner.

His room was comfortable and afforded a view over the beach and sea. His dinner, prepared by the landlord's wife, was tasty and plentiful, as Mrs. Price had predicted. He was the only occupant of the dining room, though if the sounds of boisterous voices and laughter were anything to judge by, the taproom next door was crowded. The landlord must be serving in there. It was his wife herself who brought Ben's food and lingered to talk.

"It is lovely to know there is someone in Miss Bevan's cottage again," she said. "I have hated to see it sitting empty when it is such a pretty place."

Ben could not resist doing some probing. "Mr. Bevan lives close to here, does he, Mrs. Davies?"

"Up at the big house, yes," she told him, waving a hand inland. "If you go along the street to the bridge, you will be able to see it up on the hill in among the trees. A lovely situation, it is. His father before him chose the perfect spot for it when he decided to build."

"There was no house on the land before that, then?" Ben asked.

"Only a farmhouse," she said. "But it wasn't big or grand enough for Mr. Bevan. Well, it stands to reason, doesn't it? He had that fortune he made from his coal mines, but it was here he chose to live and set up as a gentleman. He wanted a big house, and a lovely one he built. Our Marged works there as a chambermaid, and she gets a decent wage."

"This roast beef is almost tender enough to cut with a fork," Ben remarked. "And the roast potatoes are crisp on the outside and soft on the inside—just as I like them."

"I do like to see a man tuck in to a hearty meal," she said, clearly pleased.

"The present Mr. Bevan still has the mines, does he?" Ben asked.

"Those and the ironworks up the valley by Swansea there," she told him. "That is where our oldest boy has gone to work. He earns good money. A number of lads from around here go there for work, and to the mines too. He is a good employer, Mr. Bevan is. Good to his workers. But he is getting on in years, and he has no sons to carry on after him, more's the pity. Mrs. Bevan—the second one, that is—never was blessed with children before she died, poor lady."

Ben was feeling guilty. All this was none of his business—except that he probably would have been having this exact conversation even if he were a stranger here. He would have been asking questions and finding out information of interest for his book. Indeed, he probably would have been delving deeper.

He wondered what Samantha was going to make of these facts when she knew them. What had she said to him earlier?

I am a bit afraid, perhaps. Afraid of Pandora's box.

Some box!

"Perhaps he will take comfort from his granddaughter," Mrs. Davies added. "A widow, is she, sir?"

"Her husband was my friend," Ben explained. "I promised him before he died that I would see her safely settled here."

Someone called from the kitchen, and Mrs. Davies hurried away with an apology for leaving him.

Was Bevan going to be pleased to find his granddaughter living on his doorstep? And did he know yet that she was here?

One thing was sure, though, Ben thought as he cleaned off his plate. He was going to remain here until some of his questions had been answered. Samantha might yet need him.

It felt like an enormous relief, that realization.

Ben rode a horse from the inn stables to the cottage the next morning, Quinn behind him in order to help him dismount and then mount again for the return ride.

The sun was sparkling off the sea by the time they had ridden over the dunes, and there was warmth in the air. The front upstairs windows of the cottage were open, and the curtains were flapping in the breeze. The front door stood open too, and Samantha—yes, it *was* she—was bent over one of the bare beds under the parlor window, pulling out weeds. She was wearing gloves and an apron and an old, floppy-brimmed straw bonnet he had not seen before. She had left off her blacks again. Her dress was a pale lemon muslin and looked as if it had probably seen better days.

Ben drew his horse to a halt in order to enjoy a longer look at her. She looked relaxed and wholesome, as if she had always belonged here. The realization caused him a pang of something. Exclusion? Loneliness? For she would probably belong here long after he had gone.

Something alerted her even though the horse's hooves were making no great noise on the sandy grass. She straightened up and turned their way, a small trowel in her hand. She smiled. The dog, who had been stretched out in the sun at the foot of the porch steps, was on his feet too, wagging his tail and woofing.

"I always fancied myself as a gardener," she said as Ben rode up to the garden fence. "I used to dabble as a girl, but I never had a chance at Bramble Hall—Matthew always needed me in the sickroom. Now I *do* have a chance. Mr. Rhys said that my great-aunt kept a pretty flower garden here, did he not? Well, I am going to restore it, even if I have to start with some destruction. I hate killing weeds. They are plants, after all. They are living things. And who decides what are flowers and what are weeds, anyway? I love daisies and buttercups and dandelions, but everyone banishes them from their lawns as if they carry the plague."

"Perhaps because they would destroy those lawns if left to grow and spread unchecked," he said. "Did you sleep well?"

She had been in the house alone since neither her

maid nor Mrs. Price was to live in, at least for a while. He wondered if that fact had bothered her. He had worried about her a bit during the night.

"I slept with the window open," she told him. "I could hear the sea and smell it, but only for a very short while, I must admit. I fell deeply asleep and did not rouse until I could smell bacon cooking. Mrs. Price put me to shame and came early. Is the inn a decent place?"

"Very comfortable," he said. "You have a barn at the back big enough to stable the horses while I am here. I'll go back there now with Quinn, if I may, and then come visiting."

The apron and the gloves and trowel had disappeared by the time he walked back to the house from the barn, but she was still outside and still wore the floppy-brimmed bonnet, which was surely as old as the hills and made her look absurdly pretty. The dog was beside her, wagging his tail in clear expectation of being entertained. He really did assume that the world revolved around his large, ungainly self.

"You could never walk on the beach at Penderris Hall, I remember your saying," she said, "because it was at the foot of a high cliff. Was there a way down?"

"There were a few steep paths," he said. "The others went down all the time, even Vincent, despite his blindness."

"There is nothing to stop you from walking on the beach here," she said. "It is not far away and the slope down to it is not steep. The sand looks flat and smooth. Shall we go?"

"Now?"

It was human nature, he had realized long ago, always to want the one thing one could not have, even if one had been gifted with a superabundance of other blessings. He had always longed and longed to be able to go down onto the beach at Penderris. Hugo had once offered to carry him down, but he had declined so firmly that the offer had never been renewed. Not that Hugo could not have done it. He was as strong as any ox. But Ben would have been humiliated. He had consoled himself with the thought that there was nothing down there except sand to get in his hair and his mouth.

"I was hoping you would come early," she said, falling into step beside him, her hands clasped at her back, while Tramp went loping ahead of them. "I have been longing to go down there myself, but I wanted you with me the first time. I want to be able to remember that."

That? The fact that he had been with her this first time?

"I have a confession to make," she said. "I have never, ever been on a beach. Is that not strange when my mother grew up here?"

He turned his head to look at her. Her exertions in the garden and the sea breeze had whipped a healthy color into her cheeks. Her eyes were bright.

"May I suggest," he said, "that you remove your shoes and stockings before going out onto the sand? Otherwise you will have your shoes full of grit before you have walked any distance, and you will spend the rest of the day shaking sand out of everything and fighting blisters."

She laughed. "And you too?"

"I am wearing boots," he said. Besides, he was not about to expose any part of his legs in her presence.

"It sounds like a very improper suggestion, sir," she said, "but a very sensible one nonetheless."

She looked about and chose a flat-topped rock at the bottom of the slope on which to seat herself. She removed her shoes and stockings while he watched. Too late it occurred to him that it would have been far more gentlemanly to turn his back. She had slim legs, trim ankles, narrow, pretty feet—which he had seen before at the inn above the Wye Valley. She rolled her stockings neatly and placed them inside her shoes, and then she stood and set her shoes on the rock.

"Oh," she said, wriggling her toes in the mixture of grass and sand on which they stood, "that feels lovely. But it does feel sinful to be unshod outdoors."

They walked through the gap onto a wide, flat beach. Sand stretched to right and left until it met outcroppings of rock that enclosed the area into a private beach. Rocks rose behind them on either side of the gap to provide further privacy. The tide was low, though the breakers along the edge of the water indicated that it was coming in. The breeze was fresher here, though at the same time the sun was warmer. Seagulls cried overhead.

Ben's canes sank into the sand, but he found walking here somewhat easier than on hard ground. Samantha ran ahead of him a little way and then stopped and turned, her arms stretched out to the sides.

"Freedom!" she cried, just like an exuberant child. "Oh, tell me this is no illusion, Ben."

The dog pranced about her, barking.

"This is freedom," Ben said obediently, grinning at her, and she tipped back her head to look at the sky and twirled about in three complete circles while he laughed. Her dress billowed to the sides, and her bonnet brim flopped about her face.

Was *this* the austere, black-clad lady he had first met in County Durham?

"There *are* such moments, are there not?" she said. "Oh, I had forgotten. It has been *so* long. But there *are* moments of pure, unalloyed happiness, and this is one of them. I am *so* glad I waited for you to come, for such moments need to be shared. Tell me you feel it too—the freedom, the happiness." She stopped spinning to direct a look at him, and he read sudden uncertainty there.

But he *did* feel it too. As if for this moment the world had stopped and they had stepped off and nothing would ever matter again except this stopping place.

"I am glad you waited for me," he said.

Her arms fell to her sides and she gazed at him, her face alight.

"Which way shall we go?" he asked. "East? West? South?"

"Oh." She spun about to consider each direction. "South. To the water's edge. Will you be comfortable walking that far?"

The dog had already made off in that direction.

"I am on a beach at last," he said. "Let me at least dip the tip of a cane in the water."

The tide was farther out than it had looked. But walking on the sand really was relatively easy, and he would ignore any discomfort anyway for the pleasure of doing what he was doing. This was food for the future. It was her first walk on a beach. It was his first in years. And they were doing it together.

The dog was running along the edge of the water, kicking up a spray as he went.

"Dare I?" Samantha said. It was not really a question. "I suppose the water is dreadfully cold."

She was gathering up the sides of her dress even as she spoke, and she stepped into the shallow water, which barely wet the sand, and then over the nearest ripple of the incoming tide until she was ankle deep.

"Oh, it *is* cold," she said on a deep inward gasp. "And my feet are sinking into the sand. Oh, this is *lovely*, Ben." She lifted her head to look at him, her eyes sparkling. "Come in too."

He really ought not. If her feet were sinking into the sand, what would his canes do? And his boots would be white with brine after they dried, and Quinn would look reproachful and long-suffering. What if he lost his balance and fell in? How the devil would he get up again?

She had stopped moving.

"It feels cold only for the first few moments," she said. "It probably would not feel cold at all through your boots."

"That was all I needed to hear," he said and stepped into the water while she shrieked with laughter.

He *could* feel the coldness even through his boots and stockings. And his canes were indeed sinking rather alarmingly into the wet sand. But though he was only a few feet from dry land, it felt as if he had stepped into a different element. The sun beat down hot upon them. The sea sparkled about them.

He felt a sudden longing for George or Hugo or one of the others to see him now. He laughed.

She stepped closer to him, gathering her skirts into one hand as she came, and she took one of his canes in the hand that held the fabric and stepped closer still.

"Put your arm about my shoulders," she told him.

"My weight would be too much for you," he protested.

"Do it, anyway," she said. "I promise not to collapse."

He felt embarrassed, even a little humiliated, but he had no choice short of snatching back his cane and perhaps offending her—or throwing himself off balance. He made it a practice almost never to lean upon anyone. He set an arm about her slim shoulders, and she fit herself against his side and wrapped her free arm about his waist.

Oh, Lord.

"We are *not* a cripple and a poor, long-suffering nurse," she said, laughing up at him, her flushed, bright-eyed face alarmingly close, "but a man and a woman who have found a perfectly reasonable excuse for being close to each other."

He thought he was probably flushing too.

"Do we *need* an excuse?"

"It would seem so," she said, beginning to walk along the edge of the water with him. "We have been very careful to leave a decent sliver of air between us since that night we shared a room. You are lean, Ben, but you are certainly not frail, are you? Quite the contrary, in fact."

He was not going to respond with any description of her body.

"Am I leaning too heavily on you?" he asked. He was trying to put most of his weight on his cane, but that made it sink deeper.

He could feel the generous curves of her body all down his side. One firm, heavy breast was pressed against his coat. She was tall, though not quite as tall as he. He was aware of the faint scent of gardenia over the saltiness of the sea air. Her body felt warm through the flimsy barrier of her dress and stays.

And so was his body, by Jove. Warm, that was. Warmer than warm.

"You are avoiding the issue," she said.

"Which is?"

"The fact that we have needed an excuse to touch," she said.

"I promised," he reminded her, "that you would be safe from me."

"Sometimes," she said, turning her head to look out to sea, "safety seems a dull, unadventurous thing."

And by God, she was right about that.

"After you have left here," she asked him, "will you regret that you were the perfect gentleman the whole time we were together? Well, almost the whole time."

"How could I regret behaving like a gentleman?" he asked her. "That is what I am."

Would *she* regret it?

They had stopped walking. He was feeling ruffled, even a bit annoyed. Being a gentleman was important to him. And yet . . . He would have let go of her, put some distance between them, but she still held his cane.

"It is just that freedom is a precious gift," she said. "One ought to be able to use it to do whatever one most wants to do, provided one is hurting no one else in the process. We are almost never allowed to act freely, though, are we? There is always someone or some rule or convention that says, no, it is not at all the thing. And so we toe the line of propriety and deny the freedom that has been offered us and lose our chance for some happiness."

What she was suggesting, he thought, was that they become lovers before he left. And it all made perfect sense when they were out here on the beach together like this. Why should they *not* do something . . . free? Something they both wanted to do. Except that this was not the world—this beach. And they could not live out here forever.

He would regret it. For he would surely be an inadequate lover and would disappoint both her and himself. He would regret waking the sleeping devil of his sexuality—except that it had already awakened, had it not? He would regret the end of the affair. He would regret having to leave her, for he could not stay and she would not want him to. And *she* would regret it if they had an affair, even if she was not disappointed in his performance. For no one had ever been constant in her life. Even her mother had died young. She needed more than a temporary lover.

There would be pain.

There was always pain.

She was gazing into his eyes, and he was the one now gazing out to sea.

"You are tired from all the walking," she said. "I have

had my eye on that large rock over there since we started along the water's edge. Let us go and sit on it for a while."

He did not argue. He really did need to take the weight off his legs. A lower ledge of the rock she had indicated was flat enough to sit on, and it was just wide enough and at just the right height for the two of them. The dog dashed off to chase some gulls that had landed at the water's edge farther along the sands.

"Have I spoiled your first visit to a beach?" he asked her.

"By being tired and needing to sit down?" she said. "No, of course not."

He took her hand in his and laced their fingers— probably very unwisely. She dipped her head to rest on his shoulder. The soft brim of her bonnet bent easily to accommodate her.

"It is lovely here," she said. "I will always remember today. Oh, but look, your poor boots are caked with sand."

"It is more poor Quinn than poor boots," he said.

"I am going to swim here," she said after they had sat in silence for a while. "Not now, but soon. I am going to get right under that water and *swim*. Do it with me, Ben. You *can* swim. You told me so."

"That was when I was a boy and had two fully functioning legs," he said.

"I do not suppose you have forgotten how." She twisted her head so that she could look up at him. "You walk even though I daresay every physician you ever consulted warned you you never would."

"I am not exactly proficient at it," he protested.

"You *walk*," she said, lifting her head and glaring fiercely at him. "Swimming would be easier, would it not? You would not have to put weight on your legs."

"I would probably sink like a stone and never be heard from again."

He grinned at her. But could she possibly be right? What if he tried to swim and could not and was then unable to get his feet under him again? But what if he had listened to all the *what-ifs* with which his mind had bombarded him when he had tried to walk? He would still be lying on a bed or sitting confined to a chair. He may not be walking very well, but he *was* walking. He was here, was he not, sitting on a rock in the middle of a beach, a fair distance from the cottage?

"Coward," she said.

He kissed her.

She tasted warm and salty, and he reached his tongue into her mouth to taste more of her. He gathered her more closely into his arms, and she twined both her own about his neck.

They were both breathless when he drew back his head.

"When?" he asked her.

"Tomorrow," she said. "In the afternoon."

They held each other's eyes.

"I will have Mrs. Price cook dinner for two before she leaves," she said. "We are bound to be ravenous after swimming."

Ravenous.

They would be alone in the cottage.

She did not look away from him or he from her.

"I daresay I will eat every mouthful set before me, then," he said.

"If you have not drowned." She smiled dazzlingly.

He had not told her what he had learned about her grandfather, he remembered suddenly. Had anyone else told her? But he doubted it. Surely she would have greeted him with the news if she had heard.

But now was not the right time.

They were going to swim together tomorrow. And then dine alone together at the cottage. Both servants would have returned home for the night,

I promised that you would be safe from me.
Sometimes safety seems a dull, unadventurous thing.

16

❧

$\mathscr{A}$fter having luncheon together at the cottage, they rode into the village, Samantha on the horse Mr. Quinn had ridden earlier. He had found an old side-saddle in the barn during the morning and had worked on it for a couple of hours, checking it for safety, making a few repairs, and cleaning and polishing it until it looked quite respectable. He would walk back to the inn, he assured Samantha. It was not far.

And so finally they rode together, she and Ben. Matilda would have forty fits of the vapors, especially if she could see Samantha in her very old blue riding habit. But Matilda already seemed like someone from another lifetime.

"It will really be a very short ride," Ben told her, a note of apology in his voice. "It is no distance at all to the village."

Just too far for him to walk. She understood. She rode slightly behind him and watched him. He always looked so very virile and at home in the saddle. She had almost thrown herself at him this morning, she remembered. Whatever had possessed her? But it had struck her that she *would* regret it if he went away and they had shared no more than longing and a few kisses.

It would not be wrong, surely, if they enjoyed a brief affair? They were both single adults. They liked each other. They were attracted to each other. It was too soon for her to think of marrying again, if she ever did.

He had said he would never marry, and certainly he would not do so before he had found what he was searching for in life and had settled down—if he ever did.

So where would be the harm?

Would they swim tomorrow? Or would it rain, as it had that infamous day they had planned to ride together? Would he be able to swim? And what would happen afterward, when they were alone together in her cottage?

She did not have long for such thoughts. Fisherman's Bridge was indeed only just over the sand dunes.

She was eager to see it and a bit anxious too. This village and these villagers would become a part of her life, perhaps forever. She would need to find acceptance here and friends and acquaintances and things to do. For a moment she wondered if anyone knew about her, but of course everyone would. Mrs. Price lived at the smithy, and Gladys lived here. Both were talkative and sociable. And Ben was staying at the inn.

"I wonder what the people here do for a living," she said as she looked about her with interest.

"Some work here in the village," he said. "There are fishermen, as one would expect from the name. I talked briefly at breakfast this morning with a potter who sells his wares to summer visitors both here and in Tenby. I believe most people, though, are employed at Cartref in one capacity or another."

"Car—?"

"*Car,* as in *carry,*" he said, "and *trev* as in the name *Trevor.* The emphasis is on the first syllable. The *r* in both syllables is slightly rolled. It is the first Welsh word I have learned, and since it will probably also be the last, I am determined to pronounce it correctly. It means *home.*"

"You have gone through that explanation and learned

a whole new foreign word," she said, laughing, "just to inform me that most people work at home?"

"No," he said. "*Cartref* is the name of a particular home. Let's ride along to the end of the street. The road crosses the bridge there, the one that gives its name to the village. Though how anyone can fish off it when the river that flows beneath it is so close to the sea I do not know."

"Perhaps no one does," she said. "Perhaps it is so named because it leads across to where all the fishing boats are moored."

They passed a few people on the street, and Samantha inclined her head to them and smiled. She guessed that her visit here would be the subject of several conversations for the rest of the day. She wondered what the nature of those conversations would be. Would it be remembered that her great-aunt had raised a half-Gypsy girl and that that girl had been her mother? But of course it would. Mrs. Price knew it. Would these people resent the fact that she had inherited the cottage and come to live here? Or was she being oversensitive?

She would find out soon enough, she supposed.

It was a picturesque bridge, humpbacked and built of gray stone. A shallow river bubbled beneath it on its way to the sea. She gazed ahead to the small boats bobbing on the water and thought it one of the prettiest sights she had seen. Would she ever have a chance to go out in one of those boats?

"Ah," Ben said. "I was told I would be able to see it from here."

"See what?"

He was not looking at the boats. His horse was turned the other way, and his gaze was fixed upon something inland. She turned to look too.

There was no need for him to answer her question. There were low hills a mile back from the sea. Halfway up one of them, nestled within a horseshoe of trees, was a great mansion, which gleamed white in the sunshine. Even from this far away she could see that it had large windows on all three floors, diminishing in size from the ground floor to the top. There must be magnificent views from every one of those windows. A bright green lawn, which was obviously well kept, swept down the slope to the plain. The rest of the garden or park was hidden from view.

"*That* is Cartref?" she asked. "It looks very grand indeed, does it not? I did not expect to find any large estates outside of England. To whom does it belong, I wonder. Do you know?"

He did not answer. His horse had become suddenly restless, and he was concentrating upon bringing it under control.

Then the truth struck her, rather like a fist colliding with her stomach.

"Oh, no," she said.

He looked apologetically at her, as though the answer to her question was his fault.

"It is my grandfather's?"

"He is as rich as a nabob, Samantha," he told her. "He owns coal mines—plural, I understand—in the coal mining valleys in the east part of the country. He inherited those from his father. He also owns ironworks in the valleys close to Swansea, where industry has been springing up and thriving."

If she had not been on horseback, she might well have swooned.

There were seagulls crying overhead, sounding almost human.

"And I have always imagined," she said, "that he was a laborer or a wanderer, a ne'er-do-well who married a professional nomad and then, when she abandoned him, foisted his child upon a sister who had somehow gained ownership of a run-down hovel. Why did my mother never *tell* me?"

"I suppose she would have," he said, "if she had lived until you were older."

"I would *never* have come if I had known," she said. "Why not?"

She wheeled her horse about to face him. "He had no legitimate reason for abandoning my mother. He had the home and the means with which to raise her himself. He had the means with which to go after her when she went to London, and to attend her wedding, and to visit her after her marriage. He had the means to come to see *me*. And what, do you suppose, is the *tidy sum* that was left my great-aunt and then passed to my mother and so to me—with the interest it has gathered? Ben, how wealthy *am* I? I do not want to be wealthy. Not in this way. I do not want any of it."

"Think a minute." He was annoyingly calm. "That money, however much it is or is not, was left to your great-aunt by your great-grandfather. None of it came from your grandfather."

She frowned at him for a few moments. He was right, of course. But even so . . . Oh, all the sparkle and joy were gone from the afternoon.

"I *wish* I had never known," she said. "I almost wish I had not come."

"Where else would you have gone?" he asked her.

"I could have married you," she said, "and wandered footloose and carefree for the rest of my life." But the look on his face restored some of her humor and she smiled. "I had a premonition that I would be opening Pandora's box by coming here. Once that box had been opened in the myth, there was no stuffing all the troubles back inside it, was there? I cannot now leave here and forget what I have learned. Am I talking sense?"

Her grandfather had not wanted her mother or her.

John had not wanted them either. All she had ever had were her mother and father, and they were both gone. She felt awash with a terrible sense of aloneness. Yet nothing had changed. As Ben had said, everything was as it had been ten minutes ago and last week.

Oh, but *everything* had changed.

"Strangely, yes," he said. "Come to the inn for some tea."

But as they turned their horses back into the village, they were hailed by a genial-looking, gray-haired man and a plump, smiling lady.

"Mrs. McKay?" the gentleman asked, doffing his tall hat.

Samantha inclined her head.

"Pardon me for intruding when you are out enjoying your ride," he said, "but I thought it must be you and the gentleman who is staying at the inn—Major Harper, I believe? I am Ivor Jenkins, the vicar here, and this is my good wife. We are taking a stroll along the front to look at the boats, it being such a lovely day and my sermon for Sunday all written. It is my pleasure to welcome you to our community, Mrs. McKay, and to hope that we will see you at church on Sunday?"

Mrs. Jenkins did not say anything, but she beamed up at Samantha and nodded her head.

"I shall certainly be there," Samantha assured them. "Thank you, Mr. Jenkins. I shall look forward to it."

"Marvelous," he said. "I hope you will enjoy my sermon, which I think particularly clever. I always do, though my parishioners often do not agree. I *know* you will enjoy the music. It has been said that when the whole congregation sings, the roof lifts an inch or two off its moorings. I don't suppose it is true, is it, or it would blow away in a strong wind, but it *is* true that if you want to hear singing as it was meant to be heard, you must come to Wales."

He joined in Samantha and Ben's laughter.

"Ivor." His wife set a hand on his arm.

"I will not keep you any longer," the vicar said. "I have a tendency to do that when my good wife is not present to remind me that people have other things to do than stand talking with me. I look forward to serving you in my capacity as vicar, Mrs. McKay. And I hope you will enjoy the rest of your stay here, Major. We do not have much to offer here except scenery and views, but they are without compare, I always think."

He restored his hat to his head, and he and his wife proceeded on their way across the bridge to look at the boats.

"There is a welcome here for you," Ben said softly. "You can make a home here."

"Can I?" She looked at him with troubled eyes for a moment and then smiled. "The Reverend Jenkins seems kindly, and his wife looks sweet, though it would appear she knows how to keep him in line. Yes, let's go for tea, Ben."

The sky was leaden gray, Samantha could see when she woke up the following morning. And when she sat up in bed, she could see that the water was a deeper shade of the same color. There were raindrops on the window. They did not obliterate the view, and she could not hear any more pelting against the panes. But it was not a promising start to the day.

She was hugely disappointed. If they could not swim today, Ben would perhaps leave instead. There was really not much reason for his staying any longer at the village inn, was there? She had a more than decent house in which to live, she had servants, she had her own competence and more at a bank in Tenby. A few people had nodded to her in the village yesterday, and the vicar and

his wife had stopped to introduce themselves and welcome her. Both the landlord of the inn and his wife had
chatted amiably with them over tea. No, there was no
reason for him to stay any longer.

She was tempted to burrow beneath the bedcovers
again and go back to sleep. But she knew it would be
impossible. Besides, Tramp would be ready for a walk.
And she could hear Gladys in her dressing room and
Mrs. Price down in the kitchen. She could smell cooking. What a lazybones she must appear to them. They
had both walked from the village this morning.

Ben planned to spend the morning at the inn, working on all the notes he had made in his journal to see if
he could organize them into some semblance of chapters for the book he hoped to write. He was to come to
the cottage during the afternoon. It was with some surprise, then, that Samantha heard horses' hooves in the
middle of the morning. She had been sorting through
the volumes in the book room and went to the window.

It was Mr. Rhys.

He had come, he explained, to satisfy himself that
Mrs. McKay had found everything in order and that she
approved of the servants his clerk had picked out on her
behalf. He was at her service, he told her, if there was
anything more he could do for her.

She did not really want to ask. Indeed, the very idea
of doing so made her feel almost physically ill. But while
she might have remained blissfully ignorant of the answer for the rest of her life if she had stayed in England,
there was no avoiding it indefinitely now that she was
here.

"Mr. Rhys," she said, "you mentioned the money my
great-aunt left my mother and that my mother in turn
left me. I did not know of it until two days ago. Is it a
great deal?"

"I have a statement from the bank here with me," he

told her, reaching into the leather case he had set beside his chair. "I thought you would wish to know. I knew the principal but not the exact amount of interest that has accumulated. You can see for yourself, ma'am. You will be pleased, I think."

He handed her a sheaf of papers.

She lowered her eyes to the top page. Please God, let it be a smallish sum, a pleasant addition to her own modest resources, but nothing too— Her eyes focused upon the total, and then she closed her eyes and licked lips turned suddenly dry.

"It is a nice tidy sum, isn't it?" he said.

"Yes," she said. "Tidy, Mr. Rhys."

"I hope you are not disappointed," he said. "Mr. Bevan left the bulk of his property and fortune to his son, which was only natural, I suppose, when he was going to be the one continuing with the business."

"I expected only the cottage," she told him. "I wonder why my mother never drew on any of the money." And why had she never so much as mentioned it? Had Papa known about it? But he must have, after her death if not before. Why had *he* never said anything? Because his daughter had become more wealthy than his son? Because he respected her mother's wish to have nothing to do with her past? It would have been that, she decided. He would have respected her mother's rejection of her past even after her death—and even at the expense of their daughter.

Mr. Rhys was looking uncomfortable. "I know Miss Bevan was very fond of her niece," he said. "She took her in and she fed and clothed and educated her. But she was always afraid—she confided in me on a few occasions since we were in the way of being friends. She was always afraid the girl would turn wild and go chasing after her mother's people. And she did like to go barefoot out of doors and run on the beach and swim in the sea. It was what all children were like, I tried to tell Miss Bevan. My own were not much different. But she was afraid. And fear made her overstrict. And maybe a bit overcritical too. I am not sure if that was what drove your mother away. I think there may have been some sort of quarrel between your great-aunt and your grand-father, though they were scarcely on speaking terms at the best of times. And I am not even sure about the quarrel. However it was, your mother went. She was very young. Perhaps she did not know that quarrels are best made up as soon as tempers have cooled, especially with family members."

Her mother had felt rejected, then, Samantha thought— by her own mother, who had gone back to her people, leaving her child behind; by her father, who had turned her over to his sister's care; and by her aunt, who was overstrict and overcritical because she was half Gypsy. She had run away at the age of seventeen—and had met Papa, who had loved her quietly and gently and stead-fastly for the rest of her life. Perhaps it was significant that she had married an older man, a substitute father, perhaps. For though she had undoubtedly loved Papa, it had not, Samantha thought now, been a passionate re-lationship.

"I do hate to speak ill of the dead," Mr. Rhys said, "and a former client and friend at that, but Miss Bevan could be as stubborn as a mule too. When her niece ran away, she would not go after her or even write to her to beg her to come home or ask if she needed anything. And she would not go to meet your father when she heard about the marriage or to meet you when she heard of your birth. Your mother did write on both occasions, so perhaps she did try to reach out. Miss Bevan would not forgive her, though, for running away and becom-ing an actress after all she had done to make the girl into a respectable lady."

"And yet," Samantha said, "she left everything to my mother."

"And now it is yours," Mr. Rhys said. "I am glad you have come."

"Thank you," Samantha said. "I had no idea, you know."

"I hope," he said, "you are not regretting that you did come."

She gazed at him for a few moments before answering.

She had come here to escape. To hide. To break free of the oppression of a too-strictly-applied respectability. To put aside the heavy trappings of her mourning in favor of gentler memories of the man who had been her husband for seven years. To find some peace. To find some freedom. To make a new beginning.

She had not expected *this*.

"I am not sorry," she said.

"Splendid," Mr. Rhys said, rubbing his hands together, though whether his enthusiasm was for her declaration or for the tray of tea and Welsh cakes Mrs. Price was carrying into the sitting room was unclear. Perhaps it was for both.

He stayed for an hour. Samantha accompanied him to the garden gate when he was leaving since the rain had stopped. Looking up as his carriage moved off, she could see that the clouds were higher and whiter and that there were a few breaks in them, through which she could catch glimpses of blue sky. Perhaps after all the afternoon would be bright and warm.

Tramp was standing at her side, breathing heavily.

"Oh, very well," she said. "But you must give me a moment to fetch my bonnet and put on my half boots. The ground is wet."

She was rich, she thought as she stepped inside, and her stomach lurched at the realization. But *rich* was not quite a strong enough word. She was downright *wealthy*.

With property and money her mother had wanted no part of.

*O*ne thing he was not, Ben decided as he drove a hired gig over to the cottage in the afternoon, was a writer. He could see scenery and points of special interest in his head. He could people each scene with interesting characters and their stories. He could formulate his reactions to it all. He could even get it all down on paper without too much difficulty. The problem, though, was that there was an enormous difference between what he saw and heard in his head and felt in his heart on the one hand and, on the other, what was written on the three closely spaced pages with which he ended up. Somewhere between the two all the life and color and excitement had been drained away to leave cold, hard, uninspired fact.

The only thing any reader would be inspired to do if he plodded through it all was stay home and forget about any itch to travel he might have felt.

No, he was no writer. It was perhaps a bit defeatist to give up after his very first attempt. But the point was that the whole process had bored him horribly—from the daily scribblings in his journal to the organizing of ideas into some sort of outline to the attempted writing of an opening chapter. It had felt like being back at school, compelled to write essays upon subjects that were as dry as dust. This was decidedly *not* what he wanted to be doing for the rest of his life.

Which left an unsettling void—again.

Quinn was beside him in the gig, though Ben had protested that he did not need to come. His valet was going to unhitch the horse and get it settled in the barn, and then he was going to walk back to the village. He had wanted to take the gig with him and return with it later to drive Ben back to the inn, but Ben had said a firm no. He did not know what time he would be returning. It might be seven or eight o'clock, or it might be midnight. He did not want to have Quinn arriving outside the garden gate with the gig at some inconvenient time.

He tried not to think about that possible midnight departure. And he tried not to think about swimming and making an ass of himself—or drowning himself. The clouds had moved off and the sun was shining. It was warm. There was no excuse *not* to swim—unless he offered to guard her towel and clothes while she swam alone.

Coward, she had called him yesterday—just before he kissed her.

Well, he could not allow that accusation to become reality, could he, he thought as he walked from the barn to the house. A coward was something he had never been, except recently.

"Ben."

She was out in the garden again with the dog. She was wearing the floppy-brimmed bonnet and a high-waisted, short-sleeved dress of white muslin embroidered all over with peach rosebuds. It had a deep frill about the hem. And it was very obvious to him that she was wearing no stays beneath it. She was hurrying toward him, both hands extended. But she looked at his canes when she got close and clasped her hands beneath her chin instead. She was looking agitated.

"Ben, I am quite horribly wealthy."

"Horribly?" He was tempted to grin, but something about her expression stopped him.

"Mr. Rhys was here this morning," she told him. "He brought a statement from the bank. I could buy half of England."

"But would you want to?" he asked her.

"I had *no* idea," she said. "My mother did not tell me. Neither did my father after she died or later, when I married. He ought to have told me. John did not tell me."

"What are you going to do?" he asked her. "About your grandfather, I mean. I have heard that he is away from home at present. Though he is expected home soon."

"I hope he never comes back," she said vehemently. "I hope he keeps his distance from me forever. My great-aunt I *can* forgive. She was strict with my mother, but I daresay she did not mean to be cruel. I can never forgive *him*."

"Perhaps," he said, "people need to be allowed to tell their stories."

"When has he ever tried to tell his to me?" She looked stormy. "Trust you to take a man's part."

"We had better go swimming," he said.

She looked mulish for a few moments and then visibly relaxed. "Yes," she said. "Let's, or I will be quarreling with you when it is not you who has offended me. Let's forget everything except the sand and the water and the freedom and happiness of a sunny afternoon. And the fact that we are together."

Sometimes it was good just to forget all that perhaps one ought to remember and simply live for the moment.

Sometimes the moment was all that really mattered.

17

❧

$\mathcal{S}$amantha set her shoes and stockings on the rock where she had left them the day before. Her dress, bonnet, and shift were her only remaining garments. She felt very daring and really quite wicked. But there was no point in walking down onto the beach clad in all the usual finery of a lady. It would only have to come off again before she could swim.

The beach, she had decided yesterday on her first visit, was going to be her place of freedom, the place where nothing mattered but the moment in which she lived and the beauty with which she was surrounded.

As soon as she stepped onto it today, she left behind the heavy burden of her wealth; the disturbing glimpses she had had into her family past; the knowledge that her grandfather, who had abandoned her mother, was as rich as a nabob, to use Ben's words, and lived in that shining mansion on the hill ironically called *home*. She left behind the gloom of a recent bereavement, the stern disapproval of her in-laws, the fact that she could not turn for sympathy or help or affection to any member of her father's family. She ignored the fact that soon, probably *very* soon, Ben would be leaving to continue his journey and she would never see him again.

He was with her now, and that was really all that mattered.

And they were on the beach, where *nothing* else mattered but the freedom to enjoy the moment. *Everyone should have such a retreat,* she thought. How very fortunate she was.

"I have never swum in the ocean," she said, matching her pace to his, though she would have liked to stride along and even run, and watching an ever-hopeful Tramp go galloping after gulls. "I suppose it is very different from swimming in a lake."

"In several ways," he said. "The water is more buoyant because it is salty. But that makes it uglier to swallow and harder on the eyes. You have to watch out for waves breaking over your head. You may wade in until you are waist deep and then swim in the same area for five minutes only to find when you put your feet down that you are chin deep or knee deep—or out of your depth."

"What if I cannot still swim?" she asked him.

He stopped to look at her.

"Remind me," he said, "of who it was who assured me just yesterday that one does not forget."

She laughed at him.

All traces of the morning's gray weather had been blown away to leave blue sky and sunshine overhead and a sea that sparkled beneath it. The tide was higher up the beach than it had been yesterday morning, almost fully in, in fact. The rock where they had sat was not far from its edge, though the dry sand about it suggested that it was above the normal high tide mark.

"We can leave our towels there," she suggested, pointing to the rock.

He had a bag slung over his shoulder and had more in it than just a towel, she suspected. She had not brought any clothes but the ones she wore.

She set down her towel and took off her bonnet. She made sure her hair was in a tight knot at her neck and that all the pins were pushed in firmly. But Gladys had done her job thoroughly. She had also been a bit giggly when she knew that Samantha was not going to wear her stays.

"Are you just going to wear your shift in the water, Mrs. McKay?" she had asked. "I am envious, I am. It's turned into a beautiful day, hasn't it? And that major is going to swim too, is he? He is ever so gorgeous, isn't he, even if he is a little bit crippled. I wouldn't mind seeing him stripped down for a swim, I can tell you."

"Gladys!"

"Oh, sorry, Mrs. McKay," she had said, coloring.

Samantha smiled now at the memory. And she pulled her dress determinedly off over her head even though she felt very exposed in just her knee-length shift. One could hardly go swimming fully clothed, could one?

He had removed his hat and his coat and waistcoat and neckcloth, she saw when she turned. He had just sat down on the rock to pull off his boots and stockings. It was not easy for him to do, she could see.

"Would you like me to help?" she asked.

He looked up and shaded his eyes with one hand—and said nothing while his eyes roamed over her from head to foot.

"Sorry," he muttered after a few lengthy moments and lowered the hand. "No, thank you. I can manage."

She felt scorched by his glance.

It took him a while. He was so very different from Matthew, she thought as she watched. He was stubbornly independent.

There was a wicked-looking scar across the top of one of his feet, she saw when he had removed his stockings—gouged there by a stirrup, perhaps? He was fortunate that his foot had not been completely severed. He was not, she realized, going to remove his pantaloons. But he pulled his shirt free of them, crossed his arms, and hauled it off over his head.

She stood looking at him while he raised his eyes to

hers. She had lain close to his naked upper body that night at the inn, but she had not seen it, and she had not explored it with her hands. There was a nasty puckered scar between his heart and his shoulder.

"A bullet?" she asked.

"I was more fortunate than Captain McKay," he said. "The surgeon was able to dig it out."

She winced.

His chest bore other scars, some worse than others, as did both his arms. Any one of those wounds could surely have killed him. She raised her eyes to his and licked her lips.

"You were in more than one battle?"

"Eight," he said, "and a number of more minor skirmishes. Cavalry are always getting embroiled in skirmishes."

Rather than marring his appearance, the scars somehow accentuated his masculinity. And it was very clear that he worked on his physique. His muscles were firm and well defined. He looked suddenly like a tough, even brutal soldier. Brutal in battle, that was. But magnificent as a lover?

She took a step back and turned to look at the water. There was an uncomfortable throbbing in her womb, and the sun felt hotter than it had a few minutes ago.

"The water is close," she said. "Can you walk there without your canes if you set an arm about my shoulders?"

"You are not my servant," he said.

"Is it *such* a humiliation," she asked him, "to set your arm about me and lean on me for a short distance? Will it quite diminish your masculinity?"

His jaw was set hard when she turned back to him. But he nodded and then smiled.

"I believe it will *challenge* my masculinity," he said. "I have noticed, you see, that you are scantily clad."

So *that* was the reason he was reluctant to touch her?

"Are you a prude, Major Harper?" she asked him.

"Merely a normal red-blooded male, ma'am," he said brusquely, getting to his feet with the aid of his canes and then setting them back against the rock and taking two steps without them before reaching for her. "Lead me to cold water, please. And the faster the better."

It was amazing what a difference a few layers of clothing could make—or the lack of those layers. Yesterday she had been aware of his lean, strong physique as they walked in the water and it had attracted her. Today she could feel the power in his bare arm about her shoulders and was aware of the rippling muscles in his chest, pressed to her side. She was aware of his masculine hip, of the warmth of his skin. She was aware of his height—a few inches above her own. And she was aware of her own near nakedness next to him.

She felt as if some of her half-shriveled youth was gathering itself into bud getting ready to burst into bloom again.

She turned her face up to his as they reached the incoming water and laughed.

"It is c-c-cold," she said, deliberately stuttering as they stepped into it. She splashed it with her feet and sent cold droplets splashing all over them. "We are going to f-freeze."

Tramp was running along the edge of the water behind them, barking with excitement and further wetting them.

"It is too late to change your mind now," he said, grinning back at her. "I am going in, and you must too because I need you to get from here to there."

An incoming wave broke over their knees, and Samantha gasped.

"Whose silly idea *was* this?" she asked.

"I am not even going to venture an answer to that," he said. "I am ever the gentleman."

By the time the water reached her waist and then higher, Samantha thought the idea worse than just silly. His arm was a little less heavy about her shoulders, she noticed. And then it was gone altogether and he had ducked beneath the surface of the water. He came up, shaking his head so that she was showered with droplets, and spreading his arms along the water. And he was standing alone, she realized. His dark hair was plastered to his head. Water was beaded on his face and eyelashes.

He was all handsome, virile masculinity, and he was upright, unaided by either canes or her shoulders. Oh, how absolutely *gorgeous* he must once have been.

He grinned at her, and she grasped her nose between a thumb and forefinger and went under. She came up gasping and sputtering.

"Oh," she said, "I see what you mean by buoyancy and taste. Here comes a swell."

But they had come too far in for it to break over them in foam. Samantha lifted her feet and bobbed over it at the same time as Ben lay back on the water and floated. He was not, then, going to sink like a stone and drown.

She watched as he turned onto his front and began to swim in a slow crawl, his powerful arms doing most of the work, though his legs were moving too, propelling him along. She swam to catch up with him and realized that she had been right yesterday. She had not forgotten how. Neither had he. She would have whooped with delight if she had had the breath.

She drew level with him, and they swam side by side, stroke for stroke.

It seemed to Samantha that she had never been happier in her life. If only they could swim forever and never have to go back to shore.

* * *

*B*en could have wept. Not only could he remember how to swim, but also he *could* swim. He could move his legs without pain.

He could move.

Without pain.

He was free.

He did not know how far he had swum before he became aware of Samantha alongside him. And that was strange since he had been aware of her with every fiber of his being ever since he set eyes upon her back at the cottage. And when she had stripped down to her shift . . . Well, it was difficult to find words. And then when he had stepped up beside her to set his arm about her shoulders . . .

Her very dark hair was plastered to her head and held in its tight knot at her neck. Two shapely bare arms came out of the water, one after the other in a steady, graceful rhythm, and slid back beneath the surface. He could see the outline of her body through the water, her shift like a second skin. Her legs, propelling her along, were long and sturdy and shapely and mostly bare. She was not slender, but she was beautifully, perfectly proportioned. She was every man's dream of femininity.

She caught his eye and smiled. He smiled back.

She rolled onto her back and floated, her arms out to the sides. He floated beside her. There was not a cloud in the sky.

This, he thought, was one of those rare, perfect moments. He wanted to capture it and keep it and treasure it so that he could look at it from time to time and feel again what he felt now. But of course, he could do just that. It was called memory.

"You were swimming," she said.

"So were you."

"You were *swimming,* Ben."

He turned his head to look at her. "You were right. I *can* swim."

If he had been able to get down onto the beach at Penderris, perhaps he would have discovered it long ago. If he had been able to spend more time at Kenelston after leaving Penderris, perhaps he would have gone to the lake and made the discovery there. But it had never occurred to him that there was an element in which he would not be handicapped—or not completely so, anyway. So far he had tried only a very leisurely crawl. But perhaps he could build strength in the water by challenging himself to try more vigorous strokes. Perhaps he had not, after all, reached the limit of his physical capabilities.

She turned her head to look back at him. "I am right occasionally, you know."

Their fingertips touched inadvertently as they bobbed on the water, and then they touched deliberately. He rested his hand on top of hers, and she turned it so that they were palm to palm.

"I am glad there has been this day," she said.

"So am I."

"Will you remember this when you have traveled far and wide and gathered enough material for ten books?" she asked him. "And become hugely famous?"

"I will remember," he assured her. "And will *you* remember when you have an army of friends and admirers here and are busily involved in village and parish life? And when you have learned Welsh and have sung to help raise the roof off the church?"

She smiled. "I will remember."

They floated for a while longer. The dog, he could see when he looked, was stretched out by the rock and the towels and their discarded clothes. The sun was warm.

There was nothing for her in England. There was

nothing for him here. There was nothing there for him either unless he asserted himself at Kenelston or else set up house in London or Bath or somewhere else where he could establish some sort of routine and some sort of social life. He was *not* going to be a traveler. He could not bear the thought of doing it alone. And he never wanted to see a journal or a blank sheet of paper again. Perhaps he ought to try some sort of career. In business or commerce, perhaps, or the law? Or in the diplomatic service? He had never before given serious thought to actually *working,* except as a landowner on his own land. He did not need to work, after all, since he was in possession of a sizable fortune.

But now was not the time to consider his future.

Now was the time for *now.* Now was one of those rare and precious moments with which one was gifted from time to time. That was all it was. A moment. But it was one to be enjoyed to the full while it lasted and treasured for a lifetime after it was over.

"And it is not even over yet," she said, echoing his thought.

"No."

There was still dinner to be enjoyed at the cottage. And then . . .

He was not at all sure it would be wise. He could, if he chose, enumerate in his mind all the many reasons—and there *were* many, for both of them—why it would *not* be. But he was not going to think. He was going to hold on to the moment. The rest of the day would look after itself.

She had turned onto her front and had begun to swim slowly back toward the beach. He followed her.

"Stay here," she said, when she was able to stand in the water. "I shall fetch your canes."

The tide had ebbed a bit, he could see. It was a farther

walk to the rock now than it had been when they came in.

He trod water and watched her return across the sand, his canes held in one of her hands. Her shift clung to her body, leaving virtually nothing to the imagination. Yet she seemed unself-conscious.

She was beautiful beyond belief. And desirable beyond words.

"Life is really not fair," she cried, splashing back into the water. "It was freezing coming in, and now it is freezing getting out." She held the canes high as she waded toward him.

"Whoever told you," he asked her, "that life was fair?"

He took his canes from her. It was time to be earthbound again.

The dog was prancing at the edge of the water, barking at them, impatient for them to emerge.

Ben leaned one shoulder against the rock when he had reached it and rubbed his towel over his upper body and his hair. He would change into the dry pantaloons he had brought with him if she would turn her back.

"I did not bring a dry shift," she said, and his hand paused with the towel held to one side of his head. "I thought I would let it dry here in the sun."

But she did not mean what he thought she meant, he realized when he saw her spread her towel on the sand. She was not about to strip it off.

"Shall we lie down and soak up some sunshine before going back to the cottage?" she suggested.

"Have you heard of a beached whale?" he asked her.

She looked at him, arrested.

"You would not be able to get up again, would you?" she said and then laughed. "I am so sorry. I did not think of that. How foolish of me."

"Lie down," he said. "I will sit here."

She regarded the stone ledge on which they had sat yesterday.

"You can stretch out along it," she said, "and relax better. You could get up from there, could you not?"

And so they lay side by side on their towels, though she was three feet below him on the beach. He shaded his eyes with one forearm.

"Are not ladies supposed to protect their complexions from the merest suggestion of sunlight?" he asked.

"I have the complexion of a Gypsy," she said. "Even when I have not been in the sun people frown upon me because my face is not all porcelain and peaches and roses. Why bother depriving myself of feeling the heat and light of the sun on my face, then? You cannot know how irksome it was for almost four months to have to wear a black veil every time I set foot over the doorstep— when I *did* step outside, that was. Oh, Ben, there was not even any daylight in the house. Matilda insisted that the curtains be almost closed across every window. Sometimes, when she was not in the room with me, I used to stand in the band of daylight and breathe in gulps, as though I had been suffocating."

"Those days are gone," he said.

"Yes," she agreed. "Thank God. And I am *not* blaspheming."

They were probably both going to end up with some sunburn. He did not care.

"Am I horribly wicked—?"

"No," he said, not giving her time to finish.

"Just over five months ago," she said, "Matthew was alive."

"And just over five months ago," he said, "you were spending every moment of your time with him, tending him and comforting him as well as you were able."

"It is difficult to keep the world at bay, is it not?" she said. "I swore that I would not think of a thing while we were down here except the sheer enjoyment of being here."

Without thinking he stretched down a hand toward her, and she took it and held it.

"You can come here whenever you want for the rest of your life," he reminded her.

"But not with you."

He could think of no answer to that, and she did not seem to want to elaborate. They lay for a while, hand in hand. Then she got to her feet and stood looking down at him. The front of her shift had dried. It did not cling quite so provocatively.

"I shall wonder about you for the rest of my life," she said. "I shall wonder what happened to you. I shall wonder if you found what you were looking for. I suppose I will never know."

"Perhaps," he said, "you will write to my sister at some time in the future, when you feel more secure here."

"Ah, yes, of course," she said. "She will tell me about you. And then perhaps you will learn something of me too. If you wish to do so, that is."

He took one of her hands in his again and drew it to his lips.

"It would not work for us, Samantha," he said.

"No," she agreed. "A mutual attraction is not enough, is it?"

He kissed her knuckles.

"But perhaps," she said, her eyes on their hands, "just for a day—or two or three. Perhaps for a week. Can you bear to stay a week?"

He inhaled slowly. "Your grandfather is expected home in the next few days," he said. "I suppose he will discover that you are living here. Perhaps he will choose to ignore you. Or perhaps not. Perhaps *you* will choose to ignore *him*. However it is, I cannot bring myself to leave until . . . well, until things are more settled for you. I know you do not like me flexing my male muscles on your behalf. I know you can manage alone. But . . ."

"But you will stay anyway?"

"Yes," he said. "For a few more days. A week."

"Oh, Tramp." She looked down at the dog, which was making loud lapping noises. "Is my leg salty and must be licked clean? You absurd dog."

"He is a dog to be envied," Ben said, and she looked back at him, startled, and laughed.

He swung his legs carefully over the edge of the rock and sat up. He pulled his shirt on over his head. He looked at her and marveled again at the realization that she was the same woman as the morbidly black-clad figure he had almost bowled over with his horse not so very long ago. She was looking disreputable and slightly disheveled now even though most of her hair was still confined in the knot at her neck. She was looking quite scandalously sun-bronzed and bright-eyed and happy. Her nose was shining.

He set his hands on either side of her waist, drew her against him between his legs, and kissed her. She tasted of salt and summer sun.

"You taste salty," she told him. "Now I know why Tramp is enjoying licking my leg."

They grinned at each other and kissed open-eyed.

"There is a Latin phrase," she said. "Something about carps, though not really."

"Carpe diem?"

"The very one," she said. "The day flies, or the day is fleeting. Or make the most of what you have now this moment because soon it will be gone." She rested her forehead against his.

"I am afraid of hurting you, Samantha," he said with a sigh. "Or perhaps myself."

"Physically?" she said. "No, you do not mean that,

do you? I think I would be hurt more if you just simply . . . left. Is that what you want to do?"

He closed his eyes and inhaled. "No."

"Go on back to the house," she said. "You can change
your clothes there and wash with hot water. I am going
to have a run with Tramp."

And she pulled on her dress and bonnet and dashed
off along the beach with the dog in hot pursuit. Where
were the stays, and the silk stockings and slippers, and
the gloves and the parasol, and the mincing steps of
a respectable lady of *ton*? He smiled after her, admiring her bare, sandy ankles and her exuberance.

She wanted him. He wondered if he would disappoint
her—or worse.

But enough of that. He was not going to be offering
himself for a lifetime, after all, was he? He would give
as much of himself as he could for both their pleasure—
and pray God there would not be too much pain the
other side of the pleasure.

For he feared they were playing with fire.

18

❧

*M*rs. Price cooked them a chicken-and-vegetable pie, which she explained was her son's favorite dish and had been her late husband's. It was to be preceded by leek soup and followed by jellies and custard. She set out cups and saucers with sugar and milk and a cloth-covered plate of cake on a tray in the kitchen. The kettle was left to hum on the kitchen range with the tea-pot warming beside it.

Gladys laced Samantha into her stays and helped her into her rose-colored silk evening gown, which she had ironed carefully so that even the two frills about the hem and the small ones that edged the sleeves were free of wrinkles. She dressed Samantha's still slightly damp hair in an elegantly piled and curled coiffure. She clasped the pearls about her neck and clipped pearl ear-rings to her lobes before standing back to admire her handiwork.

"Oh, you do look lovely, Mrs. McKay," she said. "I bet you could turn heads even at one of them grand balls in London town."

"And all thanks to you, Gladys," Samantha said with a smile. "But all I have to attend is dinner downstairs."

"It is with the major, though," her maid said with a sigh. Clearly she was smitten with Ben. "I bet you will turn *his* head."

"If I do," Samantha said, rising from the stool in

front of her dressing table, "I shall be sure to tell him that it is all thanks to you."

"Oh, go on with you," Gladys said, blushing rosily. "He will only have to take one look at you to know how silly *that* is. You could be dressed in a sack and outshine every other lady for miles around."

Samantha did feel good, even exuberant. She had used to feel just so when dressing for assemblies and balls during her youth and the early months of her marriage. But, it struck her suddenly, perhaps it was unfair of her to dress with particular care for the evening when Ben would be wearing the clothes in which he had come from the village this afternoon, or, rather, the dry ones into which he had changed after their swim.

She was not sorry, though, when she saw the admiration in his eyes as she joined him in the parlor. And he looked very good indeed to her eyes. He must have found a brush with which to rid his coat and boots of all traces of sand. And polish too—his boots gleamed. His waistcoat was neatly buttoned beneath his coat, and he had tied a fresh neckcloth in a style more suited to evening. His hair was neatly combed into a Brutus style, which suited him.

He got to his feet, even though she signaled him with one hand to stay where he was, and made her a courtly bow.

"You look beautiful," he said.

"Despite the sunburn?"

His own face was ruddy with color, but attractively so. He looked healthy and virile.

"The sun turns your complexion bronze instead of scarlet," he said. "Yes, beautiful despite the sun."

Mrs. Price appeared in the doorway at that moment to inform them that she had set the hot dishes on the table and they must come now if they did not want their food cold and spoiled. And she would, if it was all the same to Mrs. McKay, hang up her apron and walk home with Gladys.

And so they dined alone together, Samantha and Ben, though Tramp came padding in from the kitchen to plop down in front of the empty fireplace and keep an eye out for fallen morsels of food. None did fall, but Ben fed him a few morsels anyway, to Samantha's amusement. He pretended to dislike the dog, but she had never believed him, for Tramp liked *him*, and dogs did not like people who disliked them.

The food was plain but wholesome and delicious.

He told her some stories from his military years—not anything about the fighting and the violence, but amusing anecdotes. She told him stories about her year with Matthew's regiment, mostly funny little incidents involving the other wives that she had not thought of in years. He told her stories from his Penderris years— again light, entertaining incidents involving his friends. She told him about the kittens at Leyland Abbey. A groom had discovered a litter of them in the loft of a barn and had concealed them and tended them in secret so that they would not be drowned—until Samantha had caught him at it. But she had not reported him. Rather, she had aided and abetted him and had loved those kittens until they grew into cats and deserted in order to earn their living and their daily bread as mousers.

"Ungrateful wretches," she said, laughing softly.

She had forgotten until now that there was anything at all good about that year in Kent.

"But you would not have wanted them at your heels for the rest of their lives, would you?" he asked.

"Oh, heavens, no," she said. "There were eight of them."

"The dog's nose would be severely out of joint," he said.

"Yes," she agreed. "Poor Tramp. He would have been

grossly outnumbered and would doubtless have slunk along at the back of the line instead of asserting his superior size. He does not *know* he is large, you see. He believes he is a puppy."

They both laughed, and Tramp thumped his tail on the floor where he sat.

Samantha cleared the table and carried the dishes into the kitchen, where she stacked them on the counter. She made the tea and carried the tray into the sitting room and lit the lamp. And they sat and talked more—mainly about books this time—while they drank their tea and the sky beyond the window turned a deeper blue. And then indigo.

Then it was dark.

She got up to close the curtains.

And suddenly there was no way of reviving the conversation. The very fact she had moved had acknowledged the fact that night had fallen and they were here together in her cottage, quite unchaperoned. She stood facing the window for a few moments even though she had already drawn the curtains.

"Should I leave?" he asked. "Do you *wish* me to leave?"

Perhaps she should simply say yes. Nothing much had happened between them so far, despite a rather lengthy journey that had thrown them into proximity. In another few days he would be gone. And it had to be that way. There could be no future together, for any number of reasons. Perhaps it would be better not to take that extra step into the unknown, the unpredictable.

Perhaps it would be disappointing if they did proceed. No, that was not what made her hesitate. Perhaps it would be painful. Not the act itself, but its aftermath. For he *would* leave. There *would* be a goodbye. Which would be more painful? Not to have slept with him and forever regret it? Or to have slept with him and forever . . . regret it?

He had asked her a question. Two, actually.

She shook her head as she turned. "No, don't leave."

And so she committed herself.

She watched as he got to his feet, using his canes, and she moved toward him until she was standing in front of him.

"Don't leave," she said again, and she lifted her hands to cup his face. He had even shaved, she realized. He must have brought his razor with him. He must have expected to stay.

"Are you sure you will not regret it?" he asked her. "I cannot take you with me, Samantha. I am, at least for the present, a nomad. And I cannot stay. There is nothing for me here. Besides, it is too soon for you to remarry. And I cannot . . . ever marry. I do not have wholeness to offer."

Because he was half crippled? Strangely, she would have agreed with him just a few weeks ago. She had wanted nothing more to do with wounds and disfigurement. But, slow as he was in his movements, it was hard to think of him as disabled. Except that he could not hold her now because he needed his hands for his canes.

"I was once promised a lifetime," she said, "and was given four months. Not even that, actually, as it was all illusion from the start. It was all a lie. This afternoon you promised me a week. Let us make it a week to remember."

"An affair to remember?" he said.

"With pleasure and affection," she said. "And no regrets. Will *you* regret it? Would you rather go back to the inn?"

For a few moments she thought he was going to say yes. Then he dipped his head closer to hers, closed his eyes, and set his forehead against hers.

"I am afraid," he said, "that I will be inadequate."

Did he mean impotent? Did he fear that?

"I am afraid I will disappoint you," he said.

She stepped back from him and smiled as she went to fetch the lamp.

"Come upstairs," she said. "Even if you do no more than hold me, I will not be disappointed. One of my loveliest recent memories is of waking at that inn where we were forced to share a room to find you holding me against you, one arm about me. It was so very long before that since anyone had so much as touched me—except you, when you kissed me at Bramble Hall."

Tramp padded off to the bed Mrs. Price had made him in a corner of the kitchen, next to the stove and his water bowl, and Samantha led the way upstairs, holding the lamp aloft so that he could see his way. She closed the curtains in her bedchamber and watched him remove his coat and waistcoat and neckcloth. She watched him pull off his shirt to reveal his muscled, suntanned, scarred chest. Only then did she move toward the dressing table.

"Allow me," he said, and he crossed the room, propped his canes against the side of the dressing table, sat on the bench, spread his legs wide, and drew her down to sit between them, her back against his chest.

His fingers worked at her hair, and she tipped her head downward, watching his hand as it came forward to deposit pins until her hair fell about her shoulders. He took up her brush and began to draw it through the curls Gladys had so carefully created.

"Two hundred strokes?" he asked, his voice low against her ear.

She shivered slightly. "One hundred will do."

"In a rush, are you?" he asked.

"No." She sighed and closed her eyes. "Time does not exist. I do not want it to exist."

"Then it does not," he said and drew the brush through

her hair until she could feel that all the tangles had gone—and all the curls too.

She did not count, but after a while he tossed the brush back onto the dressing table and undid the clasp of her pearls. He unclipped her earrings. And his fingers worked down the line of fasteners at the back of her dress until he could fold back the edges and set his lips against her shoulder blades, one at a time. She was holding the dress against her bosom, but he reached around and removed her hands and drew the dress down over her arms, and down over her breasts until she was bare above her shift and her stays.

His hands cupped her breasts, pushed high by her stays. His fingers were warm as they played lightly over her flesh until she could feel a stabbing of sensation down through her womb and along her inner thighs. He caught her nipples between a finger and thumb of each hand and rolled them before rubbing his thumbs over the tips. She pressed her head back against his shoulder and opened her eyes—and met his gaze in the glass in the flickering light of the lamp.

She could, she realized, watch what he did, as he was doing it.

Oh, dear God.

She spread her hands over his clad thighs on either side of her body, but lightly lest she hurt him.

And he unlaced her stays and stood her up in front of him and stripped her clothes down her body until they were pooled at her feet. Then he drew her down to sit in front of him again.

She was still wearing her silk stockings and her pink garters, she thought as she watched his hands move over her—and felt them too. Her arms and shoulders and a deep half circle above her breasts were bronzed from this afternoon's exposure to the sun. The rest of her was pale in comparison. His hands too were bronzed.

He had been celibate as long as she. But he obviously knew a great deal more than she ever had. And, as with swimming, it seemed it was not something he had forgotten. He knew just where to touch her, and just how— with his palms, with his fingers, fingertips, and thumbs, with his fingernails. And finally the fingers of one hand slid lightly through the triangle of hair at the apex of her thighs, and pushed downward and inward, cupping her heat, pressing into her most private place, lightly probing and stroking there. His thumb circled lightly a little higher until she felt such a raw ache of longing that she cried out and shuddered against him and would have doubled over if his free arm had not held her firmly back against his chest.

"Oh." She was panting for breath. She felt hot and damp and suddenly drained of energy in a thoroughly pleasurable way. "I am so sorry."

His laughter and his voice were low against her ear. "Sorry? I certainly hope not."

And she knew that she was the merest novice, that he had made love to her with his hand and given her that exquisite pleasure quite deliberately with the skill of his fingers.

"But I am not able to give *you* any pleasure," she protested.

"Are you sure?" He laughed against her ear again, and she looked at him in the mirror and saw his eyes, heavy with . . . what? Desire? Passion? Sheer enjoyment?

He was, she thought, incredibly handsome.

"You are almost fully clothed," she complained.

"That can be remedied." He stood her up again and reached for his canes. "Lie down on the bed."

She turned back the covers, sat on the edge of the

mattress, and removed her stockings while he watched. She had never been naked with a man before. She did not feel self-conscious, though. Perhaps it was because the lamplight was soft and flattering. Or perhaps it was because of that look in his eyes. Or because he had made love to her with his hand and she was still warm with pleasure.

She lay down and watched him seat himself at the bottom of the bed and pull off his boots and stockings. Poor man, it was the second time in one day he had had to do that without the aid of his valet, and it very evidently was not easy.

And then he stood and extinguished the lamp, which was standing on the table beside the bed. She could hear him removing his lower garments. It was disappointing. She wanted to watch. And she wanted them to be able to watch each other as they loved. But even through his clothes it was evident that his legs were somewhat deformed, and that the muscles were not as developed as those on the upper part of his body. It was understandable that, unlike her, he *did* mind being seen naked.

"I only hope—" he began as he lay down beside her.

But somehow in the darkness she found his mouth with her hand and covered it.

"Ben," she said, turning onto her side. "I did not know you before you were injured. The man you were then does not exist for me. Only the man you are now. And *this* is the man with whom I have chosen to have an affair. It does not matter if you do not have great prowess. I do not have any expertise either. I have known one other man, and that for only a brief time almost seven years ago when I was seventeen."

"I cannot move nimbly," he said, "even when I am lying down. Only in the water, it seems. Perhaps we ought to be doing this there."

She raised herself on one elbow and pushed at his shoulder until he was lying on his back.

"Ah," she said, lowering her mouth to his, "but I can move nimbly."

"Heaven help me." She heard him laugh softly as he reached out to hold her by the hips.

She moved over him until she lay on top of him, her legs on either side of his lest she give him pain. And she breathed in the warmth and the slightly musky smell of him mingled with the salty smell of the sea, though he had washed after coming up from the beach. Her breasts pressed against the warm, hard muscles of his chest. She set her mouth to his and opened to the pressure of his tongue.

She straddled him at the hips, raising herself onto her knees so that she could move her hands over him and feel all the magnificence of his physique. And so that she would feel his hands on her—on her breasts, up over her shoulders, down her back, over her hips and along her outer thighs to her knees, up to cup her bottom. She lowered her head to kiss his chest, to lick his nipples and nip them between her teeth, and with her hands she felt the narrowness of his waist and hips, the warmth between his thighs, the hard thickness of his arousal.

She took it in her hands and both felt and heard him inhale slowly. She caressed him with her palms and with her fingertips while he grew harder.

She lifted herself higher onto her knees, spread them wider, held him against the most tender part of herself, and lowered herself onto him as his hands came to her hips again and clasped them firmly.

For a moment, when she was deeply penetrated, she tightened inner muscles and held still, her head bent forward, her eyes tightly closed. There was surely no lovelier feeling in the world. Ah, there could not possibly be. And he was Ben. He was her lover.

It was a word she spoke consciously in her mind, savoring it.

He was her lover.

Better than husband. Ah, far better. There was freedom in being a lover. Pleasure freely given and freely received.

His hands lifted her slightly by the hips, and suddenly he was in command, moving in her, withdrawing and thrusting with firm, deep strokes that had her reaching for his chest with her fingertips to steady herself and tipping back her head so that she could *feel*. He was working fast and hard but with a steady rhythm that invited a slight turning of her hips to circle his thrusts and a contracting and relaxing of inner muscles to gather him deeper and release him. And she braced her knees and rode while his hips flexed and relaxed against her inner thighs and his breathing became labored and his chest and her hands on it became hot and slick with sweat, and always, unrelentingly, he demanded entrance to . . . where?

Where else was there to go? He was already deeper than deep.

But then something opened up anyway, something deep within, something soft, near painful, beyond words to describe, and he came in hard and deep and thrusting and she closed around him and spilled out all the inner wonder of that unknown place and whispered his name.

He came two, three, four more times into that soft, lovely place, thrusting his demand and then finding his own place. She felt heat, heard him sigh, felt him gradually relax, and went down into his waiting arms until she was lying along his body again, her legs straight beside his own. They were still joined.

Was it impotence he had feared? Perhaps she had

feared it too—for his sake. She almost laughed with de-light.

A few moments later she felt the bedcovers come up over her back and shoulders. His arms held them in place, and they lay still and relaxed in each other's arms for several minutes.

"We forgot something," he said at last, his voice soft against her ear.

"Mm?" She was more than half asleep.

"I spilled my seed in you," he said.

"Mm." She was awake now. The fingers of one of his hands were playing through her hair.

"We will have to make . . . arrangements before I leave," he said.

She opened her eyes to stare at the lighter square of the window.

"I must see to it that you have somewhere to write," he said, "if I need to come back."

She *had* thought of it but had deliberately ignored the thought, which was extremely foolish and irresponsible of her.

"I did not conceive during my marriage," she said.

"Which does not mean you are barren," he told her.

Did this mean their affair was over? Almost before it had begun? Would they not risk it again?

"I would not trap you into marriage," she told him.

"I do not doubt it," he said. "Though *trapped* would not be a pleasant word to use if there really were a child, would it?"

She did not answer him. But she did move off him to lie beside him. He reached for her hand and they laced their fingers.

"Must it end, then?" she asked him.

He did not answer immediately.

"Would it be a terrible disaster to you," he asked her, "to be with child? To have to marry me?"

"Not a disaster," she said. For a long time, while she had been living at Leyland Abbey, she had thought her life might be bearable if only she had a baby, though after Matthew was injured and came home, she had been deeply thankful that there was none. "Would it be a disaster to you?"

"If there *were* a child," he said, "I would not want to have to remember for the rest of my life that I had once called the possibility of his or her conception a disaster. Neither of us wants marriage, and the circumstances would make it difficult for us to marry even if we *did* want it. However, the needs of any child of mine will always come first in my life, and a child needs father and mother if it is humanly possible—married to each other and loving each other."

He spoke in a soft voice, obviously choosing his words with care. Samantha felt a deep welling of . . . grief? No, it was not grief. But it was something that made her ache with a nameless longing and brought tears to her eyes and the soreness of unshed tears to her throat.

. . . *married to each other and loving each other.*

How wonderful it would be to be loved by Benedict Harper and to share a child with him. If only the circumstances were different . . .

She rested her temple against his shoulder. It was not supposed to be like this. They were supposed to be having a brief affair, entirely for pleasure.

"What are we going to do?" she asked him.

"We promised each other a week of lovemaking," he said, "before we pick up the threads of our own separate lives. Shall we keep that promise and deal with any consequences that may arise if and when they do arise?"

She knew something then with a terrible clarity. She knew she was not made for casual affairs. She had thought after the first numbness of loss following Matthew's death had passed that all she wanted was to be free, to *live*. But all she really wanted to do, all she had ever wanted to do, was to love. And, if possible, to be loved.

Instead, she had begun an affair, something that by its very nature was temporary. Something that was purely carnal. Something that would leave her more bereft than she had ever felt before.

Unless there was a child.

Yet she must hope that there would *not* be, for she would not wish to bind him to her on such terms.

He squeezed her hand.

"I do not doubt," he said, "that there will be people to take note of the exact minute and hour at which I return to the inn. I would not be so late that it will be obvious I have done more here than dine with you and sit afterward over tea and conversation."

He leaned closer and kissed her on the lips, and then she swung her legs over the far side of the bed, got to her feet, and found her nightgown and dressing gown.

"I shall see you downstairs," she said and left him to get dressed.

She walked out to the barn with him fifteen minutes or so later in her slippers and dressing gown while Tramp galloped about the garden, delighted to have an outing he had not been expecting. She waited while Ben hitched up the horse to the gig.

He spread one arm to her before climbing in, and she stepped close to him and hugged him. He kissed her and smiled down at her in the moonlight.

"Thank you," he said.

"For?"

"For making me feel like a man again," he said.

"You always seem very much like one to me," she said, and she saw the flash of his smile in the darkness.

"Thank you," he said again, and he climbed slowly into the gig, settled his canes, gathered the ribbons in his hands, glanced at her once more, and gave the horse the signal to start.

"Good night, Samantha," he said.

"Good night, Ben."

She did shed tears after he had gone and after she could neither see nor hear the gig any longer. She could not help but think of the fact that in a week's time it would be goodbye, not just good night.

What had she done?

❦

$\mathcal{T}$he weather conspired in their favor. The sun shone from a cloudless sky for the next four days, and the air was unseasonably warm.

Samantha walked into the village one morning, and they borrowed the gig from the inn and drove across the bridge and along the narrow lane above the beach, stopping several times to look at the boats and breathe in the sea air. Ben chatted with a small group of fishermen while Samantha got out to take the dog for a short walk. They had luncheon together at the inn, Mrs. Price having been warned that her mistress would not be back at the cottage.

On the following morning an old friend of Miss Bevan's called at the cottage with her daughter to make Samantha's acquaintance. Ben heard all about the visit when he drove over later in the gig.

"They want me to go for tea one afternoon," she told him. "And you too, Ben, if you are still here. They were very kind. Mrs. Tudor told me so many stories about my great-aunt that I feel I almost knew her myself."

"You will go?" he asked.

"Of course," she said. "I will go as soon as— Well, as soon as I have a free afternoon."

As soon as he had gone, she had been about to say. But he was pleased for her. A few people in the village had nodded amiably to her and obviously knew who she was. The vicar and his wife had introduced themselves to her. Now an old friend of her great-aunt's and the woman's daughter had come calling and had invited her to return the visit. Yet she had been here only a few days. Soon enough she would belong here, as he gathered she had never had a chance to belong when she lived at Bramble Hall.

She would surely be happy here—though she had not yet met her grandfather, of course.

They swam each afternoon. It was almost like a drug to Ben. He was going to have to spend the rest of the summer after he left here close to the sea—perhaps at Brighton, though that was rather too fashionable a resort for his tastes. When he was swimming he could almost forget that his legs were half crippled.

In the water, he could even frolic to a certain degree. Sometimes they would race, and when he won—which was not every time—he would wait for her and then sweep her up into his arms and twirl with her, demanding kisses for a prize. Sometimes he would chase her and dive and come up beneath her and tumble her in the water until they both came up gasping and shaking water from their eyes and laughing.

He felt as if years had tumbled off him to be washed away by the tide. He felt almost like a normal man. He felt exuberant and full of energy. He felt alive. And he lived for the moment. There was no point in anticipating his departure at the end of the week. He would deal with it when the time came.

And there was no point in worrying every time they made love about impregnating her. Either they were going to have an affair or they were not—and since they *were,* then they might as well simply enjoy it. If he left her with child, she would write and tell him so—she had promised that—and he would return and marry her. It was not what either of them wanted. At least . . .

No, it was *not* what either of them wanted, but somehow they would work it out for the sake of the child.

It was perhaps a careless, irresponsible attitude to take, but Ben did not care. Sometimes one needed simply to surrender to happiness. Life offered little enough of it.

He *was* happy. He stayed at the cottage each day for dinner, which they always followed with tea and a leisurely conversation in the parlor. It somehow heightened the pleasure of their lovemaking, the fact that they did not tumble into bed at the earliest opportunity but first spent time enjoying each other's company.

They made love in darkness. He knew it disappointed her when he extinguished the lamp, but he really could not bear to have her see him as he was.

She came on top of him again on the second night. But after they had slept a short while, he turned with her and lay on her as he took her again. It was a little uncomfortable at first, and he did not know if it would be possible to continue without changing position, but passion overcame pain, and he held her arms above her head, their fingers tightly laced, and loved her with slow thoroughness until they both shuddered into release. And his legs, aching and cramped as they were afterward, survived the ordeal.

She was beautiful and voluptuous, smooth-skinned and silky-haired and fragrant with that faint scent of gardenia always clinging about her. She was warm and passionate and uninhibited in her pleasure. And he marveled over the fact that he *could* make love, and that he could give pleasure as well as receive it. He had been unnecessarily afraid that he could cause nothing but revulsion in any woman with whom he attempted intimacies. It had been foolish of him.

Except that she had not seen him.

He was always careful to return to the village and

the inn well before midnight. He supposed there was some talk and speculation anyway. It must be common knowledge, after all, that neither of her two servants lived in, that she had no lady companion, that she was alone from early evening to sometime before breakfast. But he did not want that talk to turn into open scandal.

Soon he would be gone and all talk would cease.

But he would not think of that yet. He had promised a week. He had promised it to both her and himself.

On the fifth day the sun still shone, though puffs of white cloud dotting the blue of the sky caused the occasional patch of shade and accompanying coolness. Ben went to the cottage with the gig as usual after luncheon, a towel and a dry pair of pantaloons in their bag beside him on the seat. When he drove past the house, however, there was no sign of Samantha in the garden as there usually was. Even the dog was nowhere in sight. She had still not come outside after he had unhitched the horse and walked back to the house.

She was in the sitting room, dressed smartly in a striped blue and cream muslin dress. She usually wore her oldest dresses to go swimming. And her hair had been styled in a high knot with curled tendrils at her temples and along her neck. She looked as pale as a ghost, or as pale as someone of her complexion who had spent much of the past week out in the sun could look. There was no smile on her face when she greeted him.

"Samantha?" he said, moving into the room and stopping to pat the tail-wagging dog on the head.

"I was foolish," she said. "I ought to have said no. I *did* say no but not firmly enough. I want to go swimming with you. It is a nice day, and we have so little time left."

He stood still in the middle of the room, leaning on his canes.

"What has happened?" he asked.

"I am expecting a *visitor*," she said with some venom.

"Oh?" But he could somehow guess.

"He sent his *secretary*," she said, "to discover if I am who I say I am, I suppose, though he *said* he had come to see if I would be at home for a visit from his employer this afternoon."

"Your grandfather?"

"*Mr. Bevan*," she said. "Did he think to impress me by sending his secretary?"

He sat down and propped his canes beside his chair. "Perhaps," he said, "he wished to give you some choice about whether you see him or not, Samantha. If he had come this morning instead of his secretary, you would have had no choice. Perhaps he does not wish to force himself upon you."

"Well," she said, "I know he does not wish to do *that*. He never has."

"But he is coming," he said.

"So it would seem."

She stared stormily at him, but he did not think she was really seeing him.

"I informed his secretary," she said, "that I did not want to talk with him or know him or even see him. He told me that if I intended to continue living here it was almost inevitable that I see his employer from time to time unless I meant to be a hermit. He asked me if I intend going to church here."

"Bevan goes?" he asked.

"Yes," she said. "And so I said I would receive him. I will tell him what I think and send him on his way and then the matter is dealt with and done with. Whenever chance brings us within sight of each other after today, we will be able to nod politely and continue with our own lives, undisturbed by our connection."

She did not sound at all convinced.

"Shall I leave?" he asked her.

"No!" Her hands gripped the arms of her chair. "No, please. It is horribly cowardly of me not to want to face him alone. Perhaps I ought. And I daresay you are itching to get away before he puts in an appearance. Are you?"

"Samantha," he said, "he is not my grandfather. And I daresay he is not a monster. If he is, I will be able to pose as your knight protector and fight him off with one of my canes. Either way, I will be happy to stay. I have a curiosity to see him."

And to witness their first meeting.

She tilted her head to the side suddenly, and the dog scrambled to his feet and barked once. Through the open window came the unmistakable sounds of an approaching carriage.

She wished she had gone to Leyland Abbey. Better the devil you know . . . But, no, nothing could be worse than life lived under the unyielding gaze of the Earl of Heathmoor.

Besides, this was *her* cottage. She had the power to admit or exclude whomever she wished. She had chosen to allow her grandfather to call on her—for this occasion only. Soon he would be gone again and she would be free.

But that did not seem to help much at this precise moment. She stayed where she was and Ben stayed where *he* was as the carriage drew up outside the garden gate and the sound of voices came through the window. The only one who did *not* stay where he was was Tramp. He stood at the sitting room door, his nose almost pressed against its outer edge, eagerness in every line of his ungainly body, his tail waving like a flag in a breeze.

There was a knock on the outer door, and it opened

almost immediately—Mrs. Price had obviously heard the arrival of the carriage too. There were a few moments of almost unbearable tension, and then there was a tap on the sitting room door. Mrs. Price opened it, and Tramp backed up a foot.

"Mr. Bevan, ma'am," Mrs. Price said, saucer-eyed, though she had known he was coming.

He was not a very tall man, but he was solid-looking and had *presence*. He carried himself with confidence. He was silver-haired, though there was still some darkness mixed with the silver. He had a pleasant, good-humored face. He must have been a handsome man in his younger years. Indeed, he still was distinguished looking. He was expensively, fashionably dressed.

Samantha was on her feet without having been aware of rising.

He looked at her and then down at Tramp, who was barking and prancing and generally behaving in an undisciplined manner.

"A gentleman does not make himself deliberately conspicuous in company," Mr. Bevan said with a lovely soft Welsh accent. "Sit."

And Tramp, the traitor, sat and gazed up at his new friend with intelligent eyes and lolling tongue and lightly thumping tail.

"Mrs. McKay?" Mr. Bevan said. "Samantha?"

He fixed his eyes upon her and advanced across the room with confident strides, his right hand extended. He was almost of a height with her, she realized.

She had no choice, short of being deliberately ill-mannered, but to set her hand in his. He held it in a warm clasp and set his other hand on top of it, all the while gazing at her face.

"You are not very like your mother," he said, "except in coloring. But, oh, girl, you do look like your grand-mother."

He raised her hand to his lips before relinquishing it.

"Mr. Bevan," she said. "May I present Major Sir Benedict Harper?"

Ben had also got to his feet.

"Sir." He inclined his head. "I am pleased to make your acquaintance."

Mr. Bevan's eyes swept over him. "Wounded in the wars, were you, Major?" he asked.

"Yes," Ben said.

"And a friend of the late Captain McKay's, I have heard," Mr. Bevan said. "There is not much local news and gossip that does not reach my ears at Cartref, you know. I could muzzle my servants, I suppose, but why should I? I like a bit of gossip."

He was looking keenly at Ben as he said it, and Samantha felt anger well inside her. To what gossip in particular was he referring? And what business was it of his?

"I never had the privilege of knowing Captain McKay," Ben said, and Samantha's eyes flew to his. "My acquaintance with his widow began after his death. When she decided to come here, goaded to it by circumstances she found intolerable, she had no one to accompany her. I offered my services. It was a less than satisfactory arrangement, sir, but it was the best that could be done."

Was he *apologizing* to her grandfather? Samantha raised her chin and glared at them both.

"I did not *need* the protection of any man," she said, "but Sir Benedict insisted."

They both looked at her, Ben a little sheepishly, her grandfather with a smile that revealed a fan of attractive lines at the outer corners of both eyes. He must smile frequently.

"That is my girl," he said, further incensing her.

"Oh, *do* have a seat," she said ungraciously. "Both of you."

But of course, they both waited for her to be seated first. They were being perfect gentlemen.

"I have neglected you for the last six or seven years, Samantha," Mr. Bevan said. He was smoothing one hand over Tramp's head while the dog's eyes closed in ecstasy.

"For the last six or seven years?" She raised her eyebrows.

"After your father wrote to say you were married," he said, "I decided to stop writing to you. Captain McKay was the son of an earl, wasn't he? Very high class. I did not want you embarrassed by a family member who had made his fortune in coal and iron. I knew your husband had been wounded and that you were living in the north of England. I have kept myself informed, you see, even if only from a distance. I had not heard of his passing, though. I am sorry about that. And I am deeply sorry for you, girl."

He had decided to *stop writing*? He had *kept himself informed*? He had known all about her? All her life? Samantha gazed at the hands she had clasped in her lap. She could see the whites of her knuckles.

"Thank you," she murmured just for something to say into the silence.

"I have been in Swansea for a week," he said. "When I got back yesterday and heard you were here, I thought you must be annoyed with me since you had not let me know you were coming. I sent Evans over this morning to test the waters, so to speak, and he reported back that you were indeed annoyed. Sometimes we are damned if we do and damned if we don't, if you will pardon my language, which is probably not the finest for the daughter-in-law of an earl. But would you not agree, Major? If I had kept writing, that might have been the trouble. I stopped, and it looks as if that was the wrong thing. Though you never wrote back, Samantha, except for the messages you sometimes sent."

Messages? Samantha looked up at him. A suspicion was beginning to form in her mind. More than a suspicion. Her father had written to him at least once. How much *had* her father kept from her?

"You abandoned my mother," she said, "when she was little more than an infant. You had nothing to do with her while she lived here with your sister. When she ran away to London, you did not follow. When she married and had me, you did not come. When she *died*, you did not come. There was never anything. There was *nothing*."

She wanted to be right. She did not want her world turned suddenly upside down again.

His face had turned pale. His hand was motionless on Tramp's head.

"What did they tell you, girl?" he asked her. "What did they tell you about me?"

"*Nothing*," she said, "except that early abandonment of my mother after *her* mother had gone back to her Gypsy people. Nothing at all. You disappeared from her life."

"Ah." His hand slid away from Tramp's head to rest on the arm of his chair. "It was not just that you were ashamed of me for my very middle-class wealth, then?"

"I did not *know* about your wealth," she cried. "I did not know *anything*. I assumed you were a laborer or a wanderer who had made a foolish marriage and was left with the encumbrance of a daughter, whom you then foisted upon your sister. I did not know anything about *her*, except that she had owned this cottage, which my mother described as a hovel. I assumed it *was* a hovel. I only hoped it would be somehow habitable while I made a new life for myself. I did not even know you were alive."

Ben got to his feet again, crossed to her chair, set a large handkerchief in her hand, and then made his slow way over to the window. Samantha swiped at her eyes. She had not even realized she was crying.

"Ah, my dear girl," her grandfather said.

But he had no chance to say any more for a while. The door opened and Mrs. Price came in with a large tray, her face wreathed in smiles. Samantha hastily pushed the handkerchief down the side of her chair.

"Ah, Mrs. Price," Mr. Bevan said. "Trying to fatten people up as always, are you?"

"Just a few pieces of cake to go with your tea," she said, placing the tray on the table beside Samantha and proceeding to pour the tea herself. "What else am I to do with my time but cook? Mrs. McKay is a very tidy lady and she has Gladys Jones to look after her personal needs."

"And how is your son, the blacksmith?" he asked her. "His hand has healed, has it? Hammers are always better used on anvils than on the backs of fingers. In my opinion, anyway."

"They were swollen to three times their size," she told him, "and black and painful too, though he would never admit it. He is better now, though, Mr. Bevan, and thanks for asking. I'll tell him you did. And thank you for sending—"

But she broke off at a slight motion of his hand.

"Well, it was greatly appreciated," she said. "He couldn't work much for a week."

She handed around the tea and left the room.

"I have been justly punished, it seems," he said with a sigh. "And poor Mrs. Price. The last thing I feel like doing is eating a piece of her cake, delicious as I am sure it is. I suppose you feel off your food too, Samantha. Perhaps we had better force some down anyway, had we? She will be hurt if we do not. Major, come and help us, if you will."

Ben looked over his shoulder and then came back to his chair.

"I will tell you my story, Samantha, if you will listen," Mr. Bevan continued. "But not now, perhaps. And I want to hear your story. I want to know why you would come here, expecting only a hovel of a cottage, when presumably you have a noble family to look after you as well as your father's family. But perhaps not now for that either. Major Harper, how long is it since you were wounded?"

He was a man used to command, Samantha realized, and used to doing it without bombast. Here he was in *her* sitting room, directing the conversation, taking from it the heat of emotion that had been here just a few minutes ago. And he was feeding cake to Tramp, who was quite willing to make it seem to Mrs. Price that they had all eaten her tea with hearty appetites.

Ben told him where and when he had been wounded and how, though he did not go into great detail. He told him about the years of his healing and convalescence at Penderris Hall, and about leaving there three years ago.

"You are never going to be able to walk without your canes, then?" her grandfather asked.

"No," Ben said.

"And what do you do to keep busy? Do you have a home of your own?"

Ben told him about Kenelston, and, when asked, about his brother and wife and children and his own reluctance to remove them from his home and the charge his brother had of the running of his estate.

"You are in a bit of an awkward position, then," her grandfather said.

"Yes," Ben agreed. "But I will work something out, sir. I was not made for idleness."

"You were a military officer by choice, then?" her grandfather asked. "Not just because your father had that career picked out for you as soon as you were born? I understand many noble families do that—one son to inherit, another to go into the church, another into the military."

"It was my own choice," Ben said. "I never wanted anything else."

"You like an active life, then. You like being in charge of men. And of events."

"I will never be an officer again," Ben said tersely.

Looking at him, Samantha realized fully just how that fact hurt him. Perhaps it even explained why he had not taken a firmer stand with his younger brother over his home. Running Kenelston would not be a big enough challenge for him. Perhaps nothing would ever again.

"No," her grandfather agreed, "I can see that, lad."

He talked a bit about the coal mines—he owned two of them in the Rhondda Valley—and about the iron-works in the Swansea Valley, where he had just spent a week. Ben asked a number of questions, which he answered with enthusiasm. And then he rose to take his leave.

"How long do you plan to stay, Major?" he asked.

Ben looked at Samantha. "Another two or three days," he said.

"Then maybe you will come with my granddaughter to dine with me at Cartref tomorrow," her grandfather said. He turned to look at her, a smile on his face but some uncertainty in his eyes. "Will you come, Samantha? I have a cook as good as Mrs. Price. And I would like to hear your story and to tell you mine. After that you can live here in peace from me if you choose. Though I will hope you do not so choose. You are all I have, girl."

She looked at him in some indignation until she remembered what he had said earlier. He had written to her before her marriage and she had *sent messages*. What had her father done? And after her marriage he had stopped writing for fear that she would be embarrassed by his humble origins and by the way his fortune had been made. She at least owed him one evening in which to plead his case.

But he had still abandoned his own infant daughter. There could be no excuse for that.

"Yes," she said, "I will come."

"And I would be delighted, sir," Ben said.

The older man came toward Samantha, his hand extended again. But when she set her own in it, he smiled at her, that look of uncertainty still in his eyes.

"Allow me?" he said and leaned forward to kiss her cheek. "She was very, very beautiful, you know. I had her for four years and have loved her forever."

She did not follow him from the room.

He had been talking about her grandmother. Yet he had been married to someone else after her.

She and Ben sat in silence until they heard the carriage drive away. Tramp was at the window, his tail waving as if in farewell.

"He has loved her forever," she said bitterly. "Yet he abandoned the only child he had with her."

"Listen to his story tomorrow," Ben said. "And then make a judgment if you must."

"Oh, Ben," she said, turning her eyes on him, "I *wish* I could wave a magic wand and make your legs all better so that you could resume your military career and be happy and fulfilled."

He smiled. "We are all dealt a hand of cards," he said. "Some of the originals get discarded along the way and new ones get picked up, sometimes not the ones we hoped for. That does not matter. It is how we play them that matters."

"Even if it is a losing hand?" she asked him.

"Perhaps it never needs to be," he said. "For life is not really a card game, is it?"

❧

20

*T*hey went swimming after all. And they dined to-gether after Mrs. Price and Samantha's maid had left for the day. They spent a few hours in bed before Ben returned to the village inn. They made love twice, slowly the first time, with fierce passion the second.

But there had been something a little . . . desperate about both encounters, Ben thought as he lay alone in bed at the inn later. Nothing had been quite the same. Real life, in the form of Bevan, had intruded. A small part of his story had been told, and more would be told tomorrow—Samantha had consented to listen. Her life, he suspected, was going to be very different from any-thing she had dreamed of when circumstances had led her to remember the run-down little cottage in Wales she had inherited.

She had a grandfather, a rich and influential man who, it appeared, cared for her. Whether she could care for him depended a great deal upon the story he would tell tomorrow, but she craved the closeness of some family tie, whether she fully realized it or not. Ben sus-pected that she *would* come to care for Bevan. And she needed time and space—and respectability—in which to do that. And in which to recover fully from a seven-year marriage.

It was time to leave. Almost. He had promised two more days after today.

Though they had not spoken of it, they had both been conscious tonight of the fact that their affair, their early summer idyll, was almost at an end. Ben laced his fingers behind his head and gazed upward at the ceiling. Part of him was longing to be gone, to be done with the whole business. He wished he could just click his fingers and find himself on the road back to England. He hated goodbyes at the best of times. He dreaded this particular one.

Tomorrow was Sunday. The first day of a new week. Very nearly the end of his week. He had no idea where he would be next Saturday night, except that it would be somewhere far from here. And he had no idea what he would do. No, that was not strictly true. He was going to go to London, though not in order to participate in the social whirl of the Season or to allow Beatrice to matchmake for him. He was going to explore various ways of employing his time, perhaps in business, perhaps in diplomacy, perhaps in law. He would talk to Hugo, to Gramley, to various contacts he had in the Foreign Office. It did not matter that he did not need to work. He *wanted* to work. And he would work. His elder brother had done so, after all.

But an obstacle stood between him and the rest of his life. There was the end of an affair to live through and goodbyes to be said. It was Sunday tomorrow. He had promised to go to church with Samantha. They were to dine at Cartref later in the day. And then, after tomorrow . . .

Goodbye.

Surely the saddest, most painful word in the English language.

*P*erhaps it had something to do with the fact that Ben walked with painstaking slowness and with the aid of two canes but with evident courage and determination, Samantha thought. Or perhaps it was his lean good looks, enhanced now by suntan, and the indefinable air of command that always somehow clung about him. Or perhaps it was simply that everyone loved a hint of romance, even a touch of scandal.

However it was, they were both greeted with smiles and friendly nods when they appeared at church together on Sunday morning. Samantha had been half expecting cold stares or frowns and turned shoulders, for obviously there had been talk. Her grandfather had heard it.

And though Ben looked almost austere much of the time, he was quite capable of charm. He used it that morning on the people of Fisherman's Bridge and its environs. And Samantha smiled about her too, as she had not been allowed to do after Matthew's death, and shook the hands of those who extended their own to her. She was sure she would not remember the names of all who introduced themselves and said so.

"Don't worry about it, Mrs. McKay," the doctor told her. "We have only two new names to remember, yours and Major Harper's, while you have a few dozen."

Other people within earshot smiled their agreement.

Samantha would have felt warm about the heart as they left church if her grandfather had not been there too. He had shaken hands heartily with Ben and kissed her on the cheek—while half the village looked on with interest—but he had not pressed his company on them. He had sat in the front pew, which was padded, though he did not act the part of grand gentleman after the service was over. He shook hands and exchanged a few words with everyone in his path. He dug into his pockets to bring out sweets for the very little children, coins for the older ones.

Other people's children, Samantha thought with unexpected bitterness. How she would have *loved* to have a grandpapa to beam at her thus when she was a child and give her sweets and coins. How her mother would surely have loved to have a papa to do those things.

It was a cloudy day, but it was neither cold nor windy.

"Do you want to swim this afternoon?" she asked Ben when they were walking slowly back to the inn.

She was feeling a bit depressed. She wished the sun was shining.

"What is it?" he asked without answering her question.

"It would be more appropriate to ask what it is *not*," she said with a sigh—and then laughed. "The vicar was right about the singing, was he not?"

"Well," he said, "I was disappointed not to see the roof lift off the building. I was watching for it."

She laughed again.

"But, yes," he said. "That church really does not need the choir, does it? The whole congregation is a choir."

"With harmony."

"In four parts," he added. "Yes, let's swim. There will be time."

She swallowed and heard a gurgle in her throat. *There will be time.*

Time before they went to Cartref for dinner.

Time before the week of their affair was over.

They went swimming. They raced and floated and talked, and they played silly games, the main object of which seemed to be to swim underwater and come up unexpectedly to submerge each other. It was not a very effective game since there was never any real possibility of surprise, but it kept them helpless with laughter for a time.

Laughter was better than tears.

A week had seemed a long time when they began their affair. But this was the sixth day. The knowledge weighed upon Samantha as if it were a physical thing. And she could not keep at bay the thought that they would be going to Cartref later. She wished she had not been weak enough to agree. And yet . . . Her grandfather had written, and Papa had written back to him. She ought to listen to his story, Ben had said.

When they left the water, they went to their usual rock, where they were met by a tail-wagging, bottom-wiggling Tramp, who had been guarding their belongings against seagulls. But instead of spreading her towel on the sand as she usually did, Samantha wrapped it about her shoulders.

"I gave Mrs. Price and Gladys the day off," she said. "It is Sunday. Besides, I will be out for dinner today."

He looked back at her. He was leaning against the ledge to take the weight off his legs and rubbing his towel over his chest and up under one arm.

Oh, dear, she was going to miss this—the daily swims, the sight of him, the smell of him, the touch of him. She was going to miss *him*.

"Come back to the house?" she said.

They always went to the house after their swim and after lying for a while in the sun. But she knew from the look in his eyes that he understood what she meant.

"Yes," he said.

And, shockingly, they did not stop to dress but walked back as they were, her towel about her shoulders, his draped about his neck. She insisted on carrying his boots.

She had forgotten why he must leave.

But of course he must. He could not stay here in the cottage with her, even if they married. He would have nothing to do here. He would be restless and unhappy in no time at all. And she could not go with him. It was much too soon for her to go with or marry anyone. And though he was not homeless, he had chosen to leave his brother and family in residence in his house but had established no other home for himself. He was probably the most restless, unsettled man she had ever known. It had not always been so, of course, but it was now, and she wondered unhappily if he would ever find himself and his place in life.

Yes, he must leave. Sometimes love was not enough— if it *was* love between them. It was probably not. She was lamentably naïve about affairs. Perhaps this was not love but mere physical attraction. That was undoubtedly all it was to him. Men did not fall in love as women did, did they?

They went upstairs as soon as they reached the cottage while Tramp padded off to the kitchen in search of his food bowl. Samantha led the way into her bedchamber. She drew the curtains across the window, though they were not heavy and did not block out much light. She peeled off her wet shift, toweled herself off, and rubbed at her hair, even though it was still in its tight knot at her neck.

Ben was sitting with his back to her on the side of the bed. He was pulling off his wet pantaloons, though he had drawn the bedcovers up over himself to mask her view.

"Don't," she said, kneeling up on the bed and moving across it toward him.

"Don't?" He looked over his shoulder at her.

"Don't hide yourself," she said.

He held her eyes for a few moments, his own suddenly bleak, and then pushed back the covers, finished removing his clothes, and lay back on the bed, lifting his legs onto it one at a time. He looked at her again, his eyes hard now.

His legs were thinner than they must once have been. The left one was slightly twisted, the right more noticeably so. They were horribly scarred.

"Now tell me," he said, "that you want me to make love to you."

His voice matched his eyes.

She moved a little closer and set her hand on his upper right thigh. She stroked it lightly downward, feeling the deep gouges of his old wounds and the hard, raised ridges of the scars where the surgeons had tried to mend them.

And the foolish, brave man had insisted upon walking again.

She returned her hands to her own thighs as she knelt naked beside him, and raised her eyes to his.

"Ben," she said, "my dearest, I am so very sorry. I am sorry for the pain you suffered and still suffer. I am sorry that you cannot do what you most want to do in life. I am sorry you feel diminished as a man and inadequate as a lover, that you feel ugly and undesirable. What *happened* to you was ugly, but *you* are not. I think you are the toughest, most courageous man I have ever met. I *know* you are the loveliest. You must believe me. Oh, you *must*, Ben. And yes, I want you to make love to me."

He gazed at her, his look still hard, though she had the curious feeling that he was fighting the welling of tears to his eyes.

"You are not repulsed?" His voice was still hard too, though there was a suggestion of a tremor in it.

"Idiot," she said and smiled. "Do I *look* repulsed? You are Ben. My lover. For this week anyway. And I have had enormous pleasure with you. Give me more."

She was remembering that she had called him *my dearest,* and she did not want him to believe she had fallen in love with him. And so she spoke of the pleasure she had had of him—which was no lie. He must be the most wonderful lover in the world.

He reached for her and she moved to straddle him. His hands moved over her upper thighs, over her hips, in to her waist, up to her breasts, which he cupped lightly.

"You are perfection itself," he said.

"I am not slender."

"Thank God for that," he said without contradicting her. "Do women really believe that men want them looking like sticks?"

"And I am no English rose," she said. "I am downright swarthy."

"My Gypsy Sammy." He grinned at her. "My *perfect* Gypsy Sammy."

She laughed, set her hands on either side of his head, and leaned over him to kiss him.

His legs were not quite helpless, as she had discovered on previous occasions. Before she knew it, she was on her back and he was on top of her, his legs between hers, and his lips were on hers, his tongue deep in her mouth, and his hands were fierce on her and then beneath her buttocks and holding her firm while he thrust deep into her.

She lifted her legs from the bed and wrapped them about his lean hips, and they loved each other long and hard until they were both panting and slick with sweat and they broke together into glory and collapsed into the world beyond.

They lay side by side afterward, sated and drowsy and dozing, their hands touching. Last night had felt a bit like goodbye, she thought. The melancholy of it had remained with her this morning. And now?

No, she did not want to think.

"I believe you will make a wonderful new life here," he said at last. "You have neighbors who seem very ready to accept you and welcome you into their midst. You will make friends here. And you have family here. You have a grandfather who wishes to be a part of your life. Listen to him this evening, Samantha, and think well before you reject him for all the apparent wrongs of the past."

"I have agreed to listen," she reminded him.

"I think you did the right thing," he said, "coming here. And I think it will be time for me to leave tomorrow, before speculation and a bit of gossip can blossom into scandal as they surely would if I stayed longer."

"I have delayed your travels for long enough," she said.

He did not answer her, and they lay side by side, no longer either drowsy or dozing. Samantha fought tears. She fought the urge to beg him to stay just one more day or perhaps two. For he was right. It was time for him to leave. It was time for him to go in search of his life and for her to settle to her new one.

It was time to let him go.

After a while he turned and sat up, moving his legs over the side of the bed.

"I had better return to the inn," he said. "I will bring the carriage later to take you to Cartref?"

"Yes," she said. "Thank you."

She felt about as bleak as it was possible to feel.

$\mathcal{M}$r. Bevan had the good manners and easy address of a true gentleman, Ben thought, even if he was not one by birth. And he dressed with fashionable elegance yet without any ostentation or grand display of wealth. The wealth was clearly there, however.

He took them on a tour of the house. Everything was of the finest but with not the merest suggestion of vulgarity. The room in which they lingered longest was the long gallery at the back of the house. It was filled with paintings and a few sculptures by the great masters, a few of them acquired by his father, he told them, but the majority by him. And he always purchased what he most liked, he explained to them, rather than what was most valuable. Though Ben guessed there was a fortune in that room alone. There were paintings in every other room too, some of them by acclaimed masters, some by unknown artists Mr. Bevan had admired and wanted to encourage.

And wherever he took them, there were views from the windows, over the rolling Welsh countryside, over the beach and the sea.

He plied them with sherry and conversation in the drawing room and then with good wine and food and conversation in the dining room. He told them about his travels and his reading. And he asked them about their own lives with skilled questions that would draw more than monosyllabic answers from them and yet would not seem intrusive. When Ben asked him about his businesses, he answered thoroughly but without monopolizing all their time and perhaps boring Samantha.

He appeared totally at his ease and in perfect good humor with his guests.

Samantha, Ben guessed, was troubled even as she admired the house and ate and drank and listened to her grandfather's conversation and Ben's and made her own contributions. She was looking extremely beautiful in a turquoise blue high-waisted dress he had not seen before. Her hair was elaborately styled considering the fact that she had not had the services of her maid today. It shone in the candlelight.

While they drank tea in the drawing room after dinner, Mr. Bevan told them about the male voice choir made up of eighty or so of his miners.

"There is no finer choir in all of Wales," he told them, "and that is saying something. I am not entirely impartial, of course, but they did win at the eisteddfod in Newport both last year and the year before. I always say that coal dust must do marvels for the vocal cords."

"Iced—?" Ben asked

"Eye-*steth*-fod," Mr. Bevan said, pronouncing the word clearly. "A Welsh arts festival."

He turned his eyes on Samantha, who was swirling the dregs of her tea in her cup, and watched her in silence for a few moments.

"Your grandmother was dancing when I first set eyes on her," he said. "The Gypsies had camped down by the sea, as they sometimes did, and I went to have a look with some of the other lads from around here. I was twenty-one at the time. Her feet were bare, and her bright, full skirts were swirling about her ankles and her dark hair was tumbled about her face and shoulders, and I had not seen anything as lovely or as full of life and grace in all my days. I didn't know anything at that time about not putting birds or butterflies or wild things in cages. I wooed her and I married her, all within six weeks, against everyone's advice, her own people's included. We were going to live happily ever after. She was sixteen."

Samantha's cup, held between both her hands, was still. Her eyes had lifted briefly to her grandfather's and then returned to her cup.

"We were happy for a year or so," Bevan said, "though we had to keep traveling about. She did not like to be in one place for very long. And then your mother was born, and only a few months after that my father died—my mother was already deceased. I had to take over the running of the businesses. I had been working in them, though not as much as I had before I met Esme. The baby needed a stable home. Esme did not like it, but she understood and she tried to settle. She tried hard. We went on for a few years, but then the Gypsies came back—her own group. She spent some time with them while they were here, and she went to say goodbye to them on the last night. She never came home. I thought she had stayed the night, but when I went looking the next morning, they were gone and she with them. I didn't go after them. What was the point? She had been withering away at Cartref here. She died four years after that, but I did not know it for another six."

Samantha leaned forward and set her cup down carefully on its saucer before sitting back in her chair. Ben wished he were sitting beside her.

"I took to drink," Bevan said. "I made sure your mother had a good nurse and everything she needed, and I made sure that I had a good manager who would look after running the mines, and I dedicated my life to forgetting and dulling the pain—at the bottom of a glass of liquor. A year or so after Esme left, I was in the library one night drinking and feeling sorry for myself as usual. Except it was worse than usual. It was the anniversary of our wedding. After a while I hurled my glass against the wall beside a bookcase, and the glass shattered. And someone started to cry. Gwynneth had come downstairs without her nurse's seeing her. And she had curled up under a table just below where the glass hit."

Samantha spread both hands over her knees and pleated the fabric of her dress between her fingers.

"The next morning," Mr. Bevan said, "I took her to

Dilys at the cottage where you now live, Samantha. We had never seen eye to eye. She had thought me wild and irresponsible as a boy. She had thought my marriage insanity. She was furious when she discovered that our father had left almost everything to me when she was the one with the business head. But I took your mother to her and asked her to take the child until I got myself properly sober. She told me I never would, that I would always be a worthless drunkard. She said she would take Gwynneth but only on condition that she had the sole raising of her, that I would give her up and never see her again except by chance."

Samantha was looking at him now. Ben was looking at her.

"I drank for six more months," Bevan said, "and then I stopped. I did not drink at all for years. Now I do occasionally, but only in a social way, never when I am alone. I applied myself to my work. I challenged myself by interesting myself in industries other than just coal. Hence the ironworks. And in the meanwhile, every penny of the money I ever sent to help Dilys with the upbringing of your mother and every gift I sent for birthdays or Christmas was returned. Every time I glimpsed Gwynneth, she was whisked away by my sister when she was younger—she turned away of her own accord when she was older. I wanted her back. I wanted to get her a proper governess. I wanted to get her ready for the life she could have lived as my daughter. I wanted to . . . Well, I wanted to be her father, but I had forfeited my chance with her. When I heard she was not allowed to go on picnics with the local lads and lasses, though, and was not allowed to go to the village assemblies even though she was seventeen and ready for a bit of life of her own, I went and had it out with Dilys, and we both ended up shouting like fools and behaving like two snarling dogs fighting over the same bone. And Gwyn-neth was in the house and heard it all. The day after, she was gone. Just like Esme all over again."

"And as before, you did not go after her," Samantha said.

"I did," he said. "She would not have anything to do with me. She would not let me pay for her lodgings. She would not let me give her some spending money. She would not let me help her find decent employment. And she would not come home with me. She got a job acting. I was . . . proud of her spirit of independence at the same time as I was terrified for her. And then she met your father, who was close to me in age and was everything I was not. I think maybe she was happy with him. Was she?"

"Yes," she said.

"It was the old story after her marriage," he said. "She returned my letters and my wedding gift and my christening gift to you and all the other gifts I sent. Though after she . . . died, the letters and gifts I sent you stopped coming back, and sometimes your father would write to tell me about you and to include little messages of thanks from you for the gifts. I often thought of sug-gesting that I come to see you, but I could never quite get up the courage. You were the daughter of a gentle-man, and his letters were always polite, but not exactly warm. I thought maybe the two of you would say no. And then all hope was gone. You married the son of an earl, and it seemed to me the last thing you would want was a visit from your maternal grandfather. I even stopped sending gifts after the wedding one."

Samantha was pleating her dress again.

"I daresay your father felt sorry for me," Bevan said. "But I suppose he felt even more loyalty to his wife, your mother, and agreed with her that it was best you not know me. You did not read any of those letters or see any of those gifts, did you?"

"No." Her voice was a mere whisper of sound.

"It was not wicked of either your father or your mother," he said. "I had done nothing to earn her love, and I did not deserve yours. I ruined my own life and your mother's over grief for what I could not have. And all the time I had a treasure in my grasp that I did not recognize until it was too late."

"You married again," she said.

"A year after your mother went to London." He sighed. "I wanted a son. I wanted someone to hand everything on to. Perhaps I wanted some redemption too. I wanted to try again, to see if I could do better than I had done the first time. Isabelle was a good woman. She was better than I deserved, and we were contented together despite the age difference. But we never did have children. We were denied that blessing. She died two years ago."

Samantha said nothing. But she turned her head to look at Ben, her eyes wide and blank.

"I am sorry," Bevan said. "The most useless three words in the English language when they are used together. I wish I could go back. I have wished it year after year since the night I smashed that glass above your mother's head. But that is something that is not granted to any of us. None of us can go back. I thought at least you must know about me, though. I thought your mother would have told you."

"No," she said. "But she ought to have done. Ben said to me yesterday that we all have a story to tell. My mother had a story, but she never told it. Perhaps she meant to. Perhaps she thought I was too young. I was only twelve when she died. My father did not tell it either, but I suppose he felt it was not his story to tell. Except that I ought to have known."

"You know now," he said, and he got to his feet to pull on the bell rope, "and it is not a pretty story. I cannot think of anything to add that might make you think it worth your while to accept me as your grandfather, Samantha. I wish I could, but I can't. I obviously did terrible damage to another human being, my own daughter, and I have no excuse for that. And no right to lay any claim to the affection of *her* daughter."

"I have no one," Samantha said.

"Your brother?"

"*Half* brother," she said. "No."

"Your uncles and aunts and cousins on your father's side? Your father- and mother-in-law and your sister- and brothers-in-law?"

"No."

He turned his eyes on Ben and gazed steadily at him.

"And when are you leaving, Major Harper?" he asked.

"Tomorrow," Ben said.

They looked at each other for a few moments longer, taking each other's measure, until a servant answered the summons of the bell.

"You can remove the tray," Bevan told him, "and have Major Harper's carriage brought around to the door."

He waited until the servant had withdrawn and then looked at Samantha's bowed head.

"You can have *me*," he told her. "If you want me."

She looked up at him. "I want to live in peace at my cottage," she told him. "I want to be alone. But perhaps one day I will tell you *my* story. Perhaps I will tell you everything that led up to my coming here. But not yet."

He bowed his head in acknowledgment of her words.

"It is time for you to go home, Samantha," he said. "The major will see you safely there."

"Yes," she said. "Thank you. It has been a pleasant evening."

"It has, indeed."

He shook Ben by the hand, kissed Samantha's cheek, and was again the smiling, genial host.

21

❧

*T*hey traveled back to the cottage in silence. And when the carriage stopped and the coachman opened the door and set down the steps before withdrawing, neither of them spoke for a while. He took her gloved hand in his.

"Samantha," he said at last, "would you like me to stay for a few more days? Until you have had time to digest what you have heard and made some decision?"

Ah, she was so tempted to say yes. To cling to him. To use him as an emotional prop. And to postpone the inevitable goodbye just a little longer.

"No," she said. "I need to be alone for a while. Everything I have known about my life has been turned upside down. I need to do some thinking."

Alone. She was going to be alone. Without him. Forever.

He raised her hand to his lips and kissed her fingers.

"Shall we say goodbye now?" he asked her. "Or shall I call here before I leave in the morning?"

She almost panicked then. She almost threw herself against him. She almost begged him not to go, never to go.

And yet she had spoken truth. She needed to be alone.

Would she be able to deal with goodbye better in the morning? No, she decided. There was never a good time for goodbye. And it would be unfair to him. He would want to be on his way.

"Now," she said. And she turned on her seat and took both his hands in hers and raised them to her cheeks. She closed her eyes and bowed her head. "I do thank you, Ben, for all you have done for me. And I thank you for the past week. It has been a great pleasure. Has it not?" She turned her face up to his and tried to smile.

"It has," he agreed. "Samantha—"

"If your travels ever bring you back to Wales," she said hastily, "perhaps . . . No, that would not be a good idea, would it? I will remember with pleasure. I hope you will too."

"I will," he said, and he leaned toward her and set his lips to hers in a long, lingering kiss while they clung to each other's hands.

"Goodbye, Samantha," he said. "I will wait here until you are safely indoors with a lamp lit."

He rapped on the front panel and the coachman appeared in the doorway to hand her down.

"Goodbye." She drew her hands from his. "Goodbye, Ben."

And then she was stepping down and dashing up the garden path and fumbling with the key in the lock and almost being bowled over by an exuberant Tramp. She lit a lamp in the sitting room with a trembling hand and darted to the window, desperate for one last sight of him. But the carriage door had been closed, and the coachman was up on the box, and the carriage was moving away. She could not see through the darkness into the interior.

"Oh, Tramp." She collapsed onto the nearest chair, set her arms about him, and wept against his neck.

Tramp whined and tried to lick her face.

*B*en was down early to breakfast the following morning. Everything was packed, and he was eager to be on his way as soon as possible. He did not care what direction he took, though he had told his coachman last night that they would return the way they had come. All he really wanted was to put as much distance between him and Fisherman's Bridge as he possibly could.

He was down early, but someone was earlier. Mr. Bevan rose from his place at a table by the window when Ben appeared, an open watchcase in his hand.

"Is this the time," he asked, "that the idle rich normally break their fast?"

It was shortly after seven o'clock.

"I believe it is more the time they are going to bed," Ben said, making his way toward the table and propping his canes against a chair before shaking the man by the hand.

"I have no right in the world to ask this," Bevan said when they were both seated, "and you have every right in the world to refuse an answer, but here goes anyway. What are your feelings for my granddaughter, Major?"

Ben paused in the act of spreading his napkin across his lap. Here was a man who did not believe in wasting precious time on small talk, it seemed.

"Mrs. McKay," Ben said, choosing his words with care, "lost her husband less than six months ago, sir. She needs time to recover from that loss. She needs time to adjust her life to her new home and circumstances. As she told you last evening, she needs to be alone. Not necessarily without all company, but without emotional entanglements. It would be presumptuous for me to have feelings for her stronger than respect. Besides, at present I have nothing of value to offer her except a baronet's title and fortune."

"At present," Bevan said. "And in the future?"

"I was wounded six years ago," Ben told him. "I have been well enough for the past three years to get my life in order and set on a new course, since the old one will serve no longer. But I have procrastinated. Until now. I am going to go to London. I am going to find something challenging to do."

"Other than carousing all night?" Bevan smiled.

"That sort of life has never appealed to me," Ben told him. "I must be doing something useful and meaningful."

Neither of them spoke while the landlord set their food before them and exchanged a few pleasantries about the weather with them before withdrawing.

Bevan sat back in his chair, ignoring his food for the moment. "Tell me more about the way you used to be," he said. "Tell me about being a leader of men. That is what you were, is it not? You were a major, which is not quite the same as being a general, of course, but nevertheless it put you in a position of considerable authority over men and actions and events. Tell me about that man."

Ben picked up his knife and fork and thought a moment before cutting into his food. Where to begin? And *why* begin? Why had Bevan come here this morning?

"That man was happy," he said.

He was not used to talking about himself. It was something he had never been comfortable doing. Even at Penderris he had talked less than any of the others, more content to listen to his friends' problems than divulge his own. He had always assumed that he could not possibly be of any great interest to anyone else, that he would merely bore other people by prosing on about himself. But for the next fifteen or twenty minutes he did nothing *but* that, led on by skilled, persistent, probing questions and a look of genuine interest on the other man's face. He talked about his dreams and ambitions, his war experiences, the feeling he had always had that he had been born to do just what he was doing. He talked about the battle in which he had been wounded, about his long fight for survival and his longer fight to restore himself to physical wholeness so that he could get back to the only life he knew or had ever wanted for himself. He talked about the past three years and his reasons for not going home, about his growing frustration and restlessness, about his corresponding determination to overcome lethargy and lowness of spirits by finding *something* to replace what he had lost.

"I fought hard enough to live," he said. "Now I have to prove to myself that the fight was for some purpose."

"Women?" Bevan asked. "Have there been many?"

"None since I was hurt," Ben said.

"Until now?"

Ben gave him a long, level look.

"You escorted my granddaughter here from the north of England," Bevan said, "and you have been a good friend to her. Now you are about to leave, for reasons you have just given me. But you will not pretend to me that she is no more to you than a friend, Harper. Or, if you do, I will not believe you." He smiled in a not-unfriendly manner.

"I will not pretend, then," Ben told him curtly. "Yes, I have feelings for her. *Inappropriate* and pointless feelings. And I will be leaving this morning because there is no future for us, because she needs to be left alone to find herself and her place here. I believe she will. And I believe she has a chance for happiness. She has not had much of that in her life. And I will be leaving because I need to find *myself* and my place of belonging. I will do it. You need not fear that I will linger."

"And I would not believe Samantha," Bevan said, "if she told me that you are no more to her than a friend."

"Pardon me," Ben said stiffly, "but I am not sure you have the right to offer any opinion on this matter, sir."

The older man's eyebrows rose, and he picked up his knife and fork and tackled his breakfast. "I like you,

Major," he said. "You are a man after my own heart. And you are quite correct. I have no right whatsoever."

He paused to eat, and Ben did likewise. He would excuse himself as soon as his plate was empty and be on his way. He did not know why Bevan had come except, perhaps, to warn him to leave without delay and never to return. He did not need to say it. He really did not have the right, anyway.

"I am sixty-six years old," Bevan said, picking up the conversation again. "I am not an old man—at least, I do not feel like one—but I am not young either. If I had a son, I would be gradually transferring my responsibilities to his younger shoulders, provided he showed the necessary interest and aptitude, of course. It has been one of the enduring disappointments of my life that I have no son, but that cannot be helped now. I have able and trusted men in charge at the mines and at the ironworks. I have been fortunate in my employees. What I have longed for and actively searched for in the past four or five years, however, is an overseer, a supermanager, if you will, someone with the interest and energy and ability to take charge of all my industrial concerns. Someone I can trust, and someone who trusts me. Someone who is as like a son to me as possible. Someone to replace me, in fact, after I retire and until my death, and to be well compensated afterward. He would have to be a special kind of man, for it is not enough just to understand facts or to have ideas or even to have both together. It is not enough even to have organizational skills, though they are necessary. He would have to be someone who could get work done and ensure profits while not neglecting the safety and well-being of all the workers under him. He would have to inspire trust and loyalty and even liking while at the same time demanding the best efforts of his workers. He would have to take a personal interest in what he does as well as just a professional one. He would have to be someone rather like me, in fact. He has not been easy to find, Major. Or to find at all, in fact."

Ben had stopped eating to look fixedly at the other man. "Are you offering me a job?" he asked.

Bevan set down his knife and fork and poured them each another cup of coffee before answering.

"I pride myself upon being a good judge of character," he said. "I think it is one reason for my success. I sensed something about you as soon as I met you, even though I was predisposed to dislike you, having listened to some of the local gossip—which was not particularly vicious, I must add. I sensed something about you both then and last evening, and you have confirmed that impression this morning. You liked your men, Major? You were not the sort of officer who commanded obedience with a whip?"

"I never ordered or condoned the British army's practice of whipping its soldiers," Ben said. "Yes, I liked my men. Apart from a few irredeemable rogues, most soldiers are the salt of the earth and will give their best, even their lives, when called upon to do so."

He was being offered a *job*. In Wales. Overseeing coal mines and ironworks. Could anything be more bizarre?

"Employment for me has always been about more than just making money," the older man said. "I could have lived in great luxury on what my father left me. I could have appointed managers for the mines and given them no further thought. Indeed, I did just that during the years when I was drinking and feeling sorry for myself. Fortunately, I was not cut out for idleness of either body or mind, and that fact was perhaps my salvation. I believe that in many ways we are similar, Major."

"You *are* offering me employment," Ben said.

"Knowing that you do not need the money," Bevan said, raising his coffee cup to his lips, "and that some gentlemen, maybe most, would find it demeaning to work around industry. But you do need to use your gifts and your skills, and you will never again use them in the army. I would rather you than anyone else I have met."

Ben shook his head and laughed softly. Was he actually tempted? More than tempted?

"Everything I have will be Samantha's one day," Bevan said.

Ben sobered instantly. "Are you offering the job on condition that I marry Mrs. McKay?" he asked. Sudden anger curled like a tight ball in his stomach.

"On the contrary, Major," Bevan said. "I offer the employment on condition that you leave here. An empire is not run from a country estate or even from a seaside cottage. I have homes in Swansea and in Merthyr Tydfil. You would live on site. And I do not offer permanent employment. Not yet. I do not know that you are capable of doing the job well. I do not know that it would suit you. Or if it would suit me to have you. We would need time to discover if we are a good fit for each other. As for my granddaughter, well, I will not deny that I sat up half the night thinking of how convenient it would be if you really did become my right-hand man, as capable and enthusiastic a manager as I have been, perhaps even with new, fresh ideas to bring to the task. And of how convenient it would then be if you were to marry Samantha. For then, eventually, everything would be yours as well as hers. It would be a storybook ending for an elderly man who long ago gave up all hope of happy endings. But I press nothing on you, Major Harper. Or on her. Indeed, I would insist that you leave here immediately."

"Mrs. McKay might nevertheless feel that pressure was being brought to bear upon her if I were to accept your offer," Ben said. "She might well believe that you and I were trying to manipulate her life and interfere with her newfound freedom. I have already taken my leave of her."

"I cannot speak with her," Bevan said. "She has not given me the right and perhaps never will. You must do it, then, if you feel you must. And if you accept my offer, which I believe you are inclined to do. But remember that the employment may never be permanent. There would have to be a trial period of several months before any contract can be drawn up or agreed to. When did Captain McKay die?"

"In December sometime," Ben said.

"Then perhaps we can get together at Cartref sometime just before Christmas," Bevan said, "to discuss our future association, if we are to have one."

His meaning was unmistakable. Samantha's mourning period would be over by then.

They gazed steadily at each other across the table.

Ben reached for his canes abruptly and pulled himself to his feet. "I need to do some thinking," he said. "And, depending upon the outcome of that, I need to talk with Mrs. McKay. This would *not* be a decision for me alone to make even if I would not be living anywhere close to here. For she may not want anything more to do with you, and my working for you would seem like a betrayal. Even if she *does* wish to have a relationship with you, she may not want me running the businesses that will eventually be hers. It may seem like entrapment to her."

"I perfectly understand, Major." Bevan smiled and poured himself another coffee. "You will write to me if you do not come to see me?"

Ben nodded curtly and made his slow way out of the dining room and up the stairs to his room. He felt rather as though he had been bashed over the head and had his brains scrambled.

All his baggage had been taken down to the carriage already, he could see.

$\mathcal{S}$amantha kept busy through the early part of the morning going through the linen closets with Mrs. Price, sorting out what was good, what was worth mending, and what was only good enough to be consigned to the rag bag. Tomorrow they would go through the china. Mrs. Price reported that all the cupboards were full to overflowing but that some of the pieces were mismatched or chipped or altogether not worth keeping.

She was going to go through simply everything, she decided, until the cottage felt entirely her own, until it felt like home, as Bramble Hall never had. She had not even realized that until now.

She was going to return the call of Mrs. Tudor and her daughter, who had already visited her, and she was going to make an effort to become acquainted with more of her neighbors and to discover ways of becoming active and useful in village life. She was going to ask about the availability of a tutor to teach her Welsh. Not that it was spoken a great deal just here, but she wanted to be able to speak it anyway or at least to understand it and perhaps read it. There were a few Welsh books in the book room, including a Welsh Bible. Perhaps she would even take music lessons. And perhaps . . .

And every moment of the time she thought of Ben driving away from the inn. But which direction would he have taken? She had not asked. That thought brought a moment of foolish panic. She did not even know where he was going. And where was he now, at this moment? How was he feeling? Was he thinking of her? Or had he turned his thoughts forward to the future, eager to begin something new, relieved to be away from here and away from her? Or, like her, was he thinking of the future and of her at the same time?

Would the pain lessen as time went on? But of course it would. And why was she even feeling pain? They had had a brief affair. They had agreed before it began that it would last just a week. She did not want him to stay. And he certainly would not want it. It was merely a leftover sexual passion she was feeling. Of course it would go away after a few days.

By the middle of the morning she could stay in the cottage no longer. She pulled on her old bonnet, called to Tramp, who was busy gnawing on an old soup bone in the kitchen, and went out. She hesitated only a moment at the garden gate before turning in the direction of the beach. There was no point in avoiding it unless she intended to do so for the rest of her life. Nevertheless, it felt painfully bleak to step through the gap between the rocks and onto the sand after removing her shoes.

She found a piece of driftwood to throw for Tramp and strolled along the top of the beach, trying to keep her eyes off the rock she had come to think of as *theirs*. She was on her way back, not far from the gap, when Ben stepped through it. She stopped, wondering for a dizzying moment if she was imagining him. And then she was filled with an unreasoning surge of hope.

"I thought you would have been long on your way by now," she cried, hurrying toward him.

"I had breakfast with your grandfather," he said. "He came to the inn."

She stopped abruptly while Tramp came tearing up without his driftwood and panted and wagged his tail in front of Ben.

"Why?" she asked.

"He has offered me employment," he said.

"*What?*"

"As manager of all his enterprises," he said. "As someone to oversee them as he withdraws gradually into retirement."

She gazed at him as anger balled inside her.

"You do not like the sound of it." He half smiled.

"It is an *insult*," she said. "You are a gentleman, a baronet. You have property and fortune. He is a—a *coal miner*."

"An owner," he said. "There is a difference."

"He cannot be serious," she said. "Did you tell him how insulted you were? Did you give him the set-down of his life? It is time *somebody* did."

"I did not feel insulted."

"And why *you*?" she asked. "Does he believe that by offering you employment he will be currying favor with me?"

She glared. He half smiled.

And a thought struck her.

"Why have you not set out on your journey?" she asked him. "Why did you come?"

"To say goodbye," he said. "I had been delayed anyway and thought another hour would make no great difference. Goodbye, Samantha. Try not to think too hardly of him."

She watched him turn and make his way back through the gap and move in the direction of the cottage. Tramp started to go after him and then turned to stare at her, his tail waving, waiting for her to come too.

To say goodbye.

I had been delayed anyway and thought another hour would make no great difference.

She went hurrying after him and caught up with him just above the rock where she had left her shoes.

"You came to tell me, did you not?" she said. "You have accepted his offer."

"I have not," he said. "I will be leaving as planned within the hour."

"Oh, Ben," she said, setting a hand on his arm. "Come to the house and sit down. Mrs. Price will bring us some tea. You came to ask me what I thought, then. You would not accept without my approval. Am I right?"

"I *will* not accept without your approval," he said. "And you do not approve. That is the end of the matter."

"No, it is not," she said with a sigh as they reached the garden gate and she held it open for him. "I was insulted for you. But you were not insulted. You must tell me why not. And you must tell me why on earth you would consider taking employment with the owner of a coal mine."

"Coal mines," he said. "And ironworks."

They went into the house, and Samantha went back to the kitchen to talk to Mrs. Price while he went on his way to the sitting room. It was only as she joined him there that it struck her fully—*he was still here*. She had thought never to see him again, but here he was seated in his usual chair, his canes propped beside it.

"Your grandfather claims to be a good judge of character," he told her. "He believes I have the abilities and experience and qualities of character he has been looking for in an overseer. Apart from all the knowledge and experience I would have to acquire, being in charge of everything would have certain similarities to being a military officer."

"All you ever wanted to do in life," she said softly.

"And," he said, "it is something I could do despite my disability."

"Yes," she said.

"I would not be here to trouble you," he said. "I would have to live and work in Swansea and the Rhondda Valley. I need never come here again. If I accept the offer, I will be leaving immediately, just as I planned anyway."

"Then why," she asked him, "did you need my approval?"

"I would be working for your grandfather," he said, "from whom you may choose to remain estranged. And . . . Samantha, you are his heir. If he were to die suddenly, I might be working for *you* until a replacement could be found."

She sat back in her chair and gripped the arms. Her grandfather's *heir*? But she would think of that later.

"Oh, Ben," she said, "this is something you really want to do, is it not? And now I can see why. It was blind of me not to realize it immediately. It is just the sort of thing for which you have been searching."

"I'll not do it," he said, "if it will make you uncomfortable."

"Why *did* he offer you this?" she asked, frowning. "Was it just on this instinct he says he has to judge character? Or does it have something to do with me?"

He looked steadily back at her for a few silent moments. "He wants me to do it on a trial basis for a few months," he said, "so that we can both decide if I am the right man for the job. He wants me to come to Cartref close to Christmas to discuss it and to draw up a contract if we both wish for it."

She might see him again, then?

"Before setting the month," he said, "he asked when your husband had died last year."

She thought a moment. "My year of mourning will be over by then."

"Yes."

Mrs. Price came in with the tray, and Samantha got to her feet to cross to the window.

"He is manipulating us," she said when the housekeeper had left.

"Yes," he said. "I believe he is, though it is a benevolent type of manipulation. He wants me gone without delay. I daresay he is afraid of what gossip might do to you. At the same time, he believes we have feelings for each other—both of us."

She turned her head to look back at him.

"And he genuinely believes I am the right man for the job," he said.

"*Do* we have feelings for each other?" she asked.

"I cannot answer for you," he said. "But yes, I have feelings."

She waited, but he did not say what those feelings were.

"By Christmas," she said, "everything will have changed—for you and for me."

"Yes," he agreed. "But nothing would work now, would it?"

Christmas was an eternity in the future. But not as long as his going away altogether and never coming back.

"You must accept the employment, Ben," she said. "With my approval and blessing. I believe it will work wonderfully for you, though your family will think you have taken leave of your senses when they know. Go and be happy. And we will let Christmas take care of itself, shall we?"

"Yes. No commitments. No obligations."

He got to his feet, and she noticed that she had not even poured the tea.

"Ben." She hurried toward him, and he cast aside his canes in order to wrap his arms about her. "Oh, Ben. Be happy."

"And you," he said, his breath warm against her ear, his arms like iron bands around her.

They did not kiss.

And then he took up his canes again and made his way to the door.

"Shall I come out to the barn to see you on your way?" she asked.

"No." He did not turn to look at her, but he smoothed a hand over Tramp's head. "Take care of her, you great wretch of a hound."

Tramp stood with his nose against the door after Ben had closed it on the other side, his tail wagging.

Samantha spread both hands over her face and drew a deep breath.

I have feelings.

She had not even said that much to him in reply.

❦

22

*P*erhaps the most surprising and significant thing about the next few months, Ben thought later as he looked back on them, was that he commissioned a wheeled chair to be made for himself, one with which he could propel himself about. He used it a great deal and wondered why he had not done it years ago. He had been too stubborn, of course, to give up his dream of walking unassisted again. And he could not really fault himself for that dream. Without it he probably would not have walked at all ever again. But he was very much more mobile in his chair. In fact, it set him free.

He no longer thought of himself as crippled. He could ride, he could move about freely with his chair, he could and did walk, and he could swim. He tried to do it every day when there was the sea or a lake close by.

He enjoyed those months immensely despite all the hard work that was involved—or perhaps because of it. He started from a position of total ignorance and ended up knowing as much about the working of the mines and ironworks as anyone, his employer included. And his work was indeed the next best thing to being back with his regiment. He had always liked people. And he had always had a gift for getting them to like him, even those who were subordinate to him and subject to his command. He might well have been resented in his new role. He was English, he was of the privileged classes, he was half crippled, he was lamentably ignorant and inexperienced. And perhaps he *was* resented at the beginning. Wisely, he did not worry about whether he was popular or not. He did not set about being liked. And perhaps that was the secret of his success. For respect, liking, and loyalty came gradually as he earned them.

Mr. Bevan spent a good deal of time with him. Ben liked him and learned from him. Ben had ideas of his own too, mainly about transportation and shipping, for which Bevan hired outside companies at great expense. But he kept those ideas to himself at this early stage of his career. This was the time to listen and learn.

He did not write to any of his family or friends for several months. He did not want to hear or be influenced by their opinions on what he was doing. They were bound to be negative. And he did not want to confide in anyone until he was more certain about his long-term future. There was the whole question of Samantha too. He did not want to tell anyone about her until there was something to tell—if there ever was anything. He had told her he had feelings for her. She had not said she returned those feelings. And he had not been specific about his own.

He heard very little about her during those months. He made it a point never to ask Bevan about her, and sometimes he thought the man deliberately refrained from mentioning her himself. There were only a few stray snippets of information, tantalizing in their very brevity. She had had a pianoforte delivered to the cottage, Bevan mentioned on one occasion. How did he know? Had he seen the instrument? Or had someone told him about it? She had attended an assembly at the village inn in celebration of the harvest, but she had worn lavender to indicate mourning and had refused to dance. But had Bevan seen her there? Or had he been told?

Ben did not even know if she had a relationship with

her grandfather. He did not know if time had erased him from her mind, or if she was glad he was gone. As for him, he had fallen in love during those brief weeks he had spent with her, and he remained in love, as he never had with any woman before.

Finally, in early November, Ben wrote three letters—to Calvin, to Beatrice, and to George at Penderris Hall. Calvin wrote back immediately and with a warmth Ben found surprising and rather touching. He and Julia had been frantic with worry, Calvin had written. Beatrice had informed them that he had gone traveling in Scotland, but as time had gone on and no one heard from him, they had been sick with apprehension, for they would not know where to begin looking for him if he never returned, and Scotland was a large country. Yet all the time he had been in Wales. He gave no opinion of what Ben had been doing with his time. His letter was filled with obvious relief over his brother's safety and brief details of the harvest at Kenelston and other estate matters.

It seemed after all, Ben thought, that his brother loved him.

Beatrice's letter was full of amazement and good-natured scolding for his long silence. Gramley, she reported, had given it as his opinion that his brother-in-law had taken leave of his senses, if it was true that he was working down a coal mine. Bea thought it was all vastly diverting and wondered when and if her brother would recover from the novelty of actually working for a living. She went on to complain about Mr. and Mrs. Rudolph McKay, whose presence at Bramble Hall was a severe trial to everyone else in the neighborhood—and to ask Ben if he had heard about Mrs. Samantha McKay's fleeing back in the early summer, never to be heard from again. *I do hope she is kicking up her heels somewhere exotic, enjoying life,* she wrote. *Apparently she was expected to go to Leyland Abbey under heavy guard, there to live at the tender mercy of the Earl of Heathmoor and that killjoy of a sister-in-law whom you met when you were here.*

George was delighted to hear about the new life Ben was making for himself and believed it would suit his friend down to the ground even if he *did* get some coal dust beneath his fingernails. He had some startling news too. Hugo and Lady Muir had indeed married in London, at St. George's on Hanover Square, as planned. All the Survivors had been present except Ben and Vincent, who could not be found. However, he had arrived on Hugo's doorstep two days after the wedding, bringing with him Miss Sophia Fry, a young lady whom he intended to marry without delay. And marry her he did, by special license, two days later, also at St. George's, with all his friends around him except Ben. The new Lady Darleigh was in expectation of her first confinement just before March, when the Survivors' Club usually gathered for a few weeks at Penderris Hall, and had suggested that they meet at Middlebury Park in Gloucestershire, Vincent's home, instead, since Vincent had declared that he would not leave his wife and child so soon after the birth. Now Ben would be able to give his opinion on the matter. Everyone else was in agreement, the duke reported.

Life had gone on without him, Ben realized. And Vincent, the youngest of them, the blind one, was married too. It sounded as though there must be a story behind such hasty nuptials. Ben would hear it in time, he supposed. But he hoped it was a happy marriage. Those friends of his were like brothers—and one sister.

He wrote again to George as well as to Hugo to explain why he had not replied to his wedding invitation. And he wrote to Vincent, knowing that someone—

perhaps his wife—would read the letter to him. How strange to think of Vince with a wife!

Mr. Bevan finally set a date for the planned meeting at Cartref to discuss Ben's future as his overseer. It was to be one week before Christmas, and was to coincide with a ball he had planned for his friends and neighbors. They would spend a few days together, he said, relaxing and talking things over. There would be a few other guests too to make things more sociable.

He did not say if Samantha would be at the ball.

Samantha was almost entirely happy during those months. Sometimes she felt guilty about it, for poor Matthew was dead and perhaps she ought to be far sadder than she was. But though she thought of him frequently and mourned the fact that his life had been cut off so early and so unhappily, she did not dwell upon what she could not change anyway.

She and Mrs. Price and even Gladys worked hard at making her house into a home. She changed curtains and rugs and replaced some vases and ornaments with ones she liked better. She purchased some pieces from the village potter. The only actually new piece of furniture she added was a pianoforte, which she purchased when she knew there was a music teacher in the village who had time to take on another pupil. There had been a harpsichord in the house when she was a girl, and while her mother lived she had taken lessons. But she had never enjoyed them and had abandoned them after her mother's death. Now she regretted having done so and was determined to learn to play again, at least well enough to amuse herself. More important, perhaps, the same teacher gave her voice lessons and taught her how to use her mezzo-soprano voice to best advantage.

She took Welsh lessons from Mrs. Jenkins, the vicar's

wife, and wondered if it really was the most difficult language in the world to learn or if it just seemed that way because she had never tried learning anything else but French.

She made numerous friendly acquaintances among her neighbors and one definite friend in Mari Pritchard, the schoolmaster's wife. She might have attracted the romantic interest of a number of men but took to wearing gray and lavender on public occasions so that it would be known that she was still in mourning.

Her grandfather did not come near her for a week after she and Ben had dined with him at Cartref. Finally, Samantha went to see him and was fortunate to find him at home. The next day, he told her, he would be going away and staying for a couple of weeks or so. She wondered if he would be seeing Ben, but he did not say so and she did not ask.

She sat with him in the main drawing room, from the window of which there was a magnificent view down across the park and the village beyond it to the sea. And she told him her story, ending with her decision to come to the cottage, which she had expected to be a mere run-down hovel, and Ben's decision to accompany her here.

He nodded his head slowly.

"And you knew nothing of me," he said, "and nothing of your heritage here."

"Nothing." She shook her head.

"Drink is a terrible thing," he said. "Or, rather, drink in the hands of a weak and foolish man is a terrible thing."

"You overcame it."

"For myself, yes," he said. "But that was no consolation to your mother, was it? I am glad she found a good man. And that she had you for a daughter."

"I would like," she said after a short silence, "to call you grandfather."

She watched tears brighten his eyes, but he did not shed them, and after a moment or two he went to stand by the window, his back to her.

"I loved her with an all-consuming passion," he said after a while. "Your grandmother, I mean. Unfortunately I was young, and I had no wisdom to balance out the passion. When she left, she took everything that was me with her and left behind an empty shell of raw pain. Love ought not to be like that, Samantha. One should love from a position of wholeness. One should have a firm and rich sense of self no matter what. For there is always pain—it cannot be avoided in this life, more's the pity. But pain should not destroy the person who feels it. I should not have been destroyed. I had my life and my health, this home, my work, friends. Most of all, I had Gwynneth. I loved her too, more than life, I believed before her mother left me. But it turned out that I loved my self-pity more, and the drink helped me wallow in it until I had lost my daughter as well as my wife."

He turned away from the window to look at Samantha. "You loved your husband with passion," he said, "and survived its early loss, putting duty before self-pity when he needed you. You are stronger than I was, and I am proud to call you granddaughter. You will find it again—passion, that is, and love. Perhaps you already have. But take it and offer it from a position of strength, Samantha. Use these months to—" He stopped and smiled suddenly with an expression of great warmth. "And listen to me, giving advice upon loving wisely and well."

"You are my grandfather," she said, "and someone who has had experience of life and of hell."

He nodded toward Tramp, who was lying at her feet.

"And what is the story of your dog?" he asked. "He does not look like the type one would willingly choose unless he was a tiny pup at the time and one did not know his full parentage."

"Oh, poor Tramp." She laughed and told his story, or the part of it she knew.

Her grandfather left the next day and stayed away for two weeks. He was frequently gone after that. But whenever he was at home, he would come to the cottage or she would go to Cartref. They became gradually acquainted with and fond of each other, until she realized that he had become quite central to her life. He was *family*, something she had craved since her marriage and the death of her father not long after.

They sat together at church on Sundays. He escorted her to a concert in the school hall when a visiting choir was performing there with some solo artists, and to the harvest assembly at the inn, which she enjoyed immensely though she did not dance. He invited her to dinner whenever he was entertaining guests, which happened quite frequently when he was at home. He was a sociable man.

He never mentioned Ben directly to her. She would not even have known for certain that Ben was still working for him if he had not answered an inquiry from one of his guests at a dinner one evening in October with the information that yes, the man in question was indeed a baronet—Major Sir Benedict Harper.

It was Ben who kept Samantha from being perfectly happy during those months. She had not swum since he left. She had not even walked much on the beach, and when she had, usually at Tramp's insistence, she had found it desolate rather than magical.

For she did not know for sure that he would come back. She had more or less forced him to accompany her on her journey here, after all. She had forced him to stay when she arrived and he would have resumed his own travels. Perhaps she had even half forced him into their affair. Perhaps once he had left here he had found that he was glad to be free of her.

And what about her? For such a long time she had yearned to be free. Now she *was* free. Would it be wise to give up that freedom so soon after her bereavement? If she was asked to give it up, that was.

It was only at night that all doubts fled and she knew that she loved him quite differently from the way she had loved Matthew. She liked his looks, yes, and his charm. But whereas at the age of seventeen she had not looked beyond outer appearance to wonder if Matthew had the character to match his looks, at the age of twenty-four she *had* looked. And her love was for Ben himself. His looks were unimportant. His half-crippled state was no encumbrance whatsoever to her. She loved *him*.

And surely he loved her. He would not have taken employment with her grandfather, she believed, if he did not. Or, if he had, he would not have come to consult her first. He would not have talked about coming back. He would not have told her what her grandfather had said about their having feelings for each other. He had even admitted that he had feelings, though, like a typical man, he had not elaborated.

And then, in December, her grandfather called at the cottage one morning while she was practicing at the pianoforte to tell her that he was going to host a ball at Cartref a week before Christmas for everyone in the neighborhood and a few friends from more distant places who would stay with him for a few days. He wanted her to come to stay too and to be his hostess at the ball.

"All of which you can do with a clear conscience, my

dear," he said. "For your year of mourning is at an end, is it not?"

"It is," she said. "I will be happy to come, Grandpapa."

Was Ben to be one of those more distant friends?

"Major Harper will be one of my guests," he said as if she had asked aloud.

"Ah," she said. "It will be good to see him again."

His eyes twinkled at her.

"Come into the sitting room," she said, rising from the bench to lead the way. "Mrs. Price has been baking and will be eager for you to sample her cake."

"I could smell it all the way up at Cartref," he said. "Why else do you think I walked over here?"

Ben was coming, she thought, a flutter of mingled excitement and anxiety in her stomach. It had been such a long time. It had seemed like forever. Sometimes she struggled to remember just how he looked.

He was coming, of course, to discuss business with Grandpapa.

And maybe . . .

Well. Maybe.

❦

23

It had been arranged that Ben would arrive at Cartref the day before the ball. His departure from Swansea was delayed, however, by a minor crisis at the ironworks. As a result, he did not arrive until late afternoon on the day of the ball. It did not much matter, he supposed, even though his legs were stiff and aching. It was not as though he would be dancing, after all.

The journey had been a long one across bare, windswept countryside, never far from the sight of a leaden gray, foam-flecked sea, under heavy lowering clouds. Hot bricks at his feet did not remain hot for long, and his greatcoat did not keep out as much cold as it ought. A few times there were flurries of fine pellets of snow, though fortunately they did not develop into any fall thick enough to gather on the road and make travel hazardous. There were tollgates at tediously close intervals to slow travel, though, and tollgate keepers too tired or too cold to hurry.

As he drew closer to the white house on the hill above Fisherman's Bridge, Ben could think only of the fact that he was within a couple of miles or so of Samantha, that he would see her again soon. Perhaps at the ball tonight if she was not estranged from her grandfather? Perhaps tomorrow at her cottage if she was—and if she was willing to receive him. But there was no reason, surely, why she would not even if she did not wish to continue their acquaintance.

Had she forgotten him? That was a ridiculous notion, of course. Certainly she would not have done so. But . . . had she moved on with her life to a point where he no longer had any place in it? Her official year of mourning was at an end. She had been here several months. Was there someone else by now? Someone who did not remind her in any way of the late wars? And *did* she have any sort of relationship with her grandfather? Bevan had not said either way, and Ben, of course, had not asked.

He took his canes from Quinn's hand when he had descended from the carriage and made his slow way up the steps and into the house. He was immediately cheered by the welcome warmth given off by twin fires on either side of the marbled hall, which was decorated with festoons of ivy and bright-berried holly for the season. His host was waiting for him and came forward to greet him, right hand extended, a broad beam of a smile on his face.

"Major," he said—he always called Ben that even though the rank was not really a part of his name any longer. "You must be frozen and fatigued. And you are the last of my guests to arrive. It is quite dusk out there already, isn't it, even though it is still only late afternoon. Never mind. Today is the darkest day of the year. Things can only get better from now on. What? No wheeled chair today?"

"Bevan. Good to see you." Ben clasped his hand. "Unfortunately, no one has yet invented a chair that will climb or descend steps. Besides, I am not a cripple and feel the occasional urge to prove it."

"I don't think anyone in his right mind would think of calling you any such thing," Bevan said. "Come upstairs to the drawing room. Never mind your appearance. The tea tray is still there and more hot water will be brought. I'll see that some brandy is added to your cup, purely for medicinal purposes, of course. Come and meet my other guests."

It took a while, as usual, to climb the stairs, but Quinn was waiting at the top with his chair, into which Ben sank gratefully. He would more easily be able to greet the other guests and shake hands with them if he did not have to cling to his canes while trying to ignore his discomfort.

There were a dozen people or so in the room. A few of the men, Ben had met before since they were business colleagues of Bevan's. Others were strangers, as were all the women.

Ah.

Except one. He inhaled deeply and held the breath.

She was coming toward them across the room, a smile on her face, both hands extended. She was wearing a wool day dress of deep forest green to match the greenery with which the drawing room too was decorated. It was obviously a new dress, far more elegant and fashionable than anything he had seen on her in the early summer. Her dark, almost black hair was swept back in a sleekly elegant chignon. She was smiling warmly.

He exhaled slowly.

She *was* a part of her grandfather's life, then.

"Ben." She set her hands in his, and his fingers closed tightly about them. They were warm while his were still cold from the outdoors.

"Samantha."

For a moment they gazed deeply into each other's eyes. But then she stepped back the length of her arms, though her hands remained in his.

"But what is this?" She was looking at his chair. "Oh, don't answer. It is obvious what it is. You have not—grown weaker?"

"Stronger," he said. "I am no longer ashamed to admit that my legs do not work as other people's do. I am as I am. I still walk, but I can get around much faster and more efficiently with my chair."

Her smile deepened and she squeezed his hands before releasing them and looking up at Bevan.

"Grandpapa, shall I introduce Ben to everyone else, or will you?"

She had the faintest trace of a Welsh lilt to her voice, Ben noticed. It was very attractive. Indeed, it sent a slight shiver up his spine.

"I will, my dear," her grandfather said firmly. "You look after the major's needs. Call for more hot water if you will and pour him some tea. And add a touch of brandy. He looks frozen."

"Yes," she agreed before turning away. "The tip of his nose is red."

Ben's hand went up to cover it as though he would be able to feel its redness.

He was soon involved in a round of introductions to those he did not know, an exchange of greetings with those he did. Everyone was in a sociable, festive mood. Conversation was brisk and hearty, and Ben settled to enjoying himself despite his undeniable fatigue.

And despite the fact that his head was spinning from seeing Samantha again. He had forgotten just how very vibrant her beauty was.

Had her greeting been anything more than sociable? He had thought so, but he noticed now that she spoke as warmly and with just as bright a smile to everyone else during the minutes before she brought him his tea.

Was she glad to see him? More than glad?

Of one thing he was certain. The months he had spent apart from her had not dimmed his feelings for her. Quite the opposite, if anything. Seeing her again now, he knew that he was more than just in love with her. He knew she was essential to his happiness.

And then she did come with his tea and a piece of

fruit cake on a tray. But she did not give them to him or set them down beside him. Instead she bent to speak quietly to him.

"I am going to have a servant carry the tray and show you the way to your room," she said. "You are in pain, Ben. And you may not deny it. I recognize the signs."

"I suppose," he said, "I am smiling too much."

"Not too much," she said, "but in too wolflike a way, with your teeth clenched. Quite frightening, in fact."

He laughed at her as she straightened up and led the way to the door. He made his excuses to the group around him and followed her.

She had not forgotten, then, that travel did not agree too well with him. She had noticed that he was in pain though he had made an effort to disguise the fact.

Ah, Samantha.

It should seem like a sign of defeat that he was propelling himself about in a wheeled chair instead of walking with his canes, Samantha thought as she dressed later for dinner and the grand ball. Yet it was not. Somehow it was quite the opposite.

I am no longer ashamed to admit that my legs do not work as other people's do. I am as I am.

Despite the fact that he had been in obvious pain—obvious to her, at least—she had been able to see a new confidence in him. He looked like a successful man who had found his place in the world and was at peace with it. And yet he was working for a salary for a man who was not even a gentleman by birth, while he was a titled gentleman with property and a fortune of his own.

Sir Benedict Harper was a fascinating mixture of contradictions, with which he seemed quite happy.

She had come to Cartref yesterday, bringing a delighted Gladys with her as well as Tramp, of course, who had taken up happy residence in the kitchen, where he had become a favorite during the past months. Ben had been expected yesterday but had not arrived even though she and her grandfather had waited up late for him. And today he had been the last of the guests to arrive. Each time someone else came, she had hidden her disappointment and growing sense of gloom behind smiles of welcome. He was just not going to come, she had concluded at last. Something had changed his mind. Perhaps it was the prospect of seeing her again. Perhaps he just could not face telling her that he had moved on since early summer, that he had no desire to renew or to further their acquaintance.

And then, when the gloom of early evening was already settling in, he had come.

She had forced herself to remain in the drawing room with everyone else while her grandfather went downstairs alone to greet him. It had been something of a shock to see him wheel himself into the room in a chair. She had sensed something different about him at the same time as he had looked so achingly familiar that it had amazed her she had not always been able to bring his face into clear focus in her memory.

His greeting had been warm despite his cool hands. Certainly he had watched her with steady eyes as she approached across the room. But he had been in pain, and their journey from County Durham had rushed back to her memory. Of course he was in pain—and hiding the fact behind smiles and warm handshakes, the foolish man, and so there had been no chance for further conversation with him.

Ah, but if she had ever doubted it during the last few months, she doubted no longer. She loved him utterly, totally, pain and lame legs notwithstanding. She loved *him*.

But perhaps he had come here only to discuss business with Grandpapa.

"There, Mrs. McKay," Gladys said. "I do like your hair with some curls and ringlets. And you look awfully good in royal blue. The color would swallow up most women, me included, but you can take it with your bold coloring. I wish *I* was dark like you. I bet all the single men will have an eye for you tonight and some of the married ones too, I don't doubt, though I oughtn't to say it out loud, ought I? My mam says it comes natural to men to look at women no matter if they are married or not. That major is here, isn't he? I thought he was ever so gorgeous back in the summer there. I was disappointed when he went away and nothing happened. Disappointed for you, I mean, not for me. That would be silly. But he has come back even if he *was* late and almost missed the ball. I bet *he* will have an eye for you. He did back then, but I suppose he knew you was in mourning for Mr. McKay and it wouldn't be right to press his attentions on you, didn't he? You aren't now, though. Are you glad to see him? I bet you are."

"It is very pleasant to see him again," Samantha said.

"Ho, I bet it's more than pleasant," Gladys said. "Even more than *very* pleasant. There. Your necklace is done up. I always have trouble with that particular catch. You are ready to go. Oh, you look a treat."

"Thank you," Samantha said, laughing, and she wondered for a moment what Matilda would think of a maid like Gladys. But Matilda was someone from her long distant past even though it was considerably less than a year since they had been living together at Bramble Hall.

She went downstairs early in order to step into the ballroom to see that all was ready for later. Not that it was her responsibility. Her grandfather had made all the arrangements.

The ballroom was large and two stories high. Floor-length mirrors on both long walls made the room seem even larger and multiplied the effect of all the Christmas greenery with which it was decorated. The wood floor gleamed. There were instruments on the dais—the orchestra members would be downstairs having their dinner. Three great chandeliers rested on the floor. All the candles would be lit just before the ball, and they would be raised to hang from the ceiling.

It seemed an extravagance to have such a room in the depths of the country, but her grandfather had told her it had almost always been used several times each year for balls and fetes and grand banquets.

She did not linger. It was time for dinner.

Samantha was seated at the foot of the table as her grandfather's hostess. He had arranged the seating though she had offered to do it for him. She had Mr. Morris, his white-haired lawyer, on her left, Ben on her right. She was surprised by the latter placement. She would have expected him to be seated higher at the table. But when she glanced along its length, her grandfather's eyes twinkled back at her.

He had been matchmaking from the start, of course. *Interfering,* she had called it back then. But after Ben had left, he had scarcely mentioned him, and she had concluded that she must have been mistaken. She knew now she had not been. Wily old Grandpapa had known that they must be separated so that her new neighbors would not be scandalized, that she must be given time to live out the year of her mourning. And now, just as he had planned it from the start, he had brought them back together—on the day of his grand festivity. He had set the stage and hoped they would play their parts.

Would they?

She had not seen Ben for the past several months, and

she knew something fundamental in him had changed. Did she have any part in his new life?

Samantha turned her attention to Mr. Morris while Ben conversed with Mrs. Davies, wife of one of Grandpapa's Swansea friends, on his other side. But before the first course was finished, Mrs. Fisher, wife of Grandpapa's physician from Tenby, claimed Mr. Morris, and Samantha glanced at Ben. He was gazing steadily back.

"You are in fine looks, Samantha," he said. "Finer than fine, in fact, even if you are looking a little less sun-bronzed than when I last saw you."

He was looking very fine too in his black form-fitting evening coat, gold-embroidered waistcoat, and gleaming white linen. His starched shirt points were high but not ridiculously so. His neckcloth was tied in an intricate style that had drawn glances of envy from two of the younger male guests in the drawing room earlier. A single diamond winked from its folds.

"You have changed." She leaned a little toward him. "You have found what you were looking for, have you not? Down a coal mine."

He smiled at that. "There are worse places," he said, "though I cannot for the life of me think of any."

She had always loved his smile. It was the expression she had remembered best through the past months, she realized. He had white, even teeth, and his eyes narrowed slightly and crinkled into laugh lines at the outer corners.

"You are happy?" she asked him.

"I have enjoyed the experience," he told her. "And I have learned a great deal from it, both about the job and about myself."

"*What* about yourself?"

"Mainly," he said, "that I can work with my handicap rather than let it work against me. Indeed, I do not even think of it as a handicap any longer."

She beamed at him and leaned slightly to one side while a servant removed her plate.

"But do you intend to keep working for Grandpapa?" she asked.

He seemed to give his answer some thought while his own plate was being removed. "That depends," he said.

"Upon?"

"Oh, no." He laughed softly. "This is neither the time nor the place."

Mr. Morris touched her arm at that moment and she turned to listen to what he had to say.

Upon her? Was that what he had meant?

And this was not the time and place for *what*?

Sometimes life seemed like one big tease.

*W*hat it depended upon was whether or not she would have him.

Ben had known that from the start, but he had been confirmed in his decision since arriving here this afternoon. He had known as soon as he set eyes upon her again that he would not be able to bear any association with her, even with her grandfather, if she would not marry him. He would rather go away, back to England, and start again. Though he would not be right back where he had been for three years after leaving Penderris. He knew now where his interests lay and what sort of life suited him best. It would be a dreary life, at least for a while, if there was no Samantha and no hope of her, but he would survive.

Outside guests began arriving soon after dinner, and Ben moved into the ballroom. He had seen it before, when Bevan gave him and Samantha a tour of the house. It had seemed a grand room even then. Now it looked quite magnificent enough to belong to a London mansion. The chandeliers were filled with candles, all of them burning—a splendid extravagance. Holly and ivy and pine boughs were draped everywhere, giving the effect of an indoor Christmas garden. Smells of the greenery and of cider and mulled wine from an anteroom added to the festive atmosphere.

Ben took a seat—he was using his canes this evening—and looked around at it all. His eye paused on a few sprigs of mistletoe hanging from some of the window recesses, and he smiled.

Samantha stood inside the door with her grandfather, receiving the guests. Ben recognized a few of them. She looked nothing short of stunning tonight in her royal blue gown, her hair piled high in elaborate curls and ringlets. His eyes moved down her shapely figure. He had waited for her letter for a month or two after leaving here, but it had never come. He had been glad of it, though part of him had been disappointed too.

She seemed to know everyone. She was flushed and laughing, and she occasionally turned to say something to Bevan. Ben was glad she had not held aloof from him out of some sense of loyalty to her mother. She needed him. Her husband's family had offered her no love. Neither had her half brother or any of her relatives on her father's side.

She looked happy. The thought gave him a bit of a pang.

Someone was beaming down at him, hand extended.

"Major Harper," the Reverend Jenkins said. "This *is* a pleasure."

His wife, wearing a hideous headful of plumes, beamed and nodded at his side.

No London hostess would be entirely pleased, Ben thought when everyone had arrived and the orchestra members were busy tuning their instruments. The gathering could hardly be called a grand squeeze. Nevertheless, the ballroom was pleasingly crowded and everyone would have space to dance, while those who sat or stood on the sidelines would have a clear view of the dancing.

And the first set was forming.

Bevan led out Mrs. Morris, while a young man Ben did not know led out Samantha. She stood in the line of ladies, smiling across at her partner. She was to have her wish at last, then, Ben thought a little wistfully.

I want to dance, she had once told him, a world of yearning in her voice. She had been dressed in her heavy, ill-fitting blacks at the time and standing in the gloomy, darkened sitting room of Bramble Hall. A long time ago—a lifetime.

Ben watched her perform a series of lively country dances over the next hour. Meanwhile, he did not skulk in his corner. He got to his feet a few times and moved about, exchanging greetings with people he had met in Fisherman's Bridge early in the summer and comments with his fellow guests.

He would wait until tomorrow, he decided. Or the day after. Would she be returning to her cottage? Perhaps he would call on her there. Tonight's setting, though wondrously festive, even romantic, was quite unsuited to him. He fought a return of the old frustration with his condition.

He was laughing over a story the landlord of the inn had just told him when someone touched his sleeve. He turned, and there she was.

"Ben," she said.

"Are you enjoying yourself?" He smiled at her and tried to look as if *he* was. Well, it was not difficult, was it? On a certain level he was enjoying himself. He liked this place and these people.

"Come and sit with me," she said. "The next dance is a waltz."

"You do not want to dance it?" he asked her.

She shook her head slightly and turned to lead the

way to a deep alcove at one end of the ballroom. It was the mirror image of the orchestra alcove at the other end, though without the dais. Heavy velvet curtains had been pulled across it, though they had been looped back tonight so that anyone sitting within—there was a long velvet couch there—could watch the dancing. But no one was there.

She sat on the couch, and he seated himself beside her and propped his canes against the arm.

"Is this the first time you have danced?" he asked.

"Yes," she said.

"Do you remember what you once said to me about dancing?" he asked her.

She nodded. "And I remember what you said to me."

Ah. He had told her he wanted to dance too.

"I meant," he said, "that I wanted to run free. Now I *ride* free in my chair."

She smiled at him. "But you were talking about dancing," she said.

The orchestra struck an opening chord, and the lilting music of the waltz filled the ballroom. Soon couples were twirling past the alcove.

"I always thought," she told him, "that the waltz was the most romantic of dances."

"But you do not want to dance it tonight?"

"Oh, I do," she said. "I want to dance it with you."

He laughed softly. "Perhaps," he said, "we can close our eyes and imagine it. Like rising above the rain clouds in our hot air balloon."

She wanted to *waltz* with him, he thought.

"Stand up, Ben." She got to her feet.

He gathered his canes and stood. Did she imagine he could dance? She took the canes from him, just as she had done with one of them when he had stepped into the sea with her, he remembered, and set them aside.

"Put your right arm about me," she said.

He set it about her waist and took her hand in his. She did not set her other hand on his shoulder but about his own waist to support him, and she gazed into his eyes, laughter and perhaps anxiety in her own.

Good Lord, she was serious.

And they waltzed.

They danced one whole turn about the alcove while it seemed the music became part of them and her eyes lost both the laughter and the anxiety and they simply gazed at each other and into each other.

Reality was still reality, of course. They did not, as they might have done in a fairy tale, suddenly waltz out from the alcove to twirl all about the ballroom while everyone else watched in wonder. But . . . they had danced. They had waltzed. Together.

Something drew Ben's glance upward. A sprig of mistletoe hung from the ceiling at the very center of the alcove.

"Ah," he murmured to her while he could still stand. "And for this I do not even have to beg permission. Christmas has handed me its own special permit."

He kissed her, wrapping both arms about her waist while she twined her own about his neck. And then they smiled at each other, and for the moment he felt invincible. But only for a moment.

"If I do not sit down immediately or sooner," he told her, "someone is going to have to scoop me up from the floor and bear me ignominiously hence."

And then they were sitting side by side again, their shoulders touching, hand in hand, their fingers laced. And they were both laughing as she tipped her head sideways to set her cheek against his shoulder.

"That was probably the shortest, most ungainly waltz ever danced," he said.

"And that was perhaps the shortest, most glorious kiss ever enjoyed beneath the mistletoe," she said.

He rested his cheek briefly against her dark curls. "I loved you before I left here in the summer, Samantha," he said. "I did not mean to fall in love with you. It did not seem quite fair when I came with you to protect you. But it happened anyway. And my feelings have not changed."

"Oh, you *provoking* man," she said after several moments of silence between them while the waltz proceeded in the ballroom beyond their little haven. "How dare you stop there. You cannot stop there, Ben."

He turned his head and grinned down at her. "I was giving you the chance to stop me if you did not want me to embarrass myself further," he said.

"Oh, no," she said. "I *want* you to embarrass yourself."

"Wretch," he said. "Will you marry me?"

He heard her swallow.

"Hmm," she said, her voice a little higher-pitched than usual. "Let me see. I will have to think about this."

"Right," he said. "I will go away for another six months while you do so."

She laughed softly and lifted her head so that she could turn her face to his. Her eyes were shining, he could see in the light of the chandeliers beyond the alcove. Shining with unshed tears.

"Yes," she said.

"Yes?"

"Yes."

They gazed at each other for a few moments, and then they were in each other's arms again and laughing— oh, yes, and shedding more than a tear apiece too.

"I love you," she said, her breath warm against his ear. "Oh, Ben, I have *missed* you. I have missed you so very much."

He drew back his head and smiled at her.

Samantha. His love.

Ah, the wonder of it.

"Am I forgiven?" he asked her.

She raised her eyebrows.

"For ripping up at you the day we met," he said, "and swearing most foully. You never said I was."

"I will think about it," she told him, and laughed.

❦

24

*C*hey considered waiting for a more clement time of year, but neither wanted to put off their wedding until June or July or even May. They considered Kenelston as a venue, but it had not really been Ben's home since childhood despite the fact that he owned it, and it never would be home now.

They settled upon Wales at the end of January, specifically upon the church in Fisherman's Bridge, with the Reverend Jenkins officiating. Samantha, after insisting that she would leave for her wedding from her cottage, realized that she had hurt her grandfather though he did not say so, and changed her mind. She would marry from the big house with her grandfather to accompany her and give her away. Ben would move to the village inn on the eve of the wedding. A grand wedding breakfast would be held in the ballroom at Cartref.

It was the very worst time of the year in which to expect guests to travel from any distance, but invitations were sent out anyway.

Beatrice and Gramley were the first to reply. They would come, though Beatrice reported that her husband was now quite sure his brother-in-law had taken leave of his senses. A letter came from Calvin the next day. He and Julia would also be coming. After that, while the banns were already being read at the village church, a steady stream of replies were delivered, all but one of them acceptances. Amazingly, all the Survivors were going to venture into the darkest bowels of Wales— Flavian's description—to attend Ben's nuptials. The exception was, of course, Vincent, whose wife was close to her time of confinement.

I will not leave Sophie, he had written, *though she has urged me not to miss your wedding, Ben.*

It was obvious that his wife had written the letter for him, for there followed a brief message in parentheses: (*Vincent is more nervous than I am about the coming event, Sir Benedict. It would be cruel for me to try insisting that he go to Wales when he is so anxious for my sake. You will come here in March, though, for the annual gathering of the Survivors' Club, will you not, even though you will be so recently married? And you will bring Lady Harper with you? Please? I so very much want to meet all of Vincent's friends.*)

On a separate sheet of paper, enclosed with the letter, was a charcoal drawing—a very fine caricature indeed—of a man who bore a remarkable resemblance to Vince, pacing with his head down and his hands clasped behind his back, droplets of sweat falling from his brow, and generally looking very worried indeed while a little mouse in one corner gazed kindly up at him.

"I am so sorry," Ben said, taking Samantha's hand in his as they sat together on the couch in her sitting room at the cottage one afternoon a week before the wedding. "All the outside guests will be mine."

"Ah," she said, "but all the *inside* guests will be mine, you see. All my friends and neighbors will be about me on what I expect to be the happiest day of my life. And Grandpapa will be there to give me into your keeping."

He squeezed her hand.

"Besides," she said, turning her head so that he could see that her eyes were twinkling, "I had a very civil letter from Matilda today."

"You did?" His eyebrows rose in some surprise.

"Indeed," she said. "She congratulated me upon having snared a very eligible husband for the second time despite my origins."

"Your shady Gypsy past?"

"That," she said, "and the fact that my grandfather is *in coal*. It does sound very murky and dusty, does it not? She hopes—no, she *fervently* hopes and prays— that I have learned my lesson and will not lead you a merry dance as I did her poor dear Matthew."

"No!"

"All very civil," she said. "Though she did sink just a little into spite at the end, Ben. She took leave to give it as her opinion that it would be no less than you deserve if I *do* lead you a dance, since you appear to be the type of man who believes it quite unexceptionable to ride out with a widow when she is in deepest mourning."

"We deserve each other, then?" he asked her.

"It would appear so," she said with a sigh. "Oh, she is *not*, by the way, coming to our wedding. Neither are the Earl and Countess of Heathmoor. I was rather surprised by that announcement, since my letter to them was merely to explain that I will be remarrying and was in no way an invitation."

The next day Samantha was surprised by another letter. The Reverend John Saul, her half brother, was pleased to hear that she had settled well in Wales and was happy there with her mother's people. He felt it incumbent upon himself to honor his late father by attending the wedding of the daughter of whom his parent had been so obviously fond. His dear wife would not be accompanying him.

Samantha, alone in her book room when she read the letter, unabashedly wept over it, its stiff pomposity notwithstanding.

"I *will* have an outside guest of my own," she said, thrusting the letter into Ben's hand when he drove over from Cartref with her grandfather during the afternoon.

And she turned and wept all over again in her grandfather's arms while he patted her back and read the letter over Ben's shoulder.

The preparations for the wedding were all made. All that remained was to await the arrival of those who would be traveling from England during one of the potentially most inclement months of the year. They would all acquire cricked necks, Ben remarked on one occasion, if they gazed skyward much more than they did. It was a cold month, and the wind, which blew almost constantly, was what Mrs. Price called a lazy wind.

"It can't be bothered to swerve around you," she explained. "It just blows straight through."

But the sky remained blue much of the time, and when there were clouds, they were high and unthreatening. There was no snow. There rarely was in this part of Wales, but the key word was *rarely*. They would all have relaxed a bit more, perhaps, if it had been *never*. Snow was not the only threat, of course. Rain could be just as bad or worse. It did not take a great deal of it to turn the roads to mud and sometimes to quagmires. And rain *was* common in this part of the world, especially at this time of year.

But the weather held.

And the guests began to arrive.

*A*ll the guests from England stayed at Cartref at Mr. Bevan's insistence, though Ben removed to the inn a little earlier than planned to make room for them all. Calvin, who was to be his best man, came there the evening before the wedding to stay with him.

All the Survivors came with him just for the evening, to the great pleasure of the landlord and the equal consternation of his wife, who had discovered not only that the lady and all the gentlemen were titled, which was bad enough, but that one of them was actually a *duke*.

"And there is only *that* much," she whispered to her husband even though they were in the kitchen and two closed doors stood between them and the gathered company, "between a duke and a king." She held her forefinger a quarter of an inch from her thumb.

George Crabbe, Duke of Stanbrook, meanwhile was asking Ben about his wheeled chair. "It seems a sensible notion," he said, "but you have always been quite adamantly set against using one."

"I have nothing more to prove," Ben told him. "I can and do walk. I have danced. Now I can be sensible and move around as fast as any other man."

"One is t-tempted to challenge you to a race along the village street, Ben," Flavian, Viscount Ponsonby, said. "But one would not wish to make a s-spectacle of oneself."

"Or lose ignominiously to a man in a wheeled chair, Flave," Ralph, Earl of Berwick, added.

"You will be able to race against Vince in March, Ben," Hugo, Lord Trentham, said. "He is having a race track built about the outer boundary of his park. Had you heard? That will be a sight to behold."

"A blind man and a c-cripple," Flavian said. "Heaven defend us."

"Call me that again, Flave," Ben said cheerfully, "and you may find yourself being beaten about the head with a cane."

"It might cure his stammer," George said.

"Ben." Imogen, Lady Barclay, was looking intently at him. "You have *danced*?"

"Waltzed, actually." He grinned at her. "There is an

alcove at one end of the ballroom at Cartref. I waltzed all about it with Samantha during a ball just before Christmas."

"Was that wise, Ben?" Calvin asked him. "I have always thought you may do more harm than good to your legs by insisting upon walking on them. But *dancing*? I worry about you, you know. All the time."

But the Survivors were all beaming at him.

"Bravo," the duke said quietly.

"I s-suppose," Flavian said, "this alcove is the size of an egg cup, Ben?"

"Probably a thimble, Flave," Ralph said, grinning and winking at Ben.

"It does not matter if it is the size of a pin, you fatheads," Hugo said, holding out one huge hand and giving Ben's a hearty shake. "Good for you, lad. My Gwendoline dances too, and you have all seen how she limps when she walks."

Imogen bent to kiss Ben's cheek. "It was your dream to dance one day," she said. "Everyone ought to have a dearest dream come true."

Ben caught her hand in his. "And what is yours, Imogen?" he asked her.

He immediately regretted the question, for everyone fell silent to listen to her reply, and she gazed back at him, her eyes large and luminous. Something flickered in them and then died.

"Oh," she said in her soft, cool voice, "to meet someone tall, dark, and handsome and be swept off my feet, of course."

He squeezed her hand and held it to his lips for a moment. He wanted to apologize, but that would be to admit that he knew she had not answered his question.

"I am sorry, Imogen," Hugo said, "but I am already taken."

"She said *handsome*, Hugo," Ralph said.

They all laughed and the moment passed.

"There must have been something in the air in Cornwall last spring," George said as the landlord came into the room with a loaded tray. "*Three* of our number married within the year. And my nephew too."

"The heir?" Ben asked.

"Julian, yes," George said. "And all love matches, it seems to me. One has only to look at you and Mrs. McKay, Ben, to smell May blossoms. You have done well. You will have a wife for whom you obviously care deeply and a way of life that seems to have been custom made for you, all in one neat package."

"And all in the d-darkest bowels of the wild country," Flavian said. "I expected savages to j-jump out at me from behind every r-rock as I traveled here, Ben, intent upon slitting my throat."

"It is more likely," Ben said, "that they would want to kidnap you so that they could sing to you, Flave. You should hear the miners' choir where I work. It would be enough to make you weep sentimental tears."

"S-spare me," Flavian said faintly.

Hugo had a tankard of ale in his hand. "We must not keep Ben from his beauty sleep tonight of all nights," he said, "and we will not try to get him foxed. But we will drink a toast to you, Benedict. That all your life your heart will dance as your person did in that alcove before Christmas."

"Oh, the devil!" Flavian said, getting to his feet and holding aloft his glass of port. "Marriage is t-turning Hugo embarrassingly poetic. But he has the r-rights of it, Benedict, my boy. M-may you be happy. It is all we have ever w-wanted for one another."

"To you, Benedict," Imogen said, lifting her glass of wine. "And to Samantha."

"To your happiness, Ben," Ralph said, "and Mrs. McKay's."

"To you, brother," Calvin said. "I always admired you greatly. You knew what you wanted and you went after it and did superbly well. It almost killed me when you were so badly hurt so soon after Wallace was killed. But then I learned to admire you more than I ever had. And I still do even if you *do* cause me worry when you won't come home and let me look after you and when you insist upon walking and even *dancing,* for the love of God. To you, brother—all the happiness in the world and to Samantha too."

Ben, smiling at him, felt rather as if he were seeing his brother for the first time.

"And may you always ride your wheels as fast as we can run, Benedict," the duke said.

They all drank, and Ben laughed.

"If you do not want to see me turn into a watering pot," he said, "and if you do not want to find the doors of Cartref locked against you, you had better leave. I will see you all in the morning."

"One word of advice, Ben," Hugo said as they were taking their leave. "Get your valet to tie your neckcloth looser than usual tomorrow. There is something about being at the front of the church when you are a bridegroom waiting for your bride to arrive that makes the neck expand."

"And he is not lying, Ben," Calvin told him.

Samantha's half brother arrived the day before her wedding. She had already moved into the big house and greeted him there on his arrival. They shook hands and conversed politely. She asked about her sister-in-law and nephews and nieces. He asked her about her home and her connections in the village. He shook hands with Ben and conversed politely with him.

But it was all done in company with others. Samantha

was touched that he had come so far and at the worst time of the year for her sake. But he seemed more like a stranger she had once known than someone who was close to her. She hoped he would not regret coming. But she supposed he would not. He had come out of a sense of duty to their father, not out of any fondness for her.

Ah, life was difficult sometimes.

It was not until the following morning that she finally saw him alone.

She was dressed for her wedding. She had chosen a simply styled dress of warm white velvet with a gold chain and locket about her neck and gold earrings. A small gold-colored bonnet hugged her head. Her heavy cloak, which was flung over the back of a chair in her dressing room, was also of white velvet with gold frogged fasteners at the front and fur lining.

She had considered various bright colors but had rejected them all in favor of white. She wanted simplicity. She wanted just herself on display to her bridegroom, not the brightness of her clothes.

"Ooh," Gladys said when she had fitted the bonnet carefully over Samantha's curls and tied the ribbons in a bow to one side of her chin, "you were right and I was wrong, Mrs. McKay. White is your color. *Every* color is your color. But you look perfect today. The major is going to eat you up, he is, when he sees you. Not that he'd better do it, mind, not when—"

But her monologue was interrupted by a knock on the dressing room door and she went to see who was there.

"Thank you, Gladys," Samantha said. "That will be all."

She smiled at John. She had thought everyone had left for the church by now.

"You look very fine," he said, his eyes moving over her. He was frowning. "I have always thought of you, you know, as your mother's daughter. I would never think of you as my father's too. But you were—you are. You look like your mother, of course—well, a bit like her, anyway. I was always thankful about that, for I am like my father. I can see it when I look in a glass. But you do too. Not in obvious ways. Just sometimes in a turn of the head or a fleeting expression—not anything I can put my finger on exactly. But you are his daughter. Not that I ever doubted it. I just ignored it."

"John." She stepped forward and extended her right hand. "You have come all this way and I am touched. I know it was hard for you when our father married my mother."

"You are my sister," he said. "I had to come and tell you that, Samantha. Not that you did not know it, but . . . Well, everyone needs family, and I know you have always been denied half of yours and didn't know about the other half until recently. I am glad you have discovered that half. Bevan seems a decent sort as well as being as rich as Croesus."

"John," she said hesitantly, hoping she was not about to introduce a discordant note into their meeting, "why did you keep his letters from me and all of Mr. Rhys's except the one you sent soon after Papa's death? Why did I not know about the money my aunt left me or all the gifts my grandfather sent?"

He frowned. "I knew nothing of any gifts or money," he told her. "I do know that when our father was dying he had me find two bundles of letters and burn them while he watched. He told me your mother had not wanted you to have anything to do with her Welsh relatives, that they had treated her badly and must not be allowed to bother you. He wanted to honor her wishes, especially as you had made such an advantageous marriage. All I ever had was letters asking what you wanted to do about the cottage. Father had said it was just a run-down building, not worth anything. I sent the one letter on to you after answering it myself—I thought perhaps you ought to see it so that you could send an answer of your own if you wanted. You did not write back, and your husband was in a bad way, and I didn't bother you with the other few letters that came. But they did not mention any money, Samantha—only the cottage. I had no idea it was the house it is."

"Me neither," she said, smiling at him. "As it has turned out, John, it is a good thing I knew nothing, but discovered the truth only when it would mean most to me."

"You are marrying a good man," he said, "even if he is half a cripple."

"There is no one less crippled than Ben," she said. "But thank you, John. I wept, you know, when I knew you were coming."

"You did?"

"I did." She smiled and looked beyond his shoulder.

Her grandfather had come to fetch her. He was beaming at her and then smiling genially at John.

"The bridegroom will have heart palpitations if we are late," he said. "Bridegrooms always do. It is a hazardous thing to be."

"I know." John smiled at him and looked so much like their father that Samantha's heart turned over. "I see enough of them. And I was one myself once."

He turned back and took a step closer so that he could kiss Samantha's cheek.

"Be happy," he said. "Our father loved you very dearly, you know."

"I do know," she said softly. "Just as he loved you."

He hurried away, and Samantha looked at her grandfather.

"Oh, dear God, girl," he said, "but you look like my Esme. Except that I never saw her in white. It was a color she never wore. You are beautiful. And what an inadequate word *that* is. Come, let me help you on with your cloak, and we will go rescue the major from death by heart failure, shall we?"

"Oh, by all means, Grandpapa," she said. "But I must not forget my muff."

It was her wedding day, she thought, and felt a flutter of almost unbearable excitement in her stomach.

*I*t had been decided at Christmastime that Ben would take three months during which to get married and enjoy a wedding trip and a stay with his fellow members of the Survivors' Club. After that, as Mr. Bevan's grandson-in-law rather than simply as his employee, he would gradually take over the running of the mines and ironworks while Bevan himself relaxed into a semi-retirement. The newly wedded couple would live at the cottage, though the invitation to take up their residence at Cartref was an open one. There would be homes in Swansea and the Rhondda Valley too.

All of which was satisfying, even exciting to consider, Ben thought as he sat beside his brother at the front of the church in Fisherman's Bridge while his family and friends and Samantha's murmured in soft conversation behind him. But in the meanwhile there was today.

His wedding day.

He had not really expected to be nervous. How could one feel any anxieties when one was so entirely happy? But he knew what Hugo had meant about his neckcloth. And he could not stop himself from fearing that he would drop the wedding ring just when he was about to slide it onto Samantha's finger. Indeed, he had woken up more than once during the night with just that fear. He would have to let someone else crawl around on hands and knees to retrieve it, and then he would have to go through the ordeal all over again.

"You are in pain, Ben?" Calvin asked, his voice full of concern.

"No." Ben looked at him in some surprise, but he realized he had been rubbing his hands over his upper thighs. "Make sure I have a good grip on the ring, Cal, before you let it go."

His brother grinned at him. "No one ever does drop it," he said.

Now he was in for it for sure.

And then the Reverend Jenkins, gorgeously clad in his clerical robes, was telling the congregation to stand and the pipe organ was striking a chord.

It seemed to take Ben forever to push himself to his feet with his canes, but when he had done so, she was only just coming into sight at the end of the nave, on the arm of a proudly beaming Bevan.

Oh, Lord God, Ben thought with reverence rather than blasphemy, had there ever been such beauty? Could she possibly be his? His *bride*?

And then she looked along the nave, and her eyes came to rest upon him, and she smiled. He was quite unaware of the slight little sigh that rippled through the congregation as he smiled back.

And then she was beside him, and they both turned toward Mr. Jenkins.

"Dearly beloved," he said in his lovely Welsh accent.

And just like that, all within a few minutes, the world changed.

They were married.

And not only did he not drop the ring, but he did not even think about the possibility as he took it in his hand and slid it over her finger while he spoke the words the clergyman recited ahead of him. He did not even think about how he was to manage without his canes for a few minutes.

They were married.

And then they signed the register and it was all done up right and tight.

They were man and wife.

They made their slow way back up the nave. Ben did it with one cane. Samantha's hand was through his other arm, holding it firmly without appearing to do so. In her other hand she held her white muff. He felt no pain from the walk as he looked to left and right, acknowledging their guests with nods and smiles while Samantha did the same.

And then they were outside, and a chill wind cut at them and they turned their faces toward each other and laughed.

"Lady Harper," he said.

"Absolutely," she said. "Your friends are not holding what I think they are holding, are they?"

There were a number of villagers in the street beyond the church, come to see the show and cheer the bride and groom. But in their midst, sure enough, were Flavian and Ralph, who had obviously slipped out of the church early. Where they had found flowers in January, the Lord only knew. There must be a hothouse somewhere. But those were unmistakably flower petals clutched in their hands and then raining over bride and groom as they made their slow way to the carriage that was waiting to convey them back to Cartref.

"I think the answer was yes," Ben said, laughing as he climbed in after Samantha. "And I think what is trailing behind the carriage is what I think it is too."

The church bells were ringing. The crowd was cheering. The congregation was beginning to spill out of the church.

"Here," Hugo said, "I'll close the carriage door for you."

Which he did—after tossing another great handful of petals inside.

Ben sat back on the seat and laughed. And he took Samantha's hand in his as he turned to her.

"Happy?" he asked.

She nodded.

"Words are ridiculous sometimes, aren't they?" he said.

She nodded again.

He dipped his head and kissed her while the crowd beyond the carriage cheered more loudly and there were a few piercing whistles.

The carriage lurched into motion.

Noisy motion as it dragged numerous pieces of metal hardware behind it.

"Ben," Samantha said, gazing into his eyes, "I forgive you."

"For?"

"For calling me *woman*," she said, "and for uttering a whole arsenal of foul words in my hearing and Tramp's."

He smiled slowly at her.

"I suppose," he said, "I have just married that wretch of a hound too, haven't I?"

"For better or worse," she assured him.

"Damned dog," he said and kissed his wife somewhat more ruthlessly than he had done a minute before.

Do you love historical fiction?

Want the chance to hear news about your favourite authors (and the chance to win free books)?

Mary Balogh

Charlotte Betts

Jessica Blair

Frances Brody

Gaelen Foley

Elizabeth Hoyt

Eloisa James

Lisa Kleypas

Stephanie Laurens

Claire Lorrimer

Amanda Quick

Julia Quinn

Then visit the Piatkus website and blog
www.piatkus.co.uk | www.piatkusbooks.net

And follow us on Facebook and Twitter
www.facebook.com/piatkusfiction | www.twitter.com/piatkusbooks

piatkus

LOVE READING ROMANCE?

Fall in love with
pıatkus

Entice

Temptation at your fingertips

An irresistible eBook-first list from
the pioneers of romantic fiction at
www.piatkusentice.co.uk

To receive the latest news,
reviews & competitions direct to your inbox,
sign up to our romance newsletter at
www.piatkusbooks.net/newsletters